ONE BEING'S HELL IS ANOTHER'S HEAVEN . . .

Here are sixteen glimpses of life in Hell, or tales that reveal what happens when Hell really does break loose:

"Facing Down Your Demons"—He'd thought a ghostly existence wasn't too bad until he started talking to the Devil. . . .

"The Devil May Care"—He'd fixed all sorts of heating and cooling problems, but now he had to decide what to do when Hell started freezing over. . . .

"The Curse of Beazoel"—Beazoel had discovered that being a middle manager in Hell wasn't without its pitfalls. And if his department didn't make its quota his demotion could be infernal. . . .

"That's What They All Say"—What kind of ransom do you have to pay to set Lucifer free?

ALL HELL
BREAKING
LOOSE

SCIENCE FICTION
FANTASY

More Journeys of the Imagination Brought to You by DAW:

IN THE SHADOW OF EVIL *Edited by Martin H. Greenberg and John Helfers.* The struggle between good and evil is one of the most potent themes in fiction. But what if evil had already triumphed and good was hopelessly outclassed? This was the challenge fourteen of fantasy's most imaginative tale-tellers—including Jean Rabe, Rick Hautala, Julie E. Czerneda, Jane Linskold, Mickey Zucker Reichert, Jody Lynn Nye, Gregory Benford, Tanya Huff, Michelle West, and Fiona Patton—accepted in writing these stories. From a master perfumer forced to serve the serpent god and bargain for a life with a death . . . to a king of trolls seeking justice for the wrongs done him by barbarian conquerors . . . to a cook forced to cater to the warlord who had slaughtered her people . . . to a young man raised in a world under the sway of Shadow, here are fascinating excursions into the dark side of fantasy, where every victory has its price. . . .

MAGIC TALES *Edited by Martin H. Greenberg and Janet Pack.* Let Alan Dean Foster, Elizabeth Ann Scarborough, Charles de Lint, Jody Lynn Nye, Michelle West, Lisanne Norman, Josepha Sherman, Mickey Zucker Reichert, Andre Norton, and five other masters of the cat fantastic sweep you off into enchanting feline worlds. From a cat genie who seems to have a bit of a problem fulfilling human wishes . . . to the quest which only Sleeping Beauty's cat can complete . . . to a feline desperately seeking a way to best the devil . . . to a cat-assisted solution to the Three Pigs' wolf problem, these ingenious, highly original tales are sure to cast their spell over all cat-loving readers of fantasy.

WOMEN OF WAR *Edited by Tanya Huff and Alexander Potter.* Fifteen original tales about women who are or become warriors, facing challenges in the many realms of fantasy and science fiction. From Sharon Lee and Steve Miller to Rosemary Edghill, Julie E. Czerneda, Fiona Patton, Tanya Huff, Michelle West, Bruce Holland Rogers, Robin Wayne Bailey, Lisanne Norman, and Stephen Leigh, here are remarkable stories about female protagonists who are more than able to hold their own whether in space, on distant worlds, in our own future, or in fantasy realms where a civilization's fate maybe balanced on the edge of a sword.

ALL HELL BREAKING LOOSE

Edited by

Martin H. Greenberg

DAW BOOKS, INC.

DONALD A. WOLLHEIM, FOUNDER

375 Hudson Street, New York, NY 10014

ELIZABETH R. WOLLHEIM
SHEILA E. GILBERT
PUBLISHERS

http://www.dawbooks.com

First Printing, October 2005
1 2 3 4 5 6 7 8 9

DAW TRADEMARK REGISTERED
U.S. PAT. OFF. AND FOREIGN COUNTRIES
—MARCA REGISTRADA
HECHO EN U.S.A.

PRINTED IN THE U.S.A.

ACKNOWLEDGMENTS

Introduction © 2005 by John Helfers.

The Name of the Game © 2005 by P. N. Elrod.

Facing Down Your Demons © 2005 by Alexander B. Potter.

Hell to Pay © 2005 by Donald J. Bingle.

Your World, and Welcome to It © 2005 by Ed Gorman.

The Devil May Care © 2005 by ElizaBeth Gilligan.

The Curse of Beazoel © 2005 by David D. Levine.

Poker Boy vs. a Denizen of Gambling Hell © 2005 by Dean Wesley Smith.

Water Goethe Before the Fall © 2005 by Alan L. Lickiss.

With Eyes Averted © 2005 by Tom Piccirilli.

Burning Bridges © 2005 by David Niall Wilson.

"That's What They All Say" © 2005 by Bradley H. Sinor.

Something Worse Hereafter © 2005 by Sarah A. Hoyt.

A Fly Came By © 2005 by Barbara Nickless.

Burning Down the House © 2005 by Adam Stemple.

Devil in the Details © 2005 by Daniel M. Hoyt.

Enter All Abandon, Ye Who Hope Here © 2005 by David Bischoff.

CONTENTS

INTRODUCTION

by John Helfers

IT IS RARE to find a more abstract concept—evil—that has been given a more physical form than in the idea of Hell. What with the lakes of fire and brimstone combined with demons and devils tormenting hapless souls for all eternity, one would think that people would do whatever they could to escape such a fate. Even though Lucifer (at least, according to him) led his revolt against Heaven out of a desire for free will, the teachings of Christianity have vilified him and cast him down to the netherworld, to remain there forever, plotting wickedness and leading men astray.

At least, this is what thousands of years of literature have claimed. From the ancient myths of Greeks and Romans, casting Hades/Pluto as an evil deity that kidnapped Persephone, leading to the creation of the seasons, to interpretations of the underworld by authors such as Dante Alighieri, John Milton, William Blake, and many, many others (including almost all of the world's major religions,) the theme of a plane or dimension into which all sinners and the unrepentant are cast has been an immensely popular one throughout the centuries.

But after thousands of years of bad press, one might think that the denizens of Hell might have finally had enough. In fact, one might say that they're "mad as hell, and they're not going to take it anymore."

We've assembled sixteen of today's best authors and asked them to give us their take on what Hell might be like in this enlightened age. P. N. Elrod's vagabond Myhr makes a wicked appearance as he attends a convention set—where else?—in Hell. Alexander Potter wrote about a conversation between a young man who has placed himself in a hell of his own making, and how he managed to free himself with a little help from an emissary from below. ElizaBeth Gilligan takes an even more fundamental approach to Hell—heat versus cold. And David Bischoff's inimitable rogue Whiteviper takes on an adversary that might even be a match for him—the Devil himself.

The concept of Hell means different things to different people, and the stories in this anthology have also taken a variety of different approaches to illustrating the foul pits of the netherworld. So turn the page and enter the domain of Hell—if you dare. . . .

THE NAME OF THE GAME

by P.N. Elrod

P. N. "Pat" Elrod has written over twenty novels and over twenty short stories for various print publishers. A hopelessly irredeemable chocolate addict, she resides in Texas not too many miles from the lair of the real-life Myhr, aka cover artist Jamie Murray. They occasionally do lunch so she can swipe story ideas from him. Check out www.vampwriter.com to learn more about *The Adventures of Myhr*, Elrod's novel about the cat-guy.

SUCCUBI TEND to be very giving and generous—or so went my experiences with them—so when one asked me to be her date for a Hell convention, I really couldn't turn her down. She'd just been so kind to me.

Of course, her timing was perfect; that sort of talent is in their bones. She waited until I was out-of-it exhausted, verging on an extended bout of checking my closed eyelids for leaks, then sprang her question.

"Myhr . . . ? Sweetie peetie pitty-pie pooh?" No kidding, they do speak like that.

"Hnnughungh?" And no kidding, that's how I speak, at least while in a gawd-that-was-incredible-but-

3

I-really-need-to-sleep-we'll-talk-in-the-morning-I-*promise* postcoital state.

She giggled as the thought flitted through my sex-numbed mind. Just like with any Realside female, if you spend enough time with them, they DO know what you're thinking. "I won't *be* here in the morning, you silly-billy hunny-bunny in the beddie bye-bye-bye."

Crap. I'd hoped she wouldn't have figured that out. She and her look-alike sisters tended to vanish with the dawn, thus preventing any awkward morning-after scenes on who gets to use the shower first. Bunny? I wasn't a bunny. It's pure cat DNA that improved my looks. Not to mention endurance. The human in me wanted to roll over and snore, but there was enough feline within alert enough to stay just on the edge of consciousness. I cautiously opened an eye to see how solid she was. Come morning and she'd fade along with any need to give an answer.

Yup, she was still very much with me in my rumpled bed, nubile as a vintage Varga babe right out of *Playboy,* but with fluorescent orange skin, electric blue hair, matching horns, a long, arrowhead-tipped tail, and full, full lips with a wonderfully flexible tongue. She was naked, of course. I've seen my share of naked human females (hooray!), but somehow succubi tend to be even *more* naked. I was still trying to figure out just how they did it.

"I want you to be my date at the InfernalCon," she said. "It'll be soooo much fuuuuuuun."

"Whazzat?"

"Only the biggest gathering of the year for everyone on my Side of things. You'll love-love-lovey-*dove* it, I just know."

Well, she'd been right about everything up to now concerning my likes, albeit in the specific venue that took place while I was in dreamland. Since going on a semivoluntary walk in the Hell-plane for reasons I won't go into here, I'd not lacked for Otherside female company of the horny kind. Real horns. On their heads. Though the other kind of horny was definitely involved. A bunch of the succubi there had mistaken me for a virgin, then gave their all to try to cure me of what they thought was a terrific inconvenience. I'd been in no position, so to speak, to argue and since then continued not to argue as one after another of them dropped in on my otherwise boring sleep to make sure I was happy and healthy. An all-human male might have been strung out exhausted from so much dreamtime exercise, but the cat side of me just kept singing, "Bring it on and woo hoo!"

I made myself wake up just a little more. "Where is this convention?"

"In Otherside, of course."

"In Hell?" That meant I'd have to be asleep to go there and stick side by side with my bodacious Beelzebub babe to make sure of getting back safe.

"It's at a *very* nice hotel," she added.

"Like the ones we have in Realside?"

"Where do you think *we* got the idea?"

Not as crazy as it sounds. I'd learned there's a lot of different levels to Hell, some furnished according to who's to be confined there for punishment. A nice hotel to me might be wailing perdition to someone else. One of my ideas of true Hell has to do with being stuck at a play-to-the-death canasta challenge where everyone has blue hair and wants to give me the details of their last bowel movement. That's a mental picture that keeps me on the side of the good guys for the most part.

"Oh, it's *nothing* like thaaaa-aaaat," said the succubus, picking up on my brainwaves again. I was used to it by now.

"Why me for a date?"

" 'Cause you're so ring-a-ding-dilly-billy cuuuuuute." She breathed the last, stirring the fur in one of my ears, making it twitch. Much more and I'd wake up all the way.

Okay, I was cute. Had to agree with her on that. "And what else?"

"I just don't want to go on my own." She almost pouted.

"Like a class reunion?" I couldn't remember ever going to one of those, but had seen enough movies and TV commercials to have an idea. The main characters want to show off their success to their friends; if you didn't have a pricey car or a dream job, then turn up with a dynamite date. Sounded rockin' to me. . . .

She let out with a squeal. Did I mention that succubi are *real* enthusiastic and not shy about showing it? Good thing most people on Realside couldn't hear her or my nights would get embarrassing for the noise.

"Yow! Wow! That's iiiiiiit!" she yodeled. Her long blue tail thrashed and lashed, finally winding affectionately around one of my legs. Eeek, but the tail's arrowhead-shaped tip tickled, in all the right ways.

"Yeah, okay, sure-fine-you-betcha," I said, then couldn't talk for a while because she was busy demonstrating her gratitude to me. Stage One involved some serious lip-lockage.

No rest for the not-too-terribly wicked, I thought.

The next night, right after I drifted off to sleep, the succubus was waiting for me to be her Otherside escort. There's no way to figure how she did it, but she looked even better than usual, maybe her orange skin was more orangey and she'd spruced up her horns and tail with special polish. There was definitely some blue gloss on her lips; she'd even teased her hair up twice its height so I wondered if she'd originally come from Texas. Big Hair is an art form there; I liked it.

"Whyyyyy thank youuuuuu, Myhr, the purrrrr, the hot stud with the furrrr," she crooned, doing a slow turn to give me the full effect.

"Better tone it down or I won't be able to walk," I said, my heart rate going up. Among other things.

One aspect of succubi that makes them different

from their human Realside cousins is when they get decked out for a date, they don't have a problem with a round of pregame fun. The human ladies I've gone with tend to save that for the last. No problem for me, I can be patient, if sometimes a bit frustrated for the wait. But I don't blame them for it; they went to a lot of trouble to get prettied up and want a few hours of appreciation for the effort. Succubi, on the other hand, can instantly restore themselves from a serious mussing no matter how crazy it gets. I think that's why their any-time, any-place attitude keeps them so popular with guys.

And in this case, ohhhh yeah, we were late getting to the Hotel Hell. . . .

But she looked great all over again when we appeared just like that in the lobby. She was cozied up against me and smiling, which is always nice, but had forgotten something.

"Clothes," I said.

"Never wear 'em," she sniffed. "Except for shoes." She was in some very spiky blue heels.

"Not you. Me."

The body fur goes down a long way, but still . . . mustn't scare the public. I insisted, and she finally obliged, and I was suddenly in my favorite outfit, of dark pants, boots, and a nice, soft Ren-fair style shirt with embroidery. It was suitable for all kinds of social occasions, and in this case blended just fine with the other attendees. A number of them were checking in, drifting toward the sports bar (*why* was it *always* a sports bar?) or on their way toward the convention area. They were dressed in everything from bloody skins (ick) to Fortune 500 business suits (double-ick) to polyester (off-the-scale-break-the-needle ick).

As for their physical appearance, demons come in ALL shapes, sizes, and colors, some of them able to morph into countless variations of whatever, depending on their mood. I did recognize a few types that rarely changed their looks, mostly other succubi (yow, more naked babes!) and their opposites, the incubi. The latter all tended to look (and dress) like male models for romance novels, heavy on the Schwarzenegger pecs and flowing hair, and for some reason succubi just can't stand the guys. As much as they each enjoyed nonstop nookie, you'd think they'd have common ground for having lots of mutual whoopee, but each thought the other too ugly for words. I once asked a succubus about that and she explained that I couldn't see demons the same way that demons see each other. She also told me I wouldn't want to, either. I took her at her word and left it at that, grateful the incubi were dressed. Open-to-the-navel pirate shirts and waxed chests (in a manly-man shade of orange) was the fashion this year.

Since succubi do look exactly alike—who needs a twins fantasy when you can have sextuplets, emphasis on the sex—I kept an affectionately firm grip on my girl as we strolled over to sign in.

"This gonna cost anything?" I asked, wondering if she remembered to include my wallet with the pants.

"Only your *soul*," intoned a gum-chewing demon busily writing names on badges.

"Get real," said my date, rolling her eyes.

"Dammit," he shot back, friendly.

"That's the idea. I'm prepaid and this is my guest, M-Y-H-R, rhymes with *purr*."

The demon spelled my name out on a badge using arcane glyphs and a pen with red ink. At least I hoped it was ink. The letters smoked a little until they dried. "Your name . . . ?"

"L-I-S-A."

Name? My succubus for the night had a *name*? None of them had ever hinted in the least about me calling them anything more personal than "baby-oh-baby." Then I recalled just how important names were on the demon-side of things. Once anyone knew your name they had power over you . . . and she'd just given away my REAL name. . . .

Lisa-the-succubus smiled at me. "Oh, hunny-bunny, don't worry, the rules are different now. On Realside we don't give out that kind of info, but it's okay here. Safe."

"What about when I wake up, I'll remember it."

"No, you won't."

Oh. Uhhhh. Okay. Whatever. Must have to do with Magic or something, then. Magic was boring. To me, anyway. Some went in for it big time like my roomie, who's a wizard. It's his Thing. To each his own and where was the bar . . . ?

But Lisa wanted to see the convention and began energetically hauling me around from one chamber to the next. They looked like ordinary convention rooms for a large hotel, but what with us being in Hell and all, "chamber" just seemed to work better.

This event really was huge, with no less than three huckster areas, but only one was open to me. The others were too hot or too cold. I didn't think it was a Hell Thing, just the hotel climate system living down to one's worst expectations.

The vendor decor was heavy on dark reds and blacks. Just about everyone used a black background with red lettering—or glyphs—so they looked alike to my nondemonic eyes. Lisa was in Heaven, figuratively speaking, darting from one to the other cooing over the goods, most of which I did not recognize, (scary) or did know rather well (scarier). One of the larger spreads had their name in English: Shoes from Hell, and Lisa spent a lot of time there checking out the styles, some of which were genuinely bloodcurdling because they had Realside designer labels inside.

She didn't buy anything, but the heels she did have on morphed, acquiring gold studs and a patent leather sheen. I asked why the studs were gold, not silver like the originals.

Lisa shrieked—no one seemed to notice—with horror. "Silllverrrrr!??? Sweetie pie, you wanna kill meeeee?"

Oops. She was right, certain types of metals and demons just did not get along together, like Superman and glowing green rocks. "Sorry—ahh—is that the art show?"

Fortunately, she had a short attention span, and we went for a look, or tried to; there was a waiting crowd. From what I could see of the exhibits within, some torturous performance art was going on. Literally. Lots of screaming. I'm into art, but that kind was a big turnoff, I don't care if the screamers deserved it or not.

I ducked us into the next chamber over, which was full of snickering Car Key Gnomes (I always *knew* those guys were out there). The short, Robin-Hood styled celebs at the front table were apparently well-liked in the field as the audience was roaring with laughter at their war stories of successful heists and their chaotic aftermaths. Several of the diminutive creatures were carrying autograph books, and it promised to get interesting later as other gnomes were happily picking pockets for pens. Lisa told me the next topic would be about swapping Phillips and flat head screwdrivers around, followed by "Training That New Dryer to Eat Just ONE Sock."

Oh, what joy.

"The bar," I said, firmly returning us to the hall where various demons milled, checking their program books. "That is, if it's safe for me to drink anything here."

"Suuuuure it is. This is strictly for fun. We're not doing any of the down 'n' dirty Magic stuff here. We save that for Realside."

Good. I hoped the bar stocked Shiner Bock. . . .

"Lisaaaaaa!!!!!!!" A male voice hailed her from a few yards away, and he sounded harassed. Not unexpected, given the location. How he could tell her from all the other succubi, I didn't know. Must be a Demon Thing.

Lisa took her time turning around so she could

enjoy his reaction. There's nothing like being with a woman—or whatever—who knows she can make guys trip on their own tongues. She snuggled closer to me, and I got the impression this was one of the beings she wanted to one-up on the show-off factor. "Irving," she cooed. "Loooong time."

Irving, who, from the suit looked to be a middle-mismanagement type, staggered toward us, a peculiar look on his warty face, which was saying a lot considering the surrounding company. His gray skin—and I mean real gray like for battleships—paled an unhealthy—on him—shade of pinky flesh color. He made a gasping, gagging sound, then dropped in front of us.

There was a big sword sticking out of his back. Black blood smoked from the wound, hissing. A few of the more sanguinary demon types gathered close, licking their chops.

"EEEEEEE!" squealed Lisa, her blue nails digging into my arm. She darted forward and grabbed at the weapon, then screamed very loud, yanking her hand back in pain. Her eyes were glowing with terror as she looked at me. "Help him! Take it out!"

"It'll kill him," I yelped. Was there such a thing as 911 in Hell?

"He'll die if you don't! That's cold iron!"

At that, the other demons fell back, thoroughly out of the mood for a snack.

"Pull it ouuuuuuut!" she wailed.

Okay, what the Hell, why not . . . I grabbed the pommel of the sword and yanked it clear of Irving's twitching bod. He gave an alarming cry of agony followed by aftershock moans and groans that finally wound down. Some of the gray came back to his face.

"Ohhhh, Satan, that *hurt*," he muttered. Lisa threw herself at him and helped him sit up. The crowd gave me a wide berth because of the sword. The air took on a distinct cookery tang from its coating of scorched black blood. Ugh.

"Irving? What happened? Who's got you on their shit list?" Lisa's "I'm-way-too-cool-for-you" 'tude toward Irving was gone and she sympathetically patted one of his thick warty hands.

"Hot mama, it's a heaven of a long story."

"Awww, tell me all about it."

"In the *bar*," I said firmly, not caring to stand in the middle of the hall with a bunch of gawpers. I wanted a drink *now*, and maybe I could ditch the smoking sword there. Burned demon blood smelled a lot like fajitas. I might never eat them again.

Irving-the-demon's suit was ruined for only a moment before it knitted up again along, presumably, with his perforated hide. He still seemed shaken and leaned a lot on Lisa, big hands everywhere. I'd have to remember the technique the next time I wanted to cop a feel.

The sports bar was a crowded seat-yourself place, so we grabbed a table, shoving aside beer bottles left by the last patrons. No Shiner, but they did have Dick's Dirty Devil Brew. Well, okay, in a pinch.

Irving downed his drink in one swallow and groaned again, rubbing his chest. "What a night I'm having! Hey, watch where you're pointing that thing."

Singular, so he was talking about the sword and not Lisa's prominent—uh—which were all perky and—ah—I politely put the sword on the floor, tucking it close so no one would trip on it. "Sorry. What's the headlines on the attack?

"I got an exorcist after me."

Lisa squawked. "Oh, you poor thing! Jesuits or Baptists?"

Those were the Holy Hit-Men on Realside. Either type were not the sort a demon would want to meet in a well-lighted street.

"Worse." Irving groaned. "It's a pissed-off wizard."

"Anyone I'd know?" I asked. My wizard roomie tended to be cranky at the best of times, but would happily party with demons if the chance popped up while on an Otherside stroll.

"Some guy calling himself Billy-Bob Sousane."

I shook my head, but Lisa made a *yeeping* sound.

"I've met him at a few Summonings," she said. "He's nothing special under the sheets, but has a *lot* of magical mojo. Oh, Irving, what did you do to get him mad at you?"

"Not a saved thing!" Irving was very aggrieved. "It's my do-good cousin Ralph. He's the one that screwed up the works. He's the dope of the clan, can't even get a simple possession right."

"What happened?"

"I got a Summoning. A bunch of us were hanging together and they suddenly went away, meaning that I'd been yanked over to Realside, you know how it is."

"I don't," I said.

For the first time Irving gave me a close look, taking in the badge with my name. I hoped he'd forget it. "Do I know you?"

Maybe I'd saved his life—for which he had yet to thank me—but he was still a demon and it is the nature of the beast to be boorish. "I'm Lisa's date."

"You're from *Realside?*"

"Isn't he cuuuuuute?" Lisa asked sweetly. She tickled me under the chin with the arrowhead tip of her tail, showing me off. What a babe.

Irving seemed flummoxed by my feline features on a man's bod. "Is that a mask?"

Lisa replied for me. "Of course not! Now don't be jealous and get back to telling my sweetie-peety-pittypie about Summonings."

The explanation wasn't rocket science. Anyone on Realside with the knowledge and inclination can summon a demon. Unless you command for a specific kind of demon to answer—like a succubus—there's a pool of miscellaneous mayhem makers that rotate on answering calls. I think they got the idea from telemarketers. Most of the Magically Talented I'd met rarely went in for it, having more interesting ways to play.

Except for succubi (and okay, incubi,) demons are hard to control and heavy into destroying things on Realside. The smart Talents have no need for them, and the rest are just idiots who are obligingly removed from the gene pool by the visiting demon. Hey, there's a reason *why* wizards go through decades of training to avoid that sort of thing. I've been in some less than friendly areas of Hell and the creatures there are ones you *don't* want as house guests.

Irving continued, "So one sec' I'm chillin' and the next I'm hauled over to Realside into a Circle with sage smoke so thick I could walk on it. Before I know up from down, Sousane's in my face screaming blue murder about his niece, Charlene. Man, he was pissed."

"What about?"

"Charlene, what do you think? The squirt was with her Realside buds messing around, experimenting with Magic, trying to do stuff they're not ready for. Oh, Satan, you *gotta* love Ouija boards! They're Ralph's favorite way to infiltrate to Realside. He's a dope, but he knows how to play the game, and he had these kids convinced that they'd contacted Edwin Booth."

"Edwin Booth?" I asked. "Why him?"

"Why not? Maybe one of them was a drama major. Well, Irving did his song and dance of spelling out answers to their lame questions, sounding profound and mysterious, getting the kids worked up and excited and scared—very tasty. Then little Charlene decides to call his bluff and issues one of those 'If you're Edwin Booth, prove it' ultimatums. That's all the invitation Ralph ever needs, so he jumped right into her."

"Did it hurt?"

Irving gave me a gray, withering glare. "Of *course* it did—that's the whole *point*. Haven't you ever heard 'I'm infernal, therefore I inflict pain?' Lisa, you sure can pick 'em. Where was I? Okay, Ralph goes into his Linda Blair routine, scares off the party, and settles in for a sweet filet of soul, but then Uncle Sousane barges in and queers up everything. Usually it takes weeks for the Realsiders to figure out what's happened, and by the time they get around to an exorcism the fat demon is singing and ready to vacate anyway. Ralph wasn't so lucky. He got blasted out of that little chickie and bounced around the room like a Superball on uppers. It freaked him big time, running into a wizard that strong, then Sousane got a psychic lasso on him and forced Ralph to talk."

"About what?"

"Gimme a break, he wanted Ralph's *name*."

"To control him?"

"To kill him."

"So? He'd just come back to Hell, wouldn't he?"

"No, he'd be dead. Not the same thing."

I worked to get my head around that one.

"*Dead*-dead," Lisa tried to explain. "As in doesn't exist at allllllll."

I took that to be a bad thing. "So he's trying to kill Ralph?"

"Bingo, Einstein. We got rules here and one of 'em is when a Realsider has the power and asks your name, you *have* to tell the truth."

"Why is that?"

"I just obey the rules, I don't know the why of 'em. But Ralph, the dumb ass rule breaker that he is, gave the freaking wizard *MY* name instead! While Sousane worked himself up into a death-blast to finish him, Ralph slipped his leash and shot clear. Next thing I know *I'm* in the Wizard's clutches, called up like a delivery pizza about to be turned outside-in by a frat boy."

"How did you get away?"

"Ralph knew he'd crossed the line, so he came back to help get me clear. What a night! He busted me loose and babbled the whys and warnings to me, but by the time I shed the sage-smoke fog he'd vanished. I tried the same, but Sousane dropped into a trance and followed me to Otherside. Don't know how he managed to track me here, I was going like a dove into Heaven. Thought I was safe. I saw you, Lisa, and hoped you might be able to go Realside and distract the guy till he got over his mad, and then *wham!*—I get skewered. How the heaven did he get cold iron past security?"

Speculations were not to happen. A cloud of smoke shot through with white fireworks manifested on—I should also say *through* the table between us. I was blinded for a second and the smell of sage and Nag Champa incense filled the place. Around us several demons made gagging sounds as they blundered hastily away, knocking over chairs with multiple clatters and thumps.

Familiar with his voice by now, I recognized Irving's hollow pain-filled shriek. Billy-Bob Sousane must have struck again.

Sure enough and then some. When the smoke cleared, Irving's head was on the table, leaking steaming black blood all over the hotel coasters. His body— also leaking, ick—still sat upright in the chair, arms spasming. One hit his head, knocking it nose-down into Lisa's lap.

I expected another scream, but she only picked up the head and scowled at the grimacing Irving. "Don't you *ever* get a clue? I am *off* your menu, suit-boy!" Then she plonked his head back onto the neck stump. Backward.

Irving turned his face around the right way and his skin healed up again. "All this fuss for a TINY little possession thing! Sheesh!"

"Possession is tiny?" I'd seen *The Exorcist* and knew better.

"It is on this side. Just something you do for fun. Generates a lot of negative energy to feed from. I don't go in for it much, because sooner or later they call in some big gun with Holy Water and the stress is just *not* worth it. Gimme a nice steady diet of co-dependent relationship misery. Unless they get therapy, it can go on for years and years before anyone gets cured and—"

Lisa let forth with a big raspberry, clearly bored. She was into feeding on other kinds of energy, after all.

Irving took the hint, tugging at his collar, which was losing the bloodstains. "Man, that wizard's pissed as Heaven and ready to kick ass and take names."

"He already did—yours," I said.

"Exactly, and it's a full moon night, to boot. If he keeps up with the killing mojo, I'm going to be checking out—permanently! Please Lisa, couldn't you go visit him? I know he's into succubi big time. If you could just distract him for a couple of hours and get him to sleep, I can arrange for a Visitation to reveal to him that he's after the wrong demon."

"Can't Lisa tell him for you?" I asked.

"Why should he believe another demon? Naw, I have to go through channels and see if the Powers That Be can fit in an emergency Visitation to save my ass. The paperwork's murder."

I was still getting used to how things worked on this Plane. "You mean the guys upstairs would do that for a demon? I thought you were fighting all the time."

Irving shrugged. "Hey, you gotta have *some* compromise or the whole power structure falls apart. If we were in a constant shooting war, your types wouldn't be alive. And *then* what would we fight over?"

I decided I was unqualified to answer that.

The sports bar manager—clearly not amused by the latest attack on Irving—manifested next to us and pointed toward the exit. He was large, very serious-looking, holding knobbly clubs in four of his five arms. Whatever he rumbled in a voice too deep to understand was unnecessary, we hoofed it. A number of imps popped in, armed with cleaning rags and Windex to take care of the black blood. The manager roared something at me specifically that made my hair—all of it—stand on end.

Lisa indicated the sword on the floor. "He wants that gone, too."

No problemo. I grabbed up the blade and skedaddled. I'm a lover, not a fighter, but as we emerged back into the swirl of the convention it was nice to have a hunk of cold iron clearing the way for us. No demons were curious enough to get closer than two yards.

Lisa said, "Irving, I'll give it a tidy-die-dee try, but Billy-Bob's not that easy to distract. I think you should leave before they kick us out of the convention, too. You could get the whole thing shut down."

Sounded like a Plan to me.

"Hey, by hiding here I got lots of cover . . ." Irving didn't finish because another cloud of smoke began forming in front of us.

I didn't think—one of my baaaad habits—and waved the point of the sword into the middle of the cloud. I wasn't trying to kill anything, just taking an experimental poke to see if there was any resistance. To my surprise, someone yelped and the cloud vanished.

"Myhr!" Lisa squealed, throwing her arms around me. "You're the one! YOU can save Irving!"

Hah? What? "Oh, nononononono, not me, whatever it is."

"Hey, you're right," said Irving. "He's from Realside to start with. The wizard will *have* to believe him."

I showed my teeth and not in a fun way. "Hello? What part of 'nonononononono' did you not understand? I'm staying right here until I wake up and—"

"Come *on*, cutey-pootie, sweetie-peety pie!" Carefully avoiding the sword, Lisa bodily wrapped herself around me.

Usually when she does that, it's a lot more fun, but the next thing I knew we're hurtling through a patch, vortex, dimension—oh, who *cares* what it's called this season?—and my guts weren't dealing well with the change. They caught up with me too fast, slamming back into place just as we manifested in some dark room filled with drifting incense smoke. I staggered. Lisa went "Ugh-foo!" in reaction to what I considered a pleasant smell and vanished. *Poof.*

Women. Go figure.

"Irving! I bind thee within this circle and cast silence upon thee!"

Thus intoned a very intense male voice somewhere in front of me. Definitely a wizard in Formal Mode here.

"Ahhh, hello?" I waved around with the sword again like a blind man with a cane. So long as I was here, I might as well make the best of things and do what I could to fix the situation. If I got Irving off the hook, then maybe my little succubus would be grateful enough to wake me up and then I'd never, ever agree to go to another Hell Con again.

"WHO ART THOU? I COMMAND YOU TO SPEAK THY NAME!" boomed a fella I presumed to be the pissed-off and now surprised Billy-Bob Sousane. The thick tendrils of incense parted enough for me to see him. He looked like an Old School wizard, heavy into robes, special jewelry, and other paraphernalia. He was in protective black, the magical equivalent of Kevlar.

"Hey, keep it down, I'm not deaf!" The sword blade had strayed beyond the power lines of a containing circle cast on the floor, which is probably what spooked him. What worked containing a demon hadn't done jack on me.

"WHO ART THOU?" he bellowed again. Big guy. He could have gone a few throws with the sports bar manager and held his own even with two-thirds fewer arms.

"The name's Myhr—rhymes with 'purr,' and STOP YELLING!"

Remarkably, it worked. Sousane glared at me, then my sword. Uh-oh. He must have just guessed who had poked him. There was a nick in his left palm, which he held out flat like a cop directing traffic. He had a wand in his right hand. Candles burned all over the otherwise dark room, but the wand glowed by itself. I figured he'd used it in some magical way to separate Irving from his head.

"*What* are you?" Sousane demanded.

This was no time to get snarky. He had every right to be ticked; all I had to do was smooth the waters and get out. "I are Myhr, and I'm here on behalf of Irving the demon who wants you to know he's *not* the one you're looking for."

Sousane continued to glare. Intently. I knew the look; he was checking my aura. Depending on how good he was at reading, he'd be able to tell if I was dishing him the truth.

Quickly I went through the Story As I Knew It, apologizing on behalf of demons everywhere for any inconvenience caused to him and all his kin. "And, it's really none of my business, but you should take that Ouija board away from your niece before she hurts herself or anyone else."

"Are you a wizard?"

"Nah, I just room with one and pick up stuff by osmosis. Listen, I'm getting a little cold here; if we're squared about Irving, I'd like to go back to my hot date. . . ."

"I want the demon who possessed my niece!"

"No problemo. His name is . . . uh . . . uh . . . that is . . . crap—I can't remember!" Too true. The succubus said I'd forget names on this side. I'd been able to remember Irving's only because Sousane had said it aloud.

"Too bad for you, then." Sousane raised his wand.

"Hey! Don't you go medieval on me! It's not my fault! You know how the rules work about names. I can't help you—deal with it." Just in case he wasn't planning to be sensible I held the sword in a guard position across my body. Cold iron works just as well on wizards, especially in a pointy form.

But he wasn't going to be a sport; I saw that much in one of his smoke-reddened eyes about one second before he cut loose with—well, I couldn't say what it was, because in half a second I dove the heck out of the way.

Boom crash bang rumble rumble went the sound effects, so loud I couldn't hear them. (Yes, it does happen that way.) I did *feel* them. They tromped me like a herd of elephants wearing football cleats. I rolled and took cover behind an iron cauldron big enough to do stews for cannibals. My ears rang from the aftershock of the blast. If he'd screwed up my perfect pitch, I would be severely annoyed.

"Yo, Sousane! I'm just a middleman!"

And he wasn't buying. He waved that wand and . . . *ka—wham!*

Psychic blast, a really big one, *lots* of magic in it. White hot.

It itched.

My human side didn't like it, but the cat part of me is fairly immune to magic. That didn't mean Sousane couldn't wear it down and fry both sides to a tasty golden brown, given time.

Not tonight. I dropped the sword and got my shoulder against the cauldron, heaving mightily. My muscles don't look it from the outside, but they're way better than human or I'd never have been able to shift the thing. Metal grating harshly against the floor, the cauldron tumbled toward Sousane like a drunken bowling ball. He was fast enough to dodge and did so, but I launched myself while he was distracted and tackled him square. We both hit the floor, but he was on the bottom with the breath knocked out of him.

Irving just wanted the guy busy for a few hours. The succubus had her methods; I had mine—starting with a solid clock on the jaw. It stunned Sousane for a few minutes, and by then I'd found a roll of duct tape—handy stuff—and trussed him up snug. He was fully awake and glaring over his gag when I'd finished.

"Don't be so sore," I said, dusting myself off. "You were trying to do the right thing, just aimed at the wrong being. For what it's worth, I think Irving's as mad as you are about this. If you lay off the Death Magic for a couple of hours, you'll get confirmation from a source you can trust. Don't worry about a comeuppance; Irving's probably gonna roast the dude for both of you. Won't that be nice?"

Sousane made *errrgh—arrrrrrrgh* sounds in an unfriendly tone.

"Okay, whatever. Are you alone here, or will someone be by to eventually untie you? Despite the hoorah, I wouldn't want you starving to death."

"Urrgh!"

"Was that a yes-*urrgh* or a no-*urrgh*?"

He got *real* red in the face. Some people have no sense of humor. I went to the room's only door and cracked it, listening. We were in what seemed to be an otherwise ordinary suburban house. I could hear a TV blaring and people talking a few walls away, apparently unaware of (or maybe used to) the magical pyrotechnics. No need to disturb anyone. I rummaged for paper and pen, finding some on a table. Sousane groaned as I block printed a note on the top sheet. The stuff must have been the special kind used for writing out spells. Ah, nuts, he could buy more. With a bit of duct tape I put my "do not disturb until morning—*busy!*" sign on the outside of the door. If the family below had any inkling of Sousane's work, then they'd likely leave him alone.

If not, then Irving was in for it. But I'd done my duty, above and beyond. Besides, life's a gamble—even for demons.

I left the cold iron sword behind, it not being mine, and stepped into the circle on the floor, resisting the urge to click my heels together three times.

It took a while for the magic to take hold and do its thing, like waiting for an elevator, but once started . . .

Going down. Rocket speed. With a gleeful . . . uh . . . *Lisa*—that was her name!—waiting on Other-side to greet me once my stomach settled. I decided to forgive her for whisking me off like that. She was the spontaneous sort, after all.

"Get a room!" someone bawled at us.

"No! Don't!" someone else yelled. Irving. "Did you kill him?"

I gently peeled enough of Lisa off my face to say no. "He's tied up for now. Get your Visitation paperwork started before—"

Irving vanished. *Poof.* Again, no thank you, but what d'ya expect with a demon? Lisa eventually settled down from welcoming me back and insisted we return to the convention activities. I loved her short attention span.

"Am I gonna remember any of this in the morning?" I asked.

"Only the bits you like. I'll make sure you have some gooooood times again before you wake up."

Just minus all names. Suited me fine. Lisa led me off toward another panel discussion about to start. The chamber was almost full. "Who's the speaker?"

"Oh, hunny-bunny! You're gonna *love* this guy!"

Of that I was dubious, but Lisa was in full fan-girl mode now and didn't notice my lack of enthusiasm. The attendees roared during the introduction, so I missed the speaker's name. He was one ugly critter who shape-shifted with every step he took, never the same look twice and each one scarier than the last, not unlike Michael Jackson.

A hush seized the crowd.

"He's world-famous!" Lisa whispered, passing me a book being circulated around the crowd; clearly the guest was its author and popular. Others had copies in hand. The cover read: *Coming out of the Closet*, by—oh, gawd—the Boogieman.

I checked the guy on stage again. He morphed into a blue-haired little old lady, a deck of cards in one hand and a glass of Metamucil in the other.

She looked right at me—and *smiled*.

I woke up screaming.

FACING DOWN YOUR DEMONS

by Alexander B. Potter

Alexander B. Potter resides in the wilds of Vermont, editing anthologies and writing a variety of fiction and nonfiction. His short stories have appeared in a number of anthologies including the award-winning *Bending the Landscape: Horror* volume. He edited *Assassin Fantastic, Sirius: The Dog Star,* and *Women of War* for DAW Books, and another anthology is forthcoming from DAW.

"HELL IS . . . being surrounded by people with really high metabolisms."

"Come again?"

"You know, skinny people who can eat as much as they want and never gain weight."

"Oh, *God,* yes!"

"Wait, I've got one. Hell is . . . moving back in with your parents."

From my perch on the back of Vic's recliner, I watch the group break up laughing They sprawl on Vic's living room floor in a casual circle, cards fanned in their hands, coins in a pile between them. Thinking back to my own parents, that's the best entry so far. Considering I was one of those high metabolism people back when I was alive, I don't feel qualified to comment on that one. Makes me twice as convinced Vic worries way too much about his weight, though.

"Oh, puh-lease," drawls Dave. Or is it Dan? Whichever. Something with a D. I have a hard time keeping track of Vic's friends. I don't think it's just because I'm dead. They're boring. Dave/Dan, unaware of my momentary confusion, continues. "Hell is working retail, and you all know it."

Now that I can definitely get behind. I hover up off the back of Vic's chair as I lose myself in thoughts of my first job at fourteen. Selling shoes. One year of that and I swore never again. I climb down off the chair and stretch, waiting for that shift that tells me my back has realigned. Not having a physical body but feeling like I do can be odd at times.

Usually I just try not to think too hard about it.

Just for the hell of it, I walk through the middle of their game, making the coins shift against each other and slide off the pile. Vic stiffens, and his eyes sweep the room, brows furrowing. I grin as his gaze falls on me—or should I say on the air where I would be if I were corporeal. He's getting better. He's starting to be able to sense me even when I'm not making myself visible.

Sidling around behind him, I rest my hand on the back of his neck and grin wider at his slight shudder. Easing myself down onto the worn gray carpet, I settle in behind him and drape myself against his back, leaning my face close to his ear as I breathe out a soft laugh. His hair stirs, and that shudder wracks him again.

I know he hears the laugh, feels my spectral embrace like a blanket straight from the freezer falling over his back. I stare over his shoulder at his chattering friends, tired of them. They don't amuse me like Victor amuses me. I was looking forward to having some fun with him tonight. I can't toy around with him when Evan is over, and Evan's here most of the time. Evan always sees me, whether I intend to be visible or not.

Sometimes I can pick on Vic if Evan is in another room, because he won't draw Evan's attention to me. But it's risky. Occasionally Evan senses something, even from two rooms away. And knows. Then things get complicated.

But tonight Evan is out with his sisters, and I'm tired of watching this group of would-be gamblers. They're playing with dimes and quarters, ferchrissake. Wimps. I briefly consider turning on the television, or maybe the shower, just to spook them. Or how about breaking out the fire extinguisher. That might get them out of here.

The longer I sit with my chin resting on Vic's shoulder, the more I recognize that I won't do anything of the sort. Apart from the initial shudder, he's made no move to dislodge me, and in fact leaned back into me. I make his life hard enough as it is. He's more patient with me than I would be in his place. I can't begrudge him a night with his friends, even if they are dorks. Sighing, I release him and get to my feet.

The minute my presence lifts away from him, his head whips up and around, a suspicious expression crinkling the bridge of his nose. I run my fingers down his cheek lightly in reassurance, then wander to the wall and through it, letting my hand become visible just as the rest of me is completely through, waving a quick good-bye.

Outside, the wind picks up around me, and I feel the night itself welcoming my presence. The leafless branches twist on the trees as I wander across the parking lot, letting my feet solidify enough to leave prints in the snow. I wonder briefly if Evan will know them for mine when his sisters drop him off. Evan always did notice the strangest damn details. I glance back at my meandering tracks and know he'll notice, and know. Somehow. Some strange Evan-way.

He'll burst into Vic's apartment and ask him right out, "Was Brandon here?" And all of Vic's tedious, nonseeing friends who have all heard about Evan's history with me will exchange significant looks, shift uncomfortably, toss out lame excuses and make their escape before Vic's strange "creepy" new boyfriend can say anything else about his crazy ex-lover. His crazy *dead* ex-lover.

I leave the parking lot, thinking of Vic's friends all comfortably sitting on his living room floor, playing poker and dissecting Hell. My smile tightens and bitterness creeps through my mind. You've got some good ideas, kiddies, but I can help you out on this one. Hell is being stalked by a darkness from the inside out, and Hell is losing the battle to it. Hell is the emptiness, and the apathy, and the ache . . . and losing so much of yourself that you can't stand to continue. Losing so much of yourself that you hurt the one person you don't want to, so badly.

It's funny, but Hell never seemed farther away than when I finally died.

I'm making my fourth circuit through Harmony parking lot to Elliot Street, still pondering Hell, when I realize I'm not alone. I've been walking by and through people for the better part of an hour, but I don't mean them. I mean someone—something—like me. I'm not even sure how I know. In all the time since I died, I haven't seen or talked to another ghost. But I can feel this in the wind. Another presence that the elements recognize as not of the world. A metaphysical taste on the air, the way Evan tastes snow before it starts.

The people walking the sidewalk are normal enough. Within a broad definition of normal, considering they're out wandering around on a Vermont night in December with the windchill somewhere below zero. Most of them walk right through me and don't miss a beat. Whatever cold spot I'm generating tonight is nothing compared to the weather. A few shift to go around me without breaking their stride. Repressed Sensitives, most likely. Finally, I walk out into the street, ignoring the cars passing through me, scanning both sidewalks.

I've just about decided I'm imagining things when I see him. Leaning up against the window of the music store wearing blue jeans and a dark blue wool coat. Staring straight at me with a half smile.

I finish crossing the street and walk up to him. His eyes don't waver and the smile grows. He looks solid. I can do that if I want to, but it takes a fair amount of concentration and energy, and I prefer being invisible. I solidify my hand, reach out, and poke him in the shoulder. Definitely solid.

I study him as he tips back his head and laughs. People are giving him a wide berth, but something about the way they move makes me think it's not because they see him. They swerve out around us like a school of fish turning on a dime to avoid a predator, but they do so in happy obliviousness, their eyes coasting right over him.

To me, he looks like any other man on the street, if a little more Vermontish than most. He's got that rugged, careless look of one of the hometown boys still farming or working outdoors. Too tall by a damn sight, reddish hair tangled in the wind, the start of a beard, winter clothes, a pair of beat-up black work boots. But he's standing here giving me that dopey smile, no hat to be seen, and his pale skin doesn't have even the slightest flush from the cold and wind. Standing beside him, I can feel a vague heat radiating off him, pushing back against the bitter night. No wonder I could sense something on the air.

I back up one step, not taking my eyes off his. He's got a redhead's too-pale blue eyes, ice blue, but even they aren't cold. "What are you?"

His smile stretches, and laugh lines sketch themselves across his cheeks. "You have to ask?" His voice

is pure New England. He shakes his head like one of
my old high school teachers, the guy who always
thought I could do better than I was doing. "I don't
think you do."

"Humor me." Because I really don't like where my
mind is taking me.

He sighs and gives me that disappointed look again.
"If you insist. Just call me Luke. As for 'what'—given
you're such a skeptic, I suppose you'll need visual
proof."

I start to protest that I haven't been a skeptic since
months before my death, since meeting Evan actually.
Then I'm watching horns sprout through the red hair
and I groan, "You have *got* to be kidding me." I look
down at black boots that have morphed into shiny
cloven hooves. A serpentine tail, complete with pointed
tip, curls around one ankle. My lip curls in response.
"What is this, a joke? I didn't buy that image of the
Devil when I was a kid. Nothing but a ripped off Pan
impersonation, according to my dear ex."

He shrugs, the horns already fading, the boots back.
"I know, I know . . . it's the look we trot out for the
classicists. Is this more you?" Before I can blink, my
mother is standing in front of me, lounging in the
exact position he just held.

I'm startled enough to back up again, and actually
jump when a car rushes through me. I scramble to
regain my composure, step up on the sidewalk again,
and snort. "No *way*. No way, no how. Just . . . no."

"Aw, didn't mean to scare you, Brandon." The tall
farm boy is back, the grin suddenly less dopey and
more feral. "But you are convinced?"

"I really didn't need the second showing," I grumble,
looking anywhere but at him. My mind is shying away
from what this sudden appearance means. But my per-
sonality hasn't changed much in death. Still a contrary
sonofabitch. So I force myself to meet his eyes and
bite out, "What are you doing here?"

"Waiting for you."

"That much is obvious. Why?"

He pushes away from the wall and links his arm through mine. "Walk with me." He starts down the street and I find myself moving with him. I try to go insubstantial and just waft away from his hold. Nothing doing. That's a new one. He starts talking again. "How do you know I'm not here to finally collect?"

"Collect?" I play dumb to give myself time to calm the sudden leap of fear. This is too weird, even for someone who used to live with Evan, and is therefore by definition *used* to weird.

"On you. You've been dead a while now."

"I noticed."

He laughs. All things considered, it's a nice laugh. He glances down at me. "I was wondering if you had, actually."

We've reached Main Street and we turn south, toward the bridge. "Trust me, I noticed right away."

He smiles. For the Devil, he's a good-natured guy. "Trust me," he repeats. Then he winks at me. "That's my line."

"Yeah, well, wouldn't be the first time someone accused me of having the Devil's tongue."

"Suppose it wouldn't be the first time for someone to accuse you of being damned, either, eh?"

The resurgent choking sensation of fear stops me short. I stop walking and this time my arm pulls right through his. He gets two steps in front of me before he stops, turns back.

"Coming?" He's still smiling that friendly smile and walks a few more steps backward.

I don't move. "And if I said no?"

He's beside me in a heartbeat, leaning in, face close to mine. "Doesn't make much difference, really. Wherever you go, there you are."

I didn't honestly know if I could still be scared, being dead and all. Guess I'm finding out. I manage a mostly normal, "Where we going?"

"Just down here. I want to look at the water." He

nods his head toward the bridge and starts walking
again. I follow him down the hill. His legs are long,
and I'm not in a hurry. When I reach him, he's standing at the railing, looking down at the Whetstone
Brook.

I have a sudden flash of walking this route with my
mother as a child. Walking over the bridge gripping
the cold railing, staring down into the rushing water
every time, even though it scared me to death. Turning into the parking lot just past and following the
loose wire fence that runs along the drop-off to the
brook. Pressing my hand to it and leaning over as far
as I dared. It never looked strong enough to hold
anyone back. There were holes under it big enough
for a kid to slip through.

I shake off the memory and look down at the water,
too. For a brook the water is damn fast here, when
the rains are up. Winter has it high and rushing. The
streetlights gleam off the ice on the rocks, but the
water races on, black and frigid. "Why are you suddenly appearing to me now?" I ask with a calm I
don't feel.

He turns from the water and leans against the railing. I can't shake the feeling that he ought to be wearing a John Deere baseball cap. "You've been thinking
about me all night," he says, gesturing with his hand
back up the hill we came down.

"So, what . . . I called you here?"

"In a manner of speaking."

"Manner of speaking. Right."

"Let's just say the power of concentration is highly
underrated. And incidentally, when you think, you
think very . . . hard."

Do I? That's interesting. "So you suddenly notice
me thinking real hard about Hell, and you pop up to
tell me I'm damned."

"I don't reckon that's exactly what I said," he of-
fers mildly.

"Oh, will you stop with the hick act. And you said—"

"Suppose it wouldn't be the first time for someone to accuse you of being damned, either, eh?" The words are exact down to the inflection he used the first time. Like hearing a recording. I blink.

Run through the words in my head again.

"No-o-o," I say slowly. "It wouldn't be the first time someone *accused* me of being damned. But . . . accused isn't the same as being."

He hooks a boot in the railing, swings his body up, and sits on the top rung, knees spread, grinning like an idiot. "I think that's the case *you're* trying to make."

I give an exasperated sigh, staring across the street and out over the other side of the bridge to the Connecticut River beyond. "Right. Well, fine, if you're going to be so helpful, I'll just go back to the apartment and listen to Vic's idiot friends theorizing on Hell."

His voice is suddenly soft, with a velvet edge. "What do *you* think Hell is, Brandon?"

I turn back and the bastard has a battered green John Deere ball cap on. I groan again and lean against the railing, solidifying enough not to lean straight through it. "*Will* you get out of my head?"

The grin reappears and he pushes up the brim of the cap, resettling it on his head just like all the backwoods boys I remember from high school. "Sorry, it's in the job description." He actually looks sheepish. "But seriously . . . Hell?"

I cross my arms with a huff. "Until you showed up across the street, I was pretty much convinced Hell was a construct of the human mind. Humanity's perverse need to punish itself. Scare itself. Set up a big bad consequence so morals can be imposed arbitrarily. Form of social control, really."

He laughs and rests his elbow on his knee, his chin on his hand. "Ouch. You wound me. A construct?"

"You asked."

"So if I do exist," he pokes himself in the shoulder, mimicking me, "if I'm not just a construct, what am I a consequence *of*, for you?"

I shrug. "Well, you're definitely not here because I'm gay," I toss off, refocusing on his amicable face. "And we both know it. That's just too idiotic for words."

"Well, yes, obviously." He waves a hand impatiently. "So . . . what, then?"

I pause to ponder. It's not like I haven't thought about it. As he pointed out, I was thinking hard enough about it before he showed up. Ever since I woke up dead and nowhere in particular, I've wondered why I wasn't someplace more specific. Given that an afterlife obviously did exist, it made one reconsider how that initial life got lived. Seeing him tonight, figuring who he was, I'd be willing to believe someone somewhere thought I belonged in Hell. But I still wasn't that clear on what I might have done to get there. Running over everything that had occurred to me on my rambling walk, I shrug. "I wasn't exactly the nicest person around," I begin.

"No, you definitely weren't," he agrees. I shoot him a dirty look. "Well, you weren't. Hello? I believe I've introduced myself . . . Devil? As in 'The'? With the capital D? All knowing?"

"But I pretty much lived what I believed in," I continue, still glaring at him. "I was annoyingly honest. Didn't go out of my way to hurt people. I was nice to small children and animals. Well, to animals anyway. I mostly just tried to steer clear of small children." I stop and stare at the ground. "I did hurt somebody. Badly. Not intentionally, though."

"Evan."

"Evan," I agree. "Hurting someone like Evan ought to be a damnable sin."

"But even you don't believe that it is."

I shake my head, sighing. "No." I force away the

melancholy and stand quietly, remembering all the small and not-so-small potentially damning things I'd managed to list to myself in the last hour. They don't sound any worse now than they did the first time.

"Mmm, small stuff," he agrees, even though I didn't speak any of it aloud.

"I really hate telepathy," I comment in a sour voice.

"And you have some misconception that this matters to me?" he asks innocently. After my requisite glare, he pokes me in the shoulder. "You are sidestepping a rather obvious one, though." I give him a clueless look. "Well, you *are* a suicide," he elaborates.

"Oh, *puh-lease.*" I wince when I realize I sound like Dave. Or Dan. Whoever. "That's absurd. Why should any kind of Supreme Being or Greater Power or even you for that matter *care* if I took my own life or died choking on a hard candy or got run off the road by a drunk driver? Death is death is death."

"Surely you've heard the rationale that it's an affront to the Powers That Be to squander what you've been given."

"Hey, if it was given to me, it was *mine* to do with as I wanted . . . including waste it." Even as I say the words, I realize I'm enacting a conversation I've had in my own head countless times. Trying to convince myself. The lingering panic returns.

"So you do agree it was a waste," he murmurs, eyeing me shrewdly.

I open my mouth, and snap it closed again, glowering. He's got me and he knows it. Finally the words come, feeling ripped out of my throat. "I was so far out to lunch by the time I pulled that trigger, no court of law would have even let me stand trial for my own murder."

Something like satisfaction lights up his eyes, but he just nods. "So you think you should get off on the technicality of insanity?"

"I *think* suicide is a stupid reason to condemn a person. Given you apparently exist, isn't there sup-

posed to be somebody watching out for children and
madmen?"

"Not that it's my territory, but I'm fairly sure that's
children and fools, actually."

"Fools . . . madmen . . . same difference." I sigh
and glance to my left as the Latchis Theater doors
bang open, the movie letting out. People pass, heading
to their cars illicitly parked in the Food Co-op lot.
"People who don't know any better. Isn't that the
point? And I don't think mental illness is a technicality. I think mental illness *is* Hell."

"Ah-ha! Now we're getting somewhere."

I raise an eyebrow at him. "Getting somewhere?
What is this, therapy?"

He roars with laughter and the people around us
pull back even further, all without seeming to notice
what they're doing. "I just mean, if we agree Hell isn't
a constructed form of social control—and I assume
we've agreed, given my existence—you never did answer the question of how you see Hell."

Of course, I've been thinking about that, too. Because while I do think suicide shouldn't be a damning
sin, I've never been willing to bet the farm on it. Except, I guess I did bet the farm on it, in a way. What
I mean is, I've never expected the rest of the universe
to necessarily agree with my point of view.

I solidify my foot enough to kick at the sidewalk.
A chunk of icy snow mixed with dirt comes loose and
I send it careening out into the street, causing the
teens right in front of me to ruffle like startled birds.
As they hurry on, arguing about whether or not they
actually saw a disembodied foot, I formulate my answer. The words come slow. "I've never really bought
eternal torment. It's always seemed so pointless."

Luke laughs so hard he almost falls backward off
the railing. I find myself wondering if the water would
boil, if he fell into it. "Eternal torment is *pointless?*"

"If it's truly torment, and it's eternal, you'd just be
insane in a matter of days and completely not 'there.'

An eternity of pain and suffering? It doesn't make any *sense*."

"But a ghost chatting up the Devil in downtown Brattleboro on a Friday night in December does?"

He has a point. "I didn't say that."

"I'm just saying. Being metaphysical and all, what 'makes sense' can be a little loose. You don't think I could keep someone conscious and in their right mind while torturing them forever and beyond?"

"Again, I'm kind of stuck on . . . *point?* Why would you *want* to?"

"Mmm," he sighs. "Can we say *boring?*"

"And I mean the person's dead. Who cares? It's not like you're going to make a better person out of it or make up for whatever hideousness he or she created in life. The only way an eternally tormenting Hell makes any sense at all is as a *deterrent* to behavior. A way to keep people in line out of fear of what *might* happen to them after they're dead. Very lame."

"You don't think there are people bad enough that they *deserve* an eternity of torment?"

"Ah, but that's still thinking like a *living* person," I insist. "That's revenge talking. Living people, affected by the actions of the dead, want to know that so-and-so is rotting in the deepest, darkest pit of Hell . . . which, by the way, is probably not all that dark, what with all the fire, and fire being a form of light." I snort. "I don't know. On a metaphysical scale, on the cosmic level, I just don't see punishment for past deeds being as important as the here and now. Which is pretty much *over* when a person dies."

Luke shrugs. "You've got a here and now."

"Yes, but in my here and now I'm not creating evil in the world, either. I'm not making anyone miserable."

"You're not? What *are* you doing in the world?" he murmurs.

"I'd love to know," I crack. "Shouldn't you be answering that question? Why *am* I still floating around?"

I'd love to get a definite on that one. It's been preying on my mind.

"It's just interesting, is all." He scratches at his stubble and squints at me. "Some might call your current existence a form of Hell. Wandering, caught between worlds, watching everything but not a part of it. Watching the love of your life settle in happily with someone new."

The laugh bubbles up out of me and rises into the night around me. The last movie stragglers look around, startled. "PLEASE!" I sputter. "You call *that* Hell? I thought you were the expert! Anybody who calls that Hell has never seen the real thing. That's nothing. *Hell* is knowing your mind is ready to turn on you at a moment's notice." I snap my fingers in his face. "Just like that. Hell is having this *thing* inside you, just waiting. Hovering. Hanging riiight at the very edge of your mind, just watching for a chance to strike, like it has its own consciousness. And Hell is knowing that all it needs is the barest, tiniest little crack. Just a foothold . . . a toehold. And it'll slide and stretch and reach and *ooze*. Extend a tentacle and wriggle through, and wrap around whatever it finds, the closest thought, before you know it's there. And pry. Pry that wedge just a little bit wider, an infinitesimal bit at a time.

"Once it's in there, it starts working, spreading like a contagion, one thought to the next. The ooze just inches its way into every corner. Polluting everything, just a bit at a time. All by stealth. It's a covert agent, a sleeper. Sending out reassuring messages about how things really aren't that bad and you're not sliding down *that* hill again because you'd know if you were, wouldn't you? This must just be a bad day. You're fine, really. Even though you're worthless and incompetent and a total fraud and everything good that's ever happened to you has been sheer dumb luck and everything bad is a direct result of your own actions

and fuck-ups and is in fact an accurate commentary
on who you are as a person.

"It doesn't matter what anyone else says about you
because compliments can be made up and usually are
and they never mean it because they all *want* something and you, *you* know the truth about yourself that
no one else can see. The rotten core that you keep
hidden so well. The *absent* core . . . there is no core.
But no, you're fine, really, you can get up the next
day and go through it all again, and you're fine.
You're fine.

"And every time you believe it because oh, you
want to believe it, you're just letting it in more. It
oozes a little farther and a little farther like creeping
rot and the crack gets wider and then the fog starts
to roll in. The fog that blankets everything and pushes
it all back, just out of reach. Makes you feel like
you're slogging through wet cement and why are you
so damn tired? Can't concentrate. *Need* to concentrate, but there are too many details, too many little
things cluttering. Chattering. Demanding. There's just
too much and you can't deal with any of it, because
you're truly incapable, but no one seems to understand that. And the fog makes it all harder to separate,
harder to organize. Harder to control. And control is
so important, and it's slipping. You have no control,
nothing is in your control, and it makes you so damn
mad. Everything around you has a red tinge because
everything is pissing you off and the anger is under,
over, around, everywhere and it's all because you feel
so powerless. To affect anything, to make any kind of
difference anywhere. Nothing makes a difference, and
sure as hell, not one damn thing *you* do makes a dent.

"And people are the worst. The fog is whispering
now and it makes every single person around you just
that little bit more annoying, suspicious, abrasive, con-
descending. They don't care about you. None of them
do. They tolerate you. Put up with you. You're noth-

ing but a pawn to them, just someone they want to manipulate for their own purposes and all you can think about is every single little thing they ever did to slight you.

"And the fog keeps rolling. And you start not caring. Hell," I laugh again but this time it's a weird twisted sound I don't even recognize. "Hell is not *caring*. About anything. Because you care too damn much about everything and nothing's *ever* going to change or get better and it hurts so fucking much you have to stop caring or die. But when you stop caring, you do die. Pieces of you die off and you know they're dead, but you can't make yourself stop killing off more pieces. Because not caring is at least a little bit safer and doesn't have you punching windows with your bare fist. And when you feel anything at all, you just feel so damned angry and you're *stuck*. You can't move, you can't get out, you can't get away and all you want is to crawl into a hole and curl up in the dark and make it all go away. Nothing holds any pleasure, not one thing is still enjoyable and what's the point in *that*? Pointless . . . it takes pointless to a whole new level of pointlessness.

"Depression, the real thing, not just the blues, not just a bad day, but the really serious dangerous one that leaves people curled up in a corner looking catatonic—the kind that used to get you signed up for electroshock therapy—it really is like this *beast*. You can't kill it, you can't control it, you can't fight it once it's in there and working because it uses your own mind against you. You doubt your own perceptions and you have no idea if how you're seeing the world is how the world really is or if it's just how it looks to you because your mind has been warped out of shape by the oozing fog and the *rot*.

"No matter how vigilant you are, you can't watch all the time. You just can't. You get tired, you have a bad day, you don't get enough sleep . . . and it gets by your guard. It gets in. It's always there, just lying in wait. It's got nothing but time and it's so patient. Days, months, years . . . it's all the same to it. And it never. Goes. *Away*."

I stop not because I mean to but because no more words will come. I realize I'm less than an inch from Luke's face and I back up. I feel strange, and I look around, look down, wondering suddenly if I went visible, tangible, during that little explosion. I feel solid. I'm clutching the railing so hard it almost hurts. I force myself to release it and look back up at Luke, feeling like I should apologize. Or something.

He's just sitting, watching me, expression unchanged, eyes soft. "So that would be your version of Hell, then?" he finally asks quietly.

I actually laugh. Again. Leaning back against the railing I stare at the street, watch the passing tires grinding up the dirt and snow on the road. I nod. "Caught between worlds, watching but not participating?" I shrug. "It's just not that big of a deal. My death has been more or less a significantly improved version of my life, because I was always caught between worlds, always watching without participating, always standing behind a glass wall that I couldn't get around or over and couldn't reach through."

"Aren't you tired of it?"

I stumble . . . *yes* . . . but pick up the thread again. "It's . . . familiar. And at least now I'm making Evan *happy* for a change." I exhale and shrug. "I actually kind of enjoy this life." I wince. "Death. Existence. Whatever."

"You *enjoy* this? Floating around like an eternal spectator? Hanging around your old boyfriend's new lover? What kind of masochist are you?"

"It's not as bad as it sounds. Vic's a lot of fun to poke. And I can keep a sense of Evan . . ." I trail off, realizing how lame I sound.

"But not talk to him. Or see him. Just chat with his new lover. Yeah, I can see how fun that would be." The Devil does good sarcasm.

"I'm just saying it's not as bad as being locked in a Hell inside your mind, that's all."

"No, I can imagine it's not." He nods thoughtfully.

"A Hell you feel like you should be able to get out of, get free of, fix. That you feel guilty for being in. One that people wonder why you can't just deal with, get over. Walking around invisible, trying to annoy Evan's new boyfriend? Just not that bad in comparison."

"So you're free of it now?"

I look away, back up Main Street where the shops still glow with lights. Am I? That's the question, isn't it? The beast has seemed farther away since I've been dead. But I had my good spells when I was alive, too. It always came back. Stalking me. That quiver of fear chases itself through my gut again. I was none too sane when I did myself in, but of all the things I may have thought in various suicidal frenzies, dealing with the same damn crushing fear on the other side was really not what I expected.

I realize he's waiting for an answer. I shake my head. "I don't . . . know."

He nods as if my answer is what he expected. "So why no seeing Evan, talking to him? He'd like to see you."

The sudden shift catches me off guard. "I don't know about that. I'm not at all convinced he'd like to see me. And I don't want to leave him pining over me."

"You already did that," he reminds me bluntly.

I snarl at him, but he just blinks and shrugs. It's the truth and he knows I know it. "I mean since he finally got over me, I want to let him stay over me. He's got Vic now. I made sure of that. He doesn't need me popping up reminding him of us. Of everything."

"But you just said it yourself. He's over you. He has Vic. I understood your hesitancy about appearing to him when he and Vic were just starting up. You didn't want him pining for a ghost when he could be

concentrating on a living, breathing Victor. Great.
You got your wish. They're happy."

I nod. "Vic's good for him. He's so much more . . .
stable. I mean not in the boring way, but mentally
stable. In the way that Evan needs. Not that Ev's un-
stable, it's just—" I never really knew how to explain
Evan alive, and I still don't now that dead.

"Yes, I'm familiar with Evan," he cuts in dryly.

Something about the way he says it gives me pause.
I raise my eyebrows in question.

"Honey in sunlight couldn't be more golden. Shines
so bright he hurts my eyes."

A laugh catches in my throat. "Mine, too."

He gives me a tolerant look, then his face gets serious. "So now, let's be honest, much as it pains me. I
don't think you need to worry about Evan walking
away from Victor for a ghost. Do you? Really?"

I pause to think about that. From what I've seen of
them, he's happy. Vic understands him in a way I
didn't know if anybody else could. I honestly *don't*
see Evan giving him up to go back to sitting alone on
a hillside in Dummerston, staring at gravestones night
after night, waiting to hold my spectral hand. I shake
my head slowly. "No. I guess I don't."

"And yet you're still hanging around. A lot. But
not to talk to Evan. Not that you really think he'll
start pining again. So what's the reason you're not
talking to him?"

The pause is long enough that if I was alive I might
get uncomfortable. Probably not, but maybe. Finally,
I give the most truthful answer I can find in my
head. "Habit?"

He gives that roar of a laugh again. "Good answer.
So tell me," and suddenly his gaze is razor sharp as
he watches me, "do you think Evan would let you get
away with that for one minute?"

I suddenly find I don't want to be talking about
Evan with the Devil. I don't want to be having this
conversation at all. My eyes narrow and I turn back

to watching the water. "Why are we having this conversation? Aren't you supposed to be whisking me
away to Hell or tempting me to the dark side or something?" I snap. I kick at more snow, sending it over
the edge to fall into the water with a splash.

"Let you in on a little secret," Luke stage whispers,
then leans close, laying a hand on my shoulder.
"You're already dead, Brandon. You're somewhat beyond my temptations."

That gives me a moment's pause. I frown down at
the water. Good point. "Never thought of it quite like
that. So, come on, then," I turn on him, challenging.
"If you've got all the answers, why *am* I still—" I
wave·my hand, I think rather eloquently.

He watches me silently for a moment, a small smile
twitching his lips. "Tell me something. Where do you
go when you're not—" He waves his hand in a much
more eloquent imitation of my gesture.

"I . . . where?" My brain seizes. Is it a place? Is it
a where? Something in me shies back, away. Some
part of me doesn't want to look at this.

Luke's steady voice wends its way into my ears.
"How would you describe it?"

"I . . . well, I—" I stop. Try again. "I'm just sort
of . . . I'm *not*." That's not right, either, but it's close.

His persistent voice is still pushing, like it's inside
my head, seeking out the answer on its own. "And
how does it feel?"

"Feel?"

"How does it feel when you're . . . not?"

The pause is even longer this time, but the answer
rises in my chest like a slow-breaking wave. When
it comes, I breathe it out before I realize I'm even
speaking. "Quiet."

"Quiet. It feels quiet." He smiles and we're silent
for another moment. "Do you like the quiet?"

I laugh, and even to my own ears it's a shaky sound.
"I love the quiet," I rasp, and can't quite understand
why there are tears in my eyes.

"Quiet," he repeats again in that soft velvet voice, nodding. "Anything else?"

Suddenly the words trip like water over the falls below me. The wave is crashing now, but gentle and steady. "Calm. I can let go of it all. Peaceful."

"Ah. Peaceful." He sits back and clasps his hands around one knee, rocking slightly. "Interesting choice of words." His eyes twinkle at me.

And suddenly I get where he's going with all this. Beyond temptation. Quiet, calm, peaceful. "I really am beyond your reach." I blink as it hits me full force. "I'm . . . not damned and I can't be."

One red brow wings up. "How peaceful do you suppose Hell is, Brandon? How peaceful would *your* Hell be? You ought to know. You've lived it long enough."

I can see he's trying not to laugh now, but I can't even take offense. "I never thought about it like that. I didn't realize I already *was* somewhere."

"That's usually the case with ghosts." He reaches out and brushes a hand through my hair fondly. "If you're still hanging around as much as you are, it's because you don't realize where you're at, don't know you can just let yourself be there. Most ghosts have just 'never thought about it.' Never relaxed into it. Too much else on their minds." He shakes his head, and looks sad. "Tell me, when you're 'not,' what brings you back? What makes you leave the quiet?"

I open my mouth, but nothing comes out. Finally, I manage, "I . . . just . . . do." I try to conceptualize it. I'm either here, or I'm not. Two states, and I can picture the other one, like seeing a fish through water, a silver glimmer here and then there. I can't look directly at it, only know it's there. But when I'm here, I don't think about it. Can't think about it too hard. I'm just here, wandering and thinking and poking at Vic and watching him and wondering about Evan.

My mind stutters, like a jolt of electricity jumping through it. Evan. "Evan," I breathe softly.

"Hmmm?" he asks, even though I know somehow that he knows exactly what I said.

"I . . . leave because I feel a tug." I'm speaking so slowly I almost don't recognize my voice, but it's like feeling my way blind, trying to put words to this. "Something I need to do."

"Something undone? Dare I say . . . unfinished business?"

I wince. "Shit. Well, that's just disgusting. Is there any *more* clichéd reason for a ghost to be hanging around? No, I got Evan and Vic together. I don't have unfinished business. So if I like the quiet, and it's mine for the having . . . why *do* I spend so much time walking around unquiet?"

"You're asking me?"

"Hello? We've been introduced? Devil? As in 'The'? All knowing?"

He extends his hands again and gives me a winsome look. "Prince of Lies, darling."

I roll my eyes. "You're about as helpful as nothing."

"Help is *not* in my job description."

"Should have seen *that* one coming."

"Well, really, only you can be expected to know what your unfinished business is."

"I told you, I don't *have* unfinished business." I glare at him. Then grudgingly grunt, "But all right, obviously whatever I'm still here for has to do with Evan. That's a no-brainer."

"So what about Evan? I agree not a lot of unfinished business there. You've found him a fabulous new guy, who even puts up with you. He's not hanging out in graveyards anymore. Well, any more than he did before you died. What's undone?"

I rub my forehead, trying to name that weird yanking sensation behind my breastbone. "It's not him, exactly. I mean I do want . . . to make sure he's happy, but—"

"Mmm hmm. Then why are you only talking to Vic?"

"I can usually tell how Evan is through him."

"And what would be the *point* of that, Mr. Logic?" He grins. "Except to avoid talking to Evan directly, of course. Why?"

"He's established. He's got a guy who's making him happy. Why would he want to see me?"

"Why *wouldn't* he want to see you?"

"Because he's got no reason to want to."

"How can you say that? You know how much he loved you."

"Loved, past tense. He's got someone new and seeing me would be nothing but bad memories."

"It wasn't all bad memories, was it?"

"No, but more bad than good, I'd think."

"You'd think? Isn't that reading what *you think* into what he's thinking? Just like you always did?"

"I'm not! I'm just saying I don't want to dredge up a bunch of old stuff that will make him upset. Angry, you know? He doesn't need me in his face."

"Angry?"

I pause. "Upset. Angry." I wave my hand. "You know."

"Angry at you?"

I look away. "Possibly at me. I'd be angry. In his place."

"You're not Evan."

"That's for damned sure."

"Do you think he's angry?

"I think he should be."

"But do you think he *is?*"

"I don't know."

"Do you want to know?"

"I don't know!"

"So you'd rather just hang around like a whiny, invisible third wheel every time you get jerked out of your quiet by some unnamed 'tug' that has *something* to do with Evan? You'd rather do that for time immemorial and risk your quiet peace than just face him and *find out?* Because you're too scared to actually talk to him? Too scared he might be angry?"

I jerk back as if slapped. *Scared?* I don't *think* so.
I open my mouth to tell the Devil to go to Hell, when
his words register. Have I been avoiding *facing* Evan?
I don't think of it like that. I got used to not talking
to him directly. It sort of stuck. I just don't appear to
him, or show up when he's in the room, or anywhere
around, or . . . I stop. Okay, yes, avoiding him. But
that doesn't automatically equate to being scared to
face him. It's *Evan,* ferchrissakes. I could pop in the
apartment and see him right now.

If I wanted to.

Which I don't.

Because . . . what if. What if he is finally angry, like
he should be. He certainly has reason. What I did to
him. Leaving him like that.

An ache like I haven't felt since I was alive wells
up in me, and with it the tug that keeps bringing me
back, easily identifiable in context. Guilt. That same
corroding sense of shame and desperation. What I did.
What I didn't do. How can I possibly *not* be suffering
for it? Eternal torment isn't senseless, pointless. It's
the only thing that *makes* sense.

Tears slide down my face, but I can't move. Can't
lift my hand to wipe them away, can't turn my head,
can't do anything but stand here feeling like I'm ripping right down the middle. An old recognizable sensation that makes me want to scream with the
hopelessness. Long fingers cup my chin and tilt my
face up, a thumb brushing the water from my cheek.

"You said it yourself, Brandon—you always did
have trouble hearing what other people told you about
yourself. They could say whatever they wanted, but
your inner voices were too loud. They're quieter now,
but they're still with you and you're still not very good
at ignoring them, at listening to the rest of the world.
Evan forgave you a long time ago. You just never let
yourself hear."

"How could he?" My voice is a croaking rasp.

Luke smiles. "He's Evan. He always understood

you didn't do it intentionally. You were better than most people, but even you didn't always give him enough credit." He arches his brows at me reproachfully. "And if you can think for one minute that he'd *want* you suffering, you're not giving him *any* credit. All he ever wanted was for you to make it out of your Hell."

My throat catches and I swallow back a hitching sob, nodding. "He's like that," I manage in a throaty voice.

"So, maybe, you think it might just be time to let yourself out of Hell?" He reaches up and strokes my hair back again, lets his hand fall to my shoulder. "You've been here long enough, Brandon. Let yourself out. The gate's open. Just walk through. Your guilt is the only thing holding you here. Believe me, you've served your time. If anyone should know, I should. You served your time before you ever died. Stop torturing yourself."

"I don't know how to stop feeling this way—"

"Yes, you do. The next time you feel that tug, just stay. You can let it go. The beast doesn't own you and it can't reach you now. You're already there if you just *let* yourself stay." He grins suddenly. "And if you *want* to come back and wander around on occasion? Feel free. You want to haunt Victor, go for it. Though may I advise *not* taking the fire extinguisher to his friends if you want to maintain your warm welcome. But do it because you want to, because you choose to, not because you need to torment yourself because you don't deserve the quiet."

I wrap my arms around myself in a gesture I remember from when I was alive and nod. "I can do that. I think." I give him a shaky smile. "You know, somehow this doesn't quite fit the mental image I had of the Devil."

He rolls his eyes and pushes back the ball cap. "Please. First you bitch about the horns and hooves, then you tell me I'm a construct, now this?"

I laugh. I have to. His affronted persona is just that
funny. "I just mean I'd never have pegged you for
going around letting people *out* of Hell."

That odd, sad look crosses his face again and it's
his turn to look out over the river across the road.
"You'd be surprised," he murmurs. Then he looks
back at me. "What makes you think you humans ever
got me right?" He smiles again. "You aren't mine. I
got sick of listening to you whine and obsess about
how you should be. Thought I ought to maybe set the
record straight."

"Thank you." I don't quite know how to say more
than that, so I don't.

He winks at me. "You're welcome. If you're out
wandering the world, maybe I'll stop in for a chat now
and again."

"Do that."

He jumps down off the railing and straightens his
coat, rubbing his hands together. "By the way, do me
a favor? Tell that ex of yours to tone down the glow
a little, will you? I could save a fortune in sunglasses."

I snort. "Oh, please. If being with me couldn't buff
down the shine, nothing will."

He shakes his head and sighs. "True. Well, anyway." He points a finger at me and pins me with a
hard look. "Get some rest, hear? Ta." He waggles his
fingers and he's gone, and I'm alone on the bridge.

I smile at the empty night. "I will."

I turn and walk back up Main Street, heading for
Vic's. Good bet Evan's back at the apartment by now.

HELL TO PAY

by Donald J. Bingle

Best known for more than fifteen years as the world's top-ranked player of classic role-playing games such as *Dungeons & Dragons*, Donald J. Bingle is not only a writer of a variety of role-playing adventures and gaming materials (*Advanced Dungeons & Dragons, Chill, Paranoia, Timemaster*, and more), but of movie reviews (in early issues of *Knights of the Dinner Table*), stories, and screenplays. He has fantasy stories set in the *Dragonlance* world of Krynn in *The Players of Gilean* and *The Search for Magic;* a science fiction story in *Sol's Children;* spooky stories in *Carnival, Historical Hauntings,* and *Civil War Fantastic;* and whimsical stories in *Renaissance Faire.* He is a member of the Science Fiction and Fantasy Writers of America, the Role Playing Game Association® Network, the American Bar Association, and the St. Charles Writers Group. Don works as a corporate and securities attorney at Bell, Boyd & Lloyd LLC in Chicago. He lives in St. Charles, Illinois, with his fun and creative wife, Linda, and their three puppies: Smoosh, Mauka, and Makai. He can be reached through www.orphyte.com.

"**OF** COURSE we're suing you. You're stealing from us!"

Cameron Templeton clicked off the telephone connection in irritation and wearily slid off his hands-free headset. His actions didn't deliver the same level of satisfaction that slamming down an old-fashioned receiver onto the phone cradle would have, but Templeton was a modern kind of guy. He was in a cutting edge business, attuned to the current fads and fashions, as attested by the office's plum wall covering with mustard accents and the overabundance of chrome on his furniture. But not too modern.

"Connie," he called out, ignoring the intercom switch centimeters away from his left hand. "Connie, come in here. I need you."

Connie Ingersol, the fetchingly attractive but overly formal executive secretary to Cameron Templeton, Executive Vice President of the Recording Artists Institution, Inc., walked briskly into the shiny office, leaving the office door open behind her.

"Yes, Mr. Templeton."

"Connie, my life at the RAII is a living hell, you know that, don't you?"

"Yes, Mr. Templeton."

"Be a dear and get me a raspberry lemonade and some ibuprofen, please."

"Yes, sir. Right away, sir."

"And hold my calls while I at least read the trades, will you?"

"What about your appointment?"

"What appointment?"

"There's a Mr. Santorini Andreas in the foyer. He's your 11:30."

"Who the hell is he?"

"I don't know, sir."

"How did he get an appointment?"

"I don't know, Mr. Templeton. He was in your electronic calendar. I assumed you put him there."

"Not that I recall. What the hell. Show him in, but don't forget my ibuprofen."

"Yes, sir, Mr. Templeton."

Connie moved out the door. "Mr. Templeton will see you now, Mr. Andreas."

A fit, vaguely European-looking man moved effortlessly past Connie into the office. He was wearing an expensive tailored suit with Hermes tie, French cuffs with jeweled cuff links, and eelskin shoes. He sported a fashionable and flawlessly neat ponytail that revealed just a hint of silver creeping into his black hair. He ignored Connie as he extended a hand to Templeton. Connie shut the door as the two men grasped hands firmly and a business card flicked magically from Andreas' well-manicured left hand.

Templeton looked down at the bloodred card, his brow furrowing in confusion and curiosity as he flipped it over to inspect the engraved silver lettering, which read: "Santorini Andreas, Senior Vice President of Acquisitions, BCA, A Soul Proprietorship." He had barely digested the information when the card suddenly burst into flames and disintegrated into nothingness.

Templeton looked at his visitor in surprise and some fear.

"Just flashpaper," Andreas said smoothly, with a whisper of an aristocratic accent. "I get them from a magic shop on Wilshire. So many people take your card, read it, then toss it in a file or drawer and forget it. I find this makes a more lasting impression."

"I s–s–s–see," Templeton stammered. "What exactly is this meeting supposed to be about? I'm really a very busy man, you know, Mr. Andreas."

"My apologies. I seem to have gotten our visit off to a poor start. Completely my fault. And, please, call me San."

"All right, San. What is this regarding?" Templeton looked wistfully at the door for Connie and his ibuprofen, but to no avail.

"Quite simply, Camèron, if I may call you that, I'm here to solve all of your problems."

"What problems? Who exactly are you? What is this BCA you work for? You're not in the industry. I know all the music labels, PR shills, agents, managers, producers, bands, you name it. You, I don't know."

"You know my employer—everyone does. BCA stands for the Beelzebub Collection Agency."

Templeton looked at the man in stunned silence, trying to remember the number for security. Where was Connie when he really needed her? He temporized. "You work for the Devil?"

"Yes," replied Andreas as he sat in one of the ugly, mustard-yellow-and-chrome client chairs. He continued in an offhand, relaxed manner, "But, then, almost everyone does. I'm an executive in the Acquisitions Division."

Templeton plopped down with a thud into his expensive, ergonomic, executive desk chair. "And you're here to collect my soul?" he said, his voice quavering just a bit.

Andreas gave him a sharp look of disgust. "Please, I don't do retail."

"I don't recall that I . . . I mean, I never sold. . . . What problems of mine are you here to solve?" Templeton blathered, his mind casting about for purchase in a storm of confusion.

"Really, Cameron. I'm not that interested in your soul. Individual souls, well they get lost in rounding when you look at the consolidated balance sheets. And I couldn't care less about your problems, whatever mundane little things they may be." He peered at the nervous man. "Sexual frustration, no doubt. No, I'm here businessman to businessman."

Templeton looked relieved, but still confused. "You're here for the soul of the recording industry?"

Andreas tapped the fingers of his right hand against the chrome of the client chair, leaving no discernible fingerprints. His voice expressed mild exasperation. "Everyone knows that corporations have no souls, Cameron. I really need you to focus here."

Templeton looked blankly at his visitor.

"Look, sport, you've done a fine job scaring the bejesus out of those file-swapping thieves that used to be your customers. Suing college students and eleven-year-old kids and overindulgent grandparents who let the youngsters use their computer to illegally burn CDs. Great stuff that. The world is awhir in hard drives deleting files as we speak. There'll be a bit of a dip in illegal MP3 downloads for a tad, then the news cycle will move onto something else and the hackers and geeks will find ways around your little information-gathering spyware and you'll be right back where you were. That does neither one of us any good. You need people to stop burning CDs with stolen music. I need souls, lots of them, on a wholesale basis, and I need them to burn . . . in a different way. I can accomplish what we both need with just a little help from you."

The mention of an ultimate solution to the music industry's most formidable woe—illegal sharing of digital music—wrenched Templeton's attention away from his own petty concerns. "But how?"

"It's practically done already. We call it our 'Hell to Pay' system."

"Hell toupee? Sounds like a hairpiece by Nick Nolte's stylist."

Andreas rolled his eyes heavenward. "Not 'Hell Toupee,' you idiot. 'Hell to Pay,' like 'Pay to Play' or 'Pay Per View.' "

"Of course, of course," Templeton covered. "Just having a bit of fun with you, San. Uh . . . exactly what does this 'Hell to Pay' system entail?" He grimaced slightly at his own words as he found himself looking for any signs of a devil's tail peeking out from under the back of his guest's suit jacket or for horns hidden in his visitor's dark hair. "No pun intended."

"We've had some involvement with the various file-sharing software companies for years, before the recent bubble . . ."

"Bubble?"

"The tech bubble in the market. Great way to fulfill contracts for great wealth with a huge number of people, most of them too stupid to specify the duration of their great wealth in their underlying contracts, but I stray from the point. Our access to these various companies allowed us to insert language into the 'Conditions of Use' or the 'Terms and Conditions' links on their Web sites."

"You mean all that legalese stuff you can access by clicking a link at the bottom of the page?"

"Precisely, Cameron. I knew you were a smart fellow. You see, we've spent decades, really, conditioning the marketplace to ignore legalese, boilerplate, and fine print . . . you know, that stuff you get in your credit card statement or you see in an advertising disclaimer or you are handed when you buy a car, whatever. It's technical, it's boring, it's incomprehensible. But most importantly, Cameron, it's binding."

Templeton found himself nodding as his strange visitor continued.

"Eventually, we conducted some tests. Straightaway in the middle of some legal mumbo jumbo we would drop in a sentence. 'Call this number if you read this disclosure and we will pay you $1,000.' No one called."

"Maybe they thought it was a joke or a misprint."

"Now you're getting it, Cameron. I knew you had that executive problem-solving instinct about you. Exactly our thought, so we started dropping in other things: swear words, ethnic insults, clues that would be attractive to conspiracy buffs—all the things that stir people up. No one complained; no one noticed. We became bolder. We tried **bold face,** underlining, ALL CAPS; no reaction. We inserted a paragraph in

Klingon into a car rental contract and asked people to initial the box right next to it. Nobody balked, not a single businessman, tourist, or customer of any kind. Hell, the terminally bored clerks at the rental counter didn't notice. That's when we knew we were ready."

"Ready for what?"

"We dropped a standard sale of soul agreement into the terms and conditions of use for all of the major file-swapping programs way back in 1999. Every downloader since that day has agreed to sell their soul in return for the ability to download music over the Internet."

Templeton leaned back in his office chair in utter awe. "Brilliant, simply brilliant."

"Thank you, really."

"Rock and roll actually does damn you to hell for all eternity. To think, Mom was right all along."

"Irony is really the fun part for us. But yes, even though it works for all sorts of music, rock and roll is our mainstay for filling up the pits of Hell. Believe it or not, that hasn't always been the case. This most recent method has proved much more effective in acquiring rock and roll fans than that 'I live for Satan' backmasking crap we tried in the late sixties."

Templeton no longer needed any ibuprofen. He leaned forward in his luxurious chair expectantly. "So, how does this work, exactly?"

Andreas shrugged nonchalantly. "At my signal, our lawyers will simultaneously appear in front of each of the offending file swappers who have unwittingly sold their souls and hand each one a card."

Templeton smiled. "Like the one you gave me, a card that bursts into flame?"

Andreas shook his head. "No." He reached his exquisite fingers into a breast pocket and produced a small yellow card. "Our research shows that this is the type of card that most people will voluntarily accept from a stranger."

Templeton took the card, holding it delicately in

admiration and anticipation before turning it over slowly. "It . . . It looks like a Community Chest card from a Monopoly® game."

Andreas folded his hands in a steeple in front of himself, his elbows perched on the garish chrome armrests of the designer chair. "Precisely. Nothing threatening about a Community Chest card. Years and years of promotion by Parker Brothers. has seen to that."

Templeton flipped the card over. In familiar graphics and typeface, it read simply: "Go to Hell. Go Directly to Hell. Do Not Pass Away. Do Not Collect $200."

"Two hundred dollars?"

"If people don't see it on the card, it bothers them. We're here to make the road to Hell as easy and convenient as demonly possible."

"And then what?"

"As soon as people who have sold their soul read the card, they vanish and go to Hell for all eternity."

"Poof, they just disappear, with no explanation?"

"Poof. Nobody knows where they went."

Templeton was warming to the plan. "There won't be enough milk cartons in all the world to picture the missing kids."

Andreas frowned. "Actually, we can't go for the little tykes."

"Still under God's protection?" queried Templeton.

"Still under the protection of state law. Age of consent, capacity to contract, blah, blah, blah. But we get them at eighteen in most states, twenty-one in a few, and much younger overseas, not that there is where the bulk of your problem lies."

"And you just do this simultaneously with everyone who has ever illegally copied music."

"Absolutely simultaneously."

"That's . . . that's millions and millions of people by our calculations. You have enough lawyers for that?"

Andreas tilted his head down and looked up at the

clueless executive in exasperation. "We have *all* the lawyers, Cameron. Of course we have enough."

"And that's it? There's no escape?"

"Not unless you have a 'Get out of Hell Free' card." Andreas flicked yet another card, this one orange in the manner of a Chance card, from his breast pocket faceup onto the oversized, glass-and-chrome executive desk. "Keep it with my compliments. You can also get out of Hell when you first arrive if you roll doubles on a standard pair of six-sided dice in three attempts or fail to roll doubles and pay $50. We like to keep our cultural references consistent. There's also a certain amount of fun in giving the damned yet one more way to screw up. All that's in the fine print on the ticket stub for the ferry over the River Styx, but nobody much reads that, either, even though the damned boat takes forever. And even if they do read the stub, most people who don't roll doubles don't have the $50 cash on them. We don't take Visa or MasterCard."

"But you do take American Express."

"Of course. Diners Club, too."

Templeton flushed with excitement and happiness. He had the ultimate solution to the recording industry's woes and a personal "Get out of Hell Free" card. He had some serious sinning to catch up on now that he knew that there were no consequences and he planned to start with Connie. Wine, women, and song. That was the ticket for a recording industry executive. Suddenly, his brow furrowed.

"But wait. What's the catch?"

"Catch?" replied Andreas innocently.

"You've already done all this. What exactly do you need me . . . er . . . us for?"

"Well, there are certain rules that even we must abide by." Andreas looked somewhat sheepishly heavenward. "You know. Technical limitations and parameters, commandments, that sort of thing."

"Go on."

"Well, the slipping it by in the fine print thing works fine under the legal system here on Earth, but, well, the power-that-be, He insists that someone must make a conscious decision about the transfer of a soul to Hell itself."

Templeton snorted. "Well, that guts the whole thing, doesn't it?"

"Not really. The transfer of a soul from one individual to another or to a valid corporate or other legal entity is no problem and the Beelzebub Collection Agency is in good standing in the State of California." Andreas produced with a flourish an official certificate with a gold seal and the signature of the Secretary of State of California. "The BCA stands ready, willing, and legally and cosmically able to transfer those souls to which it has otherworldwide exclusive, perpetual, and eternal rights to the RAII, provided RAII authorizes the immediate banishment and condemnation of such souls to Hell. We just can't do it ourselves. We need a middleman, an agent, a promoter. That's what you do."

Templeton hesitated over replying for a moment.

"Think it through," continued Andreas, closing the sale. "People will think twice about the consequences of copyright infringement once all the current perpetrators vanish mysteriously amid rumors of damnation to Hell for all eternity. I'm sure your PR people can get a whisper campaign going."

Templeton shrugged. What the hell did he care about the blasted music thieves? He had a "Get out of Hell Free" card and a lot of depraved good times ahead. "Sold!" he said, reaching forward to shake his guest's hand.

Andreas smiled. "Not anymore, they aren't."

Templeton tilted his head to the side in confusion.

"Souled . . . S-O-U-L-E-D. Get it?" said Andreas with a jaunty wink as he stood to leave. "I'll have our lawyers call our other lawyers and work out the documentary details."

Templeton chuckled politely and rose with his guest. "It's been great doing business with you, San. If there's ever anything else I can do for you, just let me know."

Andreas stopped. "Well, actually, if you could get rid of hip-hop, the guys at work would be dancing on the heads of pins."

Templeton snorted. "Hmmmph, I guess I figured your boss was behind that crap."

Andreas shook his head lanquidly. "No. I'm told the retail guys got several requests along those lines, but I told them that Hell would freeze over before that stuff became popular, no matter what we did. I was wrong, of course. Now all those poorly-rhyming thugs we turned down call themselves 'ice' this and 'cool' that. I think they're mocking me."

Templeton crinkled his nose slightly. "Well, if you can't stop it, there's no hope I can."

Andreas nodded. "I abandoned all hope long, long ago. I'll tell you what, though, if you could just re-release 'You Light Up My Life' and promote the hell out of it, that would be great."

Templeton was taken aback. "Debby Boone? You like Debby Boone?"

"Can't stand her or the song myself, any more than I can stand hip-hop, but nobody else can stand that damn song, either. That's the point. Keeping that song number one for ten weeks in a row, playing over and over again, did wonderful things for the suicide rate back in the summer of seventy-seven. Mass suicide, that's a plus in my column. Mortal sin, you know."

"Say no more." said Templeton as he walked Andreas to the door. "I'll get right on it."

The representative of BCA glided smoothly toward the elevator banks and pressed "Down." The button glowed a bright, flickering orange.

Templeton headed back into his office and fingered the switch on the intercom. "Connie, come in here. I need you. Oh, and close the door behind you."

Templeton leaned back in his comfy chair and smiled. Things didn't look so bad for him or the RAII after all. It was a helluva thing, that . . . practically a miracle.

YOUR WORLD, AND WELCOME TO IT

by Ed Gorman

Ed Gorman has been called "One of the most original crime writers around" by *Kirkus Reviews* and "A powerful storyteller" by Charles Champlin of the *Los Angeles Times*. He works in horror, science fiction, and westerns as well as crime. To date there have been six Gorman collections, three of which are straight crime, the most recent of which is *Such a Good Girl and Other Stories*. He is probably best known for his Sam McCain series, set in the small-town Iowa of the 1950s ("good and evil clash with the same heartbreaking results as Lawrence Block or Elmore Leonard"). He has also written a number of thrillers, including *The Marilyn Tapes, Black River Falls,* and the *The Poker Club*.

NOW THIS certainly isn't the first time our hero Sean Cameron wakes up in a lot of physical and psychic pain in a strange room he doesn't recognize.

C'mon, let's be adults about this. Handsome Sean is a serial adulterer dating back to his Bahama honeymoon when he scored a dentist's wife one late night on the beach when neither he nor the dentist's lady could sleep. She had brought along a flask of rum of which he partook, so what the hell. You know how these things go. We're adults, right?

Hotel rooms, motel rooms, bedrooms, kitchen floors, garage floors, the backseats of cars, lawns, under tables—a long list of where Sean's dick has led him to hangover mornings in unknowable locations.

But this morning—or is it morning? For the first time, just now opening both eyes and realizing that this small, completely white room has no windows— this morning there is a subtle difference in both his physical and psychic pain.

His clothes alone, white shirt, smoke-gray slacks, torn and bloody—

The physical pain isn't so much, like hangover pain, a generalized *ache*. Like the flu when you want your mommy (or wife number one, two, or three) to come in and rub some Vicks on your chest and make it all better.

The *psychic* pain is even more mysterious. He knows he knows something, but he doesn't know what he knows. Call it dread. Nameless dread as the pulp boys and girls like to say. Something he knows but doesn't know is scaring the shit out of him.

He sits up and that's when—

The wall to his right remains blank for a moment while an unseen infant begins screaming in agony and terror.

And then the wall bursts into images of an African village. You can tell this is a modern village because there is a Range Rover in the frame. But otherwise the village with its thatched huts, electrical and telephone poles nowhere to be seen, could be resting in the late 1800s.

None of this matters because the eye is fixed on the two rows of children lined up in front of one of the huts.

A white female doctor in a tan jumpsuit is holding

the infant that is crying so relentlessly. The camera zooms in on the infant's face. Or, more properly, skull. Because this tiny black child is already dead. Brain simply hasn't informed the rest of the body yet. The screaming (is this medically possible?) is strictly reflexive.

The other children lined up on the ground look even worse than the infant the doctor is holding because they are not dead, not quite yet. They are vomiting up a silky green substance that sends them into spasms so violent you can hear bones breaking—literally; have you ever heard a bone breaking? There is no other sound quite like it. They are puking with such fury that they look like crazed jitterbug dancers jerking about there on the ground. Their eyes are wild; their screams now join the infant's.

The pretty doctor begins silently crying herself as the infant flops dead in her arms . . .

By this time, Sean is covering his ears and closing his eyes. Shaking his head. What the hell is going on here?

(One of the last things he can remember—
That waitress. Yes, the waitress. God, what great eyes she had. Truly emerald-colored eyes. Very rare. And reaching across to her there in the car, sliding his hand over her wonderful breasts and her saying, "You know what my New Year's resolution was?"
"Uh-uh."
"Not to go to bed with any more married men."
Grinning that fabulous—just ask him—grin Sean Cameron smiled: "I feel flattered, then."
Her grinning her own fabulous—just ask her—grin right back at him: "We'll see. I invited you up for a drink. We'll just take it nice and slow and see what happens.)

*　　*　　*

What kind of crazy shit has he gotten himself into? Where's the waitress—Cassie? Yeah, Cassie. Dug her name a lot. Cassie. Real female sound to it. Cassie.

But what the hell did she get him into?

It has taken him this long to think about—

He opens his eyes. He uncovers his ears.

There are no windows. But that's not all—there is no door, either.

Talk about your morning-after panic.

Now would be the moment in most stories where our handsome hero asks himself if this is a dream or nightmare of some kind.

But this is Sean Cameron, a man who does not kid himself. Well, not any more than anybody else.

He knows this isn't a dream and he has evidence.

A) His entire body is shiny with cold sweat. He can see the beads of it gleaming on his arm.

B) A couple of minutes ago he caught a whiff of his morning mouth. Nothing like hangover morning mouth.

C) Also a couple of minutes ago he farted. One of those oily booze hangover farts.

Now dreams/nightmares may have all kinds of realistic special effects to convince you that they're really real. But such special effects do not include sweating, bad breath, and farting.

This is really real.

He stands there feeling pathetic and lost and scared.

This is a guy who can swagger in his sleep.

He never feels pathetic and lost and scared.

He feels pathetic and lost and scared.

(One of the last things he can remember—

"Hey, would you mind slowing down a little?"

"I'm not going that fast, babe."

"Seventy. You're going seventy."

"Seventy isn't fast."

"It is when you're drinking and when there're ice patches all over the road."

"One thing you don't have to worry about is me

driving. This little Porsche and me have been through a lot together. It's never let me down yet."

"And I hate 'babe.' "

"Huh?"

" 'Babe.' I hate being called that."

"It's a term of endearment. Like 'honey' and 'sweetie.' "

"I hate all that crap. It's all so—Vegas.' "

"What's wrong with Vegas?"

"Are you kidding? You ever *been* there?"

"Twice a year. Like clockwork."

"It's so *sterile*."

"Wow. That's quite a word. 'Sterile.' "

"You mean because I'm this stupid waitress I shouldn't know words like that?"

"Hey, hey. Chill out."

"Just don't call me 'babe.' I had a bad experience with a guy who called me 'babe.' "

"He dump you?"

"Yes, as you so elegantly put it, he dumped me."

"He married?"

"The Grand Inquisitor."

"Hey, Dostoyevsky. From college lit. I remember. You know Dostoyevsky. Wow."

"I got through three years of college myself, you know. And I'm finishing up in night school. I'm not a moron."

"I didn't say you were."

"Let's just change the subject."

"So this guy who dumped you? He married?"

"God, all these questions."

"You said to change the subject."

"Yes, he was married. And he dumped me. Now please, just pay attention to your driving. You're still going too fast. You're making me nervous.")

The thing is to take deep breaths. The thing is to take control of your panic before it takes control of you.

What he's thinking is: *Be logical. Somehow you got*

*in here. Somebody put you in here. So even though
there doesn't appear to be any door, there must be
one somewhere.*

There. Six seven eight deep breaths and he's feeling
better. He doesn't know what kind of crazy shit is
going on here, but he's damned well going to find out.

It's only logical, isn't it? If he could get in, then he
can get out, right?

He starts on the closest wall, feeling along it the
way a blind man would, waiting for his fingers to feel
any bump, division, or cleavage that would indicate
an opening of some kind.

Nothing on the first wall.

He starts toward the second wall, taking deep breaths
again because the ANXIETY is coming back and—

The wall erupts as he approaches it—

*Screaming. Only this time of a different quality. Not
the screaming of infants but the screaming of—*

*A woman in three dimensions trying to escape
toward him in the midst of an inferno of smoke and
fire, lost every few seconds in the roiling black smoke,
stumbling along on her chrome walker—*

*And a charred flaming body of an old man stepping
out of the flames that are catching up to her in this
corridor—*

The old man shouts, "Help me! Help me!"

*He is a comic book image of a flaming man, his
arms windmilling as he tries to escape the fire. But then
it just sweeps him up—he is completely flame himself
now, one with the fire itself and he literally vanishes
before Sean's eyes, fire into fire.*

*He wants to look away. He does not want to see this
old woman slip and fall to the corridor as she seems
to be doing now. He feels heat, scorching heat, suddenly, as if he's been drawn into the burning corridor.*

And her shouts. My God, her feeble, hopeless shouts.

"Don't fall!" he cries to her. "Please don't fall!"

But she does fall, slamming to the floor, raising a

trembling frail white hand toward him, sobbing, as the
old man sobbed "Help me! Help me!"

He has to turn away. Turn away. Cannot watch.
Cannot.

("You know what?"

"What?"

"I guess I'm not going to ask you to come in,
after all."

"What the hell're you talking about? That's why I
gave you a ride home."

"I changed my mind. Isn't a person allowed to
change her mind?"

"What the hell happened? I thought we were having
a good time."

"A good time? Have you been listening to yourself
since we got in this car? All your nosy questions. And
treating me like an idiot. And calling me 'babe' and
all that Vegas bullshit. And most of all, driving like a
fucking maniac."

"A fucking maniac? I'm driving like a fucking
maniac?"

And that's when it happens. When the tires of the
classic Porsche coupe meet one mean motha patch of
ice and it goes spinning out of control—accompanied
by her screaming and cursing him and letting out a
litany of dirty words—and who can blame her with
that huge oak tree on the side of the road coming up
and them still doing a good sixty miles an hour?)

Soaking. Cold shivering sweat. Every once in a
while he'd get the bad sweats and the bad shits and
the bad shakes when he'd really drink too much for
too many nights running. But never like this. Never
fetus-curled on the floor and shaking shaking shaking
like a junkie.

These scenes on the walls. First the skeleton-like
kids. And then the old people smothering in the
smoke and burning to death.

Wait. An idea. A connection. The kids and the old people. Had it and lost it, this idea. Heebie-fucking-jeebies so bad he can't think things through. They escape into the ether.

The kids and the old people. Yes. He had something there. Vague, murky. But a thought that tied it all together.

Yes!

But—

(Cheering. Huge crowd. Vast red, white, and blue scene. A football stadium so crowded that hundreds have to stand on the field.

Stand up for America, I say. *Our* America. Not their America. And I don't have to tell who you "they" are do I? That's why I'm running for president. Not for my ego. Not for my vanity. But because I am like you. I remember the old America, the pure America. The true America!

Camera shots cutting panning zooming in huge orgasm of applause foot-stamping some people crying some people laughing red white and blue and the candidate and his shining fine blonde wife so much confetti so loud Dixieland jazz music orgasm number two three four five

Candidate and shiny fine blonde wife standing on the raised podium—TV screen behind them bearing their huge images—waving and smiling waving and smiling)

And then silence.

The most absolute silence the most incomprehensible silence deep-space silence death silence he has ever heard—not heard?—in his life, our boy Sean Cameron.

The heebie-jeebies gone, though in the process he pissed his pants.

The teeth chattering and nausea gone, too, though

he realizes now that he has hot reeking puke all over his ripped shirtfront.

Just the silence and the simple profound sneaky cunning insidious bafflement of being in a white room with no windows or door, in bloody clothes and watching scenes that, he now realizes, do in fact connect to his life.

Dead she was dead when he dragged her out of the car last night.

Staggering down the middle of the street as people started streaming from their houses in bathrobes and pajamas to see who had been involved in all that horrific crashing noise this being one of the worst patches of road—especially on an icy night like this one—in the entire county.

"He's drunk!" somebody shouting at him, a man. "He's drunk and he killed her!"

And thinking now: so it does exist.

He's dead and it really does exist and he's in it.

He starts to roll over on his side and that's when a perfect door in the perfect wall opens up and a perfect man in a lounge lizard outfit of slicked-down black hair, tiny black mustache, leopard-skin smoking jacket, black slacks, black socks, and a pair of black silk slippers with the letter S embossed on them walks over to him, taking a deep drag of the cigarette fixed into the long black holder.

"If I'm not mistaken, you just figured all this out."

"You're a telepath."

"That's one of those science fiction words. I prefer to think of what I do as educated guesses. Even evil has its limits."

"Is it because I killed her in the accident?"

"The girl?" He smiles with teeth so white that not even a Beverly Hills dentist could match them. "Cassie? Oh, no. She's in the other room, Mr. Cameron. She was very jealous of her older sister and she drowned her one day. Her parents never caught on. A bad lady. No remorse at all. Perfect for our little place here."

"Then it was—"

"C'mon, Mr. Cameron. Get up and follow me. We'll get you all cleaned up and then we'll figure out what your punishment will be."

Cameron forced himself to his feet.

The man in the leopard-skin smoking jacket walked ahead of him to the door he'd created. "I'm picking up messages from your mind again, Mr. Cameron. You want to know why you're here. Think of all the things you foisted on the public. There's your answer." He spoke carelessly over his shoulder as Cameron hurried to catch up. "The contaminated milk you created and helped sell to Third World countries. All those little kids dead. The fire alarms that didn't work and people dying everywhere. And President Fitzgerald, whom your commercials put in office. He'd give Hitler nightmares."

"Then I'm not here because of Cassie, I'm here—"

The man stopped and slid a long, languid arm around Cameron's shoulder. "Don't worry, Mr. Cameron. You won't be lonely." He took a long and dramatic drag on his cigarette. "There are plenty of other advertising people here, too."

THE DEVIL MAY CARE

by ElizaBeth Gilligan

ElizaBeth Gilligan lives in the San Francisco Bay Area with husband, Doug, their children, and an assembly of furred and heavily indulged cats who are all kept under something approximating control by one very intent, peace-loving terrier. ElizaBeth has dreamed of writing professionally since she was very young and spent the last twenty-five years working on her craft. She is the author of several short stories and two books in the alternative-history *Silken Magic* series, *Magic's Silken Snare* and *The Silken Shroud*. ElizaBeth also leads a research list for genre authors called the Joys of Research.

IT BEGAN as all such endeavors do . . . shrug of the shoulders, a bored sigh, and the ubiquitous, "Sure, I haven't got anythin' else to do."

Now, that phrase ranks right up there with "Why not?" "Might as well," and "You go first" as portents of trouble. Not just any sort of trouble, but the kind where you realize—as you're flat on your back and starin' up at your inevitable fate—that you actually volunteered for this and suddenly muckin' out the Stygian stables has much greater appeal than it once had.

So, there I was, standin' at the door of an old brimstone buildin'. The doorplate declared the street number to be 666 even though this structure occupied the
entirety of this cul-de-sac immediately off the Route
00—known in these parts as the Devil's Dieway because of the hairpin turns through thick forest bogs
that were forever threatening to reclaim the ill-kempt
road. Havin' overshot the turnoff three times and
havin' gone as far as Miss Helen Bach's ranch each
time so's I could turn around, I was in a good ol'-
fashioned lather. I was thereby forced to retrace my
path over the wickedest part of the Dieway twice! In
spite of my intentions, I was still forced to make an
illegal turn onto San Angelos Court, since I was
damned if I could find a legal way onto this road!

Now, I've lived in these parts—that would be San
de Monica, Louisiana, which is the South's version of
Death Valley where even a man's fingernails sweat in
the so-called cool of the evenin'—since Pa was taken
in by some big developers when I was five or so. Even
then I understood my Pa's weakness for a sales pitch.
Pa was a fool to believe this backwater piece of . . .
uh, beggin' you ladies' pardon . . . land could be anythin' *like* that California coast city, Santa Monica,
much less a land of opportunity. We're too far from
anythin' to bring tourists by and not along even the
most indirect path to New Orleans, which o' course,
was where most folks're headed. Oh, and since I'm
givin' you the geography lesson anyway, it's pro-
nounced "Nuh Aww-lins" and the state is never pro-
nounced with an *s* cause the damned state's properly
called "Loo-zi-anna." Damned Yankee carpetbaggers . . . I think they foul the name just to see us
get worked up.

Well, there I go again—"on the tirade" as my Penny
calls it—but between the damned heat and humidity
and the drive to Helen Bach's—twice!—I was in a
mood. Then there's the nonsense with the doorplate,
yes, that's where I was.

Preacher Bob LeRoy woulda had a field day over the address and turned it into a Cause. My Penny would be first in line to coordinate the bake sale—which meant she would be bakin' from dawn to dusk, and all my favorites, too: lemon meringue, rhubarb, blueberry, and sour cream 'n' raisin pies, all nature of brownies, cookies, and more—and I wouldn't be allowed to snitch a single Snickerdoodle without makin' a contribution, even though it was my earnins that paid for the sugar and such. I never could see the sense in it. Preacher Bob LeRoy or Penny would say that was 'cause I was an indifferent Christian and the others would be noddin' their heads like one of them toy dogs in the rear window of Sheriff Tucker's new patrol car. Ever since he got it—the new patrol car—I've been longin' to have some reason to be in the back of that vehicle so's I could adjust that puppy's head and it would never wobble again, but then I have a real compulsion to be law-abidin'—which brings me back to the illegal turn from every direction to get onto this damnation backwater place and though Sheriff Tucker wasn't watchin' that stretch of road, I still didn't like bein' obliged to break the law, even a little one.

So, as I said, there I was standin' on the front stoop of this big ol' brimstone buildin'—the *only* buildin' on the whole street which made the street number irrelevant and therefore all the more irritatin'. There was no accountin' for people's senses of humor.

Though the house had a proper covered porch with a roof on it, I couldn't find me a lick of shade anywhere I stood while I thumbed through my work orders. I finally found the order sheet and pulled it out from among the others that had so far occupied my day and snapped the clip onto it and closed the metal box that made up the rest of my clipboard.

It would never do to greet a new customer in a foul temper, so I stepped back and studied the edifice. Three big chimneys rose up from the middle—or what seemed to be the middle—of the buildin'. They belched forth great volumes of thick black smoke. The smell was wretched, but one I was sorta accustomed to since there was a "wildlife preserve" down the road a bit from town. We locals just called it a swamp. Of an evenin', when a breeze sets in from the south, the smell of the sulfur bogs pretty much permeates everythin'. On the evenins when the breeze sets in from the north, well, then we can smell the paper mill which—no matter how long you live there—you never quite get used to.

Sniffin' again, I realized the smoke smelled like the bogs and the mill all mixed up as one with maybe a 'fraid polecat—Yanks call 'em skunks. In any case, it was a high stinkin' mess that woulda choked a pig, but, like I said, I was somewhat accustomed to the smell of bad eggs and sulfur bogs. Oily grime from the smokestacks settled everywhere, killin' anythin' close up to the buildin' and mixin' in the droopin' branches of the birch and willow some distance off. The Spanish moss hangin' from the trees looked kinda funny, but nothin' to laugh at, all black and limp. There wasn't a window I could see in for all the muck, not even the windows right up here on the porch.

I'm one for each of us mindin' our own business— which is why Preacher Bob LeRoy and me don't see eye to eye, if you get my drift—but still, I couldn't help wonderin' if that college kid workin' as a summer intern for the EPA had stopped by here when he was writin' up all his tickets and makin' a fine aggravation for folks in town. His name was Willow Sunbeam Smith—though he preferred to be called Will and I could understand that. I figured the kid's Pa'd been some kinda smart-ass hippie like on the Johnny Cash song "A Boy Named Sue."

Thinkin' on the kid—I refused to call a near-grown man "Willow"—he was as nice as they come if you didn't get put off by his high falutin' talk or get on his bad side for doin' somethin' to harm the land. He had a five-dollar word for it—the land, I mean. Called it an "ecosystem."

Mayor Jim Barton'd originally volunteered to keep 'im at his place since there isn't a hotel nor motel within seventy-three and a half miles, but right off the first night, the kid refuses to eat Ma Barton's venison stew, which is foolish on many accounts. First off, it's some of the best damn stew this side of the Mason-Dixon, but more important, Mayor Jim'd no doubt killed that deer himself, and refusin' to eat the stew hurt his wife's feelin's and denied the mayor the opportunity to tell one of his whoppin' tales about the hunt, which is the prelude to an after-dinner stroll through the garage to see the taxidermied remains of his kills through the years.

Host or no host, that kid flat out refused the perfectly good food, declarin' himself to be some nature of super-vegetarian that ate no animal products nor used stuff made from animals. I think he said he was a Veggin. At this point Ma Barton called up Preacher Bob LeRoy who instantly deduced that the kid was some kind of heathen and, therefore, unsuitable company for good Christians. So the mayor opened up the jailhouse and let the kid sleep in a cell with his belongings. I was ready to let the kid stay with us because he made good conversation and it would put Penny and the preacher on their ears, but he was content with the cell and powered up his fancy electric car at the station next door.

Well, the kid'd been on my mind lately. Too much, Penny said, but you just don't take a good conversationalist for granted in these parts and his rather sudden disappearance had been troublin' me for the last day or two. I'd a been more likely to give it a rest as my good wife counseled if the kid hadn't left half his stuff in the cell where he stayed. Sheriff Tucker and Preacher Bob LeRoy said it was the nature of young folks these days . . . no consideration 'tall for those who might worry 'bout 'em. I gave this pronounce-

ment the usual weight I gave anythin' Preacher Bob
said. Since my contractin' and repairs took me from
one end of the county to t'other, well, I just kept an
eye out for signs of Mr. Will Smith. He deserved some
concern, no matter his bein' a heathen Veggin or that
he had the misfortune to be born a Yankee.

So there I was, standin' on the porch and unable to
get outta the blazin' sun, ditherin' 'bout inconsequen-
tials when there was work to be done and don't let
anyone tell you I'm a slacker—less'n I get into a good
conversation, and right now the closest I was to that
was talkin' to myself. I took out my hankie and
mopped the back of my neck and forehead and took
me another look at them doors.

They was big ol' wide things and look to 've been
made outta scorched wood, which set me to wonderin'
how someone could afford a big ol' place like this and
they had to use burned up ol' wood on the front door.
Sad as it is and contrary as it might seem, 'twas somethin' I was used to . . . some ol' Southern family who
managed to fend off the Yankees in the war and the
carpetbaggers after and was left with little more'n this
ol' buildin' . . . probably spinsters or ol' widows were
all that were left of a once fine family with their ol'
house crumblin' down round their ears. Probably
meant they couldn't pay, neither, which meant I'd
likely work the afternoon for free. Times were hard
and I'd seen more than enough of such cases. The
summer's heat could be fatal for the very young and
the very old. The papers were full of stories about
grannies and old aunties found—dead or dyin'—in
front of rickety fans that did little to relieve the heat
much less stir up some air.

I sighed and looked at the humongous pair of door
knockers. Of all the things I'd seen here, this was the
first I'd seen that looked cleaned and well taken care
of. The faces of the gold knockers were like goblins,
contorted into a beastly show of teeth. Nows I consid-

ered it, even in midday the light seemed to play tricks so that the gold-plated eyes watched me while their toothy mouths chewed in apparent annoyance at the thick, gold-plated ring that kept them from takin' a serious bite outta someone so foolish as to take one of those rings in his hand.

Now, I wouldn't say the things struck terror in my heart, but I'd be a flat-out liar if I didn't admit they did cause me concern. There was somethin' about 'em that just didn' look right. I scanned the extra-wide entry doors and along the jambs hopin' to find a doorbell. Finding none, I girded my loins as David must have before meeting Goliath . . . just what exactly, I wondered, was actually girding your loins?

But before I could lose myself in further ruminations, the doors, with their baleful guardians, swung wide. The air inside the buildin' blew outward, gushin' around the cloaked woman in the doorway, and fairly knocked me off of my frosted feet.

On this hot August day, the rush of cold air was better than standin' in front of the open icebox pretendin' I was lookin' for the bread 'n' butter pickles Penny hides in the back when really all I wanted was a bit of cool—damn the energy bill!

Since most of my day is spent in my truck, all I got is the natural air conditionin'—leavin' the windows wide open and hopin' for no sudden storms. Some of the houses I visited had air-conditionin', but then that's why they usually called me: it was in the full hot of the day and their coolin' systems were doin' little or nothin' to alleviate their discomfort and, of course, once I'd fixed the conditioner I was expected to leave.

In the minute or so it took me to get accustomed to the rush of coolness from out the doors, I reckoned the problem as the goose pimples from the cold raised up on my arms. This woman or her employer or whatever had the problem eleven out ten of my customers prayed for—too much cool. It was always that way . . . the first day of spring, the fans'd come out and the heaters needed fixin' the first day a chill set in.

"Tell me you're from the repair shop!" the woman commanded.

Despite it bein' the God's honest truth, I felt a sudden and very strong urge to do or be anythin' this woman— my customer—wanted me to be and I had to work real hard to remember I was a married man and that Penny was probably making my supper at this very moment . . . and I hadn't even seen the woman's face.

She stood there, in the great yawnin' mouth of a portal, wearin' what looked like nothin' more than a deep scarlet satin robe with the hood brought up, thereby coverin' her face. The only bit of flesh I saw was her hands. This wasn't the first time a customer'd greeted me this way, some ladies, bless their hearts, met me in the altogether. Bein' a gentleman, and a married one at that, I looked in every direction but theirs till sense and a bit of propriety struck 'em. Such was the trials of a workaday repairman.

Bein' so practiced at this, it confused me then how hard it was to catch my breath and get my faculties in order, 'specially considerin' I couldn't see anythin' of the woman but her very divinely full-figure shape. A little warnin' bell went off in my head. There was nothing divine about this woman and there was a tawdriness that made me curious as to the nature of this business. The room behind her was so shadowed I couldn't be sure if it were a boudoir, family room, or the front office that I'd expected. The doors had been homey, invitin' visitors to knock before comin' right in, but the buildin' itself had an industrial look to it.

"Um—ah, yes, ma'am. I came about the heating and cooling problem," I finally managed to sputter. I handed her one of the company cards with my name scrawled in the blank space—a courtesy so folks knew who they were dealin' with. I looked down at my clipboard as she took the card. I hadn't bothered to look for the customer name and it seemed an appropriate time to look. The customer name blank was empty, which was unlike our dispatcher, Miss Marcie, to overlook. More puzzlin' still, there wasn't a name in the blank for a contact person.

"Won't you come in?" she asked.

I looked up from my paperwork, noddin'. I tucked the clipboard under one arm and picked up my toolbox. "I'm afraid I don't have your name, ma'am."

Behind her, for the first time, I could see somethin'—a long dark hallway leadin' Heaven knows where and a kinda parlor off to the right. The room made for a poor parlor. It was stark, not a lick of furniture anywhere 'sides a high bench, like in the courthouse or, on second thought, considerin' the clutter of paperwork, the nurses' station at the county hospital emergency room. Two torchlike lights on either side, behind the desk, provided what luminescence there was in that stark room. Not so much as a pew for a body to sit on occupied the expanse of the rest of the room. I shuddered; it was a tomblike place and I was happy not to have to go in it. So much for my theory this was a bawdy house.

"This way," my hostess said and turned down the hall. She stopped and looked back, her face still hidden by the cowl. "Do you have everything that you will need?"

"Depends what the problem is. I might have to go back out to the truck or maybe even order parts." I prefer to be frank with my customers, even the ones I was startin' to wonder if they had enough cash on hand to pay their bill without writin' a check . . . and that was not the way me 'n' my brothers generally operated our business.

I had the sense of her that she was not particularly pleased with my answer, but she turned and walked down the long dark corridor. She walked like one of them beauty queens down the aisle rather than some strange caretaker of an even stranger place. I had to hurry to keep up with her in spite of her slow, hip-swishing walk. It was like them horror movies where no matter how fast the girl runs and how slow and most assuredly dying the villain is, he still catches up with her . . . 'ceptin' I was no villain and if I didn't hurry to keep up I'd get lost in the maze of hallways.

Lights sprang to life, seemingly of their own accord as we stalked deeper into the buildin' and then quickly dimmed after we passed. I knew for certain that I would not be likely to find my way out easily. Even with the cold—which grew frostier and frostier the deeper we went into the buildin'—I easily felt the greasy soot outside. It kinda caked on my skin like BBQ sauce on pork ribs.

Hurryin' as I was, I didn't get much time to look around. There was no pictures or clocks or anything on the walls—'cept the torchlike lamps high up. We passed a grimy gray door now and again that blended into the grimy gray walls. There were little windows in the doors, but there were no knobs nor slots for passing things through to prisoners . . . or patients.

"Wh–What exactly is this place?" I'd smothered the question for as long as I could, but it was like holdin' your breath, you gotta give in sometime.

My hostess turned, her head still covered with the cowl. I could practically feel her eyes widenin' as though in innocent surprise, but there didn't seem any-thin' innocent nor beyond her reckonin'—which is not a nice thing to say about a lady, but then, by now, I was pretty sure there wasn't much of a lady about her other'n her sex.

"Are you serious?" she asked me.

I looked around me and wished I had my hands free to rub my bare arms. "Well . . . yeah. I don't have the proper name of your . . . your business; all's I got is your address."

"And a mighty strange one at that, isn't it?" my guide asked me silkily, swaying back to me.

I nodded tryin' to stay casual, "Well, yes. My

preacher would have a right terrible fit over the street number, never mind what he would say if he studied enough Latin in school to read the street name."

The woman's cowl slipped slightly back, enough for me to see a toothy and not at all pleasant smile. "The number of the beast Preacher Robert LeRoy would call it, no?"

I didn't wanna know how she knew who my preacher was. I was fast gettin' a real clear idea why, or rather how, she knew such things and it didn't make me any happier facin' facts that I wouldn't have believed an hour ago.

"Isn't this where you say something clever, like 'What in tarnation . . . ?'" she asked, her tone sly and cutting.

I fixed her with a stare. "I may speak Southern; it doesn't mean I speak stupid."

She laughed lazily. It mighta had more effect if she hadn't started to shiver—and she *was* naked under her robe.

I knew enough now that neither Penny nor I had to worry about wanderin' thoughts—doesn't mean a man doesn't notice things, it's just what he does with that information. I turned away from her cold nubile form barely sheathed in her red satin robe and took a real good look around.

The walls and floor were shiny with more than the greasy soot that seemed to be everywhere and in everythin'. The goin' had gotten more'n a bit slippery and what I'd taken for misty dimness I now recognized as the wafts of cold seepin' from everywhere. It was cold. It was damn cold and that gave me a grin of my own. "Hell's gone and froze over!" I laughed.

My guide's lips thinned so that pointed little teeth creased her bottom lip. "Were I you, I wouldn't find it quite so amusing."

"And why not?" I asked, turnin' round again to admire the effects of the cold on this institutional buildin'.

"You're the one that's got to fix it," she snapped . . . coldly, I noted with more than a little glee.

"I don't gotta do nothin', my fancy lady," I replied. I set my toolbox down and sat on it.

"You're a denizen of Hell now, you must do as you're told!" my guide hissed.

"Me? A denizen of Hell? First off, I didn' die, I didn' have my judgment, and—seems to me—I came in here of my own free will, which means I can leave that way, too."

"How many years late for supper will you be, trying to find your own way out of here?"

Now that did give me a turn and bore more than a little consideration. "It seems plain as the nose on my face that you aren't plannin' on lettin' me leave here whether I cooperate or not."

My hostess sighed heavily. "If you will *fix* our problem, then I promise to show you the way out." She put her hands on her hips, the way Penny did when she was about to really give me grief if I so much as hinted I was about to disagree with her.

"Like I said, I'm not stupid. Everyone with even a snitch of schoolin' knows you can't win makin' a deal with the devil," I said. I crossed my arms and stuffed my hands into my armpits to warm my fingers a bit. Now, I'm no angel by any means and I knew I wouldn't want to stay in this frigid land, but there was a higher principle than my own comforts to consider. Somehow, when the day started, I just hadn't considered that I might truly be called upon to fight this righteous battle more'n the petty little decisions that troubled a man's conscience. Doin' what was right and proper was hard enough on a man most days.

"I'm *not* the Lord of All Hells and this—" she waved around her, "—this is merely a gateway. You might say we're in collections here and, when the time comes, we send . . . we send what we've collected to that final bastion for the master's discretion."

"So, this is our very own local Hell?" I asked. I

stretched my legs out and tried to look as comfortable as I could.

"It is a dimension . . . a portal to the True Dimensions."

"Uh-huh," I said soft and calmlike. I dug an individually wrapped mint-flavored toothpick that I'd picked up at Uncle Mel's diner out of my breast pocket, slipped the splinter of wood into my mouth and put the wrapping back in the pocket. "So . . . if Hell . . . or at least this little patch of it's truly frozen over, why should I go about changin' things? Seems to me to be a good thing."

"Oh, Master, help me! It's another philosopher!" she raged, her voice raising into a shriek that could no ways I'd ever heard come from a human.

I just bided my time. My hostess, for lack of any better or polite term, had revealed a weakness. She stood, rigid, arms at her sides and hands balled into fists, her head bowed, as though some answer might come to her like writin' on the floor.

After a good long time, long enough for my nose to grow numb from the cold and my toes to curl in my work boots, feelin' like ten little icicles that were gonna fall off, and even my fanny was cold and sore from sittin' on my metal toolbox she let her breath out in a hiss. Her breath sent up a thick vapor like she'd been smokin' a pipe. "Must I explain the balance between Heaven and Earth?" she asked. Her tone was nasty.

"No," I said, shakin' my head, "I think I pretty much got that 'un covered."

"Then why . . ." She stopped speakin' and turned, I'm guessin', to study me. "No matter what you believe about Hell, it has its place in the order of things. It was made by the same divine hand that made you and everything you believe in."

I nodded, thinkin'. "So this 'divine hand' that made everythin'—includin' Hell—made those furnaces of yours, too."

"They were made by my master."

"So, why don't he fix 'em?"

The woman growled in frustration. "It doesn't work that way. We're expected to be independent."

"So, you'll be in trouble if you fail at your job, huh?"

"Not just me," she said in a kittenish purr.

I saw a gleam of dark in the shadows of the hood which I took to be her eyes.

"The retribution will reach far beyond this dimension, and beyond the earthly portal through which you came. The master's wrath will spill out of that portal and it will stretch far beyond your parish, your township . . . the longer the problem exists, the longer we cannot meet our quotas and then the master will take blindly, at his will."

That idea caused me more than a little discomfort . . . considerin' the wrath of the unholy one spreadin' trouble of all nature.

"But each of us would have our proper judgment. We would not be taken where we do not belong."

"You think not? What about those your preacher speaks of so often, those who have yet to redeem themselves? What about you—"

I raised my hand. "I'm prepared to be sacrificed for the good fight." I was bluffin,' of course, 'cause I had no intention of stayin' where I didn' belong, no matter who was the gatekeeper, but that was beside the point. "You've already so much as told me I wasn't goin' home again."

She shrugged. "It is a matter up for negotiation, but consider your final judgment should you bring the wrath of the master upon the world . . . when *you* had the opportunity to maintain the balance of All Things. You may think you're only a speck upon the divine food chain—"

Suddenly, Willow Smith came to mind. He was forever talkin' about the importance of balance, the importance of the smallest ant in the grand cycle. It gave

me a turn to consider my place in the order of things.
My "niche," as Will called it, was dominion over the
coolers, furnaces, and refrigerators in some Divine
Ecosystem. The absurdity of it made me grin.

"You smile? In the face of such peril?"

"I was just puttin' things into perspective," I said.
If I was part of a divine plan, then surely the skills I
had gathered over the years—that which made me
unique from all others, surely then my skills were
meant to be used. I put my trust in Him, and He had
brought me this far. I sighed and stood up, gathering
my things.

My guide paused in the arguments she had continued to make while I thought. She smiled—or rather,
what little of her face and lips were visible seemed to.
She had the satisfied smile of the cat who'd washed
down the canary with a saucer of milk. She was apparently convinced that she had won me over. I let her
think whatever she wanted to.

"So, tell me about this place," I said, lookin'
around. "Is there one central furnace?"

"One hundred thousand," she said, soundin' like my
brother-in-law, Kenny, when he was pitchin' to sell a
new piece of property.

The number of furnaces gave me pause. There were
so many little things that could happen within *one*
little household furnace, but these would be more'n
just industrial-sized. If the furnaces were set up in
some sort of system to always back one another up,
then the problem could be with any *one* of those furnaces and it would muck up the works of the others
in the chain . . . the cycle. We kept comin' back to
cycles and, as I'd mentioned before, suddenly cleanin'
them Stygian stables seemed a by-far-preferable chore
to face.

As though readin' my mind, she said, "The furnaces
are working properly . . . all of them have been thoroughly inspected."

"Then why . . . ?" I bit off my question. She could

come up with no answer to satisfy it, I was darn sure. If the furnaces *were* workin', then what part in the greater plan *did* I play? As if in answer to my prayers, the words of my guide came back to me . . . "Oh, no, not *another* philosopher!" Preacher Bob LeRoy was fond of tellin' me that I thought too much, that it got in the way. 'Course, I'd always figured we'd been given a brain for thinkin' and it was a damned shame not to put it to full use.

"What are you thinking?" my guide asked.

I kinda smiled. "I'm thinkin' your problem isn't those furnaces."

She looked at me, foldin' her arms in that high 'n' mighty way women have when you're gonna tell them something they already know but 've put a lot of effort into ignorin'.

"Till now, I've just been assumin' we were talkin' regular furnaces, but thinkin' on that, that would never really suit your . . . your purposes, now would it?" I asked.

"Having no idea how a 'regular furnace' works—"

"Ah now, hold on there," I said. I raised a warnin' finger and waved it at her. "Do you want your problem fixed or do you just wanna keep me here?"

"Well, you'd be another soul to feed the furnace," she said slyly.

"I'd gum up the works 'cause—at least for now—I don't belong here," I said with the full reality of it dawning on me. I looked at the chambers on either side of me. Thinkin' quick, I dropped my toolbox and stuck my face up to the little window of the closest door. I was frustrated in my attempt by the immediate foggin' caused by the warmth of my breath.

My hostess laughed, but did not stop me.

I tried to rub the sheen of ice away with my fingers, had little luck, so I pulled the cuff of my work shirt— for the first time in years, I had no complaints 'bout havin' to work in a long-sleeved shirt durin' the heat of summer—and used that. I had to squint 'cause of the low light, but after a moment or so, I saw a man in what looked to be the prime of life. I looked away, not 'cause he was naked but 'cause of his situation.

The man in the room hung in the air. Long, black and rubbery tentacles wrapped round the man and seemed to be feedin' from him. His face, though, was the worst of it, all contorted in horror . . . sheer terror . . . and there was clearly nothin' he could do about it.

"What? Doesn't the simplicity of our system appeal to you?" my hostess laughed harshly.

I shook my head and wondered if I'd manage to keep my lunch down—not 'cause I was worried about her floor, but 'cause I knew once I started, I'd be a long time stoppin'. "What are you doin' to him?" I asked, trying to wipe the image of the man's situation from my eyes. "What is that . . . that thing?"

My hostess looked into the window. I saw the flicker of a pleasurable smile with what I was able to see of her face.

"The beauty of it all is that this cell is made up of this man's own . . . inner demons, if you will," she said, the edges of her smile increased as she continued to stare inside. "He is as he sees himself—being completely healthy, in the prime of life and beautiful is not uncommon—and the fashion of his torment is of his own mind."

She turned toward me then, her smile more distinct as she faced me full on. "That 'thing' as you call it, is also of his own imagination and the method by which he fuels the 'furnaces' of Hell that torment him."

I nodded thoughtfully. I could see cycles, endless cycles feeding themselves, keeping themselves in order . . . and, if one part were missing? I could see the system in it all. "What else isn't workin'?" I asked.

"That need not concern you," my hostess retorted sharply.

"So there *are* other things . . . things important to the nature . . ." I paused thoughtfully. An idea'd come to me, but I just couldn't believe it right off. Now it was makin' more and more sense. "So," I said, feelin' much more confident, "there *are* other things that aren't workin' right as well. Hell—or this part of it—really is in the process of freezin' over. How much longer before this section begins to infect the farther reaches of Hell itself?"

She took that cross-armed stance again. She looked angry and spiteful, her eyes fairly seemin' to glow from beneath the hood. I don't admit lightly that meetin' her gaze was harder 'n anythin' I'd heretofore experienced and made the muscles in my stomach tie up in knots.

"I hardly think that's any of your affair," she finally said.

To say her tone was icy would be both redundant and more of an oxymoron than the proverbial 'military intelligence,' but it's what best fit to describe her at the moment.

I shrugged and picked up my toolbox and turned around. So far we'd headed straight in, and I was confident there was no walkin' straight out, however, I needed a direction and one preferably that led *away* from her. In either event, it quickly served my purpose.

"Where are you going?" she demanded.

I have long legs and I stretched my pace as far as I could to make as much distance as I could without breakin' out runnin'. I was pleased to see that she had to hurry to catch up to me. She caught my arm and spun me around. She was stronger 'n I'd thought—well, actually, I'd given it no thought 'tall. Her touch was hotter 'n the Fourth of July bonfires—which I had occasion to know since, for some reason, my brothers and I always started it. I was sure that the skin under my shirt blistered before I could break away.

"Where am I goin'? Lady, you got more furnaces 'n you can shake a stick at and they're all in working order . . . which was why I was called for. I don't see no point stayin'." I said it as matter-of-fact as I could, stayin' civil . . . she most certainly was not a sweet young thing, all innocent and virtuous, and most definitely a servant of the One Below, but she was female and a gentleman—I mean, a true, *southern* gentleman with more than just a lick of self-respect—was never unpleasant to those of the fairer sex.

"But you haven't fixed anything!" she protested.

I couldn't help but look at her with my mouth open like some fool waitin' to catch flies. "What, exactly, were you thinkin' that *I,* a mere mortal, might fix *here?* In *this* place?"

She smiled, an ugly, sick little thing. "Your ad in the phone book says that you can 'fix *any* heating or cooling system problem.' "

"It was assumed to mean 'any system known to man,' besides, as has been repeated, the furnaces are workin' just fine," I said. I took a very deep breath— besides the point of honor of not losing my temper with one of the female gender, there was also a certain degree of self-preservation in my concern for what she'd do to me when she figured I couldn't solve her problem.

"Do you want to negotiate those terms with the master?" she asked archly.

I was no fool to figure I could match wits and make a deal with Himself. Pretty much all I wanted to do was get out of here with my soul intact . . . 'ceptin' that wasn't quite true. I'd begun to develop a suspicion and, if it was right, well, I couldn't just go on my merry way and do nothin'. Even if Preacher Bob LeRoy were to tell me it was a pardonable sin, that each man answered to the Lord for his own doin's, I knew the guilt would be at me the rest of my life since, I prayed to my Maker, I wasn't ever gonna be called upon to enter this—or any other—mouth of Hell again.

"You know the answer, don't you?" she demanded, leapin' on my hesitation like a cat pouncin' on a mouse.

I scratched my chin, noting the fairly dense stubble. Somethin' told me that time ran differently in this neck of the woods and Penny was either gonna be ticked that dinner was ruint or she'd be worried sick enough to sic the hounds out after me. "Well, I *do* think that I know what the problem is . . ."

"Then fix it!" my hostess commanded.

I shook my head. "Not so easy as that. I reckon you have more'n your arms up your sleeves—pardon the expression."

Immediately, I sensed her guard comin' up, but by the lick of her lips, I knew she was anticipatin' what came next.

"When I've solved your problem, you must release me—"

"Done!"

"Not so fast!" I said. I wasn't a card playin' man, but I played a fair game of chess. "I must be released back to my own home—time and place, now—and the same goes for my tools."

"Yes, yes, I will agree to that," she fairly growled with impatience. "Let's get on with it."

"Not yet," I said. I stewed over how best to phrase the next part. "The thing—the part that's foulin' the system—that comes with me, too, to the same time and place and what I call 'home.' "

The woman rubbed her arms. Her lower lip was that purple blue people get when they're too cold— not that I'm overly familiar with that since, considerin' where I live, you're not often gonna get that cold. She had started doin' the two step folks do when they're either cold or their feet are bare on the hot tarmac. Nonetheless, she shook her head. "I can't just let you leave, taking whatever suits you."

Longing to have my hands free to tuck into my armpits again, I reconsidered my phrasin'. "I'll take with me nothin' that doesn't belong here at this time and place . . . and dimension!"

She shook her head again, so I shrugged and turned back toward where I was prayin' the doors to home, country, and Penny's apple-rhubarb pie awaited me.

"You'll be lost if you leave my side!" she called to me once I'd gotten a dozen yards or so.

"I figure I'm lost already. I'm leavin' my fate to my Maker," I said and continued on.

"I will pay you a thousand dollars' worth of gold coins!" she called.

I stopped and turned. "I'll take that, too."

"Too?"

"Sure. You're wastin' my time, ma'am. I'm here to provide a service and you've done just about everythin' to keep me from doin' it. You have to pay for my time," I said. I made a silent prayer that my Maker would not see this countermove as one of greed. To get what I wanted—outta here and home again with myself and such safe and sound—then I needed to raise the stakes. I almost laughed. To a demon mistress of Hell, even one who oversaw but a small part of it, these must be petty prices. "If I turn back around, I won't be persuaded by such paltry sums."

"You're willin' to risk your own soul—?"

"My body may be lost, ma'am, but not my soul. Now, do we have a deal or don't we?"

She looked frozen, a creature of ice, but the heat of the glare in her eyes was sufficient to thaw her pretty quick. "Be done with it."

"Then you agree?"

She nodded.

"Say it," I said as I came back toward her.

"I agree to return you and whatever part of the system which is not rightfully charged to Hell to the time, place, and dimension to which you refer as home," she repeated.

"Ah, there, you see, you're not cooperatin' so my

price is more specific . . . we must be in the same condition as when we came in—" I said. I held up my clipboard as I'd almost forgot, "and the money."

Her growl sounded like it came from a pack of dogs, but she nodded nonetheless. "We have terms. Now, fix this!" She waved at the ice-frosted walls.

I nodded, realizin' that now I *had* to fix this. I prayed that it was my Maker's will. I looked at the window of the closest doorway. "These cells, they're your power source."

"As I said," she snapped angrily.

I waved my clipboard at her. "No need to get nasty. I have to be sure I understand how this *system* works . . . so bear with me."

She folded her arms over her chest and her chin jutted out, but, at last, she nodded.

"So these cells provide the power source." She nodded so I continued. "Each inhabitant creates their own Hell, based upon their personal fears and traits and the energy is siphoned off that person's reaction to their personal vision of Hell."

"Yes, yes, I have confirmed this before!" she growled.

I amended my assessment of my hostess' growl—it sounded more like a pack of *rabid* dogs. I swallowed hard and focused on my task at hand. "Sometime lately . . . as in bein' from my time . . . did you have occasion to receive a gentleman? A young fella, with blondish-brown hair and mild disposition?"

The glare of her two eyes made me feel like I was just about to burst into flames. I stared back and hoped my bravado would carry me through.

"And if there was?"

"Then, if I'm right, he's the bug in your works," I said.

"How?"

"For one, he doesn't belong here . . . at least just not yet," I said. It took everythin' I had by way of intestinal fortitude to keep pressing.

My hostess continued to glower at me. She turned away slightly and snapped her fingers.

All around us the walls and ceiling began to slide as though we were inside some Rubik's Cube. After a couple of dizzying moments, the walls and ceiling slowed and finally stopped.

"Him?" she asked, noddin' toward the cell directly behind her left shoulder.

I couldn't help hopin' that whatever I was about to see was less . . . less horrible than the one I'd already seen. I closed my eyes and said a prayer before openin' them and lookin' inside. There, atop a mound of dirt in what to all appearances was a field, sat Mr. Willow Sunbeam Smith. The sky had a nasty greenish hue and dead things lay scattered around him.

"That's the one," I said. "How'd he come to be here, if I may ask?"

"He knocked on the door, hounding me about the pollution caused by my . . . 'plant,'" she said, her smile returnin'.

"So you just put him in here?" I asked. "What about judgment and—?"

"He was a pain in the nether regions of Hell and said he would not leave, so I put him here," she said. She looked at me. "How could he have caused the furnaces and everything to fail?"

"His worst fear was . . . is to be responsible for the destruction of an eco*system*. The energy he generated was like a poison to your entire network. . . ."

"I thank you most kindly," Mr. Smith murmured as he climbed out of my truck. He still looked dazed and bewildered. Even standin' there in Hell explainin' what had happened didn't seem to make a lot of sense to him.

We stared at one another in the early hours of sunset just outside the sheriff's station. The blinkin' of lightnin' bugs was a welcome sight, as was the relatively mild heat. Mr. Smith smiled as the crickets began their nightly love songs.

"It's so beautiful, isn't it?" he asked of no one in particular.

I leaned my head against the top of my steerin' wheel and contemplated the soft blues and purples of the night sky. "That it is," I said, noddin'.

He smiled again, still looking more than a little confused. He closed the door of the truck and, with a vague wave, headed into the station and a very different type of cell.

I watched him for a moment before I turned the key in the ignition. I was lookin' forward to home, though there was an injustice to it all . . . Penny would say I was blasphemin' if I told her the God's honest truth: I had one Hell of a day.

THE CURSE OF BEAZOEL

by David D. Levine

David D. Levine was a Hugo nominee in 2004, a John W. Campbell Award finalist in 2003 and 2004, the Writers of the Future Contest winner in 2002, the James White Award winner in 2001, and a Clarion West graduate in 2000. He has sold twenty stories so far, to magazines such as *Asimov's*, *F&SF*, and *Realms of Fantasy*, and anthologies including *Gateways*, *Haunted Holidays*, and three *Year's Best* volumes (two fantasy, the other SF). He lives with his wife Kate Yule in Portland, Oregon, and his web page can be found at http://www.BentoPress.com.

T HE DEMON Beazoel's pitchfork rested on two metal hooks driven into the wall behind him.

The pitchfork was ten feet long and made of pitted black iron that still smelled faintly of sulfur. Beazoel knew just how it felt in his hand, its substantial heft and comforting warmth. He had wielded it well during many centuries in the Torment and Punishment Division, and it had become so much a part of him that he had refused to be parted from it.

The wall on which the pitchfork hung was white and smooth and cool, its bland perfection unperturbed except by the hooks on which the pitchfork sat. Beazoel hated the wall, and the three others like it that surrounded his desk—hated it for its flatness, its rigidity, its uniformity. It looked like a slice of Heaven, and as such it did not belong here. But here it was, and so was Beazoel.

Beazoel himself, sitting stolidly behind his desk, was a magnificent specimen of a Demon of the Fifteenth Circle, a rugged living sculpture in obsidian and basalt. His horns curled with brute assured power from the sides of his head, his eyes glowed with baleful radiance beneath his broad, stony brow, and his massive hands could tear a sinner's torso in half in one quick motion. At the moment those hands were occupied in picking papers from the pile to his left and placing them in one of the piles to his right. Each paper singed slightly as he handled it, but though his hands were large and powerful, he had a deft touch. After his first day on the job, he hadn't let a single sheet burst into flame.

His office was equipped with a window, and this was a rare privilege, but Beazoel resolutely did not let his gaze stray from the papers before him. Beyond the glass lay a landscape out of nightmare—a chaotic, ruptured terrain of black rock and glowing lava, seething with lakes of brimstone and overcast with poisonous, corrosive miasmas. The perpetual night was lit only by flashes of lightning and the foul red glow of the lava pits.

To look upon that view would be to release a heartbreaking flood of nostalgia.

The only good thing about the window was that it did not open, so he could not smell the smoke or hear the screams of the damned as he worked. That would have been too much to bear.

Beazoel ran a finger under his collar. The asbestos fabric and the steel-mesh tie were a constant irritation to him. His neck was too large for even the largest shirt, and his shoulders too broad for his suit jacket.

Even worse, lately he found it harder and harder to button the jacket across his growing paunch.

He was becoming soft. This would never have happened if they had just let him stay in the pits where he belonged. If only he hadn't been such a good Pit Boss . . . maybe someone else would have been selected for this "promotion."

Rapidly he scanned the papers, placing each one in the appropriate pile to his right. Invoices, expenses, production reports, project plans. Approved, denied, further study. He worked quickly, but the left-hand pile replenished itself at intervals, and papers vanished from the right-hand piles, so that he was constantly in the middle of his work—never feeling the satisfaction of completion, or even the palms-rubbing contemplation of a new task.

This was the curse of Beazoel.

A knock came at his door—an event unprecedented since he had come to this office. He cleared his throat, then managed, "Come in?" The low rumble of his own voice startled him.

The door opened, revealing a massive red devil with black eyes, jutting jaw, prominent stomach, and goat's legs. "Beazoel of the Fifteenth Circle . . ." he began, mispronouncing it *be-a-ZOAL.*

"Be-AZ-o-el," Beazoel interrupted. "Sir."

The devil was taken aback for a moment, but quickly regained his poise. "Be-*AZ*-o-el of the Fifteenth Circle, you have worked diligently for the Torment and Punishment Division for many years. However, events . . ." he glanced upward, ". . . Up There, are in rapid flux, and we here must change along with them. Therefore, you are being reassigned to another position."

"Am I to be returned to the pits?" He could barely contain his joy at the prospect.

"No, Beazoel, I bring you *good* news!" Steam spurted from the devil's nostrils as he chuckled. "Effective immediately, you will be heading up a new project in the Research and Development Department of the Misery and Temptation Division."

"Thank you, sir!" Research and Development—that sounded promising. He had spent many idle years in the pits thinking of new and more terrible ways to torture the damned.

"Allow me to conduct you to your new office."

Beazoel leaped to his feet and took down the pitchfork from the wall. "I am ready."

"Oh, you won't be needing that any more."

Exciting visions of new and interesting torture implements passed behind Beazoel's eyes, but resolutely he gripped the solid metal of the pitchfork. "Please, sir. I have had this since the Beginning."

They stared at each other for a long moment, punctuated by the shuffling sound of new papers appearing on the desk. Finally, the devil snorted and said, "Oh, very well. Come along."

As the door closed behind them, a taloned fiend appeared at the desk with a surprised squawk.

The devil, whose name was Azaroth, led Beazoel down an infinite corridor, endless gray doors set in featureless white walls, all bathed in a calm sourceless illumination. The corridor bustled with imps, demons, and fiends of every description. "I can't imagine how excited you must have been to get out of the pits of torment. Why, they haven't changed in millennia!"

"Sometimes the old ways are the best, sir."

"Nonsense!" Azaroth blew a snort of acrid smoke. "Do you think our customers . . . Up There . . . are content with the old ways? Neither can we be." He stopped at a door like all the others. "Here we are. Your new office!" He flung open the door and gestured Beazoel in with a grand flourish.

It was identical to the old one, except that the window was larger. It also had a view of the pits. The Number Seven pit, where Beazoel had once been Pit

Boss, now stood cold and vacant; his people had all been reassigned after his promotion.

"Thank you, sir," Beazoel said miserably.

As soon as Beazoel had fastened his pitchfork to the wall, Azaroth led him a short way down the corridor to a door labeled MISERY AND TEMPTATION DIVISION: RESEARCH AND DEVELOPMENT LAB.

Behind the door lay a long, high-ceilinged room where dozens of demons peered into eyepieces, delicately turned knobs of shiny metal, and gingerly prodded shining disks with obscure implements. They were all garbed in pristine white outfits. "Gentlemen!" Azaroth called out, and the workers raised their heads. "Let me present your new supervisor, Beazoel of the Fifteenth Circle."

Most of them just stared at him in silence. One or two shook their heads, then went right back to what they had been doing. But one demon rose from his station and moved toward him, his hooves tap-tapping on the seamless gray flooring. He was of a type Beazoel had never before encountered, with a cheerful, handsome face and small, wicked horns. His skin was shiny and had a uniform pink color, and he wore a tie under his white coverall. "Gaznash," he introduced himself, extending his hand. It was as smooth and unyielding as the lab's walls, as cool and inoffensive as the lighting. "I am the assistant supervisor. Let me just say that I am honored and delighted to make your acquaintance, and I hope we will have a long and successful partnership."

"Pleased to meet you," Beazoel said, though he wanted to wipe his hand on his pants leg.

"Azaroth, as long as you are here . . . might I have a word?"

The superior devil gave Gaznash a dark look. "Excuse me," he said to Beazoel, and he and the pink demon stepped out into the hall.

Beazoel shuffled from one foot to another. The other demons had all gone back to work, and paid him no attention whatsoever. He peered over the shoulder of a black-winged soulsnatcher, whose wings were tightly bound up under its white coverall. It was peering into the angular metallic guts of a large, shiny machine. "What's that you're working on?" Beazoel asked it.

"This stinking developer has never worked worth shit," it spat back. "Spend all my time tweaking and poking and it still craps out ten times a week." It prodded something inside the machine with a long, thin tool. "Not that they'll listen to me when we don't make quota."

"Tell me more."

But just then a sound behind Beazoel drew his attention. Azaroth stood with his hand on the door, speaking harshly to Gaznash. "Beazoel has been carefully selected for this position, and I have every confidence that he will succeed where his predecessors have failed." Steam rose from his nostrils. "I would advise you not to try my patience any further, lest you meet the same fate as they."

Gaznash's smile never faltered. "Certainly, sir."

"I expect to see you meet quota this week. Good day." Azaroth closed the door firmly in the pink demon's face.

As Gaznash walked back from the door, Beazoel leaned down and looked into the developer's incomprehensible innards, his head close to the soulsnatcher's. "What happened to my predecessors?" he muttered low.

The soulsnatcher's face was not built for pity, but it tried. "Didn't they tell you?"

"Not yet."

It shook his head sadly. "Dispelled."

Beazoel swallowed. As Hell expanded to contain the ever-rising human population, new demons appeared to staff it—like the taloned fiend now occupying Beazoel's old office. Sometimes even new types of demon, like Gaznash, popped into existence to perform new tasks. But the opposite could also occur.

Beazoel's head whirled with questions, but before he could say anything more, Gaznash strode up. "The new supervisor has more important things to do than to help you with your maintenance, Sharoth." He whipped a clipboard out from under his arm and presented it to Beazoel. "Would you care to review the inspection reports?"

"First I need to know what we're doing here."

"We are currently at fifty-six percent of quota, but I assure you I am doing my utmost to . . ."

Beazoel fixed Gaznash with a Number Three Baleful Stare, which succeeded in stopping him in midprotestation. "No. All this . . ." he waved a hand at the machinery and the bustling demons who attended it. ". . . what is it *for?*"

"Bad ideas."

Beazoel blinked at him.

"Mass customization of bad ideas. For export—Up There. It's Azaroth's pet project."

"Mass . . . customization?" Beazoel rolled the unfamiliar syllables around in his mouth.

The soulsnatcher, Sharoth, put down its wrench. "Used to be, bad ideas were handcrafted. We'd study a customer for years before building just the right one for him . . . sweet on the outside, with a bitter center. Then, once he was softened up, the boys from Temptation would come calling. But the population's gotten too big for that kind of individual attention."

Gaznash pointed to a row of machines that stood dark and silent, covered with tarpaulins. "We used simple mass production at first. Thousands of bad ideas, all the same, distributed nationwide by radio and television. We had some great successes."

"The Red Menace," said Sharoth, and sighed. "Those were the days."

"But today's consumers are more sophisticated.

They think of themselves as individuals, and won't readily accept exactly the same ideas as their neighbors. Hence: mass customization. Millions of bad ideas, each slightly different from the others, distributed worldwide through the Internet. Botox, high-protein diets, and low-rise pants are all products of this lab. Bulletin-board and blog-comment spam are very big distribution channels for us right now."

Beazoel's head was starting to hurt. None of this made the slightest sense.

"Distribution isn't the problem," said Sharoth. "It's production. Look." It pulled a shimmering silver disk from the developer and handed it to Beazoel. "These are SUV variants. They're all essentially the same bad idea, but each one has some minor difference that appeals to different people. We do a lot with cup holders."

"Don't touch it with your *hands!*" Gaznash cried.

"This whole batch is already shot," said Sharoth. "Look at the surface."

The disk was cool to the touch, and covered with tiny, intricate designs. Each little square was slightly different from its neighbors. "Ideas," Sharoth continued, "even bad ones, are complicated things. Making them takes hundreds of steps, and if even one step gets messed up . . ." Sharoth yanked the disk from Beazoel's hand and dropped it on the floor, where it shattered into a million silvery shards. "Then we have to start over from scratch."

Gaznash crossed his arms on his chest. "You'll have to clean that up, and I expect a full spoilage report."

"You'll get your report as soon as I get this stinking developer online, and not one moment . . ."

"*I* am the assistant supervisor here, not you, and I'll have you know . . ."

"Gentlemen," Beazoel rumbled in his best Pit Boss voice—a deep sound with a layer of seeming calm overlaying more than a hint of menace—and they both stopped cold. "Sharoth, I apologize for interrupting you at your work. Please resume what you were doing. Gaznash, would you please give me a tour of the facility?"

Gaznash recovered his composure with disturbing speed. "Certainly, sir. This way."

"Good luck," Sharoth muttered as Beazoel passed.

Beazoel and Gaznash walked the long, narrow room from one end to the other, past tracers and chillers and scrubbers and derationalizers. Each hulking machine was tended by two or three demons; pink ones like Gaznash predominated, but there were also a variety of other types, including steel-skinned shriekers, red imps, and broad-shouldered mashers. One of the mashers looked familiar to Beazoel from the pits of torment, but he didn't manage to catch its attention.

Gaznash kept up a constant bright chatter that served only to deepen Beazoel's incomprehension, raining facts and figures and terminology down on his aching head. The pink demon, with skin as smooth and shiny as any of the machines under his assistant supervision, seemed to revel in their complexity. Beazoel wondered at what temperature that skin would melt.

Finally, as they stood before a machine whose very name was meaningless to Beazoel, he held up a hand to stop the flow of words. "Enough. Let me see if I have the basics. Raw materials come in here. Blank disks come out there. The machines on this side imprint the disks with ideas. That big noisy machine cuts the disks into . . . mums?"

"Memes."

"Memes. Then they get glued into carriers, and boxed for transport over there."

"Well, yes, but you've left out the whole customization process. The lexical analyzer . . ."

Beazoel put his hand over his eyes. "Let's set that aside for now. What is the *problem?*"

"Problem?"

"Everyone here keeps talking about the quota, and

how hard it is to meet it. Why? Do you not have enough raw materials?"

"No, sir, our raw materials are just words, images, and emotions, and there's never a shortage of those."

"What, then?"

"Frankly, sir . . ." Gaznash leaned in close and lowered his voice. "It's lack of discipline."

"Discipline?"

"Oh, the modern demons are all right, sir, but all those old types . . . well, they were brought in by one of your predecessors and they've been nothing but trouble. You saw how insubordinate that soulsnatcher was, and that was a mild incident. If *I* were supervisor, that kind of backtalk would never be tolerated."

Beazoel rubbed his chin, with a scraping sound of stone on stone. "I see. Can we just send them back where they came from?"

The pink demon sighed. "Apart from the paperwork, sir, which would be formidable, you simply don't have the authority. Your predecessor pulled strings and got Azaroth to transfer them in for him."

"Well, Azaroth can just transfer them back out again."

"I wouldn't advise it, sir. It wasn't at all easy for him to get them, and having gone to so much effort he's not going to let go of them. Rumor has it that he dispelled a supervisor just for asking."

Beazoel swallowed. "What *do* I have the authority to do?"

Gaznash ticked off points on his fingers. "You can reorganize your staff however you see fit. You can change the physical layout of the lab. You can requisition additional space, depending on availability. You have a limited budget for new equipment. It's all in the manual."

"What manual?"

"The New Revised Manual of Policies and Procedures. It governs everything we do here. There should be a copy in your office."

"It appears I have some reading to do." He stepped toward the door, then paused. "I don't suppose I can demote *you?*"

Gaznash chuckled. "Oh, sir, you have such a delightful sense of humor. I'm sure we'll get along famously. But, all kidding aside, the answer is no."

When Beazoel opened his office door, he was startled by the huge and growing pile of papers on his desk. At first he hoped he had accidentally walked into the wrong office, but that notion was dispelled by the sight of his pitchfork fastened to the wall. Apparently his new office came with all the responsibilities of the old as well as its own. Grimly, he set to work.

Through determined effort and brutal decisiveness—mostly making snap decisions based on the first sentence or two of each paper—he reduced the pile to a more manageable size, then looked for the manual. He soon found it in one of his desk drawers: a three-ring binder, stuffed to overflowing with dog-eared sheets in a dozen different colors. From the haphazard order of the pages, it had clearly burst open several times in the past and been put back together as quickly as possible.

He began to read. It was tough going. Every few dozen pages his mind glazed over from the effort, and he took a break by sorting some papers from the pile.

He had never dreamed that sorting paperwork could be preferable to anything else.

Beazoel was struggling through Paragraph XIII. 27.B.53(a), Revised Procedure for Revision of Previously Submitted Requisition Forms, when a tap came at the door. But his delight at the interruption was tempered by the interrupter: it was Gaznash, requesting his help with a disciplinary issue. He tucked the manual under his arm as he walked to the lab.

"These two idiots haven't the slightest notion how to run a . . ."

"So then he just up and hits me on the . . .

"I've never been so insulted in all my . . ."

"Silence," said Beazoel in his Pit Boss voice, low and firm, and the three demons immediately complied. "You first. In twenty words or less, what is the dispute here?"

Two of the pink demons—Gaznash had called them "modern demons"—were arguing with a fork-tailed banshee over a conceptual laminator, which sat wheezing and clunking in a manner that did not seem to indicate smooth operation. Beazoel had pointed at random to one of the pink demons.

"I was just getting ready to load a tray of disks into the laminator when *this* one up and hits . . ."

"That's twenty. You. Same thing."

The second pink demon paused a moment, then said, "I saw the whole thing. The banshee hit Rashnak for no reason at all. On the nose."

"Seventeen words. Very commendable. You."

The banshee was quivering with rage. "This machine's malfunctioning. I'm trying to fix it. Whole tray would have been ruined. Third one in a row."

"Third one in a row? Explain."

The banshee hesitated.

"You don't have to limit your answer to twenty words."

"The third deposition stage is overheating. It only happens when the machine is warmed up and I don't want to take it offline until I've figured out why. But as long as the machine's online, geniuses like these two keep trying to load trays into it. They managed to get past me twice already. I guess I got kind of upset."

"What would have happened if he'd loaded the tray?"

"Lamination's a late-stage process. Each of these disks represents a hundred and twenty hours of work. Losing those two trays put us a full percentage point behind quota, and that'll be hard to make up. I couldn't stand to see a whole 'nother tray go up in smoke like that."

Beazoel tapped his chin with a finger. "Your name?"

"Kaiyee of the Razor Crags."

"Kaiyee, hitting a coworker is never acceptable. Even in the pits of torment, where a certain amount of . . . physical interaction is part of the job, striking another demon is punishable by submersion in hot lava. But I'll withhold punishment if you promise never to do it again."

Then he spat in his hand, and extended it.

The banshee spat in his own hand and shook Beazoel's. "I promise."

"Good. Now get back to work."

He turned to Gaznash, who was standing with the two pink demons. All three stared rigidly back at him.

"That banshee *hit* Rashnak," said Gaznash, "and you're letting him off with a *warning?*"

"He did it because he was focused on quota. And he sealed his promise. No banshee would break a sealed promise."

Rashnak's lip quivered with indignation. "Favoritism. That's all it is. You're favoring him because he's an old-style demon like you."

Beazoel thought about that charge for a moment. There was a grain of truth to it. "I decided in Kaiyee's favor because he took action to increase this lab's production." He tapped the binder under his arm. "Continued failure to meet quota can result in disciplinary action for the *entire* staff, up to and including dispellation. A bruised nose, or being dispelled. Which would you rather have?"

The pink demon stood with his mouth open.

"However," Beazoel continued, "I am sensitive to your concerns, and I will strive to avoid the appearance of favoritism in the future. You are now free to return to your assignment."

Beazoel did try to keep his personal opinions about the pink demons separate from his professional deci-

sions after that, but it wasn't easy. They were hard
workers, efficient and polite, and their adherence to
standard procedure was unwavering. But when it came
to machinery, they were not very bright, and their
mistakes destroyed disks or caused the equipment to
malfunction or both. The old-style demons, nasty and
snappish though they were, had more technical
aptitude.

Gaznash was the only one of the pink demons who
understood the technical processes of the lab, and
even his understanding was academic—limited to how
the process was *supposed* to work. Whenever anything
went wrong, it fell to some imp or gargoyle to fix it.
Beazoel speculated that long, direct contact with
human sinners gave them an adaptability that the pink
demons, who seemed born to the sterile, third-hand
temptation of the lab, lacked.

"Try not to be too hard on him," Sharoth said to
him one day. One of the pink demons had managed
to destroy an idiomatic depositor by putting the fuser
in backward, and Beazoel was helping the soulsnatcher to fill out a requisition for a new one. "He's
an involuntary transferee, just like me and you."

"Oh?"

"The lot of them used to work for Azaroth over in
Distribution and Marketing. They're wizards at selling
ideas to customers. But when Azaroth got his big
brainstorm about mass customization, he decided to
staff the new project with his own people. That was a
big mistake. If your predecessor Thelasson hadn't
brought us in from the old handcrafted misery shop
to help them with the technical bits, the whole lab
would have been dispelled for nonproduction."

As it was, they were perilously close to it. They
were nearing the end of Beazoel's first month on the
job, and they had failed to make their weekly quota
even once. He had reorganized his staff into small
teams, with an old-style demon on each, and re-
arranged the equipment on the lab floor to improve

work flow. It had helped, but not enough. The machinery was experimental, cranky at the best of times, and even with the best of attention it kept breaking down. And though the small teams improved production, they increased the opportunities for friction between the old-style and new-style demons.

Beazoel was in his office, abstractedly sorting papers while pondering reassigning the gargoyle Umziala from the finisher team to the thematic refiner—the refiner desperately needed Umziala's technical skills, but could Daskanaz keep the finisher going without him?—when he heard a determined rap at the door.

It was Gaznash, and a half dozen other pink demons. Their faces were hard with anger as they crowded into Beazoel's office.

"We have had enough," Gaznash said. "This 'small-team' experiment of yours has ignored seniority, disrupted process flow, and created chaos for too long. We demand a return to the previous organization."

"Those taloned fiends have no respect," said one of the other demons, "and they smell!"

Gaznash silenced the demon with a glance, then presented a clipboard stuffed with papers, edges neatly squared. "The current organization simply is not working. In the last week I have received only the bare minimum of status reports, and process improvement forms are filed at the last minute—if at all!"

"Process improvement forms are optional," said Beazoel with a Number One Glare. He did not accept the clipboard.

"That isn't the *point!*" sputtered Gaznash, and slapped the clipboard down on Beazoel's desk. Papers fluttered to the floor. "If the forms aren't filed, how can we know if progress is being made?"

"Look at the bottom line. Production has gone up every week."

Gaznash picked up his clipboard and folded back some sheets. "Yes. But the curve is flattening. Without proper procedures and tracking, I can't tell you why, or whether it's going to go back down again. We *must* return some discipline to this organization soon, or I won't be held responsible for the consequences!"

Beazoel looked at the proffered chart. The amount of improvement was, indeed, going down week by week, and if the trend continued, productivity would top out at just over ninety percent of quota. Not good enough.

A harsh grinding sound filled the air, though the pink demons seemed not to notice. After a moment Beazoel realized it was his teeth grinding in frustration. What more could he do? Distributing the technically savvy old-style demons throughout the lab was the only way to keep the finicky customization equipment running, but the morale problems that caused with the majority pink demons could no longer be ignored. He had already exceeded his capital budget for the month, so there was no way to improve the situation by getting better machines—even if the new machines would really be any better than the old ones, which was by no means certain. Changing the layout of the lab floor again would only delay the inevitable.

"Perhaps you're right . . ." he began, but before he could finish the sentence he was interrupted by another knock on the door, this one hard and imperious. It was Azaroth, and he didn't look pleased.

"Come with me," said the superior devil. "Molech requires an immediate department-level report."

As Beazoel hurried through the crowded hall behind Azaroth, his feelings were an uneasy mixture of relief at the temporary reprieve and apprehension over the coming meeting. Molech was Azaroth's superior. Though Beazoel had never met him, he was known as a cold and demanding taskmaster.

"Speak only when spoken to," Azaroth said as they walked. "Be prepared to back up anything you say with hard figures. And for pity's sake, straighten your tie."

With fumbling fingers, Beazoel did his best to comply, even as his feet moved from smooth gray flooring to well-trodden volcanic stone. Azaroth led him into a cavernous space, hung with stalactites and dimly lit by flickering torches.

Molech's office.

Molech himself sat behind an enormous basalt desk, rimless glasses perched on his beaklike nose, long slim fingers steepled before him. His long red face was all angles, from the deep V of his eyebrows to the long point of his chin, and his horns were polished and delicately tipped with gold.

Beazoel joined the crowd of subordinates standing behind Azaroth. There were about a dozen others, a mix of red devils and pink demons. Beazoel stood a full head taller than any of them, and felt uncomfortably exposed.

Molech stepped out from behind his desk, a slim figure in a precisely-tailored gray suit. "I've called you here to resolve an ambiguity," he said. "Azaroth, your regular reports indicate that all is going well in your department. But though production is proceeding apace down here, actual conversion rates Up There are not meeting my superiors' expectations." He stepped closer to Azaroth. "What do you think could be the cause of this?"

"We're doing all we can, sir," said Azaroth. His tone was confident, though Beazoel could see the tip of his pointed tail trembling slightly. "Marketing and distribution are exceeding their goals by ten and a half percent, temptation has increased efficiency by over thirty-two percent, and misery levels Up There are at their highest in eighteen years."

"You haven't answered my question," Molech said, leaning forward. Azaroth bent back, almost imperceptibly. "Production and efficiency are all well and good, but what my superiors demand is results. Simply put: how many customers check in here at the end of the day, versus the Competition?" He folded his glasses and tapped them on Azaroth's chest. "What is your department doing to change that ratio in our favor, and why isn't it working?"

A bead of sweat ran down the back of Azaroth's neck. "As you know, sir, our customer base is changing rapidly, but most of our techniques are millennia old. Existing products and procedures can't keep up with the rise in population and changing technology. However, my department has several experimental projects underway to address this shortcoming. I'm particularly proud of the mass customization lab. New supervisor Beazoel has made great strides, and I'm confident we will shortly be able to take this technique out of the lab and into full production."

"Let me talk to this Beazoel," said Molech. Azaroth gestured to him.

Beazoel touched the knot on his tie and stepped forward, trying hard to control his breathing. "Sir?"

"I have read Azaroth's reports on mass customization. It certainly is a promising new technique, though until recently the results have not been satisfactory. I commend you on your progress. What would you say are the greatest challenges facing you today?"

Though Molech's face was mild, his black eyes seemed to burn right to the back of Beazoel's head. Azaroth, beside him, looked at Beazoel with an expression compounded of expectation, apprehension, and warning.

"Well, sir. The, uh, the equipment, sir. It's experimental, and unreliable." *Back up what you say with hard figures.* "We have major breakdowns every day. Or so." Inside himself, he winced at the amateurish and imprecise figure. He wished Gaznash were here with his clipboard.

"But Azaroth tells me that you have reorganized your staff to deal with this situation."

Beazoel swallowed. "That's true, sir. But the reorganization has created some, uh, friction. Among the staff. I don't think it will work in the long run." Azaroth's eyes grew wide.

Molech blinked. "How unfortunate. Do you have a plan to address this situation?"

Beazoel opened his mouth to say *No,* but then he closed it again. His brain was churning. "Well, sir . . ." He paused, and rubbed his chin. Azaroth looked at him pleadingly. "We could address the friction by dividing the lab into two completely separate teams. But the, uh, the modern demons don't have the technical skills to cope with the experimental equipment, and the old-style demons don't have the discipline to maintain a manufacturing process."

Steam came from Azaroth's nose. "This is a management decision, sir, and he's just a supervisor."

"No, let him speak," said Molech. "I think he has a useful perspective."

Emboldened, Beazoel went on, the thoughts tumbling out as fast as he could formulate them. "The lab has some old mothballed equipment for mass production. It's tried and tested. Even a pink . . . uh, I mean, it doesn't require a lot of technical skill to operate. And with the latest marketing and distribution techniques, mass-produced bad ideas can reach more people than ever before." Molech nodded. "But that isn't enough, sir! You always need custom ideas, for the more difficult customers. The old-style demons in my staff have millennia of experience in handcrafting ideas. Give them a budget and a place to work, and Internet distribution, and I'm sure they'll bring in customers by the carload."

"Mass production plus limited custom production," said Moloch. "The best of both worlds."

"Beazoel," said Azaroth, struggling to regain control of the conversation, "I want you to form a task force to implement this idea."

"Yes, sir. Thank you, sir." He started to think about who he would assign to the new task force . . . and a fierce grin bloomed on his face. "I'll need to make some . . . unorthodox organizational changes."

"Absolutely!" said Azaroth. "Whatever you need!"

The next week, Beazoel stood in his office, looking out the window. The old Number Seven pit, long cold, now bustled with activity, as demons reassigned from his lab set up the first new handcrafted idea shop in centuries. Beazoel smiled.

There was a knock at the door. It was Gaznash, with his clipboard.

"Thank you for coming, Gaznash," said Beazoel. "Have a seat."

"Sir?" There was only one chair in the office, and it was behind the desk.

"Go on." Tentatively, the pink demon sat. "Gaznash, I need you to process a reorganization for me."

"Certainly, sir." He pulled out a triplicate form.

"You'll need two forms."

"Oh?"

"I am reassigning . . . myself. To head up the custom production workshop. They need an old Pit Boss to keep them in line. But in my absence, someone else will have to supervise the mass production lab."

"Me?" A tentative smile quivered at the corner of Gaznash's lip.

"Yes."

"Oh, thank you, sir!"

"It is my pleasure." He took down the pitchfork from the wall and stepped to the door. "And if you need any help . . . don't call me."

As Beazoel closed the door behind himself, he heard the shuffling roar of a huge pile of new paperwork appearing on the desk, and a yelp of surprise. He grinned, and walked down the hall swinging his pitchfork.

POKER BOY VS. A DENIZEN OF GAMBLING HELL

by Dean Wesley Smith

Best-selling author Dean Wesley Smith has written more than seventy popular novels, both his own and tie-in projects, including *Laying the Music to Rest* and *X-Men: The Jewels of Cyttorak*. With Kristine Kathryn Rusch, he is the coauthor of *The Tenth Planet* trilogy and the motion picture novelization *X-Men*, along with more than a dozen *Star Trek* books and two original *Men in Black* novels. He has also written novels in a number of gaming universes, including *Vor*, *Final Fantasy*, and the novelization for the movie *Final Fantasy*.

THE TEN-TWENTY hold'em game at the Mirage was going just fine until Heidi sat down in the empty seat. I was up about three hundred and enjoying the game, staying out of the way of another pro at the other end of the table. We were basically taking turns slowly relieving the tourists of their money, while making sure they had a good time giving it to us.

Heidi, with her long blond hair, plunging v-neck sweater, and front-loaded assets shifted the feeling of the table. I sensed it at once, even without using my

Ultra-Intuitive Superpower. She gave everyone a bright, white smile, fumbled with her chips like she was a beginner, and then laughed at something the tourist beside her said that more than likely wasn't funny.

At once my Poker Boy Gut-Sense Power shouted at me like a voice coming up from the depths of the Grand Canyon. Normally the power never shouted at me unless I asked it to. Now the Gut-Sense Grand Canyon voice was echoing in my head.

She's a good player!
The breasts are fake!
She's evil!

As the superhero Poker Boy, I've fought my share of evil and played with more than my share of both good and bad poker players. The first because fighting evil is what superheroes do. It is the job description. The second because I make my living and pay the expenses for the next fight against evil by playing professional poker. Trust me, superheroes have to get money somewhere, and it might as well be from people who are enjoying themselves over a card game while they gave me money to cover the costs of fighting those that needed to be fought.

Since the first day I put on my leather coat and Fedora-like hat that became my superhero costume, I knew that the Gambling Gods ran anything to do with gambling. Laverne, Lady Luck herself, was head of all things corporate, with Burt the General Manager running all casino operations in the god realm.

Stan was the main God of Poker and my direct boss. I liked Stan, and over the years I had actually met both Laverne and Burt during adventures. I knew them to be powerful and damned scary. No poker player I know of screws around with Lady Luck and lives to win another pot. I always treated Laverne with the respect she deserved and so far my luck had been just fine.

Of course, over the years there had always been evil

to fight. Otherwise there would have been no need for my services as Poker Boy. But until Heidi sat down at my table, I had never faced evil over a game. And I had no real understanding that there was also a Gambling Hell where the evil I was fighting came from.

To be honest, I'm not sure why I hadn't put two and two together and come up with a Gambling Hell. The evil had to come from somewhere, didn't it? Besides, if there were Gambling Gods, I knew there had to be a Gambling Hell to keep the universe balanced. I just hadn't thought of it before I met the denizen of Gambling Hell named Heidi.

She had finished stacking her chips in a beginner-like manner, a neat triangle coming out from the rail, all chips stacked neatly in piles of five. Then she looked up at me and smiled.

Only there was nothing about that smile that reached her dark eyes.

I didn't move, didn't smile back, but it was clear from her look that she knew who I was.

And she was challenging me.

My Grand Canyon warning voice echoed in my head again.

EVIL!
Evil!
evil!

After the echo in my head died off, my next thought was to rack up my chips and just find another table, or maybe even call it a night. But I was a superhero, and superheroes didn't run from evil, they fought it, head on. Normally I had to go track it down, dig it out, and then vanquish it in some fashion or another. Evil had very seldom come to me and asked to be beaten like Heidi was doing.

But now Evil itself was sitting three chairs down the table from me in a ten-twenty game, directly across from the dealer, and I had no idea why. But I had a hunch I was about to find out.

The pro at the other end of the table, a man I respected for his great skill at poker and his ability to read just about any player, gave Heidi a quick once-over, shook his head, and racked up his chips. He knew, just as I did, that what had been a very good game had just gone sour.

"Good luck," he said to me before turning to leave.

I nodded at him and then glanced down at the two cards the dealer had just given me. Pocket kings.

I was two in front of the blinds so I raised the bet to twenty. Everyone at the table folded except Heidi, who pretended to fumble with her chips and had to have the dealer help her get her bet right.

She was good. Every man at the table was watching her, either her smooth-skinned hands or her plunging neckline.

The flop gave me another king, with two smaller cards that didn't match in suit or reach for a straight. Since I figured she was going to play the dumb blonde to the hilt and if I checked, she would check, I decided instead to bet ten more.

She again made a production out of calling. She was either giving me the first hand as part of the act, or she had aces and was playing me, pretending she didn't know what she was doing.

Then I realized there was something else going on. The calm, fun nature of the table was gone, replaced with tension and a focus that was distracted from the cards. It was almost as if the entire table had been shifted slightly out of the big Mirage Casino card room and into another dimension. The rest of the room seemed distant and a little fuzzy.

So she wasn't just after the money, she was taking the table for another reason. As Poker Boy, I had seen a lot stranger things and for the moment I was willing to ride along to see exactly where we were going. And why.

The turn came another garbage card, with a rainbow, all four suits, on the board. I still had my three kings, but this time I just checked to her, wanting to see how she played her hand next. To a pro, in certain circumstances, a check means a weak hand. At other times it's a trap, meaning the hand is strong and the pro wants someone to bet so the pro can raise.

She looked at me with a puzzled smile on her face, pretending she didn't know what a check meant.

"Up to you," the young dealer said, resting his hand in front of the woman to indicate it was her turn to bet.

"Oh, it's my turn?" Heidi said, looking down at her cards again, then pretending to study the cards on the table. Then she looked up at the dealer, "What can I bet?"

A few men around the table who were taken in by her act chuckled. When a beginning player asked how much they could bet, it always meant they had a strong hand, or thought they had a strong hand. With Heidi, I knew it was all an act.

But with that question, the room around us seemed to grow even more distant and blurry. The noise from the other tables faded farther into the background.

I had a sense of downward movement. No one else at the table noticed, including the dealer, as all their attention remained focused on Heidi, her blond hair, and her v-neck sweater.

"The bet is twenty," the dealer said.

She fumbled with her chips and then slid twenty forward.

She smiled at the dealer and then looked my way.

I knew I was going to have to make my move pretty soon to stop what she was doing with this table, but I wanted to see that last card before I did. If she had two aces in her hand, there were still two aces left out, and I wanted to be sure that third ace didn't hit the board before I moved. So I simply flat-called her twenty.

The dealer patted the table to indicate the bets were

all square, burned a card, and turned over the river card. A four of hearts that matched the four of clubs already on the board.

I had kings full of fours, the highest full house possible with the cards on the board. But not the highest hand possible. And that worried me a lot.

Around the table the rest of the Mirage poker room had become nothing more than a distant blur, the only sounds a faint rumbling. And the air was getting warmer and warmer by the moment. Heidi was moving the entire game into Gambling Hell, and no one but me seemed to be noticing.

I took a deep breath and focused on a spot between two upcoming seconds. I wanted to use what I had called my Unstuck-in-Time power. Stan the God of Poker had told me I had the power, and since then it had come in handy more than once.

My power froze everyone's movements except Heidi's. Clearly my power hadn't worked on her. She truly was evil and very powerful.

Seven of the men were frozen staring at her chest, the dealer and one of the other players were staring at her hands.

"Nice trick," she said, laughing in a way that made me shiver, even though I had on a leather jacket and the temperature around the table had gone up by twenty degrees.

By slipping myself between moments in time, I could see a little better where we were.

Granted, the Mirage poker room was a faint overlay, sort of blurred and fuzzy, but through that vision I could clearly see a huge cave with dark walls and bright lights hanging from the roof. The table I was at seemed to be up near the roof of the cavern, still sitting in the Mirage, but yet at the same time floating in space, not yet all the way down to the surface.

A river of molten lava ran through one side of the cavern, accounting for the extra heat. There had to be at least a hundred different poker games going on around the room, all frozen because I was looking at them from a moment between seconds.

A poker room in Gambling Hell. This was the last place I wanted to be.

"So, Poker Boy," she said, smiling at me, "you hoping to freeze time and come and take a quick glance at what I have in my hand?"

I laughed at her. "Not my style. That's something you'd do, I'm sure. I just wanted to stop this little elevator act you have going on."

"And you think this trick is going to stop it for long?" she asked, flaunting her chest assets by leaning forward and making sure her v-neck sweater bagged out just enough.

Granted, I was a man. But I had turned down sexual advances from a goddess far more interesting than her, so her attempts to distract me dropped short.

"Long enough to get this settled," I said.

"And just how do you plan to settle this?" she asked, smiling at me. "Knock me off my chair?"

I stared at her, looking deep into her eyes. In my years of doing superhero deeds, I had found many ways of solving problems, and for none of them, not once, had I needed to use any physical-type action. Anyone who actually looked at me would know I wouldn't be any good at that stuff anyway. I kept my poker face on and just kept staring at her, trying to get any kind of read on exactly what would work. Frighteningly enough, at the moment I didn't know. I was just playing a bluff.

She waved her arm around at the cavern. "You're in my world now."

I said nothing.

She shifted slightly, still smiling at me, still leaning forward trying to get me to look at her fake assets.

I just stared at her face, into her eyes, like I stared at any poker player who tried to make a move on me. And I made sure I kept us firmly planted between seconds of time.

After a long moment of me staring at her, she shifted slightly again, then turned to stare back, her fake smile frozen on her face.

I could tell I was getting to her. But I still had no idea what to do to get this table and all the men around it back into the Mirage poker room. I needed some answers.

"So what do you want me for?" I asked. "Why these guys?"

"Customers," she said. "Got to keep the operation running."

"No winning allowed down there," I said, indicating the tables frozen below us in the cavern.

She smiled again, and for the first time the smile reached her dark eyes. "Never."

Right at that moment I knew I had her. Just like I did in any tournament before making an all-in bet, I went quickly back over what had gone on before.

She'd been pulling a scam on the first hand after sitting down, and had gotten impatient to take the table down into her own world. And I'm sure there was a reason she was impatient.

Then I realized why. If we had reached the floor of the cavern in Hell, I'm sure I would have lost the hand we were playing. She would have been able to change her cards into pocket fours, giving her quad fours, the only cards that would beat my kings-full in this hand. That's why she was in a hurry to get the table down. She wasn't used to losing and she was going to lose the first hand.

But we hadn't reached the floor of the cavern yet. And I could still see the Mirage poker room outlined around us. That meant, I was sure, that real world rules played. That Laverne and Stan were still with me in spirit.

I leaned forward. "Any of these men actually due to arrive in your world today?"

She glanced around at the frozen faces staring at her chest. "No."

"So then you're basically after me. Right?"

She said nothing, but I could tell from her eyes that I was right. I also knew without a doubt I wasn't ever destined to go in this direction after I died. Besides, from what I understood, superheroes lived a long time, so I had no idea how long in the future any question about this issue was going to be.

"Why go after a superhero?" I asked.

She smiled. "Challenge."

"It must be getting dull in Gambling Hell."

She only shrugged and smiled.

I had played her right into my hand and there was no point in rubbing salt into a wound, even if the person was from Gambling Hell and didn't know they were even wounded yet. So instead I smiled at her for a few moments longer, just to get her squirming.

Then I said, "Well, if you like a challenge, how about we finish this hand to see which direction this table is going? I win the hand we go up, back to the Mirage, and you go somewhere else to play. You win, we go down, and I'll go with you for a while. Play your game."

The moment I put it back on the cards, I caught a slight, very slight hint of panic cross her face. She hid it well, but I still saw it. I knew I had her. She had a good hand, but she didn't have the nut hand.

"Well, let us go so the dealer can call the hand," she said.

"No," I said, not wanting this table to get any closer to that cavern floor. "Right here, right now. No more bets. We roll the cards and see who wins. Otherwise, I call in Stan and he puts this table back where it belongs and you lose the chance of getting these players and me as your toys."

Heidi stared at me, taking her turn trying to read me. She was good, of that I had no doubt. But the best players in the world had tried to put reads on me for years without luck. No chance a simple Denizen from Gambling Hell could do it.

Finally she nodded. "You have a bet."

"I win," I said, making the bet clear, "the table goes back to the Mirage and you leave. You win, I release the table and we play in your world for a while."

"Those are the stakes," she said.

With that she flipped over pocket aces.

"Nice hand," I said.

And then I did something I never do in real life because it just annoys me and every other player. I hesitated in turning over my cards. It's called slow-rolling and it is the worst thing any player can do. But I did it anyway, just to get under Heidi's skin, just to give her a brief moment when she thought she had won. Sort of a little taste of her own Hell is the way I figured it.

"Pocket kings," I said, flipping my cards onto the table faceup in front of me. "Kings-full."

For a moment I thought I caught a glimpse of what Heidi really looked like under all that fake skin and large breasts. And let me tell you, she was one ugly human being. Nightmare ugly.

She stood, pushing her chair back, and I let us go back to normal time at the same moment.

Suddenly the noise from the Mirage poker room pounded in around us. The men at the table were suddenly very surprised that Heidi was standing, and that our cards were showing without a final round of betting.

"Nice *playing* with you," she said, staring at me. Then without her false smile, she bent over and picked up her chips, giving a number of the men at the table a real show before turning and stamping off.

"What just happened there?" the dealer asked as he slid the pile of chips in the middle of the table toward me.

I shrugged. "Sore loser."

One of the men who had gotten the best show from her picking up her chips laughed. "She bends over like that a few more times and she can take all my money."

"Always be careful what you ask for," I said. "You never know where you might end up."

Everyone around the table laughed and the mood shifted back to the fun game of serious poker, playing for money instead of souls.

WATER GOETHE BEFORE
THE FALL

by Alan L. Lickiss

Alan Lickiss developed a love for short stories early in life and discovered that writing them is even more fun. He lives in the shadow of Pike's Peak in Colorado with his wife, children, and an ever changing menagerie of pets.

"WHAT DO you mean I can't leave?" asked Gimgal. He spread his wings to increase his presence in the room and his robe glowed bright, filling the room with white light.

"Just what I said," said the small man blocking the door. "And tone down the theatrics, I'm not impressed."

Gimgal folded his wings and his robes returned to their normal nonblinding white. It wasn't a reaction he was used to getting. He wasn't sure how to react. "Sorry, it's just that I want to find my unit. I stopped in here for just a minute, and now you are telling me I can't leave."

"That's correct," said the man. "You can't leave the store unattended."

Gimgal turned to look at the store. There were a dozen aisles of foodstuffs only a demon could love, a

129

variety of acids and liquid death to wash them down, and a fire pit across the back of the store with a variety of animals and organs turning on spits. Along the right side of the store there was a long stone counter with a space behind it where Gimgal had been standing a few moments before. The store was well lit, so the filth that accumulated in every corner was easily seen. It made Gimgal shudder to look at it.

Gimgal turned back to the man, who remained in front of the glass doors. The man stood only to Gimgal's shoulder, but his stiff-backed posture and piercing stare made him look like an immovable object. It was his mussed fire-red hair, thick bristling mustache, and tweed jacket that he obviously didn't mind getting wrinkled or dirty that told Gimgal he'd have a fight on his hands if he tried to move him.

"Why can't I leave, and who are you to tell me I can't?" asked Gimgal.

"Why, I run things around here. Not just this store," he said as he waved his hand toward the back of the store behind Gimgal, "but everything. You can call me Sir," said Sir.

"If you run things, why don't you take over the store until the other guy gets back?"

Sir chuckled. It wasn't a happy sound, but one filled with menace. "No, I'm too busy with all my other responsibilities. You told my last employee that you would work until he came back."

"I needed some water, but don't have any coinage. He said he had to step out for a second, and if I would take over while he was out, he'd give me some water when he got back," said Gimgal.

"And you shook hands," said Sir.

"Well, yes, he shook my hand while he was thanking me," said Gimgal. "But he's been gone for hours. I was about to leave myself when you showed up and blocked the door. He can keep the water, I just need to get going."

Gimgal moved forward and Sir stepped out of his

way. When he reached for the door handle to push it open and walk out, an invisible barrier blocked his way an inch from the door. He tried to push against it, but no amount of force could get his hand closer.

"You see, I'm not blocking your way," said Sir as he stepped into the store and began to wander down the aisles, talking over his shoulder. "Rather it's your own agreement that forces you to stay."

Gimgal turned to Sir. "You can't keep me here. I'm an angel in the army of the Lord. If you haven't noticed, you are being invaded as the Hosts of Heaven tromp through Hell for the final battle. My commander will come for me."

Sir laughed, whether at Gimgal's attempts to leave or his statement, Gimgal didn't know.

"Oh, yes, I am well aware of tromping hosts of Heaven moving though my kingdom. The problem is that most of the hosts have never been exposed to the, shall we say, products and wares, that are available in Hell but never seen in Heaven. I dare say your commander is far too busy dealing with the retreat before all of his forces are lost. Before this day is done, I think we'll have swallowed another third of the hosts of Heaven."

Gimgal rushed at Sir. "You can't keep me here, I'm an angel."

"Were an angel."

"What?"

"You were an angel, Gimgal," said Sir. "You are now a fallen angel."

Gimgal was confused. He hadn't succumbed to any of the sins and lusts that had been flaunted at the Hosts as they moved through the levels of Hell. How could he be fallen?

"I can see you are still confused," said Sir who stopped wandering around the store in front of the fire pit. He reached in with his fingers and pulled a liver off a spit. "You came in looking for water. Do you remember why? I know why, just as I now know everything about you. You soiled the hem of your pretty white robe walking through the mucky streets of Hell and you wanted to clean it."

Gimgal could only nod, a single bob of his head.

"You left the host during the campaign to find water in Hell, so you could clean a smudge from your robe. Pride, Gimgal. While not one of the big ten, it's still one of the deadly. You have fallen, and now you work for me." Sir tossed the liver whole into his mouth and began chewing.

Gimgal went back to the front door and still couldn't touch it. He moved along the dirt-streaked front windows, trying to see if he could break one and fly through the opening. He couldn't touch them either.

"I don't believe you. If I have fallen as you claim, then why am I here rather than in one of your lower pits?" Gimgal asked.

Sir sighed. "You angels take things too literally. What kind of pits and how many am I supposed to have? It's much easier to let each person choose their own form of Hell. For some it might be that lava pit. For others, it's to be surrounded by food, but never able to eat, or perhaps forced to eat everything in sight. For you, Gimgal, Hell is having to work in this place, a place filled with dirt and grease, and never be able to keep it, or yourself, clean."

Gimgal found he couldn't think. He couldn't believe what was happening to him, yet he couldn't deny that he seemed to be unable to leave. "So you're saying I can never leave? What if I refuse to work?"

Sir began walking up the main aisle, toward Gimgal and the front door.

"So you're saying I can never leave?" asked Gimgal again.

"Oh, no, not at all," said Sir, stopping in between Gimgal and the door. "I'll honor the agreement. You can leave if your predecessor returns. But I wouldn't count on that ever happening."

Gimgal hadn't moved except to turn as Sir had walked around the store. He watched Sir stand with his hand on the door handle.

"Or," said Sir, "you can leave when we close."

Gimgal looked up at Sir. "When does the store close?"

"It doesn't," said Sir. His laugh was deep and rattled the windows.

Gimgal looked at Sir's hand resting on the door. He pointed to the door. "Then why do you have locks on the front door?"

Sir sighed. "This building, like those around here, is based on corresponding entities on earth. All the components of a convenience store are here, but it doesn't mean you get to use them. There's even a bathroom, but since you never have to go, you won't be needing it, either."

Gimgal was looking around the store for a bathroom door when Sir spoke again.

"For now, I'd worry about getting this place running. I'm a demanding boss, and your customers can be testy if they have to wait too long."

It didn't take Gimgal long to find out what Sir had meant. Before the door closed as Sir left, a dozen demons entered. They ranged in size from twice as big down to a tenth of Gimgal's size, but they all paused when they saw Gimgal. Their second reaction was the same for each as well. Every one of the demons laughed when they saw him.

"Looks like we've got an angel serving us today, boys," said a blue demon that looked like a giant bat with arms and legs. "Hey, Angel, fetch me that roasting pig," said the demon as he extended a claw toward his selection.

Gimgal wasn't about to become a servant for the Adversary's minions. "Get it yourself."

"Tsk, tsk," said the demon. "That's no way to talk to your customers. Let me give you a quick lesson in service."

The blue demon extended a claw and pierced Gimgal's shoulder, shoving the six-inch talon through the meaty portion below the bone. Gimgal screamed as the searing pain stabbed through his mind as the claw sliced his skin. As the demon pulled back his claw, Gimgal could still feel the pain pulsing between his shoulder and head. When he pulled back his robe, he could see the flesh of his immortal body heal while he watched. The memory; however, remained after the flesh had healed.

"Why did you do that?" asked Gimgal.

"I'm a demon," said the demon. "I'm supposed to torture you. Now get me that pig or I'll do more."

Gimgal fled from the demon's claw extending toward him. He grabbed the roasted pig with his hands, the hot meat burning his hands and coating them in grease. Wrestling with the pig got his robe covered in grease, but he plopped it down on the counter in front of the demon.

"That's better," said the demon. He threw three dull gray coins on the counter in front of Gimgal where they bounced a couple of times with a metallic clanking sound.

Gimgal picked the coins up and examined them. "What are these?" he asked as he turned them over in his hand. On one side a flame was pressed into the metal and on the other side an impression of Sir.

Other demons were shouting at Gimgal and pointing to things around the store. The mix of sounds and attempts to speak through beaks and tusk-filled mouths made understanding them impossible for Gimgal.

"That's money," said the blue demon. "The coin of the realm as they say. But don't lose it, as that belongs to your boss. If he doesn't get his money, he might just ask me to come back and have some fun."

Gimgal looked around behind the counter and dropped the coins into a box filled with similar coins. He was about to turn back to the blue demon when he felt claws rake across his back.

"Serve me," said another demon, this one bright red with horns sticking out of his forehead.

"Just a minute, there are too many of you at once," said Gimgal.

"Serve me," the demon repeated.

"No, serve me, I was next," said another.

"Forget those nether-born wastes of space," said a third. "You must serve me next. I am more important."

The noise from the demands for service grew louder as all of the demons joined in. Gimgal put his hands over his ears to block the noise, but it didn't work.

"Quiet," he shouted over the din. "Since I am stuck here, I will help you, but you each have to wait your turn. I may be immortal, but I only have two hands."

It took some time, but finally the last demon had been served. As the group started to leave, Gimgal ran around from behind the counter and shoved his way into the middle of the group just as they were going through the door.

An inch from the doorway Gimgal hit the invisible barrier. The speed at he had been running caused him to bounce back into the store, knocking down the demons behind him. Enraged, one of the demons picked Gimgal up and threw him across the room where he slammed into the wall.

"Don't you get it? You're here to stay, Angel. You're going to be serving us forever," said the demon who threw Gimgal.

Gimgal felt and heard bones break. He fell to the floor, clutching his ribs. By the time his ribs had healed, the group had left.

Rising from the floor, Gimgal noticed that his robe was covered with grease and other filth. He almost fainted at the sight.

Gimgal began to search the store storage areas for some sort of cleaner that would bring his robe to its former shine. His search didn't find anything useful for the task at hand. He did find the bathroom Sir had mentioned, but it was occupied. A small demon was sleeping against the wall.

"Excuse me," said Gimgal. "What are you doing?

The demon jolted awake and scrambled across the floor away from Gimgal.

"Who are you? Don't hurt me," it said.

Gimgal watched as the demon that stood as tall as his knee shook and cowered in the corner. "I'm not going to hurt you," he said, "unless you try to hurt me first. What are you doing in here?"

"Oh, please don't tell Mr. Sanderson," said the little demon.

Mr. Sanderson was the man who had tricked Gimgal into getting stuck at the store. Given the way the little demon responded to the thought of Mr. Sanderson discovering him, Gimgal realized he might have a potential ally.

"I have sent Mr. Sanderson on his way. Come here. What is your name?"

"Sloth," said Sloth.

Gimgal found Sloth's name to be very appropriate. He was supposed to be working in the store, a sort of punishment from Sir. In reality, Gimgal found Sloth hardly worked at all, and had to be chased out of the bathroom constantly.

At first Gimgal had hoped that hard work and making the store cleaner would show his commander he was a changed person. But as time dragged on, Gimgal began to lose faith. His day quickly fell into a routine of cleaning and serving customers. Sir would come around once a day and collect the cash. If sales were low, Gimgal could expect to be chewed out, and sometimes worse.

One day, after Sir had left for the night, Gimgal remembered his idea about breaking out a window and flying away. The barrier might be just on the front door and not on the windows.

Taking a full, uncooked pig, Gimgal stood back from

the window and hurled it at the window. The glass shattered and a huge gaping hole appeared in the glass. Gimgal spread his wings and began to fly. He glided toward the open window, but when he reached the opening, he felt the familiar barrier push him back.

Within a couple of minutes, Sir showed up. Gimgal was picking glass shards out of his wings for days after that. He had to find another way out.

Gimgal had lost hope that his commander would come to save him. Sir must have been telling the truth, that the Host had retreated leaving many of their numbers behind. Looking around the store, Gimgal shuddered. All of his efforts to clean had resulted in naught. The store was still a mess, trash in the corners and stains mixing and blurring on the floor making them impossible to identify. His robe, once a sight of beauty in its own right, now looked like a drop cloth for the feeding frenzy that occurred regularly. There was no doubt about it. Gimgal had to escape.

The direct approach had not worked. It had always resulted in pain. Now Gimgal had to find a way to escape that involved some form of trickery. Sir used half truth and half lie to get what he wanted. Gimgal was going to have to beat Sir at his own game.

Gimgal replayed the conversation he'd had with Sir when they'd first met. There was another way Sir had said he could leave. Closing. The store had to close before he'd be able to leave. Sir had also said the store was modeled after earth stores. There was one sure way to get a store that never closed to close. Robbery. Now all Gimgal had to do was find someone foolish enough to rob the Devil in Hell.

Gimgal hesitated. While pride had caused him to fall from Heaven, destroying the money of someone else was a real sin, it was theft. He'd truly be fallen, but if he could get out of the store, he'd be able to seek forgiveness.

And Gimgal was desperate. If he didn't do something to get out, he was going to end up huddled in a corner of the bathroom, gibbering and drooling his life away. Either way, he was going to be free, or doomed.

No longer caring about the consequences, Gimgal poured the bucket of coins into the toilet. When the bucket was empty, he flushed.

Lava filled the bowl. Smoke filled the bathroom. The coins, Sir's coins, were melted and carried away down the drain. In effect, the store had been robbed of a couple of hundred coins.

Gimgal stepped out of the bathroom. There were a few demons in the store. "I'm sorry, but the store has been robbed of several hundred coins. Procedures need to be followed and after a robbery, according to standard convenience store protocol, the store must close."

Gimgal stumbled out of the door, not ready to believe he had made it. From the outside the store didn't look like the combined House of Horrors and Torture Chamber it had become.

"I'll guess you'll be heading back to Heaven now," said Sloth.

Gimgal looked down at the small demon. "There was a time when I would have raced back as fast as my wings could carry me. But now I'm thinking about another plan."

"What do you mean?" Sloth asked.

Gimgal began to stroll down the street away from the store. "I was locked in there because of my pride, my desire to look my best and reflect well on my unit. Well, it seems to me that Sir has a few sinful traits of his own. Perhaps what he needs is to experience the other side for a change."

"I still don't understand," said Sloth

"Sir told me that everyone makes their own version of Hell," said Gimgal. "I'm thinking that being overthrown by his own minions would be a fitting punishment for Sir."

"You mean you're staying?" asked Sloth.

"Yes, I am," said Gimgal. "I think I'm no longer content with serving in Heaven. I think I'd rather overthrow Sir and rule in Hell."

WITH EYES AVERTED

by Tom Piccirilli

Tom Piccirilli is the author of eleven novels, including *A Choir of Ill Children*, *The Night Class*, *A Lower Deep*, *Hexes*, *The Deceased*, *Coffin Blues*, and *Grave Men*. He's published over 140 stories in the mystery, horror, erotica, and science fiction fields. He's also been a final nominee for the World Fantasy Award and he's a three-time winner of the Bram Stoker Award, given in the categories of Novel, Short Story, and Poetry. To learn more about Tom's work, please visit his official Web site at www.tompiccirilli.com.

CHURCH IS at a party and has no idea who's throwing it or how he got there.

Okay, so—

The Satanists are on the couch, holding court over a neo-Gothic bunch sitting on the floor wearing leather, white pancake makeup, black lipstick, and contact lenses to make them look like androgynous movie vampires. Only the most alienated can form such a tight and conformed clique. If you try to say hello, they'll chop you to pieces, they've got razors under their tongues. Many of them are tattooed with spiderwebs, twining roses, ravens on their necks and wrists. Church can't help himself and begins to drift over. He's got a thing for girls who look dead.

Wands of eucalyptus incense add a sweet and cloying perfume to the place. The Satanist leaders are a transgender couple who've gone under the knife a number of times each. There's a certain simplicity to their passions when you get down to it. Church can't remember who started out as what or how many times they've gone back and forth, but he still recognizes Asriel and Mova. They're in full witchy-poo regalia tonight: ebony robes, headgear with little plastic horns, and about twelve pounds of silver jewelry clanging around their necks. Pentacles, sun wheels, pendants with Latin phrases scrawled backward on their broad faces.

If they knew anything about the black arts, they'd realize that true occultists don't give any respect to Christianity, not even by inverting crosses or spitting on the wafer. You give credence to that which you directly oppose.

Sure, all right.

The kids are in awe, alert, listening raptly. A fawn-colored pug is lying in the foyer on its side, eyes open but snoring loudly. The curve of its pudgy belly quivers with each breath, and the dog eyes Church suspiciously. Out in the den, a television blares in Cantonese.

The dead chicks pay no attention, and Church feels humbled by their indifference. Sometimes you can get shot down before they even glance at you. It's the kind of thing that makes you want to join the Foreign Legion.

He roams and finds a group of drunk frat boys staring at the widescreen television, watching the DVD of a Shaw Brothers martial arts film. Church recognizes Chen Kwan Tai and Gordon Liu flinging themselves about doing first-rate wire fu, but he can't recall the title of the flick.

One of the guys—burly in a gray college sweatshirt with the sleeves torn off, crushed corn chips sticking to his wet neck—looks up and says to Church, "Someone's looking for you."

"You sure they wanted me?"

"Yeah."

"How do you know?"

"What?"

"I've never met you. How do you know me?"

"You're the weirdo who's been standing in the corner all night."

Their dialogue ends as if a guillotine's come down. A tension packs and occupies the room, but Church isn't sure where it's coming from, who it's directed toward.

He's got to stop drinking when he's on his meds; it leaves him open to these kinds of stupid situations.

The plastic bottle remains in his pocket, but the pills are gone. Has he been handing them out again? He does that sometimes when he's bored. Gives them to children in the park, telling them the pink candy capsules will make them lighter than air . . . which they do. Boys and girls lifting off out of their tiny sneakers, flying around and waving good-bye to their parents. Funny as hell to watch folks screaming and sprinting over the lawns as the chubby tots loop above the treetops.

Did he feed them to the dog? He looks over at Pugsy Malone, who watches him carefully.

The pug's lips curl into a sneer. A rough voice issues forth and says, "Hey, see the cute ankles on that hot little patootie over there? No, the other one, the redhead in the microskirt? She's got these three inch heels on? I'm making a move on that right now. Watch me go."

Yes, he fed them to the dog.

Church has to quit doing things like that.

Malone clambers to his feet and snuffles his way over to the redheaded girl, who glances at the dog and breaks into luscious laughter. She leans over and makes a baby face at him, says, "Oh, look! He's so ugly he's absolutely adorable."

Malone freezes in shock like somebody's just threatened to have him neutered. A whine breaks from his throat—it's the same noise Church makes whenever a woman turns him down on the dance floor. Malone blinks and cocks his head, snarls savagely, and lunges for the girl's throat.

Thank Christ it's a pug and he's got no real snout, just this blunt mouth with tiny ineffective teeth, slobbering against her cleavage. Sort of a turn-on, in that disgusting under-the-counter bestiality porno sort of way. She shrieks and flings her drink in the air, and her two friends start waving their hands about their faces, helplessly prancing in circles.

With a sigh, Church rushes over, grabs the dog in midair, and waltzes him out of the room.

Asriel and Mova are in the middle of chanting. ". . . *here there be forces beyond the kith of men . . .*" Sounds about right. The Goth kids are damn near quivering with excitement, nerve-racked and waiting for dark magic to crash through the roof and swallow their commonplace lives. Hellspawn generals wear velvet blouses, you know. They speak with aristocratic accents, have long curly locks. They'd never hurt you.

They can sense the bowels of Hell opening up just for them. They think it might be fun to fuck on a grave and have skeletal hands come out of the ground and drag them down into the mud. As if somehow death might actually make them *better* than everybody else.

We all need a dream.

If any of them actually saw the inside of the ICU ward they'd shit themselves and run for mama's apron. Cancer victims coughing up their own lungs. The humming, beeping, ticking, and endless buzzing of machines that breathe for the ill and the elderly. Checking out the brain scans that graph your thoughts and lack of conscience, the gray tumors that chew their way through the raw egg of your brain. Cysts that crawl down the sterile hallways looking for a chest cavity to call home.

"Put me down," Malone says.

"Don't bite the ladies, Pugsy. You'll get us both in trouble."

"Screw off, man, I used to have an even, stable temperament until you sent me on this trip."

Church makes it out the front door carrying the dog and realizes the party is being held way beyond his usual channels. There's nothing but forest around, and only now does he notice that the place is an upscale log home, nothing but glass and lights and natural wood. A 14-point rack of antlers has been nailed over the immense front bay window. Church stares down the winding gravel driveway that twists and vanishes into undergrowth and darkness.

"Damn it," he whispers, trying to keep the mewling out of his voice. "Now where the hell am I?"

The moon slices through a wedge of adjacent hills, and he sees the silver outline of a small lake nearby. A storm brews in the air, and with the electrical pulse gradually growing stronger he allows himself to be lured away. Sooty clouds roil against the mercurial moonlight, tussling in the night sky.

He checks his watch and finds it's gone. The normally pale flesh of his wrist is as browned as the rest of his arm.

Clearly he's been off for a while.

This is something new anyhow. He's never been away quite this long before, however long it's been. Church tries to swallow down the agitation that's creeping up in him, but he can't get rid of it.

There's a heaviness in his chest. He always thought that when he finally went over the big edge there'd be a magnificent sensation of relief. Maybe he's just not all the way out of his head yet.

"I asked you to put me down," Malone says.

"Sorry."

He drops the pug and watches it saunter down the driveway, pissing on vines and clumps of leaves. Church turns and looks back through the bay window and sees Asriel and Mova slitting open their palms and letting their blood drip into an ornate goblet.

The cup appears ancient, as if it's sat in the dining halls of hoary kings—from back when witches perched on the hearth brewing potions and, you know, fucking around with Macbeth. Midget skulls encircle the base, and the handle is embellished and crafted from metal bodies twining together. Diminutive faces contort in agony and perverse pleasure. Cripes. Amazing what you can pick up on eBay for twenty bucks plus shipping.

The knife they use in the ritual is a dagger rimmed with fake jewels. Glass opals, emeralds, and rubies reflect the vapid expressions of the adoring Goths who can't wait to get their lips on the goblet. This might even be more revolting than the farm animal antics porn.

As the blade is passed around, the kids' eyes ignite with the dream of alchemy, as if this is the only way to find God, any god at all. They each poke their palms and ooh and aah as a drop or two wells and spills into the cup.

One leather-deather is done up in silk and satin, with a well-groomed devil's van dyke, wearing fake fangs he's had specially made by his dentist. He's about to burst into tears because he can't bring himself to cut his own skin.

Mova moves to him, rubs his back, speaks calming words the way any good Satanist should. The tiny plastic horns on Mova's head are a little crooked so that one juts at eight o'clock, the other at eleven.

Lucifer Jr. is still struggling to puncture his flesh. He's one of the old school Goths, pushing forty with threads of white working through his widow's peak, and he's never gone near a tattoo shop or piercing parlor. The tears plummet down his cheeks and hang in the waxed, properly curled ends of his mustache. His collar is dark with sweat and dusted with salt.

The dead kids are caught up in the moment. With rapid-fire breaths they await the drawing of blood. A few lick their lips, getting up the guts to drink. You've got to give it to them, they're certainly honest in their passion. That counts for something. Church grimaces, thinking about the swill of inherent disease in the goblet. The recessed genes, flakes of black nail polish, the STDs, the genetic predisposition toward gloss and lace.

Malone rears up, is barely able to get his chin over the sill, takes in the scene and says, "These are some seriously fucked-up people."

Church nods.

"She's calling you."

"What?"

"Over there. In the water."

"Oh, Christ. Who is it?"

"Go on."

Moving with a more resolute purpose than he's perhaps ever felt before in his life, Church wafts down to the shore of the lake, where a beautiful woman swims.

Well now.

She is luminescent, luxurious, star white, and nude in her complete splashing madness. Insanity can't hide behind a disguise to someone who can smell it. She sways her arms and kicks out, arching through her own ripples and waves.

Exotica. Maybe this is only a dream made real by the force of his own will—it's happened like that on occasion. You can find what you're looking for if you're hunting for the right thing. Usually he's not, which is what brings him to parties like this.

She is as full of sexuality as he is stuffed with carefully folded and compressed layers of fear.

Here we go.

She glows in the lake with a healthy, enormously

erotic energy. It weaves and braids around her like the glistening coils of blond hair. Fog rises from the water and wraps itself around her throat—once, twice, spiraling tighter—as the gust of her breath parts it, gently swirls and takes it in, eases it across her beautiful chest and blows it back into the twilight.

"Were you looking for me?" he asks.

"Yes," she tells him.

"Why?"

"Does it matter?"

"Sure."

Of course it does. This is when you tend to hit the wall, when you pretend that such things don't actually carry weight. Church snags the inside of his cheek with his teeth. She senses his resistance and coos, "I want you."

He tries not to say "Ohboy" with that frantic excited lilt, but he can't help himself. He can so rarely help himself these days.

"Ohboy."

"What do you need?" she asks.

It's a big question, even more mammoth for him than most folks. How do you put your desires into words on a night like this? . . . you have to figure out your need, maybe that's where the problem is.

Somehow, Church knows, he went off the rails in a slow but steady progression from the time he was about four.

"Do you need to make love to me?" she asks, kicking back in a savage sweep so the lake water bubbles and boils around her. She keeps her legs open for a moment, showing him the glory of her goodies.

"That would be nice," he tells her, aroused and feeling the standard dirtiness fill his mind, the chilling sweat prickling his scalp. There's a dock twenty yards away, and he imagines himself rushing toward it, taking off his clothes as he moves with sudden and complete grace, flinging his sneakers into the woods, catching the rhythm as he touches the first board, then

running faster and slicing into the air in a power dive
that takes him into the dark.

Until he rises from the murky depths to meet her
on the lake's surface, clouds of mist in her hair.

But it's already going bad. Church has a pretty good
intuition when it comes to naked gorgeous women in
the water who want to make love to his pudgy ass.

Something is amiss. Ohboy.

He glances at the dock again and sees a black blur
of subtle motion beside it. He takes a step toward it,
and the girl, backlit with moonlight fire, harshly whispers, "No, don't go over there. Stay with me."

"Huh?"

"Please, I want you to stay here with me."

Jesus, now she's pleading?

There are times when you call down the wrath of
fate by not looking just a little farther to the left. Or
taking the time to check under the bed for the dwarf
holding a scythe, waiting to cut you down at the
ankles. Or looking in the closet to see if her crazed
lesbian lover is in there with a garrote. Or investigat-
ing the slight reflection near the dock, the odd suggestion of circling movement. Just for not averting your
eyes.

Church frowns down at the girl again, knowing he
draws these kinds of troubles to himself.

She grins and aims her nipples at him like blow
darts. It doesn't take much to ruin a perfectly wonderful fantasy. He slips off and carefully makes his way
over the rocks and weeds to the dock, wondering how
it could've gone so wrong so quickly. In some strange
fashion he always asks for too much.

The corpse in scuba gear spins in a slow eddy.
One flipper glides along the surface tension of the
water, moving back and forth as though the diver
were still alive. The guy's rubber suit is torn in
places, great jagged rips as if a shark has mauled
him. Languidly, the girl begins to swim closer, giggling as the fog swells and lolls. She clicks her teeth

loudly, repeatedly. Church tries to hold back a scream but can only half restrain himself. A wounded goat's bleat escapes him.

"I want you," she tells him.

"Why me?"

"I need you, honey bunch."

"Uh-huh."

"Get in here! Swim with me!"

"Play with your friend some more, he won't complain."

"Come back," she insists. "I want to bear your children. Hundreds of them. Thousands!"

"Ohboy!"

Church scrambles up the path toward the cabin, groaning and grunting, tasting blood and wondering if he's actually dying somewhere, gut-shot, dreaming all of this. He's been in jail before, but he can't recall for what. Did he used to rumble and knock assholes through plate-glass windows? Did he ever rob banks?

As usual, he's screwed up what should have been simple. A wrong turn in the woods and now he's lost, wandering through the brush and having the shit scratched out of him by cat-claw briars. There's a light in the distance.

A pyre has been lit against what they used to call a coven tree.

It has to rise from the direct center of the covenstead, that area where witches draw their power, the place where natural earth energy emanates from and is at its strongest. The bonfire roars and consumes kindling, ladder-back chairs, old kitchen cabinets, torn mattresses, the widescreen TV, grandma's old steamer trunk, they're really tearing the place apart.

You can guess at what comes next. Church catches another powerful whiff of blood. They're out there with the redheaded girl that Malone was making a move on. She's being bound to the coven tree with

yellow nylon rope. He recognizes it as the sort of line
you tie to the back of a boat for water-skiing.

She's screaming and thrashing, but Lucifer Jr. and
the others have a good grip on her and she flails use-
lessly, the micro skirt rearing to show off her thong.
Lucifer Jr. squawks and throws his arm over his eyes
like she's flashed him a crucifix. Church is oddly
aroused by the whole display. The frat boys stand
around drunkenly gawking, holding their beer cans
tight to their bellies and giggling quietly to one
another.

Church may not be a hero, and he's almost certainly
out of his mind, but he doesn't suffer from inertia.
With a cool flood of adrenaline coursing through his
temples, he bursts out of the woods and rushes forward without any idea of what he's going to do next.

This is why you shouldn't draw your spirituality
from Jackie Chan movies, unless you're willing to pay
the price.

The burning girl shouts at him, "Here, take it!
Take it!"

"Take what?"

"The money!"

"What money?"

"Take it and go, please don't hurt us!"

"Me? I'm not hurting you."

He sees that his watch is back on his wrist and
knows that things are about to get bad. He's either
coming back into himself now or he's going even farther out. Which is it going to be? Which does he want
it to be?

Church blinks and abruptly he's standing in the middle of a bank, staring into the faces of terrified tellers.

A short, middle-aged woman with hair the color of
a four-day-old bruise is shoving cash at him, and he
notices he's got an open gym bag in his left hand and
a sawed-off shotgun under his arm. There's a haze he
can't shake.

Malone is running around in cute puppy circles. He's got a satchel tied around his back, stuffed with wads of fifties. "The cops! Let's go!"

Church thinks, *Oh fuck*.

Twin androgynous lovelies wheel toward him with new headgear on—ram's horns, a real wild spirit feel to them. Mova and Asriel are out of their robes and into some kind of ancient Celtic outfits now, looking half-fey, half-Cormac Mac Art. Their cheeks are rouged to a high varnish waxiness.

On the floor between them is a security guard with most of his face blown away. They eye Church with expressions of distrust and doubt.

Church goes, "God damn it," and turns into a tear gas shell smacking him in the chest, wisps of the smoke catching him full in the face. He shrieks, but the scream is as muted as his words. He realizes he's got on goggles, his own breathing apparatus, a tank of oxygen strapped to his back. The murdered scuba diver's rig has come in handy.

He grabs the canister before it spills too much gas and hurls it back out the broken front window.

Children float around the ceiling of the bank. Their parents leap and try to catch hold of their ankles, bring them back down. A moan works free from Church's chest.

He's really got to stop handing out his pills.

He tries to make a run for it, but only now understands that he's leaking all over the place—blood and black fluid spurt from his ragged stomach. He sees that he had a burger and fries for lunch. The security guard has clipped him, that's the reason for this shoot-out.

Shaking his head, Church feels the last chance for redemption drifting from him. A murderer, he's done the final deed. Man, this is what happens when you watch too many movies.

Always blame the movies.

He doesn't even know what he would use the money

for. There's nothing he's ever wanted badly enough
to pull this kind of moronic stunt. Nothing, other than
his sanity.

Sure, all right.

An eight-year-old girl in a ponytail, standing up
against the wall, breaks from the other hostages and
begins to walk toward him. She extends a hand and
he hopes she's going to help him and not suddenly go
shit-screaming maniacal on his ass. He weakly strug-
gles forward and then falls to his knees.

He'd given her a pink candy pill, and now she's
passing it back to him, the little sweetheart.

Church yanks the goggles off and eyes his medica-
tion. He holds out his palm and she drops the capsule
in. He wants to tell her thank you, but his mouth is
filling with wet copper.

Bullhorns and walkie-talkies squawk and cackle.
The cops are giving orders out in the street, about to
bust in.

Laughing kids float higher, their parents wail.

Pugsy Malone, with his corkscrew tail loosening and
straightening for a second, scowls at him and snarls,
"Think it through. You certain you want to do that?"

Oh, yeah, Church thinks.

He feels his intestines begin to slide too far forward
until they dangle against the tile floor. He should've
just jumped in the lake and let the glowing babe
drown him in all her welcoming love. At least then he
would've gotten laid before he walked off the big
edge.

Mama, mama, when you're dying you always call for
mama, that's the way of it. The hovering children glare
down at him. Church tries not to laugh, but a chortle
clambers loose anyhow. How crazy do you got to be
before it no longer hurts? Mova and Asriel are running
for the back door with their Celtic togs flapping and
showing off their naked hairy asses. Jesus, he really
could've died happily without ever seeing that. Mama.
He spits out the air hose and a mouthful of bile and

blood, unfurls his tongue and flings the pill toward it, wishing for just a momentary taste of atonement before the end of everything he's known and feared and hated, as the cops burst in firing. Okay, so—

BURNING BRIDGES

by David Niall Wilson

David Niall Wilson has been writing and publishing horror, dark fantasy, and science fiction since the mid-eighties. His novels include the *Grails Covenant* trilogy, *Star Trek Voyager: Chrysalis, Except You Go Through Shadow, This is My Blood,* and the upcoming Dark Ages Vampire clan novel *Lasombra.* He has over one hundred short stories published in two collections and various anthologies and magazines. David lives and loves with Patricia Lee Macomber in the historic William R. White House in Hertford, North Carolina, with their children, Billy and Stephanie, occasionally his boys Zach and Zane, four psychotic cats, a dwarf bunny who continues to belie his "dwarfness," a pit bull named Elvis and a fish named Doofish.

T HE SHADOWS were deeper than any Stan had ever seen. They gave the place an abandoned, cavernous appearance, and they gave him the creeps. The huge, multitiered shelving units that lined the walls loomed like eerie sentinels, stretching upward toward the amphitheater-like ceiling. Their silhouettes blended with the oozing darkness near the corners to form gray-on-black patterns of gloom.

The smell of rodents hung in the air; it was obvious that he had not been called in for just a routine job. There were rats here, lots of them, and it was going to be no picnic getting them out. Nothing he couldn't handle, but no quick fix, either.

The crawl spaces behind the shelves were the first targets to hit. Stan would eventually have to place some traps and baits higher up, among the shelves themselves, but the main nests would be on the lower levels. He suspected that there would be some breaches in the walls themselves, as well, though if his luck held they would lead to nothing more than small niches and caves, easily cleared of unwanted inhabitants.

The warehouse basement in which he stood was the lower story of the Colossus Fresh Air Food Mart. It was the largest grocery/department store in San Valencez, housed in a huge old stone building that covered a good city block. Stan wondered just how much food the citizens of San Valencez would buy from Colossus if they got a gander at—or a good whiff of—this warehouse. It was ancient, and it reeked of rot and decay. Most of the newer stock was kept in the middle sections, toward the front, but even these were poorly lit and covered with dust.

"We don't store much there anymore," Phil Barnett, Colossus' General Manager had told him the day before, "mostly bulk products and older merchandise. We've been meaning to clean the place up—put in some lighting, you know?—but we just never got around to it. Now we're having trouble getting stock workers to go down there at all. They complain about the smell, and a few people have spotted these rats . . ."

Damn surprising that they've only seen a few, Stan thought, walking over to the nearest of the shelves. *From the smell, the damned rats have more claim to this place than the people do.*

There was another scent in the air that was beginning to bother him. It was familiar, something he'd experienced before, but he couldn't quite grasp the fleeting memories it induced. One thing he did know; the memories were not pleasant. It was a sickly sweet odor, like some sort of rot.

Surely the fuckers don't keep old meat down here? he thought. He shook his head. That wasn't quite it, but it was close.

Stan moved methodically from shelf to shelf along the first wall, placing the traps in what might have seemed to one not versed in "rodent war" tactics to be an almost random pattern. He filled each crack and crevice he encountered with small poison pellets, sprinkling more in piles along the wall. Every now and then a dark form darted deeper into the shadows, or glittering red eyes glared out at him from one of the deeper holes, but none of the enemy was brave enough for open confrontation. This behavior was strange, and it was enough, combined with the sheer intensity of the damp, chilling solitude of the basement, to make Stan more than a little nervous.

The smell he'd noticed earlier grew stronger as he moved deeper. It was overpowering the scent of the rats themselves.

Rats are not a timid species, particularly when one lone animal—in this case Stan—invades their domain. Stan carried a semiautomatic .22 caliber pistol on his belt, and a large, Special-Forces-style combat knife strapped low on his right thigh. He'd had occasion more than once to use both. These rats, however, were not attacking. They seemed frightened, barely curious, and there were fewer and fewer signs of them as he neared the back of the huge room.

Stan hadn't gotten as old as he had by ignoring his senses, and they were screaming "Danger!" with a multitude of inner voices. His palms itched. Sweat gathered at the base of his neck, soaking his collar. His heart sped. That's when the memory hit him. He knew that smell, all right. Knew it like his most intimate nightmares. It was death—ignored, rotting death.

He'd seen enough of it in the war to embed that
stench in his brain, but it had taken the nervous tension of his growing fear to match it up with the
proper memories.

One set of shelves to go. It was the longest of all,
directly against the farthest wall of the warehouse.
Many of the packages in this area had crumbled, unknown contents blending with one another to coat the
floor in a powdery dusting of age and decay.

The shadows near the shelves were solid, heavier,
and more ominous. Stan knew that whatever the smell
was waited for him behind that shelf. He knew, also,
that it had nothing to do with rats. Not his concern.
He could just turn around, walk away, and no one
would know. Who would come back here to check
and see if he'd omitted to set traps behind one set of
shelves, this one in particular?

Stan started to turn. The sweat on his neck had
gone to ice—prickling at his senses. The heaviness of
the air weighed on his lungs.

Damn. He breathed. He couldn't do it. He wanted
to know what was back there. He didn't want to *see*
it, but he had to know. He reached to the holster on
his belt and pulled loose the .22. The gun felt very
small and inadequate in the face of the unknown. He
found himself, for the first time in years, yearning for
the comforting weight of his M-16, or even a .45.

Shit, he said loudly, spinning around the corner of
the shelves and stabbing into the shadows with the
flashlight's beam. If there was something waiting, it
had been damned quiet as he approached.

At first there was only pitch-black shadow. In the
flashlight's beam, he could make out a few nondescript
lumps scattered about randomly, much the same as
all the other crawl spaces had held. The stench was
overpowering, making his eyes water and further blurring his sight. He moved in, sweeping the light along
the wall until it came to rest on the first of the lumpy

objects. Stan wiped his eyes on his sleeve and squinted, concentrating.

The thing, whatever it was, was covered carefully with an oily rag. Using the toe of one boot, Stan kicked out and knocked the cover aside. He shone the light directly on the small oozing form—the tiny body. The child. He wanted to back away, to release the scream building in his throat, but his gaze was locked in morbid fascination on the rotted face, staring back at him from the dusty floor. It was wrong—three eyes, and there was a knotty, protruding lump on the side of the head—no, both sides. Like—horns.

Then Stan backed away, scrambling for purchase on the slick concrete. He skidded into the wall, cracking his head on the brick so hard it nearly drove him to his knees, but even then he was scrabbling backward. Out. Somewhere along the line he dropped the gun. The flashlight banged heavily on the stone floor, the beam flickering weakly and threatening to go out. He clutched it to his chest like a talisman as he reached the main passage between the shelves.

Without further thought, he released the screams, turned, and ran for the door at the other end of the massive warehouse. Behind him, the silence mocked his retreat. Red eyes watched from the shadows— almost with sympathy.

"There were twenty-three of them in all," Cotter was saying, running his finger down a list of statistics on his clipboard. "None of them could have been even a year old at the time of death, and none of them without—defects."

Defects. Tommy Doyle shook his head, nearly giving in to the morbid desire to chuckle at the thought. Damned psycho had killed twenty-three kids. Twenty-three kids with too many eyes, fanged overbites, and horns, and this punk-ass lab technician talks to him about "defects."

Gulping the last of his lukewarm coffee and slamming the cup on his desk, Tommy launched himself out of his chair and onto his feet. "Give me the damn report, Cotter, and leave me the hell alone long enough to read it, huh? I *can* read for myself, you know."

Tommy grabbed the small sheaf of papers off the clipboard in the young man's hands and turned toward the worn Mr. Coffee in the corner in dismissal.

As the door slammed behind him, Tommy refilled his cup and sat back down, opening the folder. Cotter was annoying as all hell, but Tommy had to admit that the kid was thorough. Every inch of the warehouse—and it was one big place—had been scoured. Every tissue had been sampled, every print dusted. Nothing had been left to chance. Swell.

Tommy let loose a long sigh. This one beat them all. How many detectives across the country could claim a murder case with twenty-three victims—all the bodies accounted for—and not the slightest shred of evidence? Not a witness, not a motive—not even a trace on the bodies. Twenty-three kids dead, killed within one year, none over the age of one, and no missing persons reports.

Not that Tommy could completely blame the parents, considering the double-D, goddamn *defects*—but how many "defective" births could one city have in the span of a year? And all of them so similar.

Tommy rose, took a last defiant gulp of his coffee, despite his stomach's complaints, and headed for the door. It was time to pay some visits—first this guy Lewis, then the Colossus Food Mart. To catch a psycho, you had to see where the bastard was coming from.

Psychos were the one constant in Detective Tommy Doyle's existence. He hated them, and he was very, very good at flushing them out and bringing them in. It was his mission—his passion. They were every-

where, and it was up to Tommy to even the odds, or
so he liked to say.

There were two things about Stan "The Exterminator" Lewis that hit Detective Doyle right off. One was
the haunted look in the man's eyes. Tommy had seen
that look before, but never quite so deeply etched.
The other thing was that the man was no coward.
Whatever he might be, and Tommy had his own ideas
about guys who made their living crawling around in
darkened rat holes, the man was not easily frightened.
But then there were those eyes.

"Detective Doyle," Stan was saying, "I'll tell it to
you like this. I ain't seen nothin' like that since 'Nam.
Hell, ain't sure I seen anything that bad there. I know
it was dumb of me to run like that, especially the way
I tore through that store, but it was just somethin' I *felt*.
Know what I mean? It was like there was something so
wrong about that place, the smell, the bodies, the fact
that two floors over my head, half of San Valencez
was walkin' around shopping for God-damned *food*
without a clue of what was down there . . . I just got
the hell on out, and I'd do it again."

Tommy did know what Stan meant. He had *feelings*
all the time, hunches. It was how he operated. Then
there was the fact that this rathole-crawling veteran
had the look of honesty in his fear—reality where it
seemed least likely.

"You didn't see anything down there that we might
have missed?" Tommy asked, hoping instinctively for
a break. "Didn't notice anything peculiar, beyond the
obvious, about the room itself, or the way things were
laid out?"

"Come to think of it," Stan said, scratching his
head, "I've been pondering over one thing ever since.
I'm a rat man, Detective. I've probably killed a million
of the little bastards, and I think I know 'em better'n
anyone walkin' this Earth. I ain't never seen one of

the little cocksuckers scared of nothin', leastways, not until that warehouse. It was like they felt it, too—and they stayed clear.

"That's what I aim to do, too. Fuck Colossus, and their money. Ain't no rat smarter than me, and if they're smart enough to steer clear, I'm gone, too."

"Thanks for your help, Mr. Lewis," Tommy said, flipping his small notebook closed. "If we need you for anything else, we'll be in touch." Tommy wanted, inwardly, to be able to laugh at the absurdity of trusting to the feelings of rats, but something in the other man's voice rendered this impossible. "Damn," he muttered quietly. "Just what the hell kind of psycho shit have I got myself involved in now?"

"So you see," Philip Barnett was saying, gesturing with a large beefy hand at the stairs that led down to the warehouse below his store, "there is only this one entrance to the warehouse. Only our staff has access to the keys. There is no other way in, or out."

Barnett, Tommy, and Tommy's partner, McCloskey, stood staring at the doorway and the stairs beyond.

"When you say staff," Tommy asked thoughtfully, "just how limited are we talking? I mean, can just any old stock boy get these keys, or are they controlled?"

"Why," and the look that crossed Barnett's face betrayed his dawning awareness, "now that you mention it, the key ring hangs right here in this maintenance room."

Barnett opened a door off to the side of the basement stairs. It was filled with mops, brooms, cleaning utensils, and, as the man had said, just inside the door hung a large set of keys on a metal ring.

"I suppose it would be possible on a busy day for just about anyone to get them, if they knew where to look." he added.

"Kind of brings us back to the staff," Tommy mused aloud, "or to someone who *knows* someone on the staff. How detailed are your personnel records?"

"Not very, I'm afraid," Barnett answered. "We're just a grocery store, after all. Beyond checking for criminal records and social security numbers, we have very little on file. Most of our employees are young, either in school or between other jobs. The turnover rate is high. We probably go through a hundred different clerks and stock boys in the span of a year."

Swell, Tommy thought. Aloud, he said, "I'd like to take a look around down there, if you have no objections."

"Of course not, Detective. If you need any assistance, anything at all, just let me know."

Tommy turned to McCloskey with a tight grin. "You up for this, partner?"

The big man looked a bit queasy, but otherwise seemed calm enough. "Guess so, Tommy. Don't know what you expect to find that the lab boys couldn't, though."

McCloskey stood around six foot four, weighed in at nearly three hundred pounds, and backed down from nothing. His unease did nothing for the condition of Tommy's stomach.

"You know me," Tommy answered, turning toward the doorway that led to the stairs, "I've got to get the feel of the place, see it for myself."

"Yeah, yeah," McCloskey muttered, following his partner into the darkness. "Psychos are everywhere. I know."

Tommy answered with a laugh. "You know it."

The basement lights were so dim they were almost useless. The shelves seemed to go on forever, like one of those damned illusion paintings by that psycho painter, what was his name, Escher? The two detectives moved straight to the back, walking slowly as Tommy scanned the walls and shadowed corners, hoping something would click.

They found the tape and chalk lines that sealed off the scene, leftovers of the lab boys' fruitless search. The smell had faded somewhat from what that guy

Lewis had described, but it was still there. Stale death. Tommy flipped on the flashlight on his belt and stepped around behind the last shelving unit.

The floor was littered with small chalk circles. Twenty-three of them. The area had been scraped clean. Nothing, not even a particle of dirt that might have been left by whatever deranged asshole had done this had been ignored. It was eerie. He played the light over the walls.

There was a vent about ten feet up, but it was too small for a man to have come in through, and the height alone would have been prohibitive without a ladder. No help. He scanned the brick. It was several different shades, all of them moldy—slightly damp. Barnett was right. Somehow, right under the noses of the staff of the city's largest grocery store, twenty-three dead kids had been smuggled down those stairs, carried through the shadows, and dumped. Damn. He turned and headed back, gesturing at his partner to follow. McCloskey said nothing, but he looked more than ready to get the hell out.

Tommy's stomach had begun to churn again, and he reached for his packet of antacid tablets. This one was going to be bad.

"I knew you were lazy," Philip Barnett was saying, his huge hand tightly gripping the neck of the man he spoke to until the other's eyes bulged, "but how in the *three thousand red boiling **Hells*** could you have been so stupid?"

Dusty Carter didn't answer. He wouldn't have, even if the hand on his throat had loosened enough to allow it. He knew there was nothing he could say that would do anything but stoke the anger, and Dusty was smart enough—at that moment—to fear for his life.

Barnett's voice echoed from the stone walls surrounding them. They boomed, impossibly loud in the utter silence of the room. "Thanks to your brilliance in ignoring me, half of the damned police force has

been within ten feet of this place for days. Do you
have any idea what you have risked? Do you *know*
what might have happened if they'd stumbled on this
room? And I don't mean what *they* might have
done, either."

Dusty shivered clear through to his soul. He knew
exactly what the bigger man meant, and the thought
of being found out came even closer to stopping his
heart than Barnett was to stopping his breathing. It
had seemed such a good idea at the time, loosening
that vent in the warehouse and dropping those bodies
through the chute, so much easier than slipping them,
one by one, to the incinerator at the other end of the
building—and who was to know? He didn't remind
Barnett that it had been his own idea to hire the
exterminator.

"We are so close!" Barnett said, finally releasing his
grip and letting Dusty slump to the floor. "It could
even be tonight."

A whimper rose from the corner of the room, and
they both turned. In a low cage, naked and hunched
over so far in her tight little prison that her long blond
hair dragged the floor, was a young woman, maybe
twenty years old. Her eyes were rolled back into her
head with fear, her movements slow and sluggish.

"Good," Barnett grinned. "She's waking up.
Quickly," he kicked Dusty roughly in the side, prodding him back to his feet, "prepare the circle. We will
proceed at once." Barnett moved to the side of the
room and ascended a set of metal rungs that pro-
truded from the wall, disappearing through the small
trapdoor at the top.

Dusty did as he was told. He'd done this enough
times to do it in his sleep. Fact was, he'd had nightmares lately where he *had* done it in his sleep. Same
spooky feeling, same chill on his scalp, like it wasn't
just Barnett watching him. Seemed reasonable, being
as how it probably *wasn't* just Barnett. He shivered
again.

Once the shackles had been opened and latched onto the rings in the floor, Dusty opened the cage door and dragged the girl out. She was only half awake, and he had her in place and fastened tightly before she even thought to put up a struggle. Once she felt the metal of those shackles, though, and the slimy floor on her back, she started to move. She was shaking her head crazily back and forth and yanking on the chains like she thought she might break them. The whimpers became sobs as the drugs slowly released their hold.

After Barnett came back, Dusty knew, they'd move on to screams right quick. It was time for him to get out. He ran a hand lightly over one young breast, lingering on the taut nipple, but he pulled himself away. Not for him . . . not yet. He headed up the ladder to the trapdoor, into the brighter light of the store above. It was almost time.

Tommy pushed the door open slowly, and slipped into the back of the Colossus Food Mart, letting the door slide closed behind him. There were lights, though few and fairly dim, and he was able to pick his way silently through the back rooms toward the warehouse steps. He slipped open the door to the cleaning room and snagged the metal ring, clamping his hand tightly about the jingling keys.

Down the hall, roughly over the area where that last shelf would stand in the basement, he thought, light seeped out from beneath one of the office doors. He moved quickly to the door leading down, and was about to open it, when sounds from the end of the passageway brought him up short. Someone was leaving that office with the light. Damn.

He slipped into the cleaning room, holding the door open a crack so he could see. It wouldn't do for one of San Valencez's finest to be caught breaking and entering, even if he did have a hunch.

A small, wiry figure darted out of the room down

the hall and into the depths of the supermarket. He couldn't make out any features, but the man's furtive, hurried movements almost distracted Tommy from his goal. What the hell was that guy doing here?

The footsteps ended and a squeaking, grinding sound marked the opening and closing of the front door. Nobody who didn't belong here would use the front door. Tommy moved back to the stairs, opened the door, and slipped inside. After carefully pulling the door closed behind him, he flipped on the basement lights. No way was he going down there in the dark, breaking and entering or not.

He just wanted another look at that damned back wall. Something was nagging at him. Something he had overlooked. It was the colors, he thought, concentrating as he moved through the darkened basement. Shadows shifted around him, tiny eyes tracing his steps. The rats were watching . . . lurking. It was as if they were waiting for something. He sensed that it was not him they watched, and it stood the hairs of his scalp on end.

The brick behind the shelves had been several different shades. It hadn't registered as strange, earlier, because he'd been hypnotized by the tiny white chalk circles—distracted by the macabre horror of it all. Different colors might mean different age—why would new bricks be placed in the farthest wall of an admittedly half-abandoned basement warehouse? He moved closer, reaching out to run his hand over the wall. That was when he heard the girl scream.

Barnett crouched low, leering at his captive. He had circled her twice now with white chalk, carefully inscribing odd symbols at evenly spaced intervals between the concentric lines. He had placed five candles, one above the girl's head, one at the tip of each set of groping fingers, and one by each of her manacled feet. He had sprinkled scented powder over her form, blowing it first in one direction, then in each of the other three, while incanting words in a language even he did not fully understand. The candles were lit, and the moment was at hand.

"You have a great honor," he crooned, stroking the girl's hair gently. "You will be the mother—the vessel. You will bring forth a son this night, a powerful son, and he will rule at my side."

Barnett's voice was hypnotic, and the girl's gaze locked onto his as her trembling lips begged for a release she knew would never come.

As the smoke from the candles rose, circling lazily toward his fingers and weaving a curtain of hazy mist about the circle, she found her voice, and she screamed. Barnett laughed, the sounds blending—her high-pitched keening scream and his laughter, which held no mirth and even less humanity. He watched her, and he felt the energy surging. It was happening.

The bridge was forming more quickly and easily than ever before. Barnett felt the power pulsing around him. He chanted on, moving slowly about the prostrate body at his feet, anointing each of her limbs from a small jar of ointment that he slipped from a fold in his robes. She screamed at each touch as she felt the bridge, burning along her limbs, opening inch-by-inch and crack-by-crack. She was that bridge, between dimensions. Between worlds.

When Barnett knelt between her shivering thighs and anointed her womanhood, the scream became one continuous, endless sound.

It only took a few seconds for Tommy to realize that the sounds were coming from the vent above his head, a moment longer for his feet to begin to move. He raced silently back up the center aisle of the warehouse, past the red, pinpoint rats' eyes and onto the stairs. His gun was already in his hand when he hit the top step and burst into the hall. The light still leaked out from under the room at the far end, and he headed there without hesitation.

Another psycho bites the dust, he thought grimly, praying he wouldn't be too late to help whoever it was that had been screaming.

The bridge was complete. Barnett had watched closely as the girl's screams reached a crescendo, then faded, and then rose again to a screeching cacophony that no human throat could have produced. He had watched, fascinated, but unmoved, as the fear-stained consciousness of the girl had drained inward, as though sucked from her mind into some other place, and he had seen the trapped, hate-filled eyes of the demon as it flowed in to replace her.

Barnett let the robes fall from his shoulders, leaving him naked in the flickering candlelight, and he finished the final incantations as his erection throbbed and pulsed, aching for the release to come. The girl's body began to vibrate, as though caught in a seizure, as the demon tried vainly to break the bond—to cross back over the bridge, but it was holding. The fire burned down the girl's limbs, and the trapped demon tore at the bonds, grinding the fingernails of its flesh prison on the floor until blood flowed, but the bridge held.

Just as Detective Tommy Doyle leaped from the trapdoor into the semidarkness below with a near maniacal yell of his own, Barnett entered the girl/demon with a grunt and a lunge, spewing his seed instantly and arching his back in ecstasy. The body beneath him bucked and shuddered, but still, the bridge held. It was going to work. He barely heard the strangled scream behind him. It did not matter. Nothing mattered beyond the circle. It was going to happen!

Tommy struggled, trapped by a thousand tiny arms that seemed to be made up of smoke and air. Razor-sharp, invisible teeth bit at his neck and ears, claws ripped at the skin on his face. He saw Barnett, saw the girl beneath him. The screams were horrible, and he couldn't stop them. Couldn't reach them. His eyes

teared with rage as he fought, inch by inch, toward
the circles. It was not fast enough. He would be too
late to help. Tommy stopped trying to move forward,
and raised his gun, fighting the threatening insanity
with all the strength of both arms and a numbed brain.
He leveled it at the form that knelt in the circle. Then,
with a single burst of will, he drew back the trigger,
and he fired. The first shot released him, and he pulled
the trigger again, and again, staggering and falling to
his knees, but holding his weapon steady. He crashed
to the floor, rolling dazedly to his feet and staring at
what lay before him.

Barnett was keeled over to one side, holding his gut
with one hand and staring, unbelieving, at the blood
that pumped out to cover the floor and the girl's body.
She had taken a bullet, too, through the shoulder.
Whatever strange force had circled them was gone,
leaving behind a fat man, bleeding to death, and a
very pale, vacant-eyed young woman.

"What have you done?" Barnett gasped, turning
with amazing ferocity to face Tommy's gun. "You
have broken the bridge—it would have held. I was so
close. I . . ."

New sound erupted from the girl, and they both
turned to her, Barnett in stupefied shock, and Tommy
with a staggering, nausea born of revulsion. The center
of the girl's abdomen was splitting, and a tiny clawlike
hand scrabbled to pull it wider—from within. There
was a horrible, wet squelching sound, and a head appeared, two horns protruding from its skull and tiny
fangs ripping and rending the flesh of its *mother*. It
continued, mindless in its fury, chewing and ripping,
slobbering over the flesh. Its eyes were open, but void
of sense—empty.

Barnett tore his eyes from it for a second, turning
to Tommy. "You broke the bridge," he repeated.
Then the big man keeled over, succumbing to his
wounds, and the thing—baby—demon was on him. It

clawed at his eyeballs, ripping a gaping gash into the flesh of his cheek.

Tommy reloaded with mechanical quickness and fired. He emptied the gun into the tiny, squirming body, continued to pull the trigger after it brought no more than the click of an empty cylinder, as though he might will more bullets from the empty weapon. The thing arched its back in a final, screaming surge of defiance, latching onto Barnett's face with its tiny jaws, and it died.

Lurching to the metal ladder rungs, careful not to look back for even a second, Tommy ascended from Hell, letting his gun clatter to the floor below. He found a phone in the office above and called the department—reporting in a few dazed words and hanging up before they could question him. Then he wandered back to the street and began to walk, wading through shadows he might never trust as empty again.

Raising his eyes to the heavens, he looked questioningly into their depths, but he got no answer . . . no reassurance. In the distance he heard the rising whine of sirens and reality reasserted itself.

As the sirens grew nearer, he turned away. The alley was open on both ends, and Tommy made his way quickly to the far end, stepping out into the street and turning right. He couldn't face them now. He couldn't explain to them what he'd seen, and he damn sure wasn't ready for a barrage of questions from reporters, or the too bright flash of cameras. He knew what they would say. Even faced with the tiny, twisted *thing* attached to Barnett's face, riddled with so many bullet holes it resembled Swiss cheese more than flesh, to back his words, they would never accept his story. How could they? How could he expect it?

To accept what he'd seen opened too many doors. It tugged the bedspread up and revealed the shadowy hole beneath. It opened the closet door a crack and revealed the bright, gleaming predator's eyes that watched from within. It took everything Tommy knew or thought he knew about his world and canted it like a car with a flat tire trying to run straight ahead on one rim.

So what, then? Tommy ducked into the doors of Sid's, a local nightclub that was big on privacy and scant on lights. He slid onto the seat at the farthest end of the bar and sat in silence as the bartender watched him. They knew Tommy here. Sid's wasn't the most upstanding establishment in San Valencez, but it served many purposes to many people, and there were times when even a cop needed a place to drink in private.

"Whiskey," Tommy managed to croak. "Might as well just leave the bottle."

No questions and no talk. The bottle appeared, a glass beside it, and Tommy poured. Three shots in, a huge, hulking shadow fell across him, and he turned slowly. Mac slipped onto the next stool and the bartender dropped a second glass on the counter and turned away.

"They looking for me?" Tommy asked.

"Captain Laroche wants to see you," Mac replied slowly, sipping the whiskey. "No hurry. They're saying Barnett's a serial killer. Kidnaps pregnant street girls. Kills the babies."

Tommy stared at the dark, amber liquid swirling in his glass. He'd known it would be something like this, and, somehow the lie was leaking into his own thoughts and diluting them. Just like that. Some sort of psychic defense system, he guessed, protecting his mind with a new wall of lies to try and patch what had been broken.

"You believe that?" Tommy asked at last.

Mac didn't answer at first, but when Tommy turned to glare at him, the big man shook his head. "I saw what I saw," Mac said. "I didn't see any street girls."

"You didn't see shit," Tommy spat, turning back to

his drink. After a moment, he felt like a shit-heel, and he continued. "It was bad, Mac. I don't know how to tell you what I saw, and I don't want to tell you. I don't want tell anyone. I *want* that bastard to be a psycho. I want him to be a killer. I don't want what I got, and I don't know what to do with it, either.

"Does that make any sense?" he asked, turning back to watch his partner's face.

The big man's face gave nothing away. He met Tommy's gaze, and shook his head again. "Everything in life doesn't make sense," he said at last. "All we can do is get on with it."

Tommy thought about that. He tossed back another shot, stared at the bottle for a moment, and pushed it away.

"Swell," he said softly. "Just fucking swell."

The two walked out into the night together, and Tommy took a deep breath. It smelled and tasted like the air of a thousand other nights. In the back of his mind, he could still hear the thing screaming, could still see it latching onto Barnett's face, but the world was coming back into focus.

"I'm going in to make my report on the 'serial killer,'" he said.

"You sure?" Mac asked.

"Yeah," Tommy said. "I'm tired as hell, but I'll tell you what, partner. I damn sure don't see myself sleeping. Not tonight. Maybe not ever. You think there's more like him out there?"

"More than a few," Mac replied calmly.

"Maybe," Tommy said, lost in memory and thought, and a little woozy from the whiskey, "it's a good thing I know, then."

"Not for them," Mac grinned.

Tommy laughed, and the sound echoed into the shadows, as if chasing something away. The faint flow of dawn was ringing the tops of the buildings to the east, and for the moment, it was enough.

"THAT'S WHAT THEY ALL SAY"

by Bradley H. Sinor

Not too long ago a friend of Brad's commented that Brad wrote family stories. "Yeah," Brad told him, "if you're related to the Addams Family or one of Dracula's relatives." Brad has seen his fiction appear in such anthologies as *Warrior Fantastic*, *Knight Fantastic*, *Dracula in London*, *Bubbas of the Apocalypse*, *Merlin*, *Lord of the Fantastic*, and others. He will have several more coming out soon. His two collections of short fiction and *Dark and Stormy Nights* and *In the Shadows*.

WHEN I SAW the demon sitting across from me, I knew that this wasn't going to be your run-of-the-mill client interview.

Demons are not the sort of folks that normally walk through the door, even at Twilight Investigations. They usually show up in a puff of smoke or some other sort of minor pyrotechnic display. If the latter happens, I generally double the fee to cover any damage to the furniture or the carpet.

For the most part Twilight Investigations did employment background checks, insurance claims, and the ever present catching of cheating spouses in the act. That had kept me and the rest of my staff in beer and hot pizza for the last couple of years.

If anyone had asked me what a demon looked like, I probably would have suggested something with horns, a tail, and green skin or—preferably—a supermodel there to talk me out of my soul. I've had both kinds sitting on the other side of my desk.

That was not what I was looking at this time.

He was short, balding, and his bottle-cap-thick eyeglasses covered sickly yellow cats'-eye slits. The rumpled white shirt and thin tie, along with a pocket protector filled with a half dozen pens of various colors, made him look like a refugee from a cubicle. I dubbed him Wally after one of the characters in my favorite comic strip.

"So who does your decorating, Humphrey Bogart?" the little guy said looking around the room.

I had leased space in an old office building that dated back to the 1930s, with heavy dark wood paneling, steam pipe radiators, and frosted glass on the office windows. The rent was reasonable. I would have preferred something more modern, but the ambience helped make the clients feel more comfortable.

"Come on, I expected better than that," I said. "The next thing you know, you'll be wanting to know if I have a half empty bottle of bourbon in my desk drawer, a trench coat in my closet, and own a dog named Asta."

Wally pulled a PDA from his pocket. "According to our records you haven't had a dog since that Chihuahua named Princess when you were twelve. You presently share your apartment with a cat named Ashe. I doubt he would tolerate a dog; he barely puts up with the dates you bring home. The strongest thing you drink is Pepsi and Dr. Pepper. Don't you think that a dozen bottles of that a day is a bit too much? You definitely don't own a trench coat. In fact, the only coat you have is an old leather flight jacket. By the way, you really need to get that seam on the left

side restitched; if you don't, it will be coming apart
soon."

Not bad; it looked like the demonic intelligence service had done its research. But it was also a relief to
see that they didn't know everything. I did own a trench
coat. Before I left the police force to open my own
agency, my captain had given it to me, something about
it being a tradition that a private eye should own one.

"So, your message said you needed something handled very discreetly."

"Yes," Wally nodded. "We need the best and
you've come highly recommended."

"By whom, if you don't mind my asking?"

"Not at all. It was Jerome Basil."

I had watched them slip a needle in Basil's arm
three years ago because of a little matter he had or-
chestrated that had ended up with a lot of people
becoming very dead, in a very messy way.

"So how is old Basil?"

"Not doing badly. We have him working on some
political campaign strategy. He sends his regards and
says there are no hard feelings. He understands it was
nothing personal, just business."

Like hell there was nothing personal; one of the
people he had killed had been a good friend. I supposed if that's what he wanted to think, then who was
I to disabuse him of that idea?

"So what do you want from me?"

"It's a simple job. There has been a kidnapping. We
want you to deliver the ransom."

"So who is the victim?"

"Lucifer."

I got up and walked up to the little fridge in the
corner. From behind the sack with the half a ham-
burger and remains of an order of fries that had been
my lunch, I pulled a can of cold Pepsi. I wasn't really
thirsty, but doing it bought me a few minutes to think
about this whole situation.

"What level are you, anyway?" Demons have been

known to lie, as had the assorted vampires, were-
wolves, succubi, and other citizens of the night nation
who had frequented my office. However, the wards I
had in the place usually let me know when someone
was not telling the complete truth. The indicator was
an itch on my right heel. So far no itch, but demons
of a certain level you could never wholly trust.

"Mr. Gordon, I will have you know I am of the
highest level in the hierarchy of the Damned, personal
assistant to Asmodaus himself."

Highest level? Yeah, right, that's what they all say.
personal assistants could be anything from company
hit men to the shmucks senior VPs sent out to pick
up their cleaning.

"Okay, let's review this. Someone has managed to
kidnap Lucifer and you want me to deliver the ransom." I think I just needed to hear myself say it.

"That's about it."

This was not going to be a good day.

I am pretty good at what I do. Five years' Special
Forces training, a few years on the police force, and
this knack for figuring out things have given me a
pretty interesting life. Of course, having an eye
toward good public relations has managed to turn a
little one-man agency into a decent-sized company.
Solving the Fraser forgery matter and the Rosen-
Gannon kidnapping didn't hurt my reputation in certain circles.

I didn't realize what kind of circles those included
until the day a six-foot-tall green guy with three eyes
and a prehensile tail walked in and wanted to hire me
to check up on his wife. The next week a group of
leprechauns showed up wanting me to investigate a
realtor who was trying to build on their fairy hill.

Since then, every once in a while, clients of a supernatural persuasion would show up. My employees
didn't seem to pay much attention to them; usually
just saying, "You need to talk to Gordon."

Hey, as long as they paid my retainer, I didn't have a problem with them; even if disposing of those four-hundred-year-old Spanish doubloons was a bit dicey. I should always have problems like that.

We had adjourned to the Starbucks across the street from my office. I couldn't tell you why, but it just felt more comfortable to be talking to a demon in Starbucks. We had the place pretty much to ourselves; the lunch crowd had dissipated and the office rats hadn't yet begun to leave their warrens for the evening. Wally had ordered a double mocha java, with whipped cream, extra chocolate flavoring, and a peppermint stick to garnish it. He nearly drained it in one swallow and called for a second one.

That really made me wonder just what they were drinking in Hell these days. It might not hurt to find out who had the Starbucks franchise for the lower realms.

I looked at the steam rising from my latte and caught myself wondering why I didn't get out of the business. It wasn't a matter of money. The last few years had been very good for Twilight Investigations, and I could afford to look for something else. Only trouble was, I really didn't want to. I liked what I did.

"So, who has kidnapped the Devil?"

"Please, his name is Lucifer. I mean, after all, he is an individual, not a stereotype."

"That doesn't answer my question."

Wally set his drink down, pursing his lips for a moment before he began to speak. "Contrary to popular belief, Lucifer does not spend all of his time in Hell. We actually have major field offices in London, Seattle, Rio, Peking, and Johannesburg. Lucifer is definitely a hands-on CEO; he likes to drop in on them and the other operations quite frequently. The company keeps expanding and there is even some talk of us going public in a year or two. Not that anyone would believe we were for real."

I wondered what the IPO for stock in Hell would be.

"Several weeks ago he had a meeting with the owners of several smaller companies that we were looking to acquire. The owners had been signed up with us for years, but it never hurts to pick up their companies as well."

"Sound business strategy."

"Unfortunately, it turned out to be a trap. Another myth is that Lucifer is omnipotent, although we do try to encourage that rumor. The people he was meeting with were in the employ of a sorcerer named Lubec. Following certain old rituals, he was able to imprison Lucifer in a mystic seal."

In terms of news, the last several weeks had been rather quiet. No great crises, no natural disasters, nothing that Old Nick would have had his hand in. Maybe having this guy locked away was not a bad idea.

"It's actually a *very* bad idea," said Wally.

"Reading minds?" I knew a few demons were reported to have that ability. Personally, I wouldn't want it; there is far too much garbage thinking running around in most human beings' heads, mine included.

"No, the spell for it gives me migraines. I'm just very good at reading body language. Yours was rather obvious, given the subject of our conversation," he said. "The furrowed brow, angle of your head, and thoughtful look on your face when I mentioned the boss being locked away told me everything."

A demon who looked like a computer nerd and talked like Sherlock Holmes; great, that somehow fit this situation just perfectly. "All right, why is it not a good idea?"

Wally pulled out his PDA and made several marks on the screen before passing it over to me. "Have a look at this."

It was a list of names, some of the top ranking demons in the hierarchy of Hell along with some from various regional mythologies such as Greek, Norse, Aztec, and Samoan. There were even a few names that I had thought were entirely fictional.

"It's Lucifer, and only Lucifer who keeps a leash on these guys. He lets them come out and play, but only under the strictest rules. If he were permanently out of the picture, you can rest assured that they would begin to take a much more active role in the everyday lives of human beings. You should pardon the expression, but all Hell would break loose. Of course there are those who agree with Lubec and will try to stop you."

"In that case, my fee just tripled. I do that when I have to add world-saving to my resume."

Wally had absented himself very quickly once I agreed to take the case. He just handed me a card with an address on Garibaldi Street on it and said that I could pick up the ransom there. A couple of years ago it had looked like the place was going to gentrify, but something went wrong and now all it had were a few stores, a lot of warehouses, and a lot of dead dreams.

That was why I was surprised to come around the corner and find myself in front of a comic book shop. I looked again at the card Wally had given me. This was the place.

The windows were covered with old sun-faded posters announcing special issues of various characters, men wearing capes and women wearing very little, both genders with bulging muscles of human proportions that just didn't work. A blinking neon sign announced that the establishment was open and that its name was simply The Comic Shop.

A small man, barely four feet tall, came out of the door, a plain brown paper sack in his hands. There was something almost feral in his manner. He shifted slightly when he saw me, eyes darting from side to side. I looked at him a moment, then he dashed off down the street.

Inside, the place wasn't very big. The walls were covered with racks and display cases. Movie one sheets for an old Flash Gordon serial and a Hong Kong martial arts flick hung on either side of an unused fireplace.

"Forget something, Rupert?"

The voice belonged to a heavyset man sitting behind the counter wearing a photographer's vest and a plain black shirt. He was looking down at several comic books spread out on the counter in front of him.

"Afraid I'm not Rupert," I said.

The man looked up, adjusted the half glasses that hung on the end of his nose, and arched an eyebrow at me. "You most certainly are not," he laughed. "And there is nothing to regret about that. Welcome to The Comic Shop."

"Highly original name," I said.

"But accurate," he said with a smile. "I'm Hugh Carpenter. I own the joint. Feel free to look around. If there is anything special you are looking for, let me know. We carry a full range of current titles and an extensive collection of back issues. Not to mention a whole line of collectibles."

"Actually, I'm not sure what I came here for," I said. "A guy just gave me this address and said I should come."

I held out the card. Carpenter took it, staring at the small rectangle for a long moment. His face went pale and he took a couple of stifled breaths.

"This guy have a name?"

"I didn't really catch it, but I call him Wally."

"Talk about your originality," the shop owner said as he got up and walked toward the front door. I heard the sound of a lock being thrown and saw him flip the switch to turn the open sign off.

"Follow me."

He led me toward the back of the shop and around the corner of a particleboard bookcase that held a statue of a black man wearing sunglasses caught in the middle of swinging a sword as his long jacket swirled around him. Next to him was a bust of a man with pins stuck through his face.

We went down a short hallway into a room half the size of the main store. A single display case stood in the center of the otherwise empty room. Inside were three comic books, each one in a protective Mylar bag. All of them looked as pristine and new as the day they rolled off the printing press.

"These?" I was not certain what I had been expecting, but this wasn't it.

"Indeed they are," he said. There was a tone of sadness in his words, "Three icons of the comic world are in front of you: *Action Comics* issue number one, the first appearance of Superman; *Detective Comics* number twenty seven, featuring this newcomer called The Batman, and *Amazing Fantasy* number fifteen, the first time that the world saw Spiderman. They originally sold for less than a quarter each. Now, collectively, those magazines are worth on the order of a million dollars or more."

Carpenter opened up the showcase; carefully gathering up the three books.

"You do know who I'm working for, don't you?" I asked after he handed them to me.

Carpenter pulled out the card I had given him, holding it up with two fingers. A tiny chimney of smoke began at the corner, and then engulfed the whole thing. He dropped it to the ground and watched the flames fade away, leaving a pile of ash on the wooden floor. He raked the edge of his shoe through it.

"I know, all too well. I've had to watch over these things for a lot of years, now I'm passing them on, let's just say, in fulfillment of a clause in a contract and leave it at that."

There didn't seem much else to say, so I headed for the door. Maybe it was it the sound of a floorboard creaking or maybe it was some subconscious instinct that made me turn. Carpenter was charging at me with a look of hatred and desperation on his face.

I was just slow enough reacting that all I could do was drop the books and manage to get my arms half-way up in some vain effort to protect myself as he crashed into me.

The impact sent us both straight into the wall. That I was able to stay on my feet was a total miracle.

I managed to get my arm around his neck. That close I could smell his sweat; it had a sickly sweet odor to it. I'm not a great fighter. I freely admit that. I prefer to talk my way out of situations, although I would like to think that I could hold my own in most fights. This apparently was not one of those. Carpenter managed to twist enough to dislodge my arm and send me flying into the display case.

Glass and wood broke beneath me as I impacted against the display case and it collapsed under me. I felt slivers driving into my cheek and arm. This wasn't one of those special breakaway, presawed plywood creations that would have shattered into nothing dangerous; it was real and it hurt.

I lay there for a few seconds as my eyes managed to focus. That was when I saw the enraged comic shop owner coming at me again.

This guy just wouldn't give up.

For some reason, right then I realized that I really wanted a fresh hot Krispy Kreme doughnut. Maybe some part of my mind had decided that that was my idea of the perfect last meal for the condemned man.

Only instead of pulling my arms and legs off to beat me to a bloody pulp with them, this enraged merchant turned maniacal killer just teetered over me for a moment, then came crashing down on top of me. I don't know which hurt more, his falling on top of me or being slammed into that display case.

I think I lost consciousness for a moment or two,

because the next thing I was really aware of was this huge mass of sweaty flesh lying on top of me, unmoving, the smell enough to knock a few years off my life. I'm not even sure if he was breathing, and I didn't really care.

"Do you need any help getting out?"

Wally was standing there to my right, along with a boy who looked to be around fourteen or fifteen.

"Yeah, I do," I said with barely enough breath to move my chest and speak.

The two of them grabbed the unconscious man's arm and pulled to the right. That was enough to get the weight off me long enough to squeeze out. I had a pretty good idea of what toothpaste felt like.

My legs didn't want to cooperate, but I forced them to support me. "How did you get here?" I asked Wally.

"Gabe called me," he gestured at the kid.

"Yeah, I just came in to get my weekly comic book fix and it sounded like you two were rehearsing for the WWE. It looked a little too real, so I whopped Carpenter with my case." He held up a musical instrument case, the handle broken, in one hand.

"I thought Carpenter worked for you?" I asked Wally.

The demon shrugged, rolling his eyes up behind those magnifying bottle-cap glasses of his. "We do have him under contract. But I did tell you that there were people who didn't want your mission to succeed. Looks to me like they have gotten their tentacles in a little deeper than we expected."

"Look, fellows," said Gabe. "I don't know what you're talking about. I don't care; I'm late for my trumpet lesson. I just hope to hell my horn isn't hurt. She can make a sweet sound, a really sweet sound."

Before I could say anything, he was out the door.

"How did that kid know you and know how to get hold of you?"

"I've known Gabe for a very long time."

*   *   *

Behind the counter in the main part of the shop I found a metal briefcase. Inside were padded slots where comics fit perfectly. My guess was that Carpenter had used it to transport some of his more valuable items.

Wally checked his PDA and then said. "We don't have a whole lot of time; we'll take my ride."

His "ride" turned out to be a twenty-year-old lime-green station wagon. It had dozens of bumper stickers and a swarm of radio antennae attached to it. Inside there were more scanners than I had seen outside of a police station in a long time.

I set the case on the floor, pushing aside a pair of shoes and what looked like a wadded-up sweatshirt. The seat belt was hidden under a pile of tabloid newspapers and old fast-food containers. There was a distinct reek of mildew and brimstone in that car.

To say that Wally drove like a maniac would be a pretty good description. We were barely away from the curb before the speed had jumped up to over ninety. I watched him maneuver that vehicle in ways that I would never have thought possible. Several times over the next half hour I had moments of my life flashing in front of my eyes. Not a good sign.

We finally pulled to a stop in front of a small strip mall, the kind that has a hundred clones in every city in the country. Most of the stores were either dark or boarded up. In fact, the only places that looked alive, if that's what you could call it, were a Chinese takeout, a single-screen movie theater, and a bar at the end of the mall.

The marquee of the theater proclaimed, in a gap-toothed announcement, that it was showing *Ca a b an a*. I took that to mean *Casablanca*. I made a mental note to find my way back here since it was one of my favorite movies and I always kept an eye out for good retro movie houses.

"There's the drop," said Wally, pointing at the bar. It figured.

Like most bars of this sort, the place was very dark. A few lights on tables were the only thing, besides some indirect lighting in the corner and a disco ball that hung above the dancers' stage, that brought parts of the place out of the shadows.

There were three people inside, but the place still had an empty feel to it. A curly-haired man stood behind the bar, putting beer bottles in a cooler, a woman in jeans and a sweatshirt was pushing a mop across the floor between tables while a long-legged girl sat on a stool by the bar, smoking as she intently worked a crossword puzzle.

"Can I get a beer?" I said, taking a seat on one of the stools. "Draw will do."

The bartender complied without saying a word. He just set a frosted glass down in front of me and went back to his inventory.

"Buy a girl a drink?" the girl said. She was a dancer; the Harley-Davidson T-shirt she wore didn't completely hide her fringed bikini panties.

"So how much commission do you get from cadging drinks from the customers?" I asked.

She just laughed, smiling a sad smile but didn't offer an answer. I dropped a couple of bills on the counter and motioned for the bartender to bring her a drink.

"So, did you bring it?" The cleaning lady had pushed her bucket over toward the bar and was leaning on her mop as she spoke.

"And just what would that be?"

"I think you know." I felt a bare foot move against my leg and then swing down to rub the case.

"Both of you?" Maybe a part of me had expected Lubec, the sorcerer who had managed to entrap Old Nick himself, to be some elderly man who had spent years mastering occult skills. Certainly not the two women I was seeing in front of me. But I am the last person to judge people by appearance. I mean, at five-foot-four and 130 pounds soaking wet, I'm not exactly the stereotype image of a private eye.

"Actually, no," said the bartender. That was when I realized that the cleaning lady and the dancer now didn't seem quite so interested in what I had brought with me.

"All of you? I'm impressed."

"Actually, only one," said the bartender, Lubec. "Let's just say it helps to be able to be in more than one place at a time."

"You should try it sometime," said the dancer. There seemed to be an extra glow to their eyes when Lubec was "in residence."

"So let's get down to business," said the bartender. "Did you bring the ransom?"

I took another drink and then pushed away the empty beer glass. "Let's say that I did bring this ransom you are talking about. So, if I'm paying for something, then I think I have the right to see just what it is I'm buying." I said.

The light in their eyes shot back and fourth among all three for a moment, faster than I could keep track of. "All right, that seems reasonable," said the bartender.

The cleaning lady motioned for me to follow her. She opened a door just beyond the bar. It was mostly storage, stacks and stacks of beer cases, boxes of pork rinds and potato chips. She put her pail and mop into a rack on one wall and then pointed toward a small alcove formed by the boxes.

"Your merchandise," she said.

Sitting cross-legged on the floor was a slim man, who looked to be somewhere between forty and sixty, wearing a paint-stained T-shirt and a plaid down jacket. In his hand was a can of beer. For the life of me he reminded me of my Uncle Bubba from Coffin's Corner, Arkansas.

"You're Lucifer?" I asked.

"Yeppers," he said, grinning with a set of perfect teeth that didn't seem to fit in with the rest of his image. "Perhaps you would prefer the more traditional look." His skin turned red, his hair inky black, and his feet were suddenly hooves. I noticed a pitchfork peeking out from the other side of a case of black cherry soda. "Or perhaps something newer." With that, in swift succession, he morphed into the forms of Peter Cook, Elizabeth Hurley, George Burns, and Al Pacino; then back into Uncle Bubba.

"Convinced?" asked the cleaning woman.

I nodded. She pulled out a feather duster and made a pass in the air with it. A moment later Lucifer vanished from the place where he had been sitting. I turned and looked back into the bar.

He was standing on the stage, next to the dancer's pole, several of the cases of beer next to him. The light from the disco ball increased as it slowly began to rotate counterclockwise.

"So you're satisfied that this really is Lucifer aka Satan aka Old Nick aka a whole mess of other names?" asked Lubec from his aspect as the dancer. She extracted a cigarette from a pack that was lying on the bar but didn't light it, even though I did see a battered old Zippo lighter lying next to it.

"I am. Now, as I understand the terms of this agreement, once I give you the contents of this case, you will release Lucifer from the spell that you are using to incarcerate him."

"That's right. The seals will be broken and he will be free to go about his business," said the bartender.

"Remembering, of course that he has agreed to seek no vengeance on me or mine."

I looked up at the figure on the stage. He was leaning back against the dancer's pole, looking rather bored with the whole matter. "Is this agreeable to you?" I asked him.

"Surely, purely is. It's my own fault; I got caught off guard and was hoisted by my own petard," he chuckled.

At that I walked over to the edge of the stage and set the case down. The dancer stood near me, but her eyes were glazed over so I didn't think that Lubec was "in residence."

One at a time I took each of the comics out, removed the Mylar bags and laid them across the front of the stage floor. After touching them, my fingers were tingling.

"So what's so special about these things?" I asked.

The bartender had come over to stand next to the dancer. He reached forward and gently ran his fingers over the surface of each of the magazines. The look on his face was like that of a junkie just after he has shot up, awash with the flush from the drug.

"Dreams," they all three said as one. "Such stuff as dreams are made of. For decades these three characters have, in one form or another, been the center of the dreams of thousands of children and adults from all across the world. There is power in dreams, and here at their beginnings, these are that power made physical."

"Why do you think I kept them locked away? Those damned books are some of the most potent magical talismans to come into existence in a long time," said Lucifer.

The cleaning woman joined the other two, taking a position in front of one of the comics. I stepped away; the bad feeling in the pit of my stomach I had had since I saw Wally across my desk had just gotten a lot worse.

"So, can the two of us leave? I've fulfilled my end of the bargain."

"I'm afraid not," were the cleaning woman's words.

"Lucifer is going nowhere," continued the bartender.

"Except to sleep," finished the dancer.

The comics had begun to glow; I could almost see ghostly images of the characters in the air over them. The light was a rainbow of colors with shapes forming and re-forming inside of it, wrapping itself around them and the stage. I noticed Lucifer looked more than a little askance at what was going on.

"I shall lock him away, with the power of these dreams. Wrap him in a core of dreams that will hold him forever and remove him from the affairs of man far more permanently than I have now. There will be no evil, no danger, only unending peace and serenity."

"Looks like they never planned to let me go," said Lucifer. "Given what I know of the power of those talismans, I somehow sort of doubt that you will be walking out of this place anytime soon, either, Gordon."

"No, he will not," said the dancer. "The life of a man is required to make the spell work."

One of the bar stools flew at me, but I managed to dodge out of the way. I had to grab the bar to keep my balance. My hand landed next to the cigarette lighter that Lubec had left behind, struck it to life, and threw it at the stage. When the lighter came in contact with the glow, it hovered in the air for a heartbeat then began to sink slowly down. The flames flared, engulfed the comics and reached out toward Lubec then pulled in on themselves and disappeared.

The three figures stood for a moment, hand in hand, facing the stage, then collapsed, in unison, onto the floor.

The whole bar began to shimmer, then faded away. I was standing in the middle of a large empty warehouse that looked to be as big as the whole strip mall. At my feet was a single form now, a man in a pinstriped suit. I presumed that this was actually Lubec. There was a bruise on the back of his neck but no other apparent injury. I checked him for a pulse and could find nothing.

"Looks like you got lucky, friend Gordon."

Lucifer, still in the form of Uncle Bubba, stood in the middle of a large design etched in white on the dusty floor. I don't pretend to be able to read any of the arcane languages, or even know some of the symbols; but I knew that this was the seal that had locked him in. The bottle of beer was still in his hand.

"That I did, that I did," I muttered.

The three comic books were lying just outside of The Seal. They didn't look like they had suffered any damage from the flames. I returned them to the briefcase.

"Let me guess," said Lucifer. "You want to make your own deal now, since you have the talismans and I am still locked up here."

In answer to that, I scraped my foot across the symbols on the ground, enough to smear them, making an opening for him to use. "I already made my deal when I took this job."

He came across the edge, looking around as if he were waiting for the proverbial other shoe to drop. "Remarkable. Then that is the reason that you disrupted their little ceremony. The world they promised sounded like a pretty good place."

"Call it enlightened self-interest. I have an innate distrust of people who claim they know what is best for me. Besides, that world they wanted, well, it sounded boring to me. I also tend to think what Wally told me was the truth; we need you around to keep some of your more nasty subordinates in line."

"I must say, you have an interesting way of looking at things." He went back across the circle to the case and pulled out another beer. This one he passed to me as we walked toward the door. "You and I should talk about possibly putting you on retainer. And I will tell you right now, you don't have to worry about any surprise clauses."

That's what they all say. I made a mental note that if I did agree to take the retainer to put in a call to my lawyers at Tatum, Kearns and Farran, and get Melissa to draw up the contract.

SOMETHING WORSE HEREAFTER

by Sarah A. Hoyt

Sarah A. Hoyt is the author of *Ill Met By Moonlight, All Night Awake,* and *Any Man So Daring,* an acclaimed trilogy which undertakes a fantasy recreation of Shakespeare's life. She's currently working on a time-travel/adventure novel with Eric Flint. She has also sold over three dozen short stories, some of which have appeared in magazines like *Absolute Magnitude, Analog,* and *Asimov's.* Sarah lives in Colorado with her husband, two sons, and four cats.

DYING IS EASY. It's staying alive afterward that's hard.

The dark portals open in front of you. You cross them. It's like a reverse birth, from light to pain and constriction and the darkness beyond. No escape.

You emerge into smoky darkness lit by a tremulous red glare. Fears of fire and damnation flee with all your memories of another life and leave you empty, vacant, alone.

You smell sulfur, but you lack a name for it. And your new eyes don't know how strange the landscape looks, how the buildings in the distance, looming and dark and diamantine, look like nothing you've ever seen. Like skyscrapers made of wax caught in the flame of a candle. Like architecture writhing in pain. Like maddened claws tearing at the crimson sky.

And then they slither out of the darkness. The creatures. To call them devils would sully a perfectly good word. They are worse than any boogeymen, more heinous than any monster, scarier than any nightmare the living mind can conjure.

They come with open maw, with dripping fang, with tearing claw and screaming hatred. Toward you.

In the new body you haven't even learned you have yet, you fight back. You fight back with your bare hands, your cunning, your monkey-mind, your puny being.

Only the strong survive the slashes and cuts and bites. Only the determined run past that first gauntlet. Only the merciless kill the demons and drink their life force.

Only those who can fight ever survive to enter Hell.

"It wasn't always like that," Len said. "It wasn't always sink or swim, survive or disappear."

Beneath our feet, the train rocked steadily on the track. It was an early-twentieth-century-type train, with lots of ironwork and uncomfortable leather seats. Not that we'd ever taken the seats. No. We stood in the space between two carriages, where a sort of little balcony abutted another and there was a gate between the two. The carriages inside and their seats were always full. Most often with desperate people. And you didn't want to sit amid hungry people when your own life force was full and glowing. As ours was, because we hunted every day.

Len's glowed around his head, its vaguely red shine probably an artifact of the smoky red light that glowed night and day from the sunless sky. Len's hair was blond, a pale silvery tone, cut short. For reasons that evaded me, he'd pierced his left eyebrow. A silvery stud shone there when he took a deep drag on his cigarette and flung it, still burning, into the darkness around the rails.

"It used to be different," he said. His gray-blue eyes shone, almost as silver as his stud, and his face—a small face with regular features and a perhaps too sharp nose—had a dreaming look that wasn't normal in him. "In the old days."

"How would you know?" I asked, as I reached casually into the pocket of his black one-piece suit for the cigarettes and pulled one out of his pack. He pulled another one out, himself, before I had a chance to put it back.

"I've read books," he said. And shook his head and corrected, "I used to read books. When I . . ." His voice trailed off.

We didn't talk about when we were alive. I'd been together with Len for years. Or perhaps millennia or aeons or however one should measure time in Hell. Hard to tell when no sun rose or fell and the sky was always a smoky red.

But you could count on the fingers of one hand the times we'd mentioned a previous existence. Our relationship had started when we crossed the dark portal together. He'd saved me from the first creature to attack me, and let me get my breath long enough that I'd saved him from the one trying to get him after that.

Acts of kindness are rare in Hell. Acts of kindness reciprocated are even rarer. We'd been bound by those acts—male and female, him blond and lean and muscular, me rounded and dark-haired and vaguely Mediterranean. Friends and hunt mates and lovers.

Friendship was rare here. It was that we watched each other's back that had allowed us to survive all this time. A kindness in Hell.

"You know, the Romans said it was just an arid landscape, where you wandered alone. Or your shade did. And the medieval theologians thought it was possible to escape Hell by swimming on tears of pure repentance."

I snorted and sucked in a mouthful of cigarette smoke. Everyone smoked in Hell. I didn't know why, save that it cut down on the taste of sulfur in your mouth, the tang of burning flesh in your nostrils. You never saw anyone burning, but you could smell it all over Hell. "And the Romans would know how? I assume the ones writing this would be predead? And the theologians?"

He grinned at me, a flash of white in the surrounding darkness. "Well," he said. "You think it's always been like this? You have to survive to enter and once here you have to keep killing other creatures, and other people—just to . . . stay here?"

"Probably," I said. "Though I think the train is recent. More recent than Rome. Unless Hell invented trains."

He chuckled as if I'd made a joke.

And then the train pulled into what looked like a deep, dark, cavernous tunnel. And stopped. The doors slid open, in a woosh of vapor and a smell of burning.

"Time to go," Len said as he flashed me a smile and reached for the weapon strapped to his back. It was no gun known on Earth. It was big and black and bulky, but it managed to have a serpentine and dark appearance to it anyway. What it did was it sucked the energy—the life—out of the demons coming after you. It stored it until you got to your pad, your hangout, your safe place. Where you could then inject that life essence into yourself. And earn another day, another week, another month here. In Hell.

After a while, the killing grounds become a habit. A routine. Just outside the dark portals, they extend what feels like a couple of miles—geography here is often a matter of opinion—through dark, sulfurous country. There is the road, and you're safe on the road, as a rule. If nothing else, because there's such a constant stream of people walking down that dark pathway that the chances of anything reaching out and snatching you out of all the others are next to none. This is not the road least traveled.

But step off the road, into the caved-up dirt, the mounded mess outside, and you get surrounded by creatures very quickly. These are the cowardly ones. Not quite the type to try to go and snatch a soul at the dark portals—where souls are known to fight desperately—but getting them here, where the souls come already tired, sometimes wounded, bleeding life force and strength. But still vital enough from the other side that their life force will last a demon for weeks.

These are the creatures we hunt—we, the ones who survive any time at all in Hell.

When you get there, you step off the road and your partner, if you're lucky enough to have one, steps off with you. You're together, each watching the other's back, guns at the ready, scanning the landscape for the monstrous shapes that would come after you. And for human shapes, too, because some people get desperate.

Len and I had it down to an art. To be down there at all, when our patterns were full, meant that we enjoyed the hunt, the chase, more than anything else.

Well, at least Len did and I went along with him. There was no point arguing. And it kept us safe. There was a legend that if you stored too much life force some horrible being, some avenger would come after you to balance the scales. An invincible being. But we'd never heard of this happening to anyone we knew or even anyone our acquaintances knew directly.

It was always something that happened to a friend of a friend, a nebulous acquaintance, a fire flicker of legend around the bars and hangouts of Hell.

And, as Len always said, every time we crossed the road to get to the killing fields, "Every one we get is one less. One less to attack the newcomers."

Put like that it was almost our civic duty. If there were civic duties in Hell.

We jumped off the road, together, me watching his back, he watching mine. The feel of the ground underneath was like that of a freshly plowed field in summer. The memory came to me, sharp and sweet, of a plowed field and the ground warm beneath, and of me, barefoot, running through it.

I had no idea how old I'd been or when this had happened. Memories are fragmentary here. Another reason you don't talk about your living days much.

But this one came with a feeling of male hands around my waist, with the memory of a kiss. I'd have sworn it was Len. I'd have—

"Look out," Len yelled.

I'd been distracted. The movement of the ground beneath my feet threw me and I fell on my back as a gross green thing—all fangs and claws and purple venom—slithered from the depths to loom over me, its little yellow eyes gloating at my helplessness, before it took a bite. Before it sucked in my life force. Before it left me, empty and discarded, like a shell, by the wayside. Gone. Dropped into oblivion.

I heard the *woosh* as Len activated his weapon, and then the thing contorted. For a moment, it looked like the gun was going to suck all of the creature—flesh and all—into its dark vortex. But then the creature withered and screamed. I saw the halo of life force leave it.

What remained slumped to the ground, barely giving me time to roll away from where it thumped, making the ground tremble.

"What was that?" Len asked. "What were you thinking?"

I shrugged. "Memory," I said. "From before."

He gave me a worried gaze.

But a dark thing with too many eyes crept up on us. And I vacuumed it away.

Our room was small and not particularly nice. Just a small room with a wooden floor, a metal bed, a sagging armchair, and two French doors that served as windows, opening only to balconies too small for us to stand up in.

Oh, we had enough life force—that was the only real currency in Hell—but we'd got this room a long time ago and we'd been oddly happy here. We didn't count on happiness in Hell, and we were afraid of doing anything to spoil it.

So now we sat, in our narrow little room, in what looked like a nineteenth-century rooming house. It was in a section of human-style architecture and most of the buildings here were just like that—vintage nineteenth, eighteenth, early twentieth century. For a moment I wondered if the only buildings in Hell were the ghosts of buildings that had once existed on Earth. But the thought slid away from me. What could a building do to end up in Hell? And what had we done, Len and I?

I looked at my lover who sat on the bed, stripped to the waist, the ratty white bedspread gathered around his lower body, hiding just enough. His life force aura shone brighter than ever, brilliant and golden.

We'd shared the energy of the monsters we'd captured. Between us, it was enough for . . . a long time.

I was naked, standing by the window, looking down on the all-too-human cobbled street. Someone, sometime, had put in gaslights, which added their quivering, wavering yellow to the immutable shining red of the sky. "Do you wonder what brought us here?" I asked Len. I turned around.

"The train," Len said automatically, while he reached from the bed for his underwear which we'd dropped to the floor sometime before making love.

"Idiot," I said. "I meant here. To Hell."

He gazed at me—or rather, at my breasts—and smiled. "There were a lot of things that could have done it," he said, and shrugged. "But I'm thinking in my case, probably concupiscence."

"Yes?"

He sighed, dropped his underwear on the floor again. "Lust," he said, and leaped out of the bed, toward me. His lips searched mine, his hands ran over my body.

Power-shots always made Len amorous.

Sometime afterward, we lounged on the bed together, my head on his chest, black hair against the pale skin. He stroked my hair absently with his long, thin fingers. A memory or something like a memory of his doing this while I lay on a plowed field came to me—a memory, a dream, or a piece of imagining. I didn't know which.

"What was that, back in the killing grounds?" Len asked, as if only then remembering.

I shrugged. I didn't want to explain, the ground under my feet, warm from the summer sun, the male hands—Len's?—on me, the feeling, the heady feeling of a beating heart, of being alive.

This flesh we had here, this new body, was of some serviceable substance. I enjoyed Len's touch and I liked our lovemaking, and his mouth on mine, and his warmth on my skin. But it wasn't the same. My mouth still tasted like sulfur and nothing made my heart beat faster.

And then there were the horrors. The things that could happen if you ran out of life force. Oh, I'd never experienced it, but I had seen others suffer it. The pain, the craving, the mindless hunger. In that state, people—souls?—here would attack everything, everyone, in search of energy.

And those who were too timid, those who were too scared to kill demons or other humans did the most

degrading things for the life force to survive one day
to the next. Outside our window, across the street, a
big neon sign scrolled, advertising "Boys, boys, boys,"
and "Girls, girls, girls," and then other, darker promises. Its red light came through our window and
stained our floor like blood.

"Why do we fight so hard to stay here?" I asked.
"Why do we have to fight so hard to stay in Hell?"

Len's hand stopped, halfway through stroking my
hair. I felt the muscles of his chest move as he
shrugged. "Because we're afraid. As the play said,
something worse hereafter." He paused, then spoke
dreamily, like someone describing a cherished fantasy.
"I mean, if we knew for sure that there was no life
after this . . . if there were nothing . . . just silence
and darkness and oblivion, don't you think most of us
would gladly go to that rest? That most of us would
gladly die again and rest in peace?" He paused. His
long fingers trailed down, caressing my face with a
butterfly touch. "But what if what's after this is so
horrible, more horrible than anything we can imagine
here? The true Hell where everything is torture and
there's no pause, no love, no comfort. Do you know
what happens to the things we kill? To the people
who vanish for lack of power?"

"No."

"Neither do I," he said, and reached for his cigarette pack, on the bedside table. He gave me a cigarette, took another one for himself, and lit them both.

I took a deep breath of the smoke and nicotine.
Cleaner than the sulfur and burn in the air.

We knew Hell. We knew the hurts, the fears, the
monsters. We did not know what would happen if we
let ourselves go. If we slid away.

I smoked, and stubbed out my cigarette, and slept,
with my head on Len's chest.

I was in a room, but it wasn't my familiar room, in
Hell. There was a moment of disorientation before I

realized it was a room in the other world. A room in the world before—a frilly, girly room with a pink curtain and a pink, frilly bedspread. The casement window was open to soft spring breezes. The air didn't smell of sulfur and the sky outside was blue, with the spring sun shining high up, and a bird singing somewhere.

But the only person in the room sat on the edge of the frilly bed and cried. In her hand was a note. Even from here, I could recognize the angular, exact handwriting. Len's.

And I could recognize the person crying, too. Myself. Myself as I'd been once—softer and younger and somehow more vulnerable. Alive. Someone who'd never held a demon down and watched it die as its life force left it.

The two recognitions felt like a blow.

And then I remembered Len, in a uniform. He'd come through my village. His regiment had been quartered there.

The name of the country, the exact time, the war and what they were fighting or fighting for, all of it had disappeared into an oblivion of forgetfulness. But I remembered Len, his hair soft as silk under my hand. And memories of a dance, and a kiss came back to me. And the memory of the plowed fields, warm against my naked back. And Len's body, smelling of clean sweat overlaid with alcohol. And the smell of the just-harvested crop warm and earthy in the air.

I remembered his body against mine, the lovemaking of which our lovemaking in Hell was a pale shadow.

And then the letter. I remembered that letter. It would have been easier—also cleaner—if he'd simply plunged a dagger into my heart. But the letter. He'd told me that he was leaving. Leaving for the front. He'd been called up. And he thanked me for the good times. The good times.

I'd thought he would marry me. Those silvery eyes, that facile tongue, that body that wrapped itself around mine as if he meant to protect me from the world, from anything bad ever happening to me.

In my dream, the girl on the bed went on crying. And I thought of the heartbreak, the sheer, searing heartbreak. And I— (She'd missed a period.)

He'd marched to war.

Villages are unforgiving. In a city one can hide lost honor and lost hope. But the only city she knew—the only city I knew—was a ruin, shattered by the war. It was a den of conflicting armies, a battleground. There, death or worse than death would meet her.

And here, her life was as good as gone.

In my dream, she went down the stairs of the quiet, comfortable house, to the garden, and got the rope and tied it securely to the branch of the old peach tree, and made a noose.

I remembered the rope against the neck, the sudden drop as she jumped from the branch and the frantic moment before her neck snapped—will against instinct, a moment for regrets.

And then the portals. Len and I had arrived at the same time.

The window broke. I woke, startled, lost, and rolled off the bed, without looking, without thinking, screaming, "Len, wake up, damn you."

Dimly, against the blood-red background of the sky, I saw creatures like man-bats—dark creatures with vast, leathery wings and only a sketch of a face, like features out of a nightmare.

They looked like men or like birds, or like bats, and I was on my knees, scrabbling on the wooden floor, scooting backward away from them, trying to escape, trying . . .

My mind had accelerated, and asked questions I could not answer. Who were they? Why were they here? Sometimes you could be attacked in the street or in your lodgings, but Len and I had never been. You heard of things like that, but—

One of the dark creatures reached for me, and I reached backward looking for my gun. I found the cold metal of it with relief and grabbed it hard in my hand. I swung around, catching the thing in the face.

It made a sound like a vulture screaming, and it let off a stench like a two-week-rotted corpse, but it backed away a little.

And I scooted backward, holding onto the gun, lifting it, reaching for the trigger and the controls.

Len had wedged himself behind the bed, with his own gun. I heard a *woosh,* and one of the bad guys vanished.

I scooted beside Len. "Who are they?" I yelled. "Who are they? Why have they come?"

"Nemesis," he said. "Or harpies. I've heard of this. When you kill too many of them. Too many . . . demons."

"Yes?" I asked.

"They come for you," he said.

And the space behind the first row of beings that had come into the room was packed—shoulder to shoulder packed with them.

Len was sucking them into his gun, one at a time, making them implode. But more were coming in, more were taking their place.

We had no chance. No chance at all.

"More expensive living quarters are warded," I screamed at Len, while I activated my gun and got one of the intruders. It hissed as its life force got sucked away, but its body just disappeared, like a soap bubble.

Another one took its place. There was no difference at all.

Holding my gun, sucking at the life force of any

being that got too close, I got up and started backing toward the door.

Len cackled. "Yes," he said. "But even spells and wards can't keep these things away. From what I've heard and read, they're like the balance keepers of Hell. You can't be allowed to get too much life force."

"Then why did we?" I asked, as I swept another the bastards and another took its place and—

"Because then there were fewer of them," he said. "I had to fight the good fight."

I thought of the village, his promises, our whirlwind romance. "No," I said.

I scrabbled for the door behind me, ready to open it, ready to run out into the hallway beyond. Where Len could follow me or not, as he pleased.

He'd gone off to war and left me a note thanking me for the good times. He'd gone without asking, without caring what would become of me once he'd left.

"Catrina," he yelled. "Don't."

Just as he yelled it, I felt it, behind me, through the wood of the door—claws scratching. And the sound like a bird-bat-human crying beyond.

I leaned against the door, but I'd unlocked it, and I could feel the pressure there.

There were too many of them. Too many of them all around. Some had wedged between Len and me. I was grabbing all of them I could, but it was never enough, and more and more came.

"Catrina," Len screamed. I couldn't see him.

"Yes," I said, my voice calm and distant and no more belonging to me than the crying of that girl on the bed, long ago. So, this is how it ended. How I found out what was there, hereafter. What we'd been fighting so hard to evade.

"I'm going to reverse power on the gun," he said.

It took me a moment to understand what he was

saying. I remembered, vaguely, dimly, the explanation the person—demon?—in the weapon shop had given us. Something about power being reversed, creating an explosion of power, igniting the life force of everything it touched. Like powder and gasoline, I remembered the thing saying.

I remembered it because at the time I'd wondered exactly what it could mean, and whether the creature talking about it had used fire and gasoline at some time, in life.

Matches and gasoline.

"Take cover," Len's voice yelled, from beyond the wall of slick, black, reptilian bodies.

I threw myself down. There was a flare.

And screams, and a smell like a charnel house, or an open coffin.

I opened my eyes, and only one creature stood in front of me. Just one, looking disoriented.

I lifted my gun and sucked it up. And then looked around the room, where all the rest of them had vanished. Soap bubbles in the air.

"Len."

He sat in the middle of the room, his head and shoulders against the metal of the bed. And he looked all right. No wounds, no hurts. Just the pale, muscular body I'd come to know so well, in this world and the one before.

But the silver eyes that focused on mine were strangely opaque and scared. Very scared.

"I was a stupid boy," he said. "Oh, I'm sure I could have married you," he said, as if I'd asked him a question. "But I didn't know how to. I didn't know how to ask for permission from my commanders. And I had no idea what I could do with you when I went back home."

His voice faltered, as if too full of tears or as if he were too short on breath. "My parents would have been very bewildered if I brought a foreigner home. Funny, I don't even remember what they looked like, but I remember that."

His life force, around his head, was almost gone. Pale and vague like the gaslights outside the window.

"And so I left. I was so scared." He shrugged. "I was so stupid. First battle, next day, and I was dead. And then . . ."

"You've known it all along?" I asked, creeping near him, on my knees, reaching for his hand, which was cold and clammy in mine.

He nodded. And smiled, a faint smile. "There are things I forgot, but none of them were you, Catrina."

His hand reached up, weakly, and tangled in my long black hair. "None of them were you."

The silver-gray eyes were distant, lost. His life force was burning out. He'd ignited it when he'd killed the demons. Fire and gasoline.

I grabbed at his wrist. "Len, don't leave me again."

And then I realized what he was doing. This time, he hadn't left me. Oh, there were things he might have done. He could have reversed that gun power and thrown it, as a grenade, to the midst of the things, and he'd probably have survived.

Probably.

But he'd chosen to ignite his huge life force reserve, to make himself into a human bomb, so that all the creatures would be wiped out. So he could save me.

"I want you to . . . go on," he said, his voice faint and distant, like a breeze through trees, like the echoing steps of a retreating regiment. "I will find out, now, if there is something worse . . ."

I'd taken the way out once, rather than face disapproval and dark glares, and fingers pointed at me. I'd forfeited my life to save my honor.

What had I done to those I'd left behind, to the family I didn't even remember?

I'd destroyed their lives to escape.

And now Len would destroy himself for me.

The guns are not needed. They're a refinement. They're a way of storing power, of trading power, of giving it to someone beyond the person who harvests it.

In fact, when Len and I got them, we got them on credit, on promise of giving our first harvest to the shopkeeper. And we had.

But before that we had killed creatures and gotten their force.

Which means, you can give your force. To someone. And someone whose life force is burning so low that they're near oblivion; can't help but take it.

"Catrina," Len said. It would have been a scream, but he simply didn't have the strength.

I brought my hand down squarely over his heart. When drinking—or giving away—life force, contact close to the heart helped.

Len tried to dislodge my hand with his. I could feel his nails scrabbling feebly at my skin, but he was too weak to do much damage.

He probably thought I was going to kill him, to take away the very little energy force he had left. To send him faster to oblivion.

As what?

A revenge against the foolish young man in that other world I only dimly remembered?

He was my hunt mate.

"Idiot," I told him tenderly, and, with my free hand, smoothed back his hair.

And then I willed my life force into him.

There is this about life force transfer. Once you start taking it—particularly if you're weak and near the end of your reserve—you can't stop.

I heard it time and again, in the train to the killing grounds or on the street, or in the dim, dark bars where those like us who could no longer taste anything, gathered to pretend to drink liquor and try to revive our memories of what would never return.

I'd heard how someone had started stealing a little life force off a friend, just to stabilize themselves, and found they couldn't stop, until the friend was gone, disappeared. Dead again. Gone to oblivion

No, once you start taking life force, you can't stop at just a little.

Even after he realized I was giving him my life force, Len struggled at first. Famished for life force as he must be, with his life force almost burned to nothing, he tried to push it away.

The young man might have been foolish. The young man might have been selfish. He might have deserved Hell. But my friend/lover in Hell was neither foolish, nor selfish.

"It's okay," I told him, and continued pushing. Pushing the life force at him, until he couldn't help but take it.

His body absorbed my life force, his hand grasped mine. His lips formed my name. His eyes shone with regret and fear.

And this time I wasn't wasting my life. I was giving it for someone else. I was trying to pay back, somehow, to erase the hurt to those people I'd left behind, those people I couldn't remember. The child whom I'd never given a chance to be born.

To pay back Len for the years of love, the millennia of care, the aeons of watching my back.

This time I would not leave someone else to pay for my mistakes. I'd have died without Len's help that first day. It was right I should go now, to whatever worse fate could wait me after Hell. It was right I should go and let Len live after me.

For a moment we merged—me and him. I was Len, he was me.

His mind, clear and protecting and mine—fearful, desperate, clinging to his.

But love shone in both.

And then I started fading, dimming, mind and memory and thought going, going, going, like a tide receding on a shore.

There would be oblivion, now, I thought.

But Len struggled. He tried to shove the life force back. It wouldn't come back. It just leaked, out of both of us, into the surroundings.

For a moment, I opened my eyes and saw him there, still pale, his silvery eyes still opaque.

"Not this time," he said. "Not this time. I will not let you go and face trouble alone. I am not that foolish."

"Foolish enough," I told him, and my voice was a whisper of wind on trees. "Foolish enough. Now we'll both go." I felt the life force seeping out of us. I was vaguely aware of creatures coming into the room, called by it.

I felt Len's hand close around mine.

And we're in water. Warm water. I start dog-paddling, without thinking.

Len is swimming beside me, looking bewildered.

Above, the sky is blue and—on the horizon—there's a clear white light shining brightly. Not the sun, but what the sun would be if it were supernatural.

Len raises his eyebrows at me. He lifts his hand to his mouth, tastes. "It's salty," he says.

Like tears.

We swim toward the light.

A FLY CAME BY

by Barbara Nickless

Barbara Nickless sold her first short story to *Pulphouse* and has been appearing in other magazines including *Dreams of Decadence* and the award-winning *Deathling* ever since. Barb holds a bachelor of arts in English with additional degree work in physics and physical anthropology. Her interest in other cultures can be seen in her new novel, *To Each Man an Island,* the 2003 mystery winner for the Colorado Gold Writing Contest. A classically-trained pianist, she is currently working on mastering "Hungarian Rhapsody No. 2" by Liszt. During her free time, Barb likes to read, hike, stargaze, cave, and collect fossils. Born on Guam, she now lives in Colorado with her husband and two children.

MIKHAIL VLADIMIROVICH Surikov tucked his head against the wind and hurried across the wet cobblestones of Red Square. His black dress shoes, shined that morning by his wife, were soaked from the melting snows, his socks already damp through the thin soles. His suit had become shiny in patches, but it would pass a casual inspection. There was nothing to be done about his haggard face, but

213

no doubt Kerensky was used to doing business with
careworn men. Why should Mikhail pretend to be anything else?

He ducked past a group of teenagers chattering on
their cell phones, then sidestepped a horse-drawn
buggy as it clattered by filled with camera-wielding
Americans. The nightmare had returned last night,
long after midnight when sleep finally claimed him.
He'd found himself staring through the glass of Lenin's sarcophagus, watching the dictator's body boil
with maggots, seeing the waxy skin bloom with monstrous patches of decay. He'd pounded on the glass,
helpless. At the last moment Lenin's eyes had opened
and he had shouted at Mikhail, "You have failed me!"
Mikhail had woken with an answering shout. His wife
had patted his back as if he were a child and given
him vodka, but Mikhail was still wide awake when she
resumed her snoring. Now he was irritable and anx-
ious and—because he had overslept after he had at
last fallen asleep—very nearly late.

He walked swiftly past the line of tourists—Russian
and foreigner—shuffling forward as they waited for
their chance to view Lenin. The deputies in Congress
could say what they liked about consigning Lenin to
an earthen grave. They could take away Mikhail's
funding, turn down his requests for assistance, reduce
him to a mere civil servant from the pinnacle he'd
once occupied. But Lenin was still venerated. Just
look at the people waiting for a glimpse of him! Not
so many as in the past, perhaps, but enough. Mikhail
thought of how these tourists would look at him with
respect if they knew he was no mere down-on-his-luck
businessman hurrying across Red Square but the man
personally responsible for the eternal preservation of
Lenin.

"Misha Surikov!" cried a voice from behind him.
"Well, I'll be blessed."

Without a backward glance, Mikhail ducked his head
and hurried on. The small bag of uncut diamonds—

lifted from the underground vault beneath the nose of the head of the State Treasury—burned against his skin where he'd sewn the little cloth bag inside his shirt. Despite his momentary fantasy of being acknowledged outside the boundaries of his own peer group, he had no wish to be delayed. Not today of all days. Even a few minutes late meeting Kerensky at St. Basil's Cathedral might cause the mob boss to change his mind and sell the chemicals to some other, less deserving person. If that happened, Vladimir Ilyich Ulyanov—better known to the world as Lenin— would begin the inexorable slide into putrefaction and corruption. Mikhail's life—indeed his whole reason for being—would be over.

The fly would have won.

"Misha, wait for an old man!" cried the voice. A few people standing in line looked over at Mikhail, past him to the source of the voice, then back again at Mikhail, glaring at his rudeness. This wouldn't do. The greatest medical doctor in all of Russia accused of being unkind to an old man. Resigned, Mikhail stopped and waited though he refused to turn around. *Two minutes,* he thought. *Two minutes and I'll send the* dyédushka *on his way.*

He grunted in surprise as an arm came heavily over his shoulder, spinning him around. Rough bristles brushed rudely against his face as his accoster deposited a kiss on each cheek. The smell of cheese and eggs, both a bit soured, washed over Mikhail's face.

"Misha," said the old man, using Mikhail's childhood nickname. "What a delight. I came to Moscow expressly looking for you, and here you are, almost as if God had put you in my path."

Mikhail looked more closely at the old man, wishing he hadn't forgotten his spectacles as he rushed from his house. The old man's bobbing head gradually came into focus. He wore the collar and robes of a priest. Bits of what looked like toast and butter clung to the tangled depths of the old man's beard.

"Well, I'll be damned," said Mikhail, using an expression he'd heard from VIPs around the world as they gazed on Lenin.

"Quite possibly," said the old man. "But let us hope not."

Before Mikhail stood Father Zhivkov, the priest of his childhood village, the man Mikhail's mother and grandmother had seen in secret after the Communist Party closed the church and broke the bells. Father Zhivkov had come to his father's house whenever his father was away on business, spending hours intoning meaningless chants through mists of incense that made young Mikhail dizzy. Mikhail had been afraid of the priest whose piercing eyes seemed to look right into his soul at all the naughty thoughts writhing there like trapped eels. How eager he had been to put away all that nonsense about gods and demons, miracles and eternal damnation for the clear path of the Communist Party.

To use your vernacular, thought Mikhail, *it was not God, but the Devil who put you in my path. Today of all days, I am in such a hurry.*

"Father Zhivkov," he said, not adding the usual pleasantries about how glad he was to see him. Because he wasn't glad. Aside from the importance of Mikhail's meeting, Zhivkov reminded Mikhail of everything he didn't wish to be reminded of, all of which lay behind in his childhood village of Simbirsk. "I'd heard you were dead in the gulag, Father." Well, that was impolite, even for the preeminent mausoleumist. "Glad to see you made it through," he added hastily.

"Now, now, Misha, it's a sin to lie. You never cared about my fate. But that's all right. How have you been? I've heard of your success, such an important man. I take it all is well in the world of preserving corpses?"

"As well as can be expected," said Mikhail. The glory days of the mausoleumists were over. Where Mikhail's predecessors had enjoyed handsome paychecks, unlimited travel, and the latest equipment, Mikhail and his nine assistants had virtually no funding, no secretary, and precious little office space, and that shared with a boorish travel agent and a grubby little insurance broker. Worst of all, Mikhail was almost out of the embalming fluids that kept Lenin looking as fresh and whole as on the day he died. Mikhail had no funds to purchase new chemicals. Thus the stolen diamonds and the meeting with Kerensky.

He sneaked a look at his watch. The seconds were ticking away, grains of sand dropping with the sound of thunder in the hourglass that held his future. It occurred to him that he was probably the only man alive in Russia today who was still afraid of Lenin.

"I really must—"

"I remember when your *babushka* brought you to me in greatest secrecy," the old man babbled on, "so that I could baptize you. Such a little thing, and how you wailed."

Another grain of sand roared down. "Are you in Moscow for long, Father?" Mikhail asked, glancing again at his watch, this time pointedly. "We must arrange to meet. I'll take you to dinner at the French restaurant. You'd like that, eh, Father? You always were one for the table."

"Not anymore," said the priest, glumly. "Not since the gulag. Got an ulcer there. Actually, that was the least of what I got there," he continued in a morose voice. "No, I'm only here for an hour, so I am happy I ran into you. You're the one man who can help me."

Mikhail glanced around the square as if there were someone who could offer escape. That was when he noticed a man watching him and Father Zhivkov. The man stood twenty meters or so away from them on the far side of the line. Dressed in a well-tailored overcoat and sporting immense sunglasses so that Mikhail couldn't see his eyes, his body was nonetheless planted so that he faced sternly toward Mikhail. He stood with a sinister stiffness that made him seem anything but a tourist. Mikhail felt a shiver of unease. Probably it was nothing. Probably, behind the sunglasses, the man wasn't even looking at him.

A shimmer of flames danced in the mirrored sunglasses and then vanished. Mikhail blinked. Nerves and not enough sleep, he thought.

But what if Kerensky *had* sent someone to spy on him? The man might think that Father Zhivkov was a policeman and that Mikhail was setting up Kerensky for a fall. Or the man could be an agent of the treasury looking for the diamond thief. His hand rose to rub the small lump formed by the bag beneath his shirt. He removed his handkerchief and mopped his face. Despite the late winter chill, he was suddenly hot in his coat.

The priest, in contrast, wrapped his buttonless coat more tightly around his thin chest. He leaned forward and whispered in Mikhail's ear, exactly like a policeman offering secret instructions. "I am cold and you are hot, though today's weather is nothing like the extremes you might suffer beyond the grave."

Mikhail couldn't stop a sniff of irritation. "Is that why you've sought me out, Father? You're worried about my immortal soul?"

"Let us just say, Misha, that things aren't quite settled. Your fate and the fate of your client are tied together."

There was something about Zhivkov nagging at Mikhail. Something he'd forgotten and should have remembered. He scratched his head. "Which client?" he asked.

"The only one that matters."

Whatever it was he was supposed to remember now sank like a stone. Mikhail's irritation grew as he ran through a mental list of his patrons. His most recent customers were mob bosses. The famous clients were far away and couldn't affect him. That left Lenin. He mopped his face again. The man with the sunglasses

took a few steps in their direction. "I don't understand," he said. He felt the vein in his forehead throb.

"Lenin is destined for Hell, my dear Misha, as soon
as his body is allowed to decay in the natural way and
he is freed from Limbo."

"Is that what this is all about?" Mikhail was furious.
"You tracked me down to convince me to let Lenin
slide into corruption! How dare you! You risk my life
with such an arrogant idea? Who sent you? Those
sniveling dogs from Congress? Reducing me to pov-
erty didn't work so now they try to employ God
against me?"

People in line glanced their way. Mikhail forced
himself to lower his voice. "You realize the way you
are behaving, you could get me killed?"

A beatific smile. "It would be acceptable, Misha, if
it saved your immortal soul."

"I have no immortal soul!" What he did have was
a mortal soul that was now mortally afraid. He feared,
not the flames of Hell, but an early arrival at the
grave. He glanced back at the sunglassed tourist. The
man was continuing to slowly and, oh so casually,
work his way along the line toward Mikhail and the
priest. "I'm a card-carrying member of the Society for
the Promotion of Atheism, for God's sake!" he
shouted.

"My point exactly."

"I really must go, Father. Look me up at home."
He turned to flee, but the priest's hands snatched
him back.

"No, Misha," said Father Zhivkov. "I'm not long for
this world, but there is one thing I must do before I go."

"Tonight. Whatever you want I'll get you tonight.
But right now I'm horribly late for a very important
meeting."

"I want to look in the eyes of my enemy," the priest
went on, ignoring Mikhail's attempt to escape. "And
you are the one man who can help me. You can see

for yourself that were I to wait in this line, I would collapse before I ever reached Lenin. But you can get me right there, isn't that so, Misha?"

"Please, Father." He was practically weeping. "I'll put you up in my house tonight. I'll give you a private tour. I can even get you inside the laboratory."

"No, no, that won't be necessary." The priest pulled Mikhail toward the front of the line with a strength that was alarming. Perhaps, coincidentally, the man Mikhail was now thinking of as the Agent also began walking faster. Mikhail struggled, but the old priest had superhuman strength.

"You don't understand, Father!"

"What I understand is that you've made many mistakes in your life, Misha. You abandoned your parents, very nearly sold your brother to the KGB. There was that affair early in your marriage, and a whole string thereafter. Isn't that right, Misha?"

"How could you—?"

"It's that 'very nearly' that's got you still teetering on the edge, dear Misha, instead of already condemned. But now you're about to make another mistake. Dealing with the mob." The old man clicked his tongue. "The proverbial fox skin that broke the sled."

Mikhail tried to dig in his heels, failed. The priest jerked him forward a few more feet.

"How can you be so strong?" Mikhail gasped.

"Years of moving mountains," answered Zhivkov.

Of course, the gulag. That which does not kill a man makes him stronger. The gulag probably also gave him connections he didn't have before.

Zhivkov, or whoever employed him, had gone to a great deal of trouble to learn about Mikhail's background. Mikhail racked his brain trying to decide who would have done this. Was Zhivkov a spy for Kerensky, testing Mikhail's loyalty? Certainly the Russian mob had the kind of resources it took to pry into a man's background. Or maybe the priest worked for a delegate of Congress. A few loose lips and an attentive ear could have ferreted out information about Mikhail. And what about agents of the treasury?

The priest yanked on his arm.

"Then we have Lenin," the priest was saying. "Misha, Misha, you must let him go. If ever a man deserved to go to his fate, it is Vladimir. Creating concentration camps, shooting priests, instituting a reign of terror. But he rests peacefully in Limbo because of your work, Misha. Your work. You've upset the entire balance."

The man with the sunglasses elbowed aside a few tourists and bore down on them with the strength and conviction of Russia's famous icebreaker ships. The priest moved faster, dragging Mikhail along until they reached the gaping door at the base of the mausoleum.

"We must hurry," Zhivkov said. "Show your badge to the guard."

Unable to think for himself anymore, Mikhail obeyed. The guard halted the tourists with a raised hand, then saluted Mikhail and waved him and Zhivkov on. Father Zhivkov pulled him into the dark of the tomb. The sunlight winked out. At their feet, the red granite stairs fell into blackness like the gateway to Dante's Hell. Mikhail rubbed at an ache now throbbing in the center of his chest.

"You see, Misha," said Zhivkov, "the worst of it is the irony."

The pain was growing worse. "What irony?" he gasped, stumbling on the steps. He could hardly catch his breath.

"Lenin went after the priests with such viciousness that he asked daily to see the list of the clergymen who had been put to death. He seized church property, outlawed God. But his enthusiasm left a void in the hearts of the people. No saints, no martyrs. No one to worship. So upon Lenin's death, Stalin hatched a brilliant plan. In place of the Orthodox saints preserved under glass in cathedrals across Russia—the incorruptibles—he offered them Lenin."

So Zhivkov was working for himself after all, thought Mikhail triumphantly. This was all about God and he could deal with God.

That still left the Agent.

Mikhail could see the man in the sunglasses silhouetted at the door, arguing with the guard. Mikhail tried to say something, but the pain in his chest made speech impossible. The priest was now literally dragging him down the steps.

"People look at Lenin and they are confused," said the priest. "Worship God or worship Lenin?" He gave a great sigh and patted Mikhail's hand. "But it is you we are talking about right now, Misha. You must make a decision before the Agent reaches us."

Mikhail drew a short, wheezing gasp, well beyond all thought of conversation.

"You're out of shape," said the priest as they raced down the hallway. Walls of gray stone flew past and the cold grew deeper. Their footsteps rang like weapons being forged on anvils, echoing the hammer in Mikhail's chest.

At last a faint glow appeared in the darkness. The lights around Lenin's coffin.

"Here we are," said Zhivkov. "The sarcophagus. Sit. Catch your breath."

Mikhail collapsed in the gloom on the bottom step of the stairs leading up to the lighted glass coffin. To his vast relief, the pain in his chest eased and the roar of his own blood returned to a whisper in his ears. The hush of decades fell back into place. The few tourists creeping past the sarcophagus took one look as Zhivkov approached the coffin, then hurried down the stairs on the other side and out the door. No guard was in sight. The local police had never taken the job as seriously as their Kremlin predecessors.

"So," called Zhivkov from the highest stair. "Decide."

"Decide what?" Mikhail managed at length.

"Why, Lenin's fate, Misha. And your own, of course."

"You're trying to save my soul."

"Yes."

"And to do that, I must let Lenin decay."

"Now you understand."

"You can't expect me to just—" he waved an arm vaguely toward the sarcophagus, "—let him go."

"Why not?"

"I'd be reviled. Loathed. Spit upon. Out of a job." He clutched his chest. Tears of pain and frustration squeezed from his eyes.

"It's your diet," said the old priest. "You really need to eat better. And get some exercise. Don't worry, you aren't going to die today, Misha. But you are fat."

"So what?" said Mikhail, glumly. "The Agent is surely almost here. I'm late for my meeting. I think I *will* die today."

The priest pressed his hands against the glass, staring at the lifelike figure of Lenin. "Beautiful job you've done. A bit waxy, but still, the man looks better in death than he ever did in life." He turned back and sat on the stair next to Mikhail. He seemed abruptly older, as if accomplishing his goal had eroded away the last barrier to old age.

"Don't you have a cousin in America?" Zhivkov asked. "Surely you could get a job there."

"They're having a recession."

"But you would be a hero. Write your memoirs, join a gym, live practically forever. Now, here are your choices. You may give the diamonds to the agent who is even now rushing down the stairs. He will see that they are delivered to Kerensky and that the embalming chemicals are sent to your office. Your worries will be over. You will still have your reputation as the brilliant mausoleumist, and it is a reputation you will take to your grave."

"And my other choice?" asked Mikhail, not really interested. If Father Zhivkov knew about the diamonds and Kerensky, then he must be right about the Agent. Mikhail's worries were over. He wasn't going to die. Not from a heart attack, not from a gun.

The priest patted his shoulder. "You may do what is right." He uncurled Mikhail's fingers and deposited a smooth, glass vial in the embalmer's hand.

"Farewell, Mikhail Vladimirovich Surikov. And good luck."

Mikhail blinked. Father Zhivkov had vanished. The Agent stood before him, breathing heavily, his breath like a dragon's plume in the chill air.

"You're not going to disappoint Mr. Kerensky, are you?" asked the man.

"Of course not." Mikhail glanced at the vial. Within, a tiny green fly hurled itself against the glass walls of its cage. Mikhail recognized *Sarcophaga canaria,* the flesh fly.

He thought about his mother and father, to whom he'd always *meant* to send money. His *babushka,* whose funeral he'd *meant* to attend. He thought about the beautiful women he'd known in the most intimate ways and how that knowledge had made his faithful Lena weep. Mostly, he thought about his brother, dead in a car accident that maybe wasn't an accident only days after Mikhail had nearly turned him in. Mikhail had slept with the wife of a powerful man, and Yuri had threatened to expose him if Mikhail didn't change his ways. Yuri hadn't *meant* it, but Mikhail had still almost turned him over.

All the mistakes a man can make, given a little money, a little power. A huge ego.

Like Lenin behind him. What an ego. Even dead, the man had an ego.

Mikhail looked again at the fly batting its wings desperately against the glass. Suddenly he remembered what he had forgotten about Zhivkov.

Not from Hell, he thought, but from Heaven.

He struggled to his feet.

"Give me a minute," he said to the Agent, "to pay my respects."

He felt the Agent watching him as he staggered up the stairs to the coffin. Within, Lenin slumbered on. The man's wife, his family, his comrades had all gone to their eternal rest or damnation. But Lenin looked as if he could rise and resume control of Russia.

Mikhail leaned closer. A narrow crack ran across the glass where the priest had laid his hands. The nearly invisible rift ran to the corner, where it widened to a few millimeters. A whiff of formaldehyde tainted the air.

Mikhail turned back to the Agent.

"I've changed my mind," he said. "Tell Kerensky I don't need the chemicals."

The Agent frowned. "That would be a serious mistake."

"Quite possibly."

The Agent drew closer. His breath fell over Mikhail with a chill like the wind across Siberia. Mikhail backed against the coffin.

"Mr. Kerensky doesn't like being stood up," said the Agent.

"Send him my apologies. He'll find another customer."

The Agent frowned. There came from him the faintest hint of smoke, an even fainter scent of sulfur. He studied Mikhail for what seemed an eternity before at last he shook his head and stepped away.

"You are but a mortal, susceptible to the corruption of the flesh," he said. "There is always tomorrow." He turned and clattered down the stairs, vanishing just as Zhivkov had before him.

Mikhail shivered in the cold. What curious forces were at work today, he thought. Zhivkov, after all, had been dead three years. The news had been in the last letter he'd received from his mother before her own death. The Agent . . . well, perhaps it was better not to think about him.

He turned back to the cracked glass with a philosophical shrug. Communist or Orthodox. Agents or demons. What did it matter?

Use or be used, it was the way of Mother Russia.

He lifted the vial, heard the beating of the fly's wings as a faint echo from far away places. It was the only sound in the darkness.

He smiled. The fly, at least, was his. Nightmare or salvation, it was his.

BURNING DOWN THE HOUSE

by Adam Stemple

Adam Stemple is an author and musician who lives in Minneapolis with his wife, Betsy, his two children, Alison and David, and a very confused tomcat named Lucy. He spends his days watching the children (and the cat), his nights playing guitar with his Irish band, The Tim Malloys, and the few hours he may once have used for sleep, he now spends writing. Adam Stemple is very tired.

I'M NOT the sharpest guy in the world, but I probably ain't one of the smallest, either. I go maybe six-seven, two-seventy-five, and I can hold a piece of Sheetrock over my head with one hand and drill it into place with the other. Give me a pry bar and a ten-pound sledge, and I can take an entire house down to subfloor and studs in an afternoon. Then me and the team would put it back together the next day.

The team. We were good at what we did. The best, maybe. As a team. Individually, we couldn't have finished a job with a six-month deadline and a copy of *An Idiot's Guide to Home Remodeling*. I mean, I could do demo and Sheetrock, but hand me a roller and a bucket of primer? I've seen five year olds do cleaner work with finger paints.

The other guys were like that, too. Mickey was an ace carpenter—and not bad with a paintbrush, either. But he couldn't hook up an electrical outlet if you attached everything but the ground for him. We left that kind of stuff to Sparks, the electrician. Sparks could change out the outlets, install light fixtures and appliances, rig a house from top to bottom—and do it live, never turning the main power off, so the rest of the team could keep running their power tools. But his wrists were as thin as the wires he worked with, and he wasn't much use when it came to the heavy lifting.

Mother was plenty strong, but too damn lazy to help with anything but the skill that had earned him his nickname. After I hung the Sheetrock, but before we primed, Mother would come through and cover up all the joints with mud. Screwheads, too. Any unevenness, any imperfections, Mother smoothed them over real nice, like butter on a bun. Apparently, there was an art to it, something to do with putting variable pressure on your blade as the mud on your palette knife decreased. Mother had tried to explain it to me once, but my efforts still ended up looking like I'd squashed a sand castle onto the wall. A good mudder could save you hours of sanding time. And Mother must have been a real genius at it, given the amount of time he wasted sitting on the ground flipping playing cards into a hat.

Mudder. Mother. Get it?

Well, I never said any of us were clever, just that we were good at our particular tasks. There were other guys on the team, too, working inside and out, showing up at different stages of the job: Ken the Finisher, Don Lawn, Plumber Paul . . .

And Chief. Chief, with his big black Suburban and his slicked-back hair. Chief, dropping by unannounced, towing some pretty young thing in a tight skirt, leading her around the work site, telling her to watch her step. "Careful, there, darlin'," he'd say, one hand on her arm, the other on her ass. "You don't want to trip in those heels."

Chief was the boss, the money man. And he never let you forget it.

We were working on an old house down the end of Weathersby Lane. A real broke-down nineteenth-century place, all crooked doorways and rotten beams, lath and plaster walls like to crumble away if you breathed on them too hard. In fact, the whole thing looked ready to fall over in a stiff wind. But Chief thought he could rehab it and sell it at a hefty profit, so the team was going in hard and heavy. We were going to do a full retrofit, top to bottom, take it down to studs and then build it back up, turn that old shack into a palace for some rich couple to retire in.

Mickey took one look at the state of things and threw his hands in the air.

"I won't know what we're going to need for lumber till you knock it all down, J.T."

"Okay." I didn't need any more instruction than that, and as Mickey drove away, I headed to the basement to get started.

There was no art to what I did; it was all about swinging hard and not stopping till my arms were falling out of their sockets. I set up a steady rhythm with the sledge, crushing things indiscriminately until the ancient plaster dust got to be too much for even the breather strapped over my mouth to handle. Then I went upstairs to clear my throat with a beer.

"Five hundred to one, Sparks! Five hundred to freaking one!" Mother was sitting on a milk crate brandishing a handful of cards at Sparks, who had his back to him.

"Five hundred what?" I asked as I came up the stairs.

"Five hearts," Mother said, showing me the cards

he was holding. They were, indeed, all hearts. "I dealt myself a pat flush. That's five hundred to one against."

"Wow." I had no idea what he was talking about. "That happen a lot?"

"No, of course not. It's five hundred to . . ." Mother sighed. Flipped one of the cards neatly into an upside hat some ten feet away. "Oh, never mind."

Sparks chuckled without turning from the tangle of wires he had his face stuffed into. "We've seen you pull stranger hands than that out when you needed to."

Snick. The jack of hearts sliced through the air. Right into the hat.

"Yeah. But that's when there's money on the line." Mother pushed himself to his feet. "How's it going down there, Dummy?"

I felt heat in my face. "You know I don't like it when you call me that, Mother."

"All right, all right. How's it going down there, J.T.?" He said the letters of my name real slow and loud.

"Okay, I guess." I pulled a beer out of the cooler and popped it open. Took a long draught, the chill of it scraping the dust off my throat. "Something weird in that center wall, though."

"Weird?" Sparks asked with a quick glance over his shoulder at me. "Weird how?"

I shrugged, but he'd already turned back to his wires. "Dunno. Just weird."

Mother stood and moved to his hat. "I'll check it out, Sparks." He pulled what looked like an entire deck of cards out of his hat before flipping it onto his head. With a quick riffle, he smoothed the cards out, then wrapped a rubber band around them and stuffed them into his back pocket. He glanced at me. "The center wall?"

I nodded. "Yeah. Something . . ."

"Weird. Yeah, you said."

"What are you guys doing here, anyway?" I asked as we trudged downstairs.

"The wiring is so old in this place, Chief wanted

Sparks to get a head start on it. See how much trouble he was in. And me . . ." I could feel Mother shrugging behind me. "I had nothing better to do. Chief said I could hang out."

I knew what that meant. "You owe somebody money again?"

"Just show me this wall."

We stepped carefully over the piles of shattered lumber. The dust wasn't as bad now and I kept my breather off so I could talk.

"See?" I said when we reached the center wall.

Mother peered curiously at it. "No. Looks like a wall. Like they wanted to partition the basement."

"It's newer than all the other work in the house. Can't be more than five or six years old. The rest of the stuff hasn't been touched in decades." I held my hands out, like a fisherman telling a story. "And it's too big. Too thick to be just a partition. It's built around something. To hide it, maybe."

Mother scratched his cheek. It looked like he hadn't shaved in a couple of days.

"Well," he said. "Knock it down. Let's see what it's hiding."

"There's more, though."

"What?"

"Something . . ." Despite the dust, I took a deep breath. "Something weird. I can't explain it."

Mother leaned to one side then the other, looking at either side of the wall. "Looks fine to me. Knock it down. I want to see what's in there."

"I don't want to."

"Come on! Knock it down, Dummy!"

I shook my head.

"J.T. . . ."

"No," I said, folding my arms. "There's something weird."

Mother blew air through his lips like a horse. "Sparks!" he called upstairs. "I'm gonna need you down here."

I could hear tools getting set on the counter, then the light footsteps of Sparks coming down the stairs.

"What's the problem?"

"J.T.," Mother said. "He's getting stubborn. Doesn't want to knock that center wall down."

Sparks came toward us, picking his way gingerly across the debris covered floor.

"Now, J.T. . . ." He spoke soothingly, as if I were a child. Or a large dog. "Why don't you just finish knocking stuff down so we can all go about our business?"

His tone made my ears red, and I found my teeth were clenched. I shook my head, more to relax my jaw than to signal a negative. I didn't want to get angry. I get angry, people tend to get hurt.

"J.T.," Sparks said, oil dripping off each letter. "Let's get back to work, eh?" When I didn't move, he turned to Mother. "Maybe we should call Mickey. He's the one talked Chief into hiring him."

Mother snapped at me. "C'mon, Dummy!"

Then a low, stern voice came from the top of the stairs—a voice that made Mother and Sparks snap to attention like a couple of army recruits.

"Knock it down."

I looked over my workmates' shoulders. "Morning, Chief."

The boss himself stood at the top of the stairs, wearing a shiny black tracksuit with a white racing stripe. He had designer sunglasses perched on top of his head and a toothpick clenched in his teeth. I'd never seen him on the work site so early in a project. And unaccompanied, as well.

"There's something weird about that wall," I told him.

He peered at the wall in question, then shrugged.

"Knock it down, J.T.," he said again. "It's what I pay you for."

Well, I thought. *He's got me there.*

I slipped my breather back on. Hefted my sledge.

"Okay." The word died in my mask, unheard by any-one but me.

I took an easy looping swing at the wall, hoping to maybe catch a stud and knock the whole thing down in one blow. But the sledge nearly jarred out of my hands as it came up against something harder than the plaster or wood I'd been expecting.

"Weird," Sparks said.

"That's what I've been saying." But I didn't think anyone could understand me through my mask.

We peered at the fresh hole I'd made. Another wall was laid behind the first, old red brick, now dented in the middle. I looked back at Chief. He nodded twice—once at me, once at the wall.

Adjusting my grip and lifting the sledge, I coiled like a spring. Arms, hips, shoulders—I wound them all to full extension, then stepped into it and let fly, roaring like a wounded lion. It was an all or nothing shot: either the wall would break or I would break against it. Stinging pain shot up my arms as the sledge landed and I thought my collarbone might shoot out of my neck. But no bones broke and the hammer punched a hole in the wall, bricks crumbling to dust or squirting away like soap squeezed in your hands.

Then a blast of heat shot out, singeing my eyebrows, and sending me scampering backward in a panic.

"What the . . .?" Mother said.

Flames licked out of the hole I'd just made, and the cheap wallpaper blackened and curled away. There was something burning behind the center wall. Some-thing big.

"Look out, boys." Chief was down in the basement with us now, shouldering his way past Mother and Sparks. He had a fire extinguisher in either hand, and he flipped them to the ready position with his thumbs. "Hit it again, J.T."

Well, I would have much rather run out of that basement and called the fire department. But like Chief had already said, it's what he paid me for. And he looked as ready as any fireman to fight whatever was burning behind the wall.

Trying to ignore the heat, I stepped forward and swung my sledge. Chief was right behind me, giving the outer wall short bursts with both extinguishers.

"Again!" he shouted. "Give it another!"

The brick wall gave way easier now that it had a hole in it, and the drywall never had a chance to begin with. I pounded away, ash and debris flying, Chief firing away with the extinguishers, until we couldn't see a thing from the dust and smoke and chemical powder that filled the air.

"Enough," Chief finally said.

I stepped back, arms limp at my sides, the sledge slipping from my grasp and falling to the ground with a loud thunk. My eyes stung. My head hurt. And my arms were too weak to fend Mother off when he ran up and crushed his hat onto my head, pushing it down hard and rubbing it around.

"What are you doing?" I said, finally summoning the strength to push him away. I pulled my breather down and asked again. "What are you doing?"

"Hair was on fire."

I blinked twice, removed the hat, and ran my fingers through my hair. My fingers came away black with soot.

"Oh. Thanks." I handed Mother his hat back and watched as he tried in vain to shape it back to normal.

"What is that?" breathed Sparks. He was standing right in front of the hole in the wall, staring through as the dust settled and normal visibility returned. Mother and I came up on either side of him.

"The lake which burneth with fire and brimstone," Chief intoned from behind us. "Which is the second death."

Whatever that meant.

There seemed to be more room behind the wall than there should have been. A lot more. The hole—now big enough for Mother, Sparks, and me to walk through side by side—opened up into a gaping cavern. There was fire everywhere. It dripped from the ends of giant stalactites, or ran in thin lines across the rock walls and mineral formations. It flowed in rivulets of molten lava, cracking the floor into uneven sections. Oily puddles burst into flames then subsided quickly, only to flare up again seconds later. In the near distance, I could see a dark lake, flames skittering across its glassy surface. I thought I could hear screaming.

"Forward, boys," Chief said.

"No way, Chief," Mother replied. "I ain't going in there for love or money."

Sparks and I both nodded in agreement.

Chief sighed and pulled a glossy black pistol out of his jacket pocket. He poked it into Mother's back.

"Move."

We all took a step forward.

It was still hot once we were inside, but not enough to singe any more of my hair.

"Chief?" I said, turning to look at him. "What are we . . ."

I stopped speaking. The hole was gone. The basement, too. Just more cavern. Flames. Screams.

Chief checked his watch. "Won't be long, boys. Won't be long."

Suddenly, a fat froglike creature leaped out from behind a flaming stalagmite. It was roughly man-sized, with eyes the size of cantaloupes perched on its bulbous head. Where it wasn't marred by open sores or oozing pustules, its hide was the chartreuse of a good walleye lure.

"Jesus!" yelped Sparks.

The frog-creature became mostly mouth as it smiled wide.

"Jesus ain't in it, gentlemen." Unlike the deep croak I would have expected, the frog-creature's voice was kind of high-pitched—but still recognizably male—and used-car-salesman smooth. "Been a while, Levi."

Who's Levi? I thought.

But then Chief gave a curt nod. "Seven years. Same as always."

"What the hell is this, Chief?" hissed Mother.

But it was the frog-creature who answered. "Exactly."

"Exactly?" I looked at Mother. "What does he mean, 'Exactly'?"

Mother pushed his hat brim up with one finger. "Aw, Hell."

"That's right," Chief said. "Now you boys stand over there." He waved his gun toward the thick stalagmite that frog-creature had leaped out from.

I followed orders, stepping over to the stalagmite, my workmates beside me—Sparks shuffling like a zombie, Mother with his eyes darting back and forth looking for escape. No one said a word. We lined up like prisoners waiting to be shot, with Chief and the frog-creature as the firing squad.

"Well, then," the frog-creature said. "I'll get straight to the point." He waved a thin arm at Chief. "Levi here has sold you three to me."

"Why, Chief?" Sparks said, his voice cracking.

Chief wouldn't look Sparks in the eye. "Let's get this over with."

"Why?" Mother asking this time.

Chief shuffled his feet before answering. "Because I saw enough of death in the war to know that I didn't want any part of it."

"What war, Chief?" I asked. "I didn't know you were a soldier."

He looked up at me. "The Civil War."

"The Civil War?"

"That's right," the frog-creature said, bouncing once on thick legs. "The Civil War. The War Between the States. The Late Unpleasantness. Levi here was a full-blown colonel." He swiveled on his thick legs to face Chief. "Had yourself a big horse and a sharp sword, didn't you, Levi?"

Chief didn't answer. But he seemed to stand a little straighter, maybe remembering his days in uniform.

"And you sent more than your fair share of souls to us with that sharp sword of yours, didn't you?" The frog-creature's squat head bobbed crazily with every word he spoke, sending pus and spittle flying.

Chief looked down at his shoes. Nodded once.

The frog-creature turned his attention back to us. "Levi was quite industrious in his quest to avoid death. And he followed a few paths that most would have thought dead ends. But they weren't. They led to the house you were working on, and to the portal you came through." Long teeth in a wide grin again. *I wonder how far he can open that mouth.* "And they led to me."

I saw Sparks' Adam's apple bob as he gave a sort of choking swallow. Mother shifted from one foot to the other. Chief stared at his shoelaces.

Hopping closer, the frog-creature continued. "We came to an agreement, Levi and I. To keep his very tainted soul out of my master's rightful possession, Levi promised to bring me three fresh souls every seven years. A tithe, if you will. Like you'd give to church." The frog-creature spread his spindly arms out wide, before clasping them in mock prayer. "But our church gives true immortality, not some vague promise of an 'afterlife' like our competitor." Another hop and he was right in front of us. He looked us each in the eye. "But I'm a fair man. Least I was when I walked the earth. I'm going to give you gentlemen a sporting chance."

Sparks' head shot up. "A chance?"

"That's right!" In one bound, the frog-creature was back next to Chief, who spared the ugly thing one glance before looking down at his feet again. "A sporting chance. You play a game against me. And if you win, you get the same deal Chief here got."

"And if we lose?" Sparks asked.

"Well," the frog-creature said, indicating our sur-

roundings with a sweep of his hand. I looked out at
the flames and darkness and shivered despite the heat.
"Let's just say, you don't want to lose."

Mother pulled his deck of cards out of his back
pocket. "What kind of game?" He asked.

The frog-creature grinned wide. "Any game you
like, young man."

Mother slipped the rubber band off his cards and
cut them nimbly with one hand.

"High card. One cut, one card, ranked by suit."

"With your deck?" laughed the frog-creature. "I
don't think . . ."

"You said any game!" Sparks cut him off. "Any
game you like."

"Well . . ."

"That's right," Mother said. "And I pick high card.
With my deck."

The frog-creature frowned. "Hoisted on my own petard, eh, Levi?" Chief didn't look up. "Okay. High
card it is. But I pick first."

Mother's face broke into a knowing smile. "No
problem."

I knew why Mother was smiling: he was a wizard
with that deck. It didn't matter who picked first.
Mother could force a deuce into someone else's hand,
just as easily as pass himself an ace. It was in the bag.

"I want to play Mother's game," Sparks spoke up.

"You want to cut a card, too?" asked the frog-
creature.

"No. I want to play Mother's card with him."

The frog-creature stopped and thought while
Mother shuffled. "Oh, what the Hell," he finally said.
"Why not?" Then he turned to me. "You want in on
this, too, big fella?"

I didn't see why not. It was a done deal. Mother
would force a two or a three on this guy, and we'd
all walk out of here. Get drunk for a week.

Mother gave the cards one last riffle and placed
them facedown in his palm.

"J.T.?" Sparks said.

I wasn't the smartest guy in the world. And people could tell. I'd been the target for every stupid bar bet and drunken dare ever invented. I must have lost hundreds of dollars over the years to guys with tattoos that said "Your Name" or "It" or had schnauzers that could drink beer or smoke cigarettes or juggle freaking tennis balls. But if I wasn't smart, I was, at least, experienced. I'd learned that it didn't matter how unlikely the wager seemed—if someone wanted to bet, the money was already theirs.

It was a done deal. And Mother and Sparks were doomed.

I shook my head. "No."

Mother shrugged. "Your funeral." He fanned the cards. Held them out to the frog-creature. "Pick a card. Any card."

The frog-creature hemmed and hawed, poking at one card then another with his long bony fingers.

"Hrmmm. This one. No, that one! No, wait!" He put his finger in his mouth. Chewed on the long nail. "It's so hard to choose."

"Take your time," Mother said, in his element, now, the hustler about to land his mark. "You only get one chance."

"I suppose you're right."

The frog-creature pulled a card from the middle and cupping it in his hands, peeked at an edge. The corners of his mouth drooped into a long frown.

"What is it?" Sparks asked anxiously.

The frog-creature gave an exaggerated sigh. I could smell his breath from where I stood, even over the reek of brimstone: old fish bones and rotten fruit.

"It's not good," he said.

"Well," Mother said, smiling. "It ain't over yet. I still have to pick. I'm sure . . ."

"No," the frog-creature interrupted. "It's not good for you." And he flipped his card over, showing us the ace of spades. "High card. You lose."

"What? How?" Mother sputtered.

"You were expecting something different? Something smaller, perhaps?" The frog-creature's voice was getting louder and lowering in pitch. "You thought you could cheat me?" he bellowed. "Me? Manservant to the Prince of Darkness himself? You are a petty thief and swindler! A two-bit cardsharp with a gambler's soul." The frog-creature smiled. "A soul that I now claim."

Mother turned to flee. I had no idea where he thought he'd run to, but he never got the chance anyway. The frog-creature's mouth opened impossibly wide, his jaw unhinging like a snake's preparing to feed. Then with a lightning fast hop, he leaped into the air, landing mouth first on top of Mother. There was a muffled scream and the frog-creature righted himself. Two worn sneakers poked out of his mouth. Then he gulped once and the shoes were gone.

Sparks squealed and took off. The frog-creature winked one of his big eyes at me, then shot a thick rope of tongue out of his huge mouth. It caught Sparks around the midsection, winding around twice and sticking fast. Sparks dug his heels into the ground and clawed at the tongue, trying to work his hands underneath it, pry himself free. But nothing he did stopped the frog-creature from reeling that long tongue back in. Sparks had time for one strangled scream, before he got popped into the frog-creature's gaping maw.

Gulp. And he was gone, too.

I stood there, blinking rapidly. It had happened so fast. My thoughts scampered around my brain like cockroaches when the lights came on, and random muscles in my arms and legs twitched and flexed as my brain sent conflicting messages to my body to *Run! Fight! Stand still!*

"Looks like you made the right call, big fella," said the frog-creature. He ran his tongue—just the tip—

around his lips. "Don't want to throw your lot in on a game of chance. Too many ways to fix the odds."

I nodded without speaking. Couldn't think of anything to say that would save me.

"Perhaps a game of skill." He looked me up and down. "You good at anything?"

I took a slow breath. Got my body under some sort of control. "Not so's you'd notice."

"Hrmph." He hopped up close. I didn't flinch. Small victory. "Look at those arms." He reached out and pinched me on the bicep. "Huge. Now look at mine." He held up one of his own. It was spindly, weak. Barely more than an inch of gristle on a twig. "Let's arm wrestle. I wouldn't stand a chance."

It certainly looked like he was right. My arms must have been five times the size as his, and I'd arm wrestled before. I was good at it. As big as my arms were, I'd beaten men with bigger. It was all in the wrist. And the heart.

I shook my head. I couldn't get around the fact that he'd suggested it. And if he wanted to play, I figured I couldn't win.

"Well," he said. "How about we wrestle? Greco-Roman or Indian Leg, your choice."

I shook my head.

"Box? Bare-knuckle brawl?"

Still no.

"Weight lift for it? Shot put? Caber toss? C'mon, you're a natural for the caber toss!"

I could lift more weight than a pickup truck could haul; I could fling a shot put farther than most people could throw a baseball. And I probably *was* a natural for the caber toss—whatever that was. But I shook my head after each suggestion. The way I figured it, the only way to win was not to play. The frog-creature was starting to sound frustrated.

"Well, pick something already!" His melon-eyes squinted momentarily. "Or maybe I'll rescind my gen-

erous offer of a sporting chance." He frowned.
"You're mine anyway. Even if Levi hadn't brought
you here."

His? "What do you mean?"

The frog-creature's frown resolved into a sly grin.
"You didn't think you could kill someone and not end
up here did you?"

"What? I never killed . . ."

"Sure you did. In that bar upstate."

I thought I knew the incident he was talking about.
But I hadn't killed anyone, had I? "I only hit him
once. He hit me with a chair. His buddies were trying to . . ."

"He died. You saw him go into convulsions, didn't
you? Or were you too busy running?"

My legs were suddenly wobbly, and I had to sit
down before I collapsed. The ground was hot.

"I . . ."

I'd seen the guy start shaking, but I hadn't known
what it had meant.

"He was twenty-four years old." The frog-creature
let loose with a theatrical sigh. "Kind of young to die,
don't you think?"

I nodded. "Yeah."

He bobbed his head once in response. "So let's end
this charade, J.T. Pick a game and join your friends."

I've killed a man, I thought. *I'm a killer.* It sounded
strange in my mind. I didn't feel like a killer. I didn't
feel like a bad man. But maybe no one did. I looked
at Chief, a backlit silhouette now, his shoulders hunched
and his eyes glued to the ground as he waited for his
every-seven-years ordeal to be over. Maybe the biggest bastards around thought they were just regular
guys struggling to get by in a cold hard world.

Maybe not.

I pushed myself back to my feet. It still didn't make
sense. *Why do I need to play his game?*

"Let me ask you a question," I said to the frog-
creature.

"Why?"

"Exactly," I said.

Chief looked up, his expression hard to read.

"What do you mean, 'exactly?'" said the frog-creature slowly.

"Why? Why should I pick a game?"

"Because . . ." the frog-creature sputtered. "A sporting chance. I'm a gentleman . . ."

"No. That doesn't make any sense." I scratched my head, trying to put it all together. "You said I'm yours because I killed a guy. Okay. I think he had it coming, him and his buddies picking on that poor girl. But if I'm yours already, why pick a game? Why not just take me?"

"Well, if you insist," the frog-creature said. "I thought you'd at least like the opportunity to escape."

"Of course I would."

"Then pick a game."

"No."

Suddenly, the frog-creature leaped in close. He stood on his toes and opened his gigantic mouth right in my face. I thought I could smell Mother's aftershave on his breath. He snapped his jaws inches from my nose.

"Pick a game," he hissed. "Or I eat you now."

I was too terrified to speak. But I was able to shake my head.

"That's it! Your soul is mine!"

I stared at him, not moving. "No," I said as calmly as I could.

He snapped his jaws, he roared, he leaped back and forth in front of me raging.

"No," I said again. The more he fumed, the more certain I became. "You won't eat me. You won't claim my soul. You won't even keep me from walking out of here." I raised an eyebrow at him. "Will you?"

The frog-creature came to a stop. He seemed much smaller all of a sudden. Breathing a deep sigh he said, "No."

"Chief didn't give Mother and Sparks to you, did he?

He just brought them here. They gave themselves. Win and they get to live forever, lose and you eat their souls. You tricked them into gambling their souls away."

The frog-creature grinned. "You're smarter than you look."

"No, I don't think I'm smart at all," I said, shaking my head. "But I *am* walking out of here."

"Well, you're right," the frog-creature said. "I can't stop you from leaving." I liked the sound of that. But before I could turn and go, he added, "But he can."

And the frog-creature pointed at Chief. Who was aiming his little pistol right at my head.

"Sorry, J.T." Chief said. "But I can't let you go." He raised his shoulders once and dropped them hard.

A century's worth of bad deeds weighing down that shrug, I thought. *And more to come.*

"Makes no difference, anyway," Chief went on. "Play his game or get shot dead. If you die in this place, you're his anyway."

Suddenly, I was angry. Like flipping a switch. I'd just been scared before. Scared and without hope. But now, to *know* that I was getting out alive, and then to have that snatched away . . .

It made me want to hurt someone.

"Chief, don't do this." My voice was perfectly calm, not giving a hint of the killing rage I was feeling. "We can both—"

And in the middle of that sentence, I threw myself at him.

Every bar I ever drank in, there was someone who wanted a shot at the biggest guy there. Which was usually me. I'd learned that if you could attack in the middle of a sentence, without letting your voice change at all, it usually gave you that little edge that allowed you to get the first shot in.

And as everyone here now knew, I only had to hit a guy once.

Chief managed to get a bullet off, but he flinched as he fired and he pulled his shot, knocking my earlobe off and deafening me, but not doing much else. My left hook was a much better blow, and knocked Chief flying. I jumped on him and wrested the gun away, flinging it as far as I could. Then I set about pummeling his face in. But I only hit him twice more before catching a glimpse of the frog-creature out of the corner of my eye. He was positively beaming, watching me take Chief apart.

And suddenly, I knew: if I killed Chief, I wasn't getting out of here. It was like the frog-creature said: you can't expect to kill someone and not end up here. It wasn't like upstate, where I was fighting first for an abused girl, and then for my life. Chief was down; he was out. If I killed him now, it'd just be because I could.

"Chief," I whispered in his ear. "Chief!" Louder now and shaking him. "C'mon, Chief. Let's go."

Chief was a bad man. Maybe the worst I'd ever known. But nobody deserved this. Certainly not Mother and Sparks. And not Chief, either.

"C'mon, Chief. Let's get out of here."

Chief's eyes cleared and he looked up at me. Saw his own blood spattered on my face. With a surge of panicked strength, he threw me off of him.

"Chief!" I grabbed for him, snagging a jacket sleeve, but he shrugged it off in my hands and rolled away. He pushed himself to hands and knees, scuttling off backward.

"Chief, look out!"

But he didn't look out. Maybe he wanted to keep his eyes on me while he got himself a safe distance away, look for his gun or a sword or something. But a person should watch where they're going in a place with a lot of open flames around.

Chief banged into the fiery stalagmite, and a small flame jumped from it to his pant leg. He looked down. Patted at it. Then slapped at it furiously when it continued to burn. It seemed to dance away from his hand, jumping to his other leg and shooting up it, tracing the white racing stripe in orange and red. Chief dropped and rolled, trying to strip his flaming sweatpants off at the same time. It did no good, just seemed to attract more flames' attention. They burst from the ground and shot down stalactites, swarming over him, engulfing his body in fire. He screamed as he burned, but his vocal cords soon melted away and his cries were replaced by the sizzle of molten nylon dripping to the ground.

I turned to the frog-creature. He was smiling contentedly.

"Three is what I came for," he said. "Three is what I received." He winked at me. "But perhaps I'll see you again, J.T."

"I don't think so."

He shrugged. "Well, when time has hunched those big shoulders and old age has stolen your strength, you know where to find me." He glanced at the charred skeleton that used to be Chief. "And it seems I'm in need of a new agent."

I shook my head. Looked over my shoulder. I could see the basement again. I turned and walked to it without looking back.

"You know where to find me," the frog-creature called after me.

I stepped back into the basement.

Standing for a moment, I let the cool air wash over me. But not for long. I had a wall to build.

A quick trip to the lumberyard and I had supplies: two by fours, Sheetrock, fireplace bricks. I plugged in the table saw, hooked up the compressor and pneumatic drill, mixed up some cement. The bricks took the longest, but once I had them in place, a rough framing job, a professional drywall hang, and a couple of sloppy coats of paint took care of the rest, and the wall was rebuilt. It wasn't pretty. It *really* wasn't pretty. But it was done. And all before Mickey returned that evening.

"Where's Mother?" he said. "I figured he'd still be hanging around." He frowned at my bloody ear. "And what happened to your ear?"

"Mother said he had to leave town. Owed some-one money."

"And the ear?" Pointing.

"Caught it on a nail. Think the lobe's still around here somewhere."

"Ouch," Mickey said, shuddering. He took stock of the main floor. "Doesn't look like you did much demo."

"Had to fix something in the basement first."

"Show me."

We walked down the stairs. Inspecting my handi-work, I said, "Not the best paint job, but Chief wanted it done first."

Mickey stared at the new wall, eyeing it up and down and side to side. Then he shrugged. "Wonder why he wanted that done first."

"Don't know." I tapped Mickey on the shoulder, getting his attention off the wall. "Another thing, Mickey. Chief is starting another crew. Out of town. He's moving."

"Oh?"

"Yeah, and he, um . . ." I waved Chief's company checkbook at Mickey. It had been in his jacket pocket. "He left me in charge."

"You?"

"Yeah." I dangled the Suburban's keys in front of him. Also from the jacket pocket. "Even gave me a company car."

Mickey stared at me hard for what felt like a min-ute. Then shrugged. "All right. What do you want to do now?"

I gave an inward sigh of relief. "Well, with Mother and Sparks gone . . ."

"What happened to Sparks?"

"Oh." *Yeah, what did happen to Sparks?* "Chief had to let him go."

"Why?"

"I don't know. I was out getting lunch when it happened. And you know Chief. I wasn't going to ask any questions."

"Yeah, I guess."

I put my arm around Mickey's shoulders. Started walking him up the stairs. "So with the team short-handed now, we're going to forget about this house. It'd take too long. We're going to find something smaller. Something we can turn around quicker."

"Makes sense," Mickey said, shooting one last look over his shoulder at the new basement wall. "But what about this place?"

"I'm going to move in. Work on it in my spare time. Keep an eye on it." *Make sure no one ever gets through that wall.* We reached the main floor and I propelled Mickey toward the door. "No profit in it for the full team, though."

"All right." Mickey stopped at the front door. Looked at me one more time. "Chief put you in charge?"

I looked him in the eye. Nodded once.

"I think it's a good choice, J.T." He smiled at me. "I always knew you weren't as dumb as everyone thought. I didn't think Chief had noticed, though. And . . ." He paused.

"Yeah?"

"And you're a good man, J.T. Honest, hard-working, trustworthy."

"Well," I said, thinking about the whoppers I had just fed him about Mother and Sparks. Chief, too. "As honest as the next guy, I guess."

Mickey shrugged. "We carpenters have a sense about these things. You're a good man. A good choice to watch over this house."

"Thanks, Mickey," I said, but he was already out the door and gone, and I was left alone in my new home. I thought I could hear screams drifting up from the basement, and maybe the crackling of an eternal fire.

DEVIL IN THE DETAILS

by Daniel M. Hoyt

When not working as a rocket scientist, Daniel M. Hoyt writes fiction, poetry, and music. His short stories have sold to markets as diverse as *Analog Science Fiction & Fact* and *Dreams of Decadence*. He currently lives in Colorado Springs, Colorado, with his wife, author Sarah A. Hoyt, two rambunctious boys, and a pride of cats. Catch up with him at www.danielmhoyt.com.

"WILL YOU be leaving Hell on business or pleasure?"

The One Who Causes Migraines scratched her spiky head carefully with a reddened, callused talon and stared blankly at the border guard, who waited patiently for an answer as if he had all the time in the world—which he did.

Not far away, the ground ripped loudly and erupted a bleachy, sulfurous cloud, strong enough to cause the guard's eyes to water and choke The One Who Causes Migraines.

Apparently bored after only a few seconds of silence from his customer, the guard dropped his gaze and scribbled furiously on a yellow pad to the side of the visa applications. The guard (definitely humanoid and evidently a he, given his male-pattern-baldness shiny dome and chunky knuckles sporting tiny, curved black hair—oh, and his name tag read Dick) wore a bright red jumper (as did all the border guards) that should have made him stand out, but somehow failed. Diminutive in both height and girth (and not just in comparison to The One Who Causes Migraines, whose enormous bulk beside the guard resembled nothing less than a huge, carnivorous beast regarding its prey), Dick the guard faded farther away into inconsequentiality with each passing moment.

The One Who Causes Migraines twitched her bony tail and, with visible effort, cocked her massive head slightly on what little neck she possessed to see how the others she knew were faring. As far as all twelve of her strategically-located eyes could see, there was no more progress anywhere else.

No walls or doors here, just a long line of glass booths in open space, stretching to infinity in either direction, each one manned by a standing, red-jumpered minor bureaucrat of that strange no-demon's land between Hell and the living, and the legions of Hell queued up in neat little rows to one side of the booths. Demons and devils, humans and animals—cats, of course, since everyone knew all dogs go to Heaven, and cats wanted no part of that if dogs were there—they all waited nervously, shuffling from one supporting appendage to another, what passed for heads swiveling impatiently, each hoping for a short interview with a border guard before being allowed to pass.

Except that nobody seemed to be going anywhere.

The One Who Causes Migraines watched for a minute, pointedly ignoring the border guard ignoring her. Every few seconds, a candidate at a booth would turn back, shaking its head or stamping its feet, and disappear into the crowd. The other side of the border booths—the land of the living—remained empty, all the way to the shore of the great river dividing Hell from the living.

(Hope, that is—the *real* river, not the Styx, which is only a child's fantasy version of the Hope.)

It had all seemed so easy that morning, when the Big Bad had gathered them all to announce that it was time for Armageddon. The End of the World, he'd said, as the first of the hell-suns peeked red over the horizon and bathed the Big Bad in purple hell-light. The legions of Hell would ride to victory today, before the dark green hell-sun set!

They'd worked themselves up to a murderous frenzy, but their maddened, red-eyed rush to the border had been stopped dead by the endless line of grim-faced border guards in glass booths.

"Business," The One Who Causes Migraines said meekly, looking away from the guard. She wondered if she'd *ever* get to Armageddon at this pace.

A few booths away, The One Who Causes Migraines spied someone she knew, Henry the Masturbator, who'd enticed by his example many a teenager here to Hell. Henry was humanoid, naturally, being one of the humans' personal demons, and he could have passed for someone's favorite uncle on pretty much any street among the living. But here, he showed his true colors without shame. A permanent leer decorated his pale face, drawing your notice away from his pale gray eyes flitting this way and that like a madman. At odd moments, in the middle of a sentence, for no apparent reason, he'd reach down and grab himself, grinning wickedly, all without missing a breath. Humans thought of him as rather creepy; The One Who Causes Migraines found him sweet and charming.

The border guard handling Henry looked calm, nodding sagely without speaking, but Henry was going purple trying to explain his case sufficiently to get past the bureaucrat and join the ultimate battle.

The One Who Causes Migraines tilted one of her ears in Henry's direction so she could eavesdrop.

"Well, yeah, I *guess* somebody among the living

could do what I do there," Henry said slowly, carefully. "But there ain't been any volunteers, so I'm it. Just let me pass, okay?"

Henry's guard shook his head.

"Article 19, section 3, paragraph 12 of the Living Law states quite clearly—" the bureaucrat shrilled defiantly.

Henry stamped his foot and his face colored scarlet. "I don't give a rat's rectum on Dante's balls what the Law says!" He grabbed himself and grinned.

"—that all Hell entities entering for business," the guard droned on without paying any attention to Henry, "must have written proof—in triplicate—of the necessity of their visit. If you can show that no living being can do your job, we'll let you in."

A heated debate ensued for a couple of minutes, during which Henry got so worked up he turned deep purple. Finally, the guard said something that seemed to settle the matter and Henry deflated visibly. Sagging against the booth, defeated, Henry moaned something unintelligible at a distance, even with The One Who Causes Migraines' sharp hearing, but the guard still shook his head. "Next," the guard shouted brightly, looking past an embarrassed Henry, who turned to slink back into the crowd.

Dick the guard cleared his throat. The One Who Causes Migraines turned all of her eyes to him quickly. Dick produced heavy black glasses from somewhere below the countertop in his booth and twirled them in his hand.

"Did you say business?" he asked tartly.

"Pleasure," The One Who Causes Migraines said in a growl.

"Ah, good," the guard said, nodding, and looked down, placing the glasses carefully on his counter. "There seems to be some business convention or something today; I'm glad you're not one of *them*. Businesspeop—"

He glanced up at The One Who Causes Migraines.

"Business *entities* take so long to process, sometimes we deny them just so we can get lunch." Dick glanced at his watch, stifled a single, nervous laugh, and looked up again.

Great. Just great. It was almost lunchtime. The One Who Causes Migraines felt her hopes evaporate for making Armageddon while the good battles were still going on. She'd heard that a favorite stunt of the border guards was to take lunch mid-interview, leaving you to stew in your anger, unable to leave for fear of losing your place in line, even to get your *own* lunch. Nothing to do except wait an hour or two for the petty, heartless bureaucrat to return.

"Do you think this will take much longer?" The One Who Causes Migraines asked politely through clenched teeth. "My friends will be expecting me soon."

"No problem," Dick the guard said, scribbling something on her forms. "No problem at all." He pointed vaguely behind her without looking up, waggling his outstretched finger. "There's a pay phone back there." He looked up and smiled, propping up a sign against the glass in front of her, then Dick disappeared in a wisp of smoke and sulfur.

Out to Lunch.

The One Who Causes Migraines stared for a moment, stunned, then turned around. Scanning for phones, she found one easily—just one, currently in use by a skinny guy with a flaming red afro—far away, past hundreds of other warriors itching for Armageddon. She slumped to the ground, leaning against the glass booth for support, and prepared to wait for a long, long time.

She daydreamed. Bloody daydream fantasies. Fantasies about her talons embedded deep in Dick's head. It would only take a moment, and then she could just pass, unnoticed. Hell, the people in line behind her would thank her.

Who were these stupid bureaucrats, anyway? They weren't Living, and they weren't even proper denizens of Hell. They just *were,* somewhere in between the two realms. And it's not like they actually *did* anything, either. The One Who Causes Migraines snorted. These bureaucrats from nowhere, these in-betweeners, didn't deserve even a moment of respect. Who did they think they were to deny warriors of the legions of Hell entrance to Armageddon?

She'd kill Dick the guard. That's all there was to it, The One Who Causes Migraines decided. Hope he liked his damned lunch, 'cause it'd be his last meal. She'd see to it—the moment he returned from lunch. Meanwhile, she fumed.

After what seemed like only a few minutes, The One Who Causes Migraines noticed another old friend step up to a booth recently vacated by a short demon retreating into the crowd, its long tail (probably twice its height!) draped over a bobbing arm.

Actually, she *smelled* her friend first. Tiny the Runner was one of those rare dragons that didn't like to smell like a dragon. For some reason known only to him—or her, The One Who Causes Migraines wasn't actually sure of Tiny's gender, or even what genders dragons *had*—Tiny liked the smell of bacon grease. Every morning, Tiny would dull his magnificent, iridescent green scales with bacon grease, until he could no longer smell himself. With a standing shoulder-height of nearly twenty feet, Tiny needed a *lot* of bacon grease. So, most of the time, Tiny smelled like breakfast walking. Or flying breakfast.

The One Who Causes Migraines was getting angrier and hungrier the longer she waited, and Tiny wasn't helping. She decided to watch and listen in on him, just out of spite.

"—business or pleasure?" a tall, blonde woman in a red jumpsuit asked Tiny. She smiled broadly, as if she were Tiny's best friend. Her name tag read Chipper. It suited her.

"Both," Tiny said without a moment's hesitation.

Oh, Hell, thought The One Who Causes Migraines. *Here we go again.*

The border guard, Chipper, raised an eyebrow and licked her lips. "Oh?"

"Yeah," Tiny said through a half smile that looked particularly demonic with his wide maw and jagged rows of sharp, crooked teeth. "It's my *business* to eat humans, and a real *pleasure,* too."

"We'll just say pleasure, then," Chipper said brightly and handed Tiny a stack of papers through a small slot in the glass. "Just fill out your complete itinerary—in detail, say to the nearest one-hour increments is fine, nothing too restrictive—and include contact information for each human day." The guard passed over another stack of papers. "And we'll need to know everything you're taking over there, along with receipts for anything valued more than one U.S. dollar." She passed through yet *another* stack. "Oh, yes, and we'll need to know the names and addresses of all of the humans you plan to eat." Chipper smiled benevolently. "So we can identify next of kin, of course."

The One Who Causes Migraines was pissed. She had told Dick the guard *she* was here on pleasure, too, and now he'd expect her to fill out all those forms after he got back. He could've at least had the decency to leave her the forms to fill out while he was at lunch.

Dead. Dead as a bureaucrat's heart, that's what he'd be. *You're mine, Dick. Soon as you come back, you little bureaucratic bastard, I'm going to lunch on your head!*

Evidently, Tiny shared her opinion, despite Chipper's cheery countenance. Tiny's black eyes narrowed and his nostrils flared and belched smoke. His wings unfolded slightly, knocking over at least half a dozen demons in the line behind Tiny and to either side. The One Who Causes Migraines saw it coming and scooted away just in time to avoid a massive bacon smear to her head spikes.

Tiny's head jerked back like he was about to hawk up a wad of phlegm, and he spit out a tongue of flame through wide open jaws. The blonde border guard disintegrated into a pile of ashes, and Tiny flailed his mighty wings, trying to take flight.

Instantly, the space around Tiny was crammed with palm-sized baby-blue devils armed with miniature spears attached to long cords. They attacked *en masse,* like Lilliputans capturing Gulliver, until Tiny was so wrapped up, he fell with a ground-shuddering thump, his head landing just inches from The One Who Causes Migraines.

"Oh, hi," Tiny said, seemingly oblivious to both his plight and the bacon grease he'd just splattered on The One Who Causes Migraines. "Didn't see you there, Migraines. You trying to get to Armageddon, too?"

The blue devils dragged Tiny away just then, before The One Who Causes Migraines could answer. The crowd parted for Tiny's passing, an open space moving among the sea of heads like a negative Tiny-shaped ship, sailing away rapidly. In its wake, heads tottered uncertainly as hell-beasts and demons tried to regain their places in line, only to find the ground slicked with bacon grease.

"You wouldn't have any agricultural products with you, would you?" The muffled voice came from above, and The One Who Causes Migraines looked up to see Dick the guard's face pressed against the glass. She scrambled to stand, which took some effort with her bulk.

You don't know how lucky you are, Dick. If it hadn't been for Tiny, you'd be dead now. But then, there'd also be a The-One-Who-Causes-Migraines-shaped negative ship sailing that sea of warriors' heads back there. Dickie-boy, you just won the lottery of life for today.

"No," she said aloud, between heaving breaths. "But don't you usually ask that coming *into* Hell?"

The guard grinned. "Yeah, but I didn't get any veg-
gies for lunch. Hoping you had some on you."

"Sorry."

"It's okay. I won't hold it against your process.
Now, where were we?" Dick squinted quizzically, as
if seeing The One Who Causes Migraines for the
first time.

The One Who Causes Migraines paused. Did Dick
really not remember? Perhaps, just perhaps, she could
speed up this process a little. She took a deep breath.
Despite being a hell beast, lying didn't come easily
to her.

"Pleasure trip," she blurted out. "Quick out-and-
back thing, you said there was minimal paperwork?
Just a declaration of belongings, I believe? Which I
don't have, as you can plainly see." She lifted every
appendage she had to show Dick she had no baggage.
Flippers, legs one after the other, tails, talon arms,
vestigial wings—everything.

Dick narrowed his eyes at her at first, but seemed
to accept her word finally. He shrugged and punched
a button on the counter.

Bing. Bing. Bing. Bi—

"You're overweight," Dick the guard said flatly.
"You and your luggage can only be four hundred
pounds combined. You're four-oh-seven."

—ng. Bing. Bing. Bi—

"Are all those talons *strictly* necessary for a *pleasure* trip?"

—ing. B—

The One Who Causes Migraines stared, dumb-
founded.

"I mean," Dick asked, "can you maybe *remove* a
few? Probably save a few pounds that way."

—g. Bing. Bin—

Each chime of the overweight bell pounded in The
One Who Causes Migraines' head, like a countdown
to insanity.

"What about those vestigial wings there?" Dick asked,

oblivious to the rising fury in the creature before him.
"Are they removable? No? Can we just cut them off?"

—*Bing. Bing. B*—

"No? Nothing?"

The One Who Causes Migraines glared at Dick.
"*Nothing's* removable. They're all attached. Sorry."

Dick the guard rubbed at his temples and squeezed
his eyes shut in pain.

—*Bing. Bing. B*—

"Perhaps," he said, massaging his temples frantically, "we can overlook it just this once." He punched
a button.

—*ng. Bing.*

The cursed bell silenced.

"Sorry," Dick said. "I seem to be having a migraine
or something." He stamped a form and handed it to
The One Who Causes Migraines.

She shrugged and snagged the form before Dick the
guard could change his mind. "That's me," she said
sheepishly. "If you spend too much time around me,
that's what happens. It goes away in a few minutes.
Sorry. Nothing I can do about it. Have a nice day."

"Yeah," Dick said, "you, too." He rubbed at his
temples. "Next," he announced, tentatively, and The
One Who Causes Migraines moved aside for a yellow
demon with pink teeth, its eyes squinting nearly closed
in obvious migraine pain. The demon glared at her as
she stepped away.

"Sorry," she repeated to the demon. "It's what I
do. Can't control it. Sorry." The One Who Causes
Migraines hurried away to the Hope River and, across
it, Armageddon.

Armageddon seemed a bit empty to The One Who
Causes Migraines. She'd expected, you know, a battle
or something. As near as she could tell, she was the
only one there. She didn't even see any of the Living.
Looking around frantically, The One Who Causes Migraines wondered if she was in the right place.

But, then, would Armageddon even *have* a specific place? Shouldn't it be *everywhere?* Or was it a by-invitation-only thing? Her head spun. She found a large rock and sat down to think. *If I were the Big Bad, where would I have Armageddon? Think! Think!*

"So it's just you, then?"

The One Who Causes Migraines looked up, startled by a familiar voice. Gravelly, dead serious, not a hint of humor in that voice. The smell of sulfur carried by the sound of fire crackling in that voice. A voice that could only belong to the Big Bad.

"Sir?" she said and leaped to her feet. All of her eyes swiveled to face the Big Bad.

He looked hungover.

Big, bad, red. With a little pair of horns on his fore-head and a pointy tail, just like the Living expected. No doubt for their benefit, too, just for Armageddon. The One Who Causes Migraines had seen the Big Bad on several occasions, and he looked different every time. A natural shape changer, he was a master at The Right Look for any occasion.

She was sure there was a good reason for his des-perate, pinched expression. There always was.

"Reporting for Armageddon, sir!" She snapped off a smart, six-taloned salute.

"Uh-huh," he said, squinting a little. "Only I've been waiting right here for some time now, and it's just you. Where are my legions?"

"At the border, sir!" The One Who Causes Mi-graines shouted. "Coming soon, I'm sure, sir, to bring you glory at the ultimate battle, sir!"

"Damnation," the Big Bad said, cringing. "Could you keep it down? You're giving me a migraine. Jeez!" He rubbed his temples.

The One Who Causes Migraines gulped. Whoops. Just how long *had* the Big Bad been waiting for her to notice him?

"At the border, you say?"

The One Who Causes Migraines nodded slowly.

"Damned bureaucrats," the Big Bad muttered. "Should never have let them in." He glanced up at the sky, where the azure sun shone high in the sky. The red sun was already gone. "Damn," he said. "It's too late now for a decent Armageddon. We'll have to reschedule." He wandered away, slowly, painfully.

The One Who Causes Migraines stared after the Big Bad, shrugged, and went home, confident she'd catch the *next* Armageddon.

ENTER ALL ABANDON, YE WHO HOPE HERE

by David Bischoff

David Bischoff was born in 1951 a graduated from the University of Maryland in 1973 and worked for NBC Washington until 1980 when he shifted to a full-time career in freelance writing. Since then he has written or edited dozens of novels, anthologies, and nonfiction books, as well as worked on many TV scripts, including two for *Star Trek: The Next Generation*. His favorite mystery writers are John D. MacDonald, Janet Evanovich, Lawrence Block, and Donald Westlake. His recent novels include *Philip K. Dick High*, and *H.P. Lovecraft Institute*. The second most amount of fun he's had writing, though, was in his recently ended stint as a writer for *Rampage*, a professional wrestling magazine.

HELL?
Been there, done that.

You think I speak in metaphor? Not surprising. We of the Middle Dimensions are known for our languages rife with tropes. No, I speak most literally. I have set foot on at least a few of the many layers of Hades, have supped with the Devil himself, and all

for a woman. And in truth, I know why the sages of
the aeons say Love is Hell.

Wormtoes! Get that dictagem out of your nose before you get more snot on it, or I shall skewer your
guts! See Sharptongue, here, my sword? No metaphor
will pierce your tripes.

Roll out the vellum, uncork the inkpot, commence
to quill-scribble. I, Vincemole Whiteviper, feel a mem-
oir coming on.

You say, "love," Lord Whiteviper. You must have
been a youth then, to have felt the touch of love and
gone to Hell for it. But not so. Should have known
better. I was dead center in my prime when I met
Chanandra of the Stardust. I had dipped my quill in
the distaff pool more than many times. Should have
known far better. But, as the poets say, "Love is like
the Bitch of Levantathor. Turn your back to it and it
will bite you in the ass."

A moment, Wormtoes. Is the door closed and se-
cure? Set about the Silent Spell. It is best that the
Lady of the Citadel not get wind of these musings. I
have suffered enough for this particular love, believe
me.

Oh, sparkle and thrill! Lovely enchantment. It even
pricks up this villain's heart to see such crystalline
designs in the air and to smell the pepperment of its
musics. There you are. Ah, and let me decant a little
more claret to set my brain abuzz and let Memory
bray!

Aye. I believe I was forty and five years of age
when I met Chanandra. I had long abandoned these
climes and found a faerie portal into the Upper Layers. My larceny and grift had put a price on my head
in many mortal kingdoms, and I felt much safer for a
time in lands of the High Folk, boring farts that they
tend to be. With my manly build, my way with a
sword, my sharp mind, my military skill, and my facility not just with languages but in the way they can

trill and flatter and maneuver, they would welcome me. I found a nice island in the sky by the name of P'Nartha, and in very short order worked my way up into the echelons of its military forces. Pomp and circumstance: these were the main purposes of this particular army, with some security as well, I suppose, though I never saw action there. I was good at the march, and the presentation of arms, and looked manly and handsome in bangles and epaulets and filigree. Medals sparkled nicely on my broad chest, and the feathers on my cap of rank matched my blue eyes particularly well. It was a pleasant enough duty, and I made a good deal of gold coins in teaching the rank and file the sting of a good dicer and cards man.

My reputation as a gambler spread through the island quickly enough, and as the High Folk get as bored as anyone, and they'd been smart and lucky enough not to have any invasions for almost a century, betting and racing and many games of chance and sport were popular. A fox in the henhouse? Perhaps. Although those people loved me for the rogue I was with a dice cup.

Ah, I remember the day well when Chanandra first breezed into my life. Or should I say night, for all the suns had set and the Moons of Mithir silvered the clouds upon which the High Island sat like a ship on a peaceful sea. I was high upon a gaming cupola, with the mild breezes blowing wafts of jasmine and archangel's breath from the gardens below. There had been a banquet that night in the High Halls, and we had marched a bit and fired our muskets to beat the band, and it was all a grand success with much applause from the visitors from some exotic realm. A celebration was in order, and so the troops were sent remnants of the feast and kegs of good brew, which is more or less like eating scraps and drips from beneath tables of the gods.

The evening had settled in its trappings. Melodies squeezed from arabesque windows, flavors ancient hung in drapes of mist around the casual mirthmakers. A cup or two of willowslip wine north of sobriety, I'd been dragged in for a game of Slap Deal Cards with a group of visiting nobles from even more exotic climes. Their cards were filigreed with gold and pearl, and each individual face and number upon them looked hand painted. I thought I smelled magic in them and liked it not playing with them in ignorance. However, I liked the jangle of the nobles' purses, and also thought these cards might be worth examining more intimately.

"So Whiteviper," said Lord Soth at my elbow as he sucked on an ivory pipette and blew smoke toward the pot. "Have you got your Upper Design Quadrant?" We were the last two in the hand, and he'd just called my bluff with a hundred. I took my two face-down cards and examined them thoughtfully, wondering if I'd missed some elegance of strategy. I needed a King Divine or a King Opaque. I had a Queen Majestic and a Jester Mild.

"Please forgive me, sir, but your rundown of the rules. Did you mention that Jesters might add luster to Court Cards?"

He frowned at me and lifted an eyebrow. "You mean are they wild? I did no such thing, and my fellows will bear witness."

I shrugged. No great loss. But just as I was about to fold, the Queen—an elegant tart with the tops of her breasts exposed—seemed to wink at me. I blinked with surprise and suddenly the Queen was a King— and of the Opaque sort, just as I needed.

I laid down the hand in the order needed for a win. "Then this will have to do."

Lord Soth grinned, showing teeth a bit sharper than they had to be for human repasts. "Most amusing. And you say you have never played this version of the Royal Slap?"

"That is true."

"It looks as though Colonel Princetip and General

Matchskin were correct. They do have a gamer of note in their midst."

I nodded politely as I dragged in my new coins. "Both men give as good as they get in the pits."

"Ah, but I sense something special about you. My daughter will be pleased."

"Daughter, milord?"

He blew a burst of opalescent smoke toward door. "Yes. Princess Chanandra. She enjoys a game of cards from time to time, and if the play in the Lesser Hall tonight leaves her unsatisfied for the nights' quota of entertainment, she may join us."

I finished piling up my loot. "A gambling maiden? There are lands where such is unheard of and shocking."

"Ah, but I assure you, Sergeant at Arms Whiteviper. My daughter is no maiden." His jade eyes glinted with mischief and he happily attended to the next hand.

I lost two straight, but for little cost in actual coinage.

"These cards, Lord Soth. They are most remarkable. May I request their provenance?"

"There is a whole chapter of the artisan's guild in the Southern City of Murr on my continent that specializes in creating them."

"Ah. I thought these looked hand painted."

"Indeed." He looked quite jolly, for he himself had just won the hands I'd lost and his piles of coin were high.

"May I ask where I may purchase such a set as this?"

"You may, sir, but it will be useless. They must be specially ordered. My father delighted in them and ordered many. Thus I carry a set with me. I still trust you find them satisfactory for our play."

"They are sufficient for play, but it is their design I admire."

"Oh?" He stroked his graying mustache thoughtfully. "Then if I propose that this deck itself be a part of the winner's spoils tonight, you will play with your full abilities?"

I was caught a bit off guard. The man had discerned that I wasn't taking too much note of the cards of all the four players, which I often do. In truth, the wine had mellowed me much and I'd lost some of the savagery of my play.

"Well, sir, are you saying that if I take home much of the money we see here on the table, I will also win this set of cards?"

"It will be a gift of respect in such circumstances."

"I humbly accept your challenge. I did not want to see our city's guest go home wearing rain barrels."

Lord Soth and the other men barked with joy to hear this, and I saw the glints of sharp teeth in the other gamblers' mouths as well as they bent to the game.

I pushed away my wineglass and took a smoke of rush-weed and commenced to play with seriousness and diligence.

I had just won three hands in a row when there was a stirring. Velvet draperies at the doorway shifted. A whisper of incense insinuated into the room, followed by a sweep of torchlight, casting a shadow before it and catching up faceted gleams in jewelry. Thus attracted, I lifted my eyes fully and saw, like some vision descending down a stairway to the stars, a woman. Nor was I the only one to notice the entrance. All heads turned.

"Ah," said Soth. "Chanandra. You've come!"

The woman walked light as a dancer only tenuously affected by gravity. Veils shivered and rich clothes whispered along the floor. She carried her bosom high and dignified, but her eyes were soft and mysterious as chants echoing in an ancient priory. Her hair was long with tendrils hanging over her cape: auburn hair catching highlights from the torchlight. Her eyes were chestnut dark, clear and magical.

"Yes, Father. I've spent enough money tonight.

Now is the time to earn some." She swept her robe
out of her way and alighted upon a new chair, which
had been immediately placed at the table. "If I
might."

"Oh, yes, of course, you may join us. But we will
see about you winning any money, young lady!" said
Soth merrily. "We seem to be in the company of
true talent."

"Oh?"

"Oh, indeed, Daughter. But pull up your purses and
let's see what you can contribute in money here. A
fresh supply might afford a change to bash this harle-
quin down some."

"And, pray tell—who is this, then?" said Chanadra.

I managed to break myself from the spell cast upon
me. I arose and clicked my heels and bowed in a military fashion. "Milady. Sergeant at arms Vincemole
Whiteviper. At your service."

She smiled. Her voice was lovely. "Charmed, I'm
sure. Service, you say? Serve me up some of your
gold!"

The smell and sight of her were thick in me, but I
was more than familiar with sensuous ploys of women.
No, this woman had an impact, a visceral touch that
rocked me.

I confess I lost the next hand. Chanandra won the
pot. By the time a specially ordered wine was at her
elbow, she'd won two pots. At three pots, she was
chatting merrily about the performance she'd just seen
in the theater. The men in the room seemed more
interested in her smooth, friendly talk than in the
game at hand. I myself managed to recover somewhat.
The woman was beautiful by any measure, but I also
sensed a wit and intelligence below her prattle.

"And, pray tell, Sergeant Whiteviper. Are you a
native of these parts?"

"No. I come from lower lands."

"Earthier lands, more like. You have quite a handsome body to you, in good trim, I think."

"Such is my duty in martial matters."

"And marital?"

"I am not married, madam."

"If you were, you'd be in trouble, I should think. Losing at cards!" Those dark eyes twinkled mischievously.

And as I looked at her closer, I realized part of the reason I was so shaken by this woman.

This image before me now was the very same one that had winked at me from the queen's card.

I covered up my discomfort by staring down at my cards. I had smelled magic in the cards, and this woman was pure magic. Magic plus magic, I had always found, equaled not just magic, but trouble. Best to proceed with caution.

I saw nothing of interest in the cards before me. I folded. I folded two more times, before I saw my chance. And then, sober once more in all senses, I played and played hard with all the tricks at my command and not a few I made up on the fly.

Lord Soth whistled with admiration as he placed the deck of playing cards in a box, and then the box into a pouch. He threw the pouch at me. It landed by a large pile of gold coins. "We take our instruction duly. Bloodied but admiring."

The other men had already left, muttering and shaking their heads. Chanandra was staring down at her empty purse.

"Buy a broke girl a glass of wine?" she said.

"Hang onto your money as long as you can, my boy!" said Lord Soth. "I have lost some money tonight, but I have gained much as well, I think. Now, an older man needs his sleep. Mind that you two get some tonight as well, eh?"

I called for the garçon. It was too late to go anywhere else, but a capon and some sack would not go amiss at the moment. I was far too hungry and far too sober. I had played intensely and truly, measuring my statistics and using a little tricky math I had been taught by a reformed sorcerer. He claimed I had a knack, but I found it a little dry, save for use in gambling. That, intuition, facial expressions, paying close attention to game play and the players: all helped. But there was something else that was rather odd, for even though I played at a high level, I seemed to be very lucky indeed, for luck is still the Supreme Goddess in such things, barring cards up the sleeve and such (tricks I had been known to perform when using more standardized cards.) No, it was as though these cards— these cards *liked* me. They smiled on me.

I should have been suspicious.

"Wine, then, and some food," I said, feeling very full of myself, almost a cocky youth again. "You play cards well, Chanandra."

"You play better."

"Tonight there seemed something in the wind. These cards . . . I will have a theomancer look at them sometime. In the meanwhile, they are a beautiful trophy."

"I have been called such myself by some men," she said, a low purring in her voice. "Now then, handsome and brilliant gambler—tell me about yourself."

Oh, ho, the spell those words weave! For as these memoirs may suggest, I do enjoy talking about myself. There are such depths to me, such insights, such experiences! Oh, and she was intensely interested and she leaned her lips so, and sighed so, and her breasts heaved at the exciting parts of my tales. Well, I need not tell you that by the end of our meal and drink, the seduction was complete—and fool that I was, I thought I was the seducer!

Oh, my heart, it beat! Oh, my brain, it was on fire. I hadn't felt like I felt with that woman since I was a lad. She invited me to her chambers to show me some artifact, and I happily accompanied her. We took an air sled to the palace where she was staying, and I may assure you, her rooms were a sight more luxurious than a soldier's. In a trice, I was bedded in silk and tresses, and soft murmurs of ardent admiration. I was covered in the sweet smell of her, and her tongue tasted sweeter than any wine. The little sergeant volunteered for immediate duty, but she tenderly danced and teased until finally the world itself came to an explosion of delicious fire and I lay in the ashy rubble, an angel gently sending ripples of heaven up my back. Nor was this the end. Before dawn, I was swearing my complete and utter devotion to this woman, for she revealed to me a needy and vulnerable princess lost in the mazes of male power and chicanery, and I knew I must champion her.

"Oh, I feel your power, your bravery, your . . . amazing soul!" she cried at a moment of rapture of which I was the author.

Now usually by this time women were either calling me a bastard or collecting coins, usually shortchanged if I perceived a lack of counting ability to them. I was totally surrendered, smitten, tied and bound in enchantment strong as life itself. I found myself crying out my love, and it wasn't a bald-faced lie as was often the case with women. By dawn, after a few moments of peaceful and contented sleep, I felt I was headed straight for the upper tiers of Heaven. Oh, the irony!

"You say you love me, and I have much love for my brave soldier," she said. "I have given things to you I have never given a man before. I have fallen in love with you, Sergeant Whiteviper, as I have loved no other before."

Amazingly after such a night, her ministrations were awakening the little sergeant as well. He was gaining rank to a major and saluting proudly.

"And I do love you, my little princess. Please . . . more . . . more . . ."

"Would you follow me to the ends of the earth?"

"Yes . . . ooh, yes . . . ohhhhhh."

"As I bring you to the gates of Heaven, will you also save me, if need be, in the depths of Hell?"

"Oh stars . . . stars . . . yes . . . yess . . ."

"Would you swear such to me?"

"I swear!"

"Swear on your new cards!"

"Easily. Oh . . . don't stop that . . . oh . . . yes, here they be. I swear. I swear!"

With a swirl of eternal relief she sent me off into a dimension of gasping pleasure, and I passed out or surely I would have passed away.

When I awoke, the suns were fully up and the day was radiant with sweet spring breezes and birdsong. I lay in a sweep of silken abandon beneath a velvet canopy, the appointments of luxury all about me.

"Chanandra," I whispered.

I should have been on duty I know, teaching drill to some poor new recruits, but such seemed very unimportant now as I lay in the bed of my love, after a visit to paradise.

"Good morning, Sergeant Whiteviper, I trust you slept pleasantly. Would you like some tea and toast before our journey?"

I looked up from the scene of carousal, rumpled as the sheets, and was surprised to find Chanandra sitting at a table covered in white linen, boasting a tea service with a tray of cooked food. She herself was sipping delicately at a china cup. Dressed in a sharp red riding outfit, she seemed all ready to hunt fox, right down to the crop dangling off the table.

"Journey, my love?" I said dreamily. Some godforsaken piece of me languidly glimpsed sails heading off for a sunset, all away from military service among the High Folk. "Where?"

"Why, exactly where you promised to go with me, darling Whiteviper."

"I remember going around the world with you several times last night, dearest peach."

She stood and picked up the riding crop. "To Hell, Whiteviper. To Hell."

"Did you say 'Hale?' Why, I do believe I heard of a city by that name at one time."

"Hell. Hades. The Inferno."

I arose to a sitting position and scratched my head. There was something of a headache back between my eyeballs.

"No, no, I don't think so. You must be mistaken."

"You refuse to acknowledge your promise, Whiteviper." The whip of the crop thwacked against the bedpost and she leaned her gorgeous face toward me. She was every bit as beautiful in the day as at night, but somehow holding a riding crop and snapping nonsense about traveling to blazes didn't add much allure.

"Oh, I don't know what I said last night. Goodness."

"Badness. Just as well. It simply proves that I have found the right man for the job."

"Oh, even if there's a remote chance of you being correct here, Chanandra, I don't think that's possible. You see I have sworn a term of duty in service to Count Farafel of the Dangling Berries. I cannot leave here."

"You can, indeed, sir, and you will."

The voice boomed from the doorway. A man dressed in ornate High Folk clothing walked smartly in and threw an envelope onto the bed. I recognized the seal immediately. It was from the effeminate old pig's ring, all right.

"A moment, please. Very well," said I, backpedaling. "Lord Soth? You pandered your daughter to me in some odd plan to get me to accompany her on some strange journey to a place that is surely merely fable and old wives' tales? This is very odd indeed, sir."

"Fables?" Lord Soth sighed. "Would it were so, Whiteviper. Come on up, then. Get some clothes on. Might as well get on with this, don't you think?"

"I think, sir, that you are mad."

"If force is needed, then force shall be used!" said

Lord Soth. He gestured and suddenly the doorway started spewing forth oddly attired soldiers.

I hopped from the bed and made for the window. Many a time Whiteviper has made his slip from jealous husbands via balconies and such. The palace had trellises and awnings galore, and I knew we weren't very far up. I also knew if I could get back to the barracks, I could muster up some aid from the bonnie lads there.

Alas, a bizarre and dreadful thing occurred.

Last night, before I availed myself of the further treasures Chanandra proffered, I had placed on the floor the sack containing the cards that I had won for my gambling expertise. This sack arose, and gave issue to the cards, which commenced to fan out into an alarming and magical array that resembled a wall.

And felt like one, too.

I bumped nose and face directly into it as I attempted my getaway, and I rocketed back onto the bed, where I was shortly apprehended by Soth's ruffians. They manhandled me up before my captors.

I wish I could say I felt a valiant speech coming on at the time, but in truth I opened my mouth and started to blubber.

"Chanandra! Darling. How could you betray me? I thought our love was real."

"Oh it's real enough, dear." She smacked me playfully on my bare behind. "Why should I chance eternity with someone I hate?"

Well, needless to say, my head continued to be a buzz of confusion for some time. I suspect the hot tea I was given when I clothed myself had some drugs in it as well, but the situation was sufficient to truly confound all my faculties. I remember blubbering a bit as I was strapped into a saddle with Lord Soth's retinue, I remember the deck of magic cards being tucked into my jacket pocket, and I remember the frustration I felt as we trotted along, peaceful as you please, our horses rich and regal, and the townspeople waving ta-da at us.

God speed, Sergeant at Arms Whiteviper.

Go to Hell!

I felt the powers of the cards again, and this time they were not helping me through a game, they were keeping me clamped on that horse, headed to perdition.

Wherever that was.

A way from the city gates but still within sight of the rings of cloud that draped their crenellations and towers upon the low mountains, I felt the restraints of the damned cards lift from my throat, and thus eased I was able to speak.

"And where are we going?"

Lord Soth said, "To Hell, Whiteviper."

"Yes, yes, but the fables . . . now that I am in my right mind . . . there are many fables. Hell is just the common word for where the enemies of a particular religion go. Is there only one True Hell, then?"

"It is a complex situation," said Lord Soth, riding up to my side, friendly again and casual now that I was safely tucked away into his plans. "Let us simply say that this is the Hell that I've dealt with, in any case."

"Dealt?"

Lord Soth sighed. "Yes, alas. When Chanandra was not yet conceived, and I was a lowly royal in my realm with a pittance for an income, and precious few opportunities for me to achieve the fame and riches and success for which I longed, I searched for a way to make my fortune easily. I met a creature . . . He seemed a man to me at the time, though not of the High Folk . . . And after a serious loss at lots, he bought me drink and asked me my heart's desire. I told him. He laughed, and oh, the laugh was eerie. 'Easy enough,' says the demon, for that indeed what he was, and of a most high caliber. 'I have just extended a bit of influence into these climes, and am trying the waters, as it were. I should like to see how well I do. Consider me a salesman. I would like to sell you your hearts' desire.'

" 'But the cost?' Surely it would be great.

" 'Oh, yes, back where I normally conduct business, I request the client's immortal soul for his worldly requests. Here I shall strike an easier bargain for us both.' "

" 'You are some kind of god?'

" 'Some kind . . . indeed. I have power enough to grant your request here, your wish, in most particulars, I think. You only have to sign a contract, and not even in blood as I have others do.'

" 'What is it you wish from me for this?'

" 'You shall need an heir. I am not greedy. When you marry your lady, your firstborn shall be a healthy strapping lad. He will be yours. But your second will be a beautiful girl. You must deliver her to me upon her twenty-second birthday.'

"So I think, well, this is fine. I'll just have one child. There are ways to prevent conception.

"And so I shook his hand. It was furry and it had claws. I saw below his hood then: horns. There were such folk as these I heard of, and many were magical. I thought no more of it, and went about my forlorn ways.

"But then, an incredible series of misfortunes fell upon the ten people that stood before me and much money, much property, and my present title. I married well, and to a woman for love. I was a happy man, and my wife bore a son. We were good to our people and to others, and I obtained a good reputation everywhere. I was a happy man. This was enough. No more children. Alas, as I loved my wife, I obtained spells and preventions against further pregnancies. They did not work. My daughter Chanandra was born, and I thought, well . . . perhaps it was but a dream. We had three more children and were happy. And I grew to love my Chanandra, my clever and brilliant girl, most

of my children. Upon her eighteenth birthday, a
stranger arrived to call at my court. He was elegantly
garbed and wore no hood. He had hooves, and horns,
and claws for hands. He presented himself as Lucifer,
Angel of the Diadem Lower and I recognized him and
allowed him to enter, sick at heart.

" 'You are the . . . magical creature that has allowed
me this wonderful life,' " I said.

"He said yes, that would be him, and he was very
happy with the deal. He dabbled with this and that in
the High Folk realms, but had decided he didn't care
for the elevated real estate. However, he would take
Chanandra as per the deal. 'The girl has not matured
sufficiently for my needs, though.' He presented me
with a map. 'Bring her to this spot four years from
today.' 'And if I do not?' 'What has been done can
be undone. For you, for your beloved wife, for your
lands, for your country. And you will lose your daughter nonetheless. So why not simply your daughter?
She seems to be an adaptable piece. She will be mine.
There are worse fates.' "

"And he looked at me and he laughed, and in that
laugh I heard a strange kind of evil I'd never encountered.

"And so I just nodded and said very well. But there
were four years to figure out what to do. And finally,
almost too late, we found a plan that might work."

"What? Send me along to suffer as well? What good
will that do you or Chanandra . . . or this Lucifer
fellow, come to think of it?"

"We have consulted necromancers and astrologers.
Among many creatures, you seem appropriate. You
have escaped many times. Escape from Hell itself,
with my daughter, Whiteviper . . . and your reward
will be great . . . Not the least of all, preserving your
mode of existence in these dimensions for a time."

I gulped and blubbered a bit more.

I turned to Chanandra who had galloped alongside.

"How can you abide this . . . this deal with Evil."

Chanandra shrugged eloquently. "If not for this deal, I would not exist. I have had an excellent twenty-two years. Perhaps I will have more. In all ways, my father has been good to me and my siblings. I shall be a good daughter. Perhaps you can be a good man, Sergeant Whiteviper. Or at least a man."

Well, that shut me up for a time. Survival for a cutpurse, rogue, and dastard like me is paramount, of course. But a chiding from a harlot bitch, that stung. That shut up the tears for a bit.

I cannot say exactly what happened next. But after a meal and a rest, we entered a valley. As we traveled, the countryside began to blur, and shift, from river views to ocean views and landscapes of desert, from night to day and back again, from stars to moons to comets wheeling in the sky. And finally down a slope between two hills to a dark valley.

"This is the place, yes," said the man beside Lord Soth who served as navigator. He tapped upon a map that seemed to glow and char at the edges. "The Valley of Doom."

"Oh, lovely, lovely," I sniveled. I felt hopeless, but still within my confines, I waited for the slightest chance to escape.

We entered the valley, and a damp chill invaded my bones unlike I'd ever felt before. Gloom seeped from the sky and the very ground. At the base of the hills, fires sprouted from swamps. In the distance I saw mad demons cavorting among the shadows. This did not attract my principal attention, however.

No, that attention was directed toward the most frightful edifice I have ever glimpsed.

"Hellmouth," whispered the navigator in awe. "Ah, it is good that I love you, my lord. For not even riches would have brought me here otherwise." The swarthy man made some sort of religious sign.

Fear glimmered in the eyes of the other men, but both Lord Soth and Chanandra seemed impassive and resigned.

As for me, I was so afraid I whimpered.

For ahead of us, in the shape of the hill, was the face of a hideous beast-thing, rising up to the size of a small palace. It had horns and sharp ears. Crimson fires glittered in its eyes. Its contorted rocky features were the parody of a man, and streams of steam poured from its nose. Its mouth was open wide, wide, incredibly wide. From the top were fangs, from the bottom fangs, and down its gullet glowed fires of counter-numinous majesty. A breath of death and rot, sulfur and burning oil issued from this chasm, and if I hadn't just peed myself with fear, I would have been overtaken by awe at the very spectacle.

A dark river lit with hither-thither pieces of floating fire flowed into this maw. On the banks of this river was a pier, and on the end of this pier was a gondola of dark glimmering wood. Standing on the end of this pier was a figure in a hood.

As we approached a voice emerged from the figure, from deeper than its feet.

"Lord Soth. Lady Chanandra. You have come. You keep your bargain. We of the Underworld are pleased."

"Yes," said Lord Soth. "And a little early, I think."

"All the better."

Lord Soth reared up, stretching his muscles in a casual way. "We ask a favor. A boon as it were. Perhaps one that will work for you."

"Oh?"

"Another soul."

"Another soul? Hell is always in the market for another soul. But why?"

"She would like to bring a servant. I think also this fellow, by the name of Whiteviper, is an excellent gambler. I know that Lord Lucifer enjoys testing his mettle with new gamblers."

"Indeed," said the cloaked and hooded figure. I could not see within his mask, nor did I particularly care to. Nonetheless the effect was spooky enough. "There is plenty of room in the boat and I must make the classic announcement. Abandon all hope, ye who enter here."

I should think that perhaps if I might have been able to wriggle and writhe a bit, fall off and beg not to be taken, showed myself to be a spineless worm, this chap—and by inference, Lord Lucifer—would want to have nothing to do with me. I am the only gambler I know who is also a good whiner. However, whatever magical effect the cards had not only clamped me down, but force my lips up into a grin.

"You see, boatsman," said Chanandra. "My servant is eager for the challenge. But what is your name, sir? I have heard whispered such possibilities as Charon and Dante and Milton."

"Joe," said the wraith.

"Ah," said Chanandra. "Pleased to meet you, Joe. Well, Father . . . farewell."

"And farewell to you, Daughter," said Lord Soth solemnly.

With hardly any more ceremony, I was carried off the horse and placed on the boat. Chanandra stepped in under her own steam.

The boatsman named Joe did not seem to take much note of my bonds, or—if he did—he cared about them little.

He pushed the gondola off into the swirling, stinking river. I looked back in horror.

And, damn him, Lord Soth winked at me.

Mercifully, I fainted with the strain of it all.

When I awoke, I was untied. For a moment I thought it was all a dream. However soon enough the smell of sulfur, the flickering fires, and the ominous figure of the boatman and his pole alerted me to my situation.

I heard a wail and a gnashing of teeth.

"Would you be quiet, please," said Lady Chanandra. "I'm trying to concentrate."

I turned and there she was, at my side, scribbling in a notebook.

"What are you doing?"

"I'm writing in my journal. This has been a remarkable day indeed. This will help me remember everything."

"Oh, just let me forget! I curse the moment I laid eyes on you."

"Still love me?"

I looked at her, at her smile. She was a brazen hussy all right, proud and noble. I ached for her arms again. Perhaps it was the cards.

"Only with my heart."

"There you go, Whitey. Good enough. By the way, where did you learn that little trick with your big toe? My goodness, I almost fell off the bed."

"In a Majarashi's houri," I said.

"Jolly good one." She scribbled a bit more, and then shut her book with a sigh of satisfaction. "Oh, my. I do think I need to go wee wee. Joe, I don't suppose we could stop in one of these little caves so I can lift my dress and have a polite, private whiz?"

Without a word, the boatman guided the boat into a small lagoonlike thing, and beached.

"Thank you. Whitey? Care to use the Hell loo?"

I was surprised to find that there was still moisture in me. Joe did not object to the request, so I got out of the boat as well.

"I will go behind that rock there, Whiteviper. You can use that one over there."

I scurried over and was about to unzip and let fly my pressure in a more agreeable fashion than my previous piss, when I gasped. Hovering in the cavern behind the rock was a cauldron set above a pile of fiery wood. Two devils with pitchforks were prodding a

man in the cauldron. With astonishment, I realized
that it was none other than Cadwallader Humperdink,
an agent I had once used when I wrote my first novel
and tried to sell it. Unsuccessful, he was, however,
able to pander me as a gigolo for a bit—but then
absconded with all his clients' cash one day, never to
be heard from again.

"Hullo," I said. "It's old Cad."

"My moans and groans," said the man, looking pro-
foundly in the pink. "Whiteviper! What are you
doing here?"

"I could ask the same, you villain!"

"On the boat? But you seem to be quite of the
flesh?"

"I am. Long story." I scowled. "Have you got my
money?"

The man in the boiling cauldron broke into hearty
laughter. "Do you here that, Sneeze? Barb, he wants
his money. He's come all the way to Hell for his
money. Can you give me my break now?"

The demons shrugged. "Sure. We're due ours as
well." One of the twisted devils leered at me. "Just
don't you be telling the bosses about this frater-
natization."

They scampered off. They brought back almost immediately a table stacked with teacups, teakettles, and
tea cakes. Then one popped out a flash, giggled, and
they scampered off into dark recesses.

Cadwallader Humperdink clambered out of the
cauldron. He shook his head. "Something to do here
in the Underworld, this cauldron. Next week, though,
I get to trade off with Sisyphus and that rock of his.
It's just Styrofoam, you know, so it's not too bad."

"I haven't an inkling of what you're talking about."

He was wearing a simple tunic, dripping, but for all
his redness, he looked healthy enough. "Tea?"

"Very well. I haven't time to jabber, though. I must
get back to the ship. And mind if I have a pee?"

"Why not?"

I peed and he poured. I took the cup and sipped. It was amazingly delicious.

"Pardon me, but the fable is that there's supposed to be something of punishment down here . . . like for absconding with clients' money."

"Oh, yes, dear boy, I suppose the afterlife could be better." He waggled his eyebrows. "It's really just strange, that's all. Sorry, but I haven't got your money. Can't take it with you, you know. We are all in servitude to Lord Lucifer down here. But behind his back, we don't have a bad spirit existence, I suppose."

"I guess I'm at a loss. I just want to get out." I took down the rest of the tea. "Look, you rapscallion. There should be some honor among thieves. Tell me how to get out of here, and I'll offer up some incense at a temple for your soul or some such nonsense."

"Fair enough. I sense some cards about your person, Whiteviper. You are here to gamble in the flesh for your soul with Lucifer."

"Something like that."

"And knowing you, there's a woman involved."

I sighed.

A voice resounded through the chamber: the boatman's deep rumble. "Whiteviper!"

"Be off with you, then. See you perhaps soon, but definitely later. In the meantime, Whiteviper, take note of this advice to all who gamble with the Lord of Hell in his own halls. 'Enter All Abandon, Ye Who Hope Here.' Now I'll if you'll excuse me, I'll help myself to these luscious cakes before I climb back into the boiling oil."

I hadn't the faintest idea of what he was talking about, but I trotted back to the boat, thinking deeply.

Well, I'll spare you most of the details of the journey. You've probably got the gist of the place by now. Rivers of lava. Screaming souls. Demons poking contorted souls with pitchforks. It was all rather like a stinking perverted carnival, and after a while I sort of got used to it, especially when I noticed that not just demons had flasks in their hip pockets, but the souls as well.

This is not to say that I wanted to linger there in that nether dimension. I simply slumped in the boat, conserving my energy.

Eventually we rounded a bend in the river, and before us was a mighty castle, very much like those bulbous behemoths favored by trolls. Black and ponderous, jagged glass crenellations, twisting towers. All very grand in a macabre way, and I couldn't suppress a shiver. But I realized something very important about myself now, some positive quality. I thought of what old Cadwallader Humperdink had said, and I realized I belonged to the membership of his last clause, always had, always will.

I had hope.

Double damn Lucifer and all his minions, I wasn't going to abandon it!

There were slimy tentacles wiggling here and there in the moat, but they all seemed very much for show. A portcullis raised and Joe guided the gondola into a slanted dock.

"We are here," he said as he slipped a mooring rope about a stump of wood.

A wooden door on grating hinges opened. A great batlike thing scuttled out. He had goggles on and some sort of uniform. If he wasn't so frightening, I would have laughed at the ridiculousness of the sight.

"Come," he hissed. "Lucifer's own . . . come."

After a number of winding and tilting passageways, we came to a series of rooms.

"Thissss issss yourssss," said the bat-thing, opening one of the doors.

Oh, dear. What, my own personal cauldron of boiling mucus? A couple of drunk, giggling mutant devils, to prod me with tridents?

But no. Instead, it was just a rather nicely appointed bedroom.

"The flessh must resst. The meeting is at inferno-ssssummit. Food and drink are on the dresser. Enjoy your damnation."

Bloody hell. I will, I thought.

"Toodle-loo, my lady," I said, and quickly shut the door behind me. In truth, the room was fabulous. Not only was there wine to drink, which I did and much of it, but there was a nice roast ham with potatoes in gnosh. When I'd had enough to sate me, I explored. No windows, of course. No escape likely here. There was a door, however. I opened it. An odd porcelain bowl connected to pipes sat by a white bath, also attached to pipes. Oh my, I had heard of these things, fabled as devils—Hell had Indoor Plumbing. I gave the bowl a quick mouthful. It made a terrible watery noise when I removed my buttocks, and swallowed. I was duly impressed, yes, but when I went to the sink, I refrained from washing my hands for fear of hot and cold running brimstone.

I was examining an odd square box with a front surface of glass, when the door opened. Damn, I'd forgotten to lock it.

The next thing I knew, there was Chanandra. She was wearing a gorgeous long silk robe. In her hand was a bottle.

"Is not this the most remarkable place!" she said.

I scowled at her.

"You expect me to be friendly to you?"

She shrugged and wiggled over to the dresser, where there were two fresh crystal glasses. She poured out amber stuff into them.

"I'm being friendly to you." She handed me one of the glasses.

"What is this?"

"Try it."

I was suspicious, but also curious. I sniffed. Definitely alcoholic. I took a sip. The stuff went down hot.

"Hellfire!" I gasped. "You've poisoned me."

"Of course not, ninny. Any moment for a long period of time I could have killed you if I wanted, right?''

Even as she spoke, the stuff lit up my insides into warmth. It tasted rather peaty, earthy, like a great stein of beer reduced into a thimble.

"The label reads 'Whiskey,' " she said.

"Dreadful stuff," I said. "Somehow, though, I love it."

I swallowed a larger portion, with proportionate effects. I was starting, in fact, to feel rather fine, which is no mean feat after such an ordeal as mine, and right in the middle of Hell as well.

"Peace?" she said.

"Damn your eyes. Why'd you drag me to the bottomless pit, woman. There are plenty of good gamesmen and smarter than me, too."

She chuckled throatily. "Because you're so bad, Whiteviper. There was no other talented soul who deserved the trip so much. No, take another snort, then shut your mouth and kiss me."

She stepped forward.

"Well, I'll have another drink, yes," I said. "But I'll not touch you. You belong to the fellow in charge here, and he's got the most fiendish imagination, it would seem, for torture."

"Oh, come on, Whiteviper. You know you want me," she said, and she untied her robe.

I drained the rest of my glass and woozily opened my arms to my fate. Damnation maybe, and definitely betrayed. Yes, Whiteviper was a fool, but then there were sometimes benefits to the role.

"I had expected something," said Lady Chanandra. "Well, a little more gaudy."

"Spare, yes," I agreed, sipping at a cup of excellent stuff that was doing wonders for my slight hangover. "But elegant and tasteful, I think."

The room we sat in looked like a parlor that also served as a study. There were leather-bound books in bookcases, neatly ordered and kept. A nice candelabra sat upon a table. The rug seemed a particularly splendid version of the Oriental persuasion. There was a nice scent of pipe tobacco to the air. A set of crystal sherry decanters glittered on the sideboard. In short, it looked like the room of a gentlemen and a statesman.

"Most interesting."

"You don't seem terribly downfallen at this whole business, Chanandra."

"I'm not dead. And I've still a chance with you here . . ." She fingered my sleeve knowingly. "And also with you here, Whiteviper, Eternity will have its diversions."

"Depending on what Lucifer wants with you."

The clacking of steps sounded upon the floor outside. "Looks like we'll find out soon."

The double doors opened.

In stepped a man. He wore a topcoat and a hat and carried a walking cane. He took off his hat and placed it on a rack. Then he took off his gloves and his topcoat and placed these upon a side table. He wore a waistcoat with a watch chain stretched between its two side pockets. He kept the walking stick as he turned and took a few steps toward us, fixing us with dark and powerful eyes.

"Good day, sinners," he said.

"You . . . you are Lord Lucifer?" said Chanandra.

"I am."

"But my father. He spoke of horns and hooves."

"When they are appropriate." Lord Lucifer touched the top of his head. Horns sprouted from his close-cropped black hair, then immediately retracted.

Chanandra said, "I am here, the cost of my father's good fortunes. I do not know why I am here, beyond your general desire to collect souls. Yet I am not dead. Why have you worked so hard to bring me here?"

Lord Lucifer smiled. "It's what I do, my dear. It's my little joys that keep me going."

"This is Whiteviper—my valet."

"Yes, I know of Whiteviper and am most intrigued."

"Actually," I spoke up. "With all due respect, I should say that I was tricked here and if you'd rather not have me taking up space and eating and drinking up your stocks, I'd be quite happy to get on Joe's boat and go back topside."

Chanandra gave me a harsh look.

Lord Lucifer lifted his head up and laughed. It was a chilling, trilling, nasty laugh. "Oh, Whiteviper, how you wriggle on my pitchfork!!" He shook his head. He went over and poured himself a drink of sherry. However he didn't offer us one. "I like that. I must have my amusements you know. It keeps me sane in my imprisonment."

"Imprisonment?"

"Yes. Oh, of course, you're from another dimension, aren't you? One that I don't dabble in much . . . except to extract the occasional beauty and commit the odd mischief. It really is a simple and sad story. I was once the highest archangel of Jehovah, or God as he likes to be called sometimes. The creator and commander of all."

"But gods are a farthing a dozen," I said.

"Don't tell that to Jehovah! He got all uppity when a bunch of straggly desert people on the World Above decided there should be only one. Out went Baal, out went lots of others, up went God and with a remarkable amount of hocus-pocus, scribblings, stories, Torahs, commandments, burning bushes, psalms, prophecies, and plagues. But I'm putting the Revelation before the Genesis. As I was saying up in Heaven, God's crib, I was his Number One. We got on. But, I tell you, he was a little nuts, Jehovah was, especially after he decided he was the only true God around. Well, that was all well and good I suppose, but then he started saying, 'You know, Luce—I'm thinking I'll be three gods for the price of one.' And I said, 'Jehovah. You know I have a degree in Celestial Psychology. I specialize in cherubim and seraphim, but I'm sure I have plenty of time for you as well.' But no. Pretty soon, he decided he was a Trinity and started doing nutty things like declaring that human beings on the World Above were destined to become doomed unless he impregnated some virgin and let his son save them. 'Son?' I said. 'What son?' 'Oh, that would be me.' 'But you're God.' 'Oh, but I'm also my own son.' Well, I said to myself. Maybe God should get a forced vacation for a bit to think things over and heal his brain. So I cooked up a little retirement party that didn't work well, and got booted out of Heaven. Didn't know this place was down here, let me tell you, or maybe I would have just forgotten my malcontent and chirped the music of the spheres for eternity. But I didn't and here I was. Fortunately, I helped steered mankind to the place God feared they'd be and then did my damnedest to foul up his plan. Believe me, there have been snags."

I noticed as Lord Lucifer spoke, his face was getting redder and redder. His eyes began to protrude and his breath came thick and harsh, adding a touch of sulfur to the otherwise pleasant taste in the atmosphere.

Lucifer raised a fist, and shook it emphatically.

"But I will have my retribution! When the time is right, as the prophecies say, I shall triumph and take over all the earth—and from the highest mountain, I will bend over and moon the bastard." He seethed down a bit. "In the meantime, I shall have my mischief. I shall frolic and oversee the torturing of the damned. Not bad, eh?"

"Pardon me, Lucifer," I ventured. "You mentioned prophecies?"

"Yes! In the damned scriptures this mental case beamed down. There's even a whole last chapter in the section they call the New Testament devoted to the subject called Revelations."

"And what's the outcome?"

The Devil grew sullen. "That blasted book claims I'll fail."

"And what's been the accuracy of these prophecies so far in this book for this Earth?"

"Disquietingly dead on."

"So let me get this straight. This Jehovah flattened you once already. He's in charge of a whole universe of many stars and planets, with so much power that he actually created them . . . as well as you, come to think of it. And you honestly think you have, pardon the expression, a snowball's chance in Hell of defeating Him and thwarting a run of positive prophecies from a God who also seems pretty handy with time as well as space?"

Lucifer's eyes bulged again, only this time incredibly. Steam literally blew from both ears. Fire licked out of his mouth like a tongue. He began hopping up and down, shrieking, "I will! I will! I will!" He fell to his knees and began pounding the floor. "Bastard! The bloody bastard!"

He rolled around a bit, spasming and kicking his legs, spewing up no end of smoke. I noticed that his nicely polished leather shoes had turned to nicely polished hooves. He then got up and clacked over to a door. He opened the door. A rubber dummy issued out. The dummy was the size of a man, and wore white robes, a long white beard, and a great sunlike halo about his head. Holy chants issued from behind him.

"I'll whip your butt, you son of a bitch!" Lucifer then took a bat from inside the closet and commenced to beat the rubber out of the doll, until it was busted up quite properly. He then kicked it back into the closet and slammed the door.

"Now then, my new friends," he said, the sudden picture of calm control. "I gather you both enjoy a nice game of cards."

Lucifer's face still had an occasional tic to it as he seated himself at the table with his glass of sherry before him, but obviously he'd managed to check his blaring temper for a time. "Actually that was a good question," he said, counting out colored chips. "A takeover of the earth itself is a gamble. Perhaps the best answer is that I, Lord Lucifer, am the Great Gambler. In fact, in my universe, I invented it!"

"Remarkable!" I said, sucking up to the fellow as I do so well.

"Oh, yes. So, as you might imagine, I'm the greatest gambler in the universe. Well, my universe." He smiled. "Which is why I'm so interested in testing my mettle with gamblers in other universes lately. This is ultimately why I was so interested in you, Chanandra. You see, I divined that your father was a superb gambler. I did some scrying and discovered that there was a good chance he'd sire remarkable gamblers and that the second would be a female. Well, not only in this bargain would I procure a good gambler to game with . . . I should have one that would not be hard to look upon. And perhaps be of service to me . . ." He rubbed the back of his head ironically. ". . . in my hornier phases."

"I see. You are truly magical, sirrah! This is why you've allowed my lady to drag me here."

"Indeed. All evidence would indicate that you are a good gambler as well."

"I have my moments."

"That's fine."

"Sherry?"

"Maybe a glass of cold water," I said.

"In Hell?"

"Excellent point, sirrah. I will take a small sherry, then."

Chanandra took one as well.

Lucifer procured a carved box and set it down upon the table. "Now then. I shall, of course, provide the deck of cards and choose the game of chance."

"It's your pit," I said.

"Yes, it is." He took out a deck of cards with red markings on the back. "Now here is the deck we shall play with." He took out a pack and unwrapped some transparent crackling material.

He slapped the deck into the center of the table that had been brought into the room by a brace of burly demons, smoking stumpy cigars and wearing sleeveless T-shirts.

"You may examine them if you like. I assure you they are fresh and not fixed. My gambling is based on ability, intelligence, and factors other than magic."

"But are these cards the ones we are familar with?"

"Good point. If memory serves from playing in your lands, the principles are the same. In this case . . ." Slickly, like the ultimate stage magician he was, he turned over the cards and fanned them out. "Four suits. Hearts and Diamonds are the red cards, spades and Clubs are black. 1 through 10. Jack. Queen. King. Ace. In order of ascendancy. Jokers here: wild. Decent gamblers should understand the concepts, true."

"True. Five suits in ours. A few more cards in each run, and cards very similar to jokers," said Chanandra.

I examined the cards. It was simple enough and, with fewer cards, perhaps easier. However, I concentrated hard to learn the faces of the cards and the order.

"Now then. We will be playing a game called poker."

"Why?" I said. "If we're playing with your cards, can't we play one of our games?"

One of his furry eyebrows arose at my insolence. "I like it. I invented it."

I nodded. I had to test him a bit, and show him that I had some backbone. Otherwise I'd never be able to bluff.

"I have taken the liberty of drawing up the order of the winning hands for you." He snapped his fingers, and one of the demons handed us both an illustrated scroll.

"Allow me to run them down for you."

Quickly, he ordered cards to reveal examples of hand rank. I picked it up immediately. I pick up rules to games quickly, just as I pick up the basics of a language. It is a useful talent for survival, being a quick study.

"Excellent. We will play with chips. At the end of two hours of play, the player with the highest number of chips wins." Lucifer snapped his fingers again. More servants lugged in a large hourglass and stood on hand to turn it over upon request.

"And the rewards?"

"If I win, you both will be mine to do with as I please. Your wills will dwindle, keeping enough only for me to amuse myself. And what would you like if one of you wins?"

"We should like to be returned to our homelands," said Chanandra.

"Excellent. I shall lose you both, doubling my loss, and making the game play intensely interesting to me. Now, I have decided that we shall play one form of poker only, a form I relish. When I return, I shall tell you the rules. I shall not be gone long."

He arose and sped off into another room.

The demons left as well. Probably for a quick nip, I thought.

"The cards in your pocket!" whispered Chanandra. "Take them out and replace this deck."

"But they're not similar at all! He'll know we've tried to cheat, kill us, and our spirits will be trapped here forever."

"Do it!" she said emphatically.

I felt the familiar sensation of being taken command of by the cards. In a trice, the larger deck was out in the middle of the table, and the smaller was in my pocket. Sweat began to drip down the back of my neck.

Almost immediately, the door banged open.

In strolled Lord Lucifer, wearing chaps, holstered

firearms, a leather vest, a scarf, and a ridiculous round hat with a wide brim.

"Ye doggies," cried Lucifer, Prince of Darkness. "The poker game, folks, is called Texas Hold 'Em."

Now say what you like about some of the villains I've dealt with in my time. They were all as bad as me, maybe worse, but I could at least relate to them. This Lucifer fellow obviously was of a different stamp entirely.

"He's a loony!" I whispered to Chanandra.

"Shhh. Take a look at the cards."

I did.

For a moment I thought I'd made a terrible mistake. But then I remembered there was definitely magic in the cards that we'd brought down with us.

The cards I'd replaced the others with had changed themselves into the exact same shape and coloration as Lucifer's deck. I just hoped it got the suits right. A Duchess of Pearls in this game would go down like a turd in a mead bowl.

"Yee haw," said Lucifer, his eyes glowing. "My favorite place in the world, Texas. I'm out of here, but I still feel like home. Now, rules, rules, rules. Let's go over some rules. They're simple enough."

It seemed as though each hand had seven cards, but five of them are community cards. Each player is dealt two cards down, private cards, then after a card is discarded from the top of the deck ("the burn—and they say I didn't invent this"), three cards are dealt faceup in the middle of the table, the community cards. Meanwhile, betting. Then another burn. Another faceup card. Bet. Another burn, another face up card. Bet. Raises, checks, folds, all that stuff, which makes me think that Lucifer didn't invent poker so much as stole it from one of our dimensions.

Lucifer poured another round of drinks and we

commenced to play. I must say, I picked the game up quite speedily. My gambler's mind immediately grasped hold of the odds, and I wasn't fooled at all by the boisterous, hearty, and obnoxious behavior old Lucifer was exhibiting. Loony as a mattress worm he could well be, but he was old and crafty. He played cunningly as well, and won the most of the first five pots. But of course Chanandra was no more foolish than I—we kept the bets low, folded a great deal, and lost little chips while we learned the game.

It was when I was dealt two kings facedown that I began to think I might have a victory streak on my hands. But as the cards and bets continued, an odd thing happened.

The King of Hearts in my hand began to speak to me.

"Psst. Whiteviper."

"What?"

"Not so loud. It's me. Subvocalize and I promise you'll not be heard."

I looked down. The King of Hearts was slowly turning into a man with a white beard and a halo about his head.

"God?"

"No. They call me Saint Peter. I do house calls. Not as much as the Virgin Mary."

"Her house calls can't be much fun. Who is she?"

"The mother of God."

"Wait a minute. I thought God created your universe."

"No. She was the mother of God's son. Jesus. Who was also God."

"Oh." The second flip of community cards turned into another king. I started piling on the chips. "Wait a minute. How can she be a virgin, then?"

"Let's not get into biology or theology, okay? We always try to trip this nut up as much as possible, and that's why we're collaborating on a special attack today."

"Attack?"

"Yes. On the Fallen Archangel's greatest failing. His pride."

"Hmmm. Yes, we have a saying where I come from. Pride comes in summer. It's right before fall."

"Hmm. Amazing the similarities in our universe! See. Look at the next card."

The next card was a King of Diamonds.

My heart skipped a beat, but I kept a blank face and checked, letting Lucifer plunk down a hefty amount.

"You did that?"

"Well, it's a collaboration. I won't go into the celestial mechanics."

"You're going to get us out of here?"

"I'm certainly going to try. But I thought I'd take a moment to have a chat with you."

"Just don't put out another king, okay?"

"Verily, my son, I have got my cards straight. Whiteviper, I must say, you are not a good man."

"Depends on what you mean by good."

"You are selfish, nasty, prideful, vicious, backstabbing. You lie, cheat, steal, commit adultery constantly. You are a braggart, you deal in chicanery. You kill, you perjure, and when you act out your soldierly roles, you are a hypocrite. You play as though you're brave, but at heart you are a coward. Your principle interests in life are strong drink and debauchery."

I took a drink of sherry.

"I am a survivor. I do what I do."

The next card was a queen. I couldn't help but notice that Lucifer got excited. *Lovely, lovely,* I thought. *Let the bastard have four queens in the end!* I bet a hefty amount and sure enough he raised.

"Perhaps you should concentrate on the card play, and allow me to do so as well. I loathe sermons," I told the goody two shoes in my hand.

Peter glowered at me, but I ignored him and played.

"We'll discuss this later," he intoned self-righteously.

I was irked. Something bothered me terribly. Nonetheless, I finished off the last betting round, brilliantly suckering in Lucifer.

"Observe these, and sob!" he said, revealing that his cards, matched with those in the middle, produced what he termed a "full house"—three queens and two kings.

Chanandra had fortunately folded toward the end.

I laid down my kings. "I believe this is high, correct!"

The arch-demon's mouth dropped. He snarled. Soon enough though, he recovered and as I gathered in the chips, he even complimented my play. Although he hated to lose, it was clear that he relished the competition.

And so play proceeded. Chanandra performed admirably, winning a pot here and there, and vexing Lucifer no end by taking away a particularly large amount of stakes he'd placed on a straight by trumping it with a flush. I, on the other hand, cleverly utilized the good hands I received to chip away at the arch-fiend's gains and reserves. Also, I was wise enough to read Chanandra to guess what she had, and so bow out when she was a winner, so as to bleed Lucifer and minimize the damage to myself. Chanandra, in turn, played well with me. Apparently, in his arrogance, Lucifer had neglected to think that we might not play as singles, but as a team against him.

Finally, with half an hour to go in the hourglass, Lucifer's piles of colored wooden chips were clearly lower in number than both my piles and Chanandra's piles. His absurd hat was off, and he was no longer speaking in a drawl or behaving obnoxiously.

"I think," he said, "I need a break. Therefore, I call a five-minute recess. You should not mind, since you are ahead and I have less time to catch up."

"Of course not. And being a creature of flesh and blood, I need a visit to the toilet," said Chanandra.

"One of my servants will show you the way." Lucifer stood up. "And be sure, Whiteviper, I will cut those cards when I return."

He pointed to the deck, twirled and departed, followed immediately by the guards—doubtless for another booze break themselves.

The thought of drink made me hurry over to the bar. Sure enough, there was some of that stuff that Chanandra had imported to my room last night. I poured a large splash and quaffed it. Another. My hand was shaking as I brought it up to my lips. I was already feeling a little better. This was a tension-filled game, to say the least.

"Psst," said a voice. "I need to speak to you."

I recognized the voice. That holier-than-thou Saint Peter chap. "I don't need to speak to you. I need to speak to my glass."

I did so.

"You do want to win this game and defeat Lucifer, do you not?"

I did. And I knew that the cards had been going our way because they were our cards, and somehow this heavenly clown had helped effect that. I poured in a little more whiskey and stumped back over to the table. Sat down heavily. Sighing, I cut the deck in front of me, and there he was, the king again, speaking to me from under a halo.

"Now, as I was saying, Whiteviper . . . whew! What is that stench you're breathing at me?"

"Whiskey," I said.

"As though wine isn't damaging enough. Well now, let me tell you, son, you may revel and carouse all your days. But you see what comes of it. Have you not seen the fates of revelers and carousers down here? But in any case, in this time I have, I appeal to you. You are a person of great charisma and magnitude, and your potential is surely great. If not for heavenly rewards or to avoid the ghastly eternity in some even smellier Other-dimensional Underworld . . . If not for that, then not for the sake of goodness itself, but to ease the pain of others and to shed some light in the vast amount of darkness in all the universes. Please! I beseech you. Consider."

"I am my own man. I do what I like. I work for others as I please. I have needs. What more can I say?"

"Are you so talented in that respect? I mean, surely you would lose this card game quickly were it not for the enchantment of this deck."

"That's nonsense!" I snapped. "I'm the best gambler I've ever met. I'm better than this Lucifer, that's for certain. And at his own game."

"Tch. Tch," he said. "Oh it is so good to associate with the humble where I reside. You're worse than a fool and what's more—"

Zounds! I admit that the whiskey was going to my head. My fury hit it dead center. There was an immediate explosion of rage in my head. The next thing I knew, I'd hefted up the charmed cards, and stomped over to the fire in the hearth.

"Whiteviper!" squeaked this Saint Peter. "What in Heaven's name are you doing?"

I felt a strong sensation buzz up my arm: the magic again, seeking to take control again. My rage however grew so mighty, I forced it back. With all my might I threw the cards into the roaring hearth.

"Aaaaaaaaaaaaaaaaaahhh." Whether that was Saint Peter or the cards themselves, I didn't care. The act was quite satisfying. For a time.

I immediately marched back. From my pocket, I withdrew the pack of cards Lucifer had initially given me and placed these precisely where he'd left the others. After a quick shuffle of course. I sat back in my chair, and finished off what was left in my glass.

I felt like a god. I felt alive and powerful. I had broken the chain about me, and now I was about to take on all comers. The magic was in me! I, Whiteviper, was the master gambler.

However, this surge of enthusiasm lasted for a whole fifteen seconds. Then doubt and its cousin, dread, began to creep in. Ye gads! What had I done?

In another fifteen seconds I was back at the bar. It

was then that Lucifer entered, looking confident and refreshed again, and ready to play. Chanandra followed, looking a bit perplexed and a little tousled. She must have had a rather strenuous pee, I thought.

"Ah, Whiteviper, at the whiskey I see. Good fellow. Slurp up all you like." Lucifer sat down, cracking his fingers. "But do bring the bottle over here and let's get on with it."

Lucifer had changed. He now wore his previous style of outfit, only this time a bit more elaborate and expensive looking. An immaculate cut of cloth, with a little flower in his lapel. He actually looked rather dashing—and totally in control.

I wish I could say the same for me. Rather than comforting me, the whiskey began to eat a hole in my stomach and start seeping like acid into my bowels. They gurgled with complaint.

Chanandra sat down. I sat down with more whiskey. Chanandra gave me an odd look. Then Lucifer dealt out the cards.

My spirirts picked up. I had a pair of jacks dealt me and another jack was in the flop. The last card matched another in the flop, giving me a full house. I bet confidently . . . and lost to a queen high full house belonging to Lucifer. The hands kept going in that direction for the next ten minutes. Chanandra was looking at the cards in a vexed way, and feeling them, as though their feel wasn't right. And of course it wasn't. They weren't her cards. I'd chucked the lot into the fire.

Despite my better judgment, I continued drinking the whiskey. I continued losing most of the hands, so that my pile dwindled. Chanandra was holding her own, though, and of course Lucifer was heading back to his healthy state. And with that sand coursing through that glass ceaselessly, the seconds shusshed onward to my doom.

I drained my whiskey.

"More, Whiteviper?" asked Lucifer convivially.

"I will have a bottle of champagne or two to cele-
brate my victory, Lucy," I said.

He lifted his head and laughed. "Ah, spirit! How I
love to squash it!"

Chanandra by now obviously realized somehow the
cards were no longer what they had been. She looked
panicked. I looked at her directly and I winked. She
just shook her head and continued playing.

I had, alas, in my own panic, forgotten that this
wasn't a game I needed to gain money from, nor a
game I had to win. It was only a game in which either
I or Chanandra needed to have more chips than Lucifer. I began to calculate feverishly.

The cards were much more erratic than they had
been before, often coming up with low values, so that
it seemed anything could win. I looked over the hourglass. By my calculation, there were ten minutes left.
For one brief second I felt like following those cards
into a fiery demise. But then, suddenly, I remembered something.

One possible and very strange ace in the hole, to
use a phrase Lucifer had supplied.

I began to weave a bit. I made it appear I was even
drunker than I actually was (although with the strain
I felt quite alert, thank you). It took another bad hand
until I obtained a good one—four fives. A pair of
the fives were showing, which meant that Lucifer and
Chanandra could only build a full house around them
at best, and that was likely what they would do. Less
than five minutes left, I followed the advice I'd received and entered abandon as I'd never entered
abandon before.

"All right, Cadwallader," I whispered. "This is it."

I bet my final gold pieces, still looking very drunk
indeed.

"All right, Lucy," I said. "Guess this is it."

He smiled at me and happily matched the bet.

Chanandra folded.

I was terrified, of course, but at the same time I felt elated. It would seem I did have some faith in my life, though in no gods or religions. I had faith in Whiteviper!

"Excellent. You will be entertaining here, Whiteviper. For an hour and a half, you gave me a game. Alas, I have cleaned you out this time."

He showed his cards. Not only was it indeed a full house, but the top three cards were aces.

"Two pair, I presume?" he said.

"Yes. Two pair," I said.

He laughed and began to reach for the pot.

"Two pairs of fives, Lord Lucifer!" I said, turning my cards over.

He looked at my cards, stunned. Chanandra couldn't help but giggle. Lucifer fell back into his chair as I reached over and pulled in the chips. Immediately, he began to deal another hand. However, I folded early.

One more hand. Again I folded.

The sands ran out.

The chips were counted. My calculations were correct. I had taken enough chips in to rise above Lucifer's piles by just a small margin, but quite sufficient for my needs.

"Now," I said. "You mentioned champagne?"

Lucifer stood up. Again, his face was a beet red. He went to the fireplace, where he found a poker and commenced to beat his servant demons senseless. He turned to me, seething. "That's why I called this a poker!" He stormed about a bit, cursing and swearing, and then fell to the floor where he kicked and shrieked like a spoiled little child. "Impossible. Impossible! I have never been beaten! It's my game! MY game! Unless . . ."

He went to the door and roared out a command. A demon arrived, took orders, left.

Lucifer strode over to the table. "Unless, somehow, these cards have been fixed." He sniffed them as a dog sniffs an arsehole. He thumbed through them and gave me a glare, then turned toward Chanandra. "Whiteviper smells of mere perfidy. You, my dear, smell a little of magic."

"Can't you just accept that I played well?" said I.

"The champagne will not be poured yet," said Lucifer.

The next thing I knew a hunchback demon was scuttling into the room, pulling a monstrous dog with three heads.

"This is Cerberus. He can sniff out all manner of magic, mushrooms, and marijuana."

He gave the cards to the demon, who stuck them under one of Cerberus' snouts. The dog's head drooled on them. The other heads canted and sniffed. Cerberus then lay down and began to lick its genitals with three tongues.

"My Lord, there is no magic on these cards but yours!"

Furiously, Lucifer took the champagne bottle and smashed it over the hunchback's head. After kicking him a few times, he turned to us, calm again.

"Don't worry. I have more bubbly."

From thence forward, Lucifer was utterly charming although I would catch him giving me strange looks. We drank some champagne, we had some supper. Lucifer assured us that he would keep his promise, but that at the moment, Joe the Styx boatman was busy. Seems as though a minor war had broken out above. Tomorrow, after a good rest, we would be escorted back to our dimension. Lucifer would even provide a retinue to carry us back to the High Folk.

We were entertained by dancers and a band of musicians. Very tired, Chanandra and I begged to be allowed back to our quarters for some sleep. Lucifer assented.

Back there, I tried the faucet in the bathroom. Just water. I splashed my face, then continued my ablutions. I sprayed on a little cologne, humming to myself.

I grabbed a bottle of wine, and then snuck out, silently creeping down to Chanandra's door.

I tapped. No answer. It was unlocked. I opened. Chanandra was not inside.

"Good morning, Whiteviper."

I woke up. Immediately, I felt the headache. Nothing better in the evening, I say, than strong drink. Nothing worse, though, the morning after. I thought, Where am I? *Oh, yes.*

Hell.

I opened gummy eyes to examine the speaker.

It was Chanandra. She was dressed in some new outfit, a woolen suit with a white shirt. She wore a black tie about her neck, and her hair was up in the back. She looked different, otherworldly—but not a jot less lovely. My heart went beat beat beat.

"Darling," I said reaching out for her. "We did it."

She stepped back a pace, smiling playfully at me.

"Damn it, get in here with me. I'm your plaything, remember?"

"What happened to my cards, Whiteviper?"

"Sorry about those. However, I am now a free man—to throw myself at your feet with praise and adoration."

"Where did you put them?"

When I told her, I could tell she was angry, but she just nodded. "I suppose it turned out well enough."

"Quite. Now get your pretty self down here and let's have a few minutes of rowdy celebration."

A woman can be a headache out of bed, but there is nothing better for a headache than one IN bed.

"No, Whiteviper. I'm here to speak with you on an important matter."

"Yes. Right. We're not going to spend the rest of our lives and then eternity in this forsaken place."

"No. I've made an important decision."

I smiled. "You wish to take me as your official consort. Together we will live in your ivory tower and cavort through the flowers every day and make passionate love all night?"

I got up and scratched myself.

"No. Lucifer, at my request, showed me his world tonight."

"You mean this place?"

"No. The World Above. The place he calls Earth." She shook her head sadly. "It is a sorry place. Hunger. Misery. Plenty of bad taste. And in the most civilized of nations, women have no political power, and precious little in the home, unless they are very rich. Whiteviper, my kingdom does not need me. Earth needs me."

"Pardon, my lady?"

"Lucifer is quite loony . . . yes. But he's rather cute. And he's just a male, after all . . ." She chuckled throatily. "I think I'm going to stay here and do what I can with his power to help the earth."

"What?" I was aghast.

"And influence him, of course."

"Foolishness!"

"Whiteviper, it's the beginning of what they call the twentieth century on Earth. A new dawn of something the Earthlings call 'technology.' There is such promise for this planet . . . and for the whole of the cosmic universes. Peace. The end of hunger. The human race can make something of itself—under the guidance of women, in the proper positions of power and respect. Whiteviper, with my help, in a hundred years this planet will be in much better shape . . . and so will the human race, thanks to me!"

"But what about this nut's crazy plan to invade?"

"Doomed, of course, which is why I'm not worried about it. It will keep the poor dear busy."

"Dear? He's the Devil?"

"So are all you men." She put her hand on her hip and narrowed her eyes at me.

"He's not a man. He's a Fallen Angel. An arch-demon!"

"You're just jealous."

Well, I couldn't say much to that. I guess I was. I felt wounded. For all she'd put me through, I had feelings for this woman, dammit. And now though I was happy to abandon Hell, I didn't want to abandon her.

I got up and stretched my arms out. "One more for the road, then, eh?"

"You're so coarse, Whiteviper. Please. Pull up those pants and brush your teeth. You smell like a brewery sinking into a sewage pit."

That shut my mouth properly. I sat back down onto the bed.

"I'll see you off in an hour, Whiteviper," she said, and marched away.

We were at the dock. Joe was in his boat, waiting for me. I stood with Chanandra, and we said good-bye.

"Good-bye," I said.

"Good-bye, Whiteviper."

Chanandra wore a straw hat. There was a banner draped across her imposing bosom labeled: VOTES FOR WOMEN.

"Just a moment!" called a voice.

We turned. Coming across a drawbridge was Lord Lucifer.

"Good morning, Lucy," I said, feeling pretty full of myself despite the ache in my heart. "Been doing some card practice this morning."

"Don't press your luck, Whiteviper," said Lucifer. He, too, wore a straw hat. The ribbon around it proclaimed. WOMEN'S SUFFRAGE. "It's hard enough for me to swallow my pride, but I wanted to thank you."

"Thank me?"

"Yes. If you hadn't won that game, I wouldn't have realized all the weaknesses of my goals and procedures. I must reevaluate. Just remember, if you ever want a job in MY army, just draw a pentacle, slaughter an innocent goat or something, and give me a call."

"Sure. Thanks, Lucy."

"Oh, dear, Luce," said Chanandra affectionately. "There's a spot on your shirt."

"There is?"

"Yes, and you really do need some new cuffs. And that hair in your nose and ears. Can we get a good barber?"

"Of course, my dear."

"Now I've been looking at those reports you gave me and I have to tell you, there's a lot of work to be done. But on the Russian front, I was looking at this fellow Rasputin. He seems a very arresting fellow. We should put a little push behind him, don't you think?"

"If you like, my love."

Oh. So that was it. Lucifer had dipped his wick in the lake of fire so much, he'd thought he could handle the Lady of the Lake of Fire.

Ha. Ha.

"And maybe these countries in Europe should just have a go at each other. You know, let off some steam. It won't take but a blink and they'll sign treaties or whatever and we can get on with the serious business of getting some women in offices of power."

"As you say, my dear. Travel well, Whiteviper. And remember, a good damnation is only a dead goat away!"

He turned and offered his arm to his new lady.

"Let's try this a different way, Luce," she said. She offered him her arm. He shrugged and hooked a claw in it, and they were off.

"Are we going to mope around here all day?" said Joe. "I've got so many dead guys piling up in South Africa their souls are starting to stink."

"Just a moment," I said.

Sure enough, even as she walked, Chanandra turned around and winked at me.

I sighed and got into the boat, and look dolefully at Joe. "Something tells me," I said, as he pushed off into the dark. "That is the start of a beautiful relationship."

So that's it. That's how I went to Hell. Now take that dictagem, and do up a good manuscript, Wormtoes, and then bring it back to me for the odd tweak here and there.

What? Well yes, of course . . . I still miss her. I miss 'em all, damn 'em. Women!

Thanks, I will take a drink. You're a helpful fellow and . . . . Just a moment. What's that in your pocket. A full purse. Oh that's right, you've just been paid.

Have a drink there, yourself, my friend. That's a good fellow. My best plunk, yes, it is. You've been a good servant.

Just a moment. I've got a brainstorm.

You want to know a little more about poker?

What do you say to a few hands of cards?

Tanya Huff

Victory Nelson, Investigator:
Otherworldly Crimes a Specialty

"Smashing entertainment for a wide audience"
—*Romantic Times*

"One series that deserves to continue"
—*Science Fiction Chronicle*

BLOOD PRICE
0-88677-471-3

BLOOD TRAIL
0-88677-502-7

BLOOD LINES
0-88677-530-2

BLOOD PACT
0-88677-582-5

To Order Call: 1-800-788-6262

Tanya Huff

The Finest in Fantasy

SING THE FOUR QUARTERS	0-88677-628-7
FIFTH QUARTER	0-88677-651-1
NO QUARTER	0-88677-698-8
THE QUARTERED SEA	0-88677-839-5

The Keeper's Chronicles

SUMMON THE KEEPER	0-88677-784-4
THE SECOND SUMMONING	0-88677-975-8
LONG HOT SUMMONING	0-7564-0136-4

Omnibus Editions:

WIZARD OF THE GROVE　　　0-88677-819-0
(Child of the Grove & The Last Wizard)
OF DARKNESS, LIGHT & FIRE　　0-7564-0038-4
(Gate of Darkness, Circle of Light & The Fire's Stone)

To Order Call: 1-800-788-6262

DAW 21

Kristen Britain

GREEN RIDER

As Karigan G'ladheon, on the run from school, makes her way through the deep forest, a galloping horse plunges out of the brush, its rider impaled by two black arrows. With his dying breath, he tells her he is a Green Rider, one of the king's special messengers. Giving her his green coat with its symbolic brooch of office, he makes Karigan swear to deliver the message he was carrying. Pursued by unknown assassins, following a path only the horse seems to know, Karigan finds herself thrust into in a world of danger and complex magic....   0-88677-858-1

FIRST RIDER'S CALL

With evil forces once again at large in the kingdom and with the messenger service depleted and weakened, can Karigan reach through the walls of time to get help from the First Rider, a woman dead for a millennium?   0-7564-0209-3

To Order Call: 1-800-788-6262

OTHERLAND

TAD WILLIAMS

"The Otherland books are a
major accomplishment."
—Publishers Weekly

"It will captivate you."
—Cinescape

In many ways it is humankind's most stunning
achievement. This most exclusive of places is also
one of the world's best-kept secrets, but somehow,
bit by bit, it is claiming Earth's most valuable
resource: its children.

CITY OF GOLDEN SHADOW (Vol. One)
0-88677-763-1

RIVER OF BLUE FIRE (Vol. Two)
0-88677-844-1

MOUNTAIN OF BLACK GLASS (Vol. Three)
0-88677-906-5

SEA OF SILVER LIGHT (Vol. Four)
0-75640-030-9

To Order Call: 1-800-788-6262

Tad Williams

THE **WAR** OF THE **FLOWERS**

"A masterpiece of fairytale worldbuilding."
—*Locus*

"Williams's imagination is boundless."
—*Publishers Weekly*
(Starred Review)

"A great introduction to an accomplished
and ambitious fantasist."
—*San Francisco Chronicle*

"An addictive world ... masterfully plays
with the tropes and traditions of
generations of fantasy writers."
—*Salon*

"A very elaborate and fully realized setting
for adventure, intrigue, and more
than an occasional chill."
—*Science Fiction Chronicle*

0-7564-0181-X

To Order Call: 1-800-788-6262